Dear Reade

These two r

Winters we

are delighted to be able to bring them to you in
one volume.

Rebecca Winters is known for writing deeply
emotional stories and these two are no
exception. What must it be like for a wife to be
reunited with the husband she believed to be
dead? And what about a woman who is carrying
her husband's child but knows their relationship
is in serious trouble?

Read on to find out…

The Editors

All the characters in this book have no existence outside the imagination of the author, and have no relation whatsoever to anyone bearing the same name or names. They are not even distantly inspired by any individual known or unknown to the author, and all the incidents are pure invention.

All Rights Reserved including the right of reproduction in whole or in part in any form. This edition is published by arrangement with Harlequin Enterprises II B.V. The text of this publication or any part thereof may not be reproduced or transmitted in any form or by any means, electronic or mechanical, including photocopying, recording, storage in an information retrieval system, or otherwise, without the written permission of the publisher.

This book is sold subject to the condition that it shall not, by way of trade or otherwise, be lent, resold, hired out or otherwise circulated without the prior consent of the publisher in any form of binding or cover other than that in which it is published and without a similar condition including this condition being imposed on the subsequent purchaser.

Harlequin, Harlequin Duets and Colophon are trademarks used under licence.

First published in Great Britain 1999
by Harlequin Mills & Boon Limited,
Eton House, 18-24 Paradise Road, Richmond, Surrey TW9 1SR

STRANGERS WHEN WE MEET © Rebecca Winters 1997
LAURA'S BABY © Rebecca Winters 1997

ISBN 0 373 59690 1

20-9908

Printed and bound in Great Britain
by Caledonian International Book Manufacturing Ltd, Glasgow

Strangers When We Meet
REBECCA WINTERS

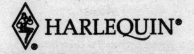

HARLEQUIN®

TORONTO • NEW YORK • LONDON
AMSTERDAM • PARIS • SYDNEY • HAMBURG
STOCKHOLM • ATHENS • TOKYO • MILAN • MADRID
PRAGUE • WARSAW • BUDAPEST • AUCKLAND

My sincerest thanks to First Lieutenant Edwin V. Rawley of the Army-Air Force for sharing some of his war experiences and helping me get inside the mind and heart of a soldier who lost limbs in combat, yet is still serving God and country by helping others adjust to similar losses. *He's what being a hero is all about!*

Credit also goes to Jerry D. Braza, Ph.D., and Kathleen Braza, M.A., who most graciously consented to let me use some of the valuable information in their book, *Coping with War and its Aftermath*, copyright 1991. Though out of print now, it can probably be found in your local library. I obtained other information by phoning Kathleen Braza, Bereavement Consultant at Healing Resources (1-800-473-HEAL).

A special thanks to Ronald L. Webb, C.P.O. of Shield's Orthotic Prosthetic Services in Salt Lake City, Utah, who gave his valuable time to help me understand in a small way the adjustments a vet or any other person who has lost a limb must make.

*To all veterans and their families
this book is lovingly dedicated.*

CHAPTER ONE

"ZACH?"

"Rosie? Good morning, sweetheart." The huskiness in his tone told her he hadn't been awake long. It was barely seven.

"Good morning."

Dear God. Help me.

"I've been dreaming about us. Our cruise didn't last nearly long enough. The only thing that keeps me going is the knowledge that you're going to be my wife in June. I wish you were here right now," he murmured. "Why don't you come over for a little while before you have to leave for work? I want to *show* you how much I love you."

She wouldn't be going to the university today; in fact, she'd already called Chow Ping, one of the graduate students, to cover her classes.

"Rosie? Why aren't you saying anything?"

A shudder passed through her body. She wished she could tell him everything he wanted to hear. But the last urgent message, one of many left on her answering machine by her in-laws, had turned her world upside down for the second time in her life. They'd called again from a hotel in Ogden, Utah—

not five minutes after she and Cody had walked in the door from their trip with Zach.

"Zach…we have to t-talk!" She swallowed hard. "I'm just glad I caught you before you left for work."

"Sweetheart? Something's really wrong. What is it?" She could feel his concern. There wasn't a more understanding man than Zachery Wilde. But when she told him…

"Rosie?" he prodded. "Don't go all quiet on me."

"I-it's about Nick."

"What about him?"

Zach's voice had dropped to a lower register. Nick had been the ghost between them far too long for Zach's liking. Rosie was terrified of what this news was going to do to him, but she couldn't put it off any longer.

"H-he didn't die in the war, Zach."

As soon as she'd said those words, the silence on the other end was so eloquent with shock, Rosie didn't know if she could bear it.

When she'd been given that news, she'd gone into shock herself, unable to tell her in-laws what had happened on the cruise—that she'd accepted Zachery Wilde's proposal and would be marrying him at the end of the spring quarter, hopefully with their blessing.

She hadn't been counting on it of course, because Nick's parents were still in mourning over their only son's death. She was well aware that they would have trouble allowing Zach into their grandson's life on a permanent basis, let alone accepting him as her husband.

But with one phone call, everything had changed, and her world no longer made sense. After six and a half hours of soul-searching agony, it still didn't. She was in love with Zach, but she'd never stopped loving Nick.

The joy she'd experienced on hearing he wasn't dead, after all, that he'd be home in a few hours, was indescribable. Everything had taken on the properties of a fantastic dream.

When her normally sober Cody heard the news, he ran around the house making whooping noises, leaping in the air at odd moments—behavior so uncharacteristic she barely recognized him—while she'd been in a sort of stupor.

Not until she could function well enough to carry her suitcases into the bedroom did thoughts of Zach intrude on her consciousness. Then she was overwhelmed by guilt. *Consumed* by it.

Zach was in love with her. And she adored him. She couldn't wait to become his wife.

But Nick was alive! Her beloved husband who'd been missing in action and was presumed dead. The husband she hadn't seen for seven years.

Zach's sharp intake of breath sounded like ripping silk. "So what are you saying? Is he a POW?"

"He *was*." Rosie couldn't keep the tremor out of her voice. She couldn't stand the thought of what Nick had been forced to live through.

"Was?"

"He's been released, a-and is on his way home."

"You mean to Germany?"

"No. I—I mean he was in Germany for debriefing, but that's over. The air force is flying him into Hill Air Force Base this morning."

Another ghastly silence. "I'm coming over."

"No, Zach!" She panicked. "You can't!"

"Rosie—"

The anguish in his voice devastated her.

"There's no time, Zach. His plane is landing at nine-thirty this morning. As it is, Cody and I are going to have to rush to make it. His parents drove up there yesterday. They're meeting us at the base."

God forgive her for putting off this phone call until the last minute, but she didn't know any other way to do it. She dreaded the idea of causing Zach any more pain when he'd waited two years for her to agree to marry him.

"I don't believe this is happening. I just put my ring on your finger ten days ago. *Rosie...*" he cried in agony.

She reeled, clutching the headboard of her bed for support. *The bed she'd shared with Nick for seven years.* In eight weeks she'd be sharing Zach's bed. Now Nick was coming home....

"Will you be wearing it when you see him?" She knew it was anger that had made Zach lash out, anger and pain.

This was only the beginning.

"Zach—" her voice shook as tears gushed down her cheeks "—you know how much I love you. You *know* it."

"Mom?" Cody hollered. "Hurry up! What if

Dad's plane gets in early? I want to see him come in!"

"I'll be right there," she called.

Cody was in shock, too. Euphoric shock. The kind only a thirteen-year-old boy could experience. A boy who'd just learned that his hero father, the man whose memory he'd always idolized to the exclusion of every other male, including Zach—especially Zach—was alive.

To Cody, everything was so simple. His dad was coming home to be his dad again. Cody had huge plans for them, plans that toppled the foundation Zach had been carefully laying to reach some sort of understanding with her son.

One phone call had wiped out two years of work. Already Zach was a memory. No one could compete with Cody's flesh-and-blood father, who was coming home to stay. What more could one ask of life? End of story.

A groan escaped her throat. "I—I've put your ring in my jewelry box."

"And where are Nick's rings?"

She closed her eyes in fresh pain. "The same place."

"For how long?" he demanded, his voice fierce with hurt.

Dear God. That was a question she couldn't answer.

He muttered a few bitter curses, sounding as out of control as she felt. "I had no right to ask that of you. No right at all. But I'm warning you, Rosie. I haven't spent the last two years loving you, only to give up now. Remember *that,* even if you can't remember *me* after today!''

"*Zach!* I'm in love with you, darling. I swear I'll call you before the day's out. *I swear it!*"

"Don't make promises you can't keep."

"Have you so little faith in me?" she cried.

"Mom?" Cody opened the door of her bedroom and poked his head in. "Hurry up!"

She nodded, signaling that he should close it again and leave her some privacy. He frowned his impatience before the door clicked shut. He knew she was on the phone with Zach.

"*Lord,* Rosie. This has nothing to do with faith and everything to do with the kind of marriage you and Nick once had. So let's not pretend."

She flinched from his bitterness. "I—I'm not pretending."

"Oh, hell, Rosie—"

"I have to go," she whispered.

"I know, and I'm being an insensitive bastard." She could hear the tears in his voice. "But I also know that the next time I see you, things'll be different. You won't be the same Rosie who finally made every damn dream of mine come true."

"I haven't been the same Rosie since I got that phone call," she admitted in a dull voice. "To be honest, I don't know who I am, Zach. Right now there's only one reality—I'm terrified."

"You don't know the half of it, sweetheart."

The line went dead.

"I'VE GOT A PIT in my stomach bigger than Kennecott," R. T. Ellis muttered, his fingers clawing the armrest.

Nick Armstrong gazed dispassionately at the bandaged stump below his left wrist, then flexed his right hand, as if reminding himself it was still there. He leaned across the man who was closer than a brother to look out the window of their C-141 transport plane.

They were passing over the huge Kennecott open-pit copper mine, reputed to be the largest in the world. Nick surmised that heavy air traffic or high winds must have caused the pilot to swing this far south before turning around to make the rare southerly approach to the base.

In the distance the Great Salt Lake, surrounded by scorched desert, shimmered a pale blue. A few more minutes and they'd be landing at Hill. What an incredible irony that after six and a half years of being held prisoner in a godforsaken desert, they were returning to one.

He sat back and closed his eyes. "I know the feeling."

The plane engines droned on, filling the eerie silence that had been building the nearer they came to their destination. Both he and R.T. had survived captivity at various locations inside Iraq, but they'd never known the names of places or the coordinates. The Iraqi soldiers had moved them by truck a total of fifteen times, and each time they'd been blindfolded.

Both Nick and R.T. had agreed that when they got out, they didn't want their family reunions to happen in Germany. They just wanted to be debriefed, receive any medical attention at Fitzsimmons Army Hospital in Colorado, then fly home without losing any more precious time.

There was to be no press coverage, no news leak that would result in their pictures being plastered all over the *Salt Lake Tribune* or *Deseret News*. No gruesome details to recount of an experience they preferred to forget. All they wanted was their privacy and the right to carry on with their lives.

The powers-that-be in Germany didn't like the idea, not with the politicians breathing down their necks. But Nick reminded them that there were POWs released in Vietnam who were able to arrive at their own front doors without prior notice. No one could refute Nick's argument, and he got his wish.

R.T. and Nick had discussed every conceivable problem they might face after being gone this long and presumed dead. All POWs did. The worst fear among the married ones was the very real possibility that their wives had moved on and remarried. The prisoners with children had the additional worry that some other guy was raising their family.

Nick's thoughts fastened on Rosie, who'd never been out of his heart for a moment. Theirs was the kind of love destined to last a lifetime and beyond. They'd talked about everything before he'd left with his unit, everything that could happen—except the chance that he might be taken prisoner, a subject Rosie refused to even contemplate.

But it didn't matter, because he knew she'd wait for him, till the end of time if necessary. That knowledge had been the only thing to keep him sane during his long incarceration.

But nothing—not hope or even faith—could have prepared Nick or R.T. for the hell of not being able to talk to their wives yet. Rosie had a new phone number and address, listed under R. Armstrong, which came as a jolt. All he got was a U.S. West answering-machine voice telling him to leave a message, which he didn't feel ready to do. He preferred his first contact with Rosie to be in person.

R.T. couldn't even find his old phone number. The operator had insisted there was no listing for a Cynthia Ellis or anything close.

He'd been raised by an aunt before his marriage to Cynthia. She was the only relative of his still living in Salt Lake. But when he called her, he'd been forced to leave a message, asking her to get in touch with his wife to inform her that he was alive and on his way home.

As Nick watched R.T. retch into a bag, he realized that the trauma of not knowing anything had finally caught up with him. The thrill of coming home had been swallowed up in the anxiety of being this close to loved ones without having made that first vital contact.

Neither of them spoke aloud what they were thinking—that his bride of a year had remarried. Nick grimaced; R.T. had lost his breakfast after leaving Denver and still couldn't keep anything down.

Not until Nick had undergone an emotional reunion over the phone with his parents did the tight band around his own chest relax a little. His overjoyed mom and dad not only reassured him that they were in good health, thank God, but they answered his single most important question.

Rosie hadn't remarried. She was doing a wonderful job of raising Nick's look-alike son, who was thirteen now and already approaching five foot ten. Nick's mother forgot her tears long enough to add laughingly that it wouldn't be much longer before Cody rivaled his father's six foot two.

Nick couldn't talk after that. Nothing else mattered. The details of their lives he'd catch up on later.

Rosie was still waiting for him. She'd never given up hope.

If there was a black cloud on the horizon, it hung over R.T., who had no idea what future awaited him. It wasn't fair, Nick thought, not when R.T. had just been released from the depths of hell, only to be thrust down all over again if it turned out he'd lost his wife because of a damn war over oil.

"She isn't going to be there, Nick."

They'd been through too much to lie to each other.

"Maybe, maybe not. If that's the case, plan on coming home with me."

AS SOON AS HE'D YANKED on a pullover, Zach phoned his secretary at home, but she'd already left for work. When he called his office, he got the answering machine.

He waited for the beep. "Barb? I'm back from the Caribbean, but I won't be in until tomorrow. Reschedule all my apppointments for another day."

Within minutes he'd locked up his condo, located

at the base of the foothills, and sped off on his racing bike toward the mountains. Mid-April meant spring in the valley and snow on the peaks, but he gave no thought to his surroundings as he headed up Little Cottonwood Canyon.

Strong winds buffeted him during the steep climb to the ten-thousand-foot summit. When he got up there, he hoped he'd pass out from overexertion and find forgetfulness, if only for a few minutes.

Until two years ago, he'd always lived in California. But after losing his fiancée two years before that to a rare form of brain cancer, he'd needed an outlet for his restlessness. Biking had always been one of his favorite sports, and now it became a necessity of life.

In the beginning, the pain of his loss had been so acute he'd deliberately pushed himself to the extreme, with the result that for a few hours each day, the physical agony camouflaged his heartache. As time went by, he found a certain satisfaction in seeing how hard he could drive himself. He began entering national bike races and eventually traveled to Europe to race. Two summers ago, he'd ended up in Park City, Utah, not far from Salt Lake. Having turned pro, he'd attended a special racing camp to train for the Tour de France.

Utah was where he'd met Rosie Armstrong. She'd been out cycling with her son and his friend. They were in the middle of a private mountain road when Zach came upon them at full speed. He'd almost crashed into them on his bike. Once apologies were made on both sides, he realized he wanted to get to know her better. From that moment on, his world had started to right itself.

Though he continued to compete in cycling races both in Europe and America, he never did enter the Tour de France. Everything he'd wanted was right here in Utah, where he intended to put down roots— where there was the promise of love, marriage and a ready-made family.

Virtually overnight he'd relocated, expanding his family's lucrative outdoor-sign business to Salt Lake City. Wilde Outdoors was a successful enterprise he'd helped his father and brothers build throughout high school and college.

It had taken two years to make Rosie see *him,* instead of Nick. Finally, on that cruise, she'd turned the tables and reached out to him, telling him she loved him, begging him to ask her one more time to marry him.

That was what he'd been waiting for.

He'd pulled out the diamond ring he'd purchased three months after meeting her—a promise to himself that one day he'd win her love and be allowed to put it on her finger—then slid it home with an over-whelming sense of fulfillment and joy.

All that was shattered by her phone call an hour ago.

He didn't die in the war, Zach. The gut-wrenching premonition that the pain he was experi-encing now might never go away, might become worse than anything he'd ever known before, tore through him like a jagged shard.

Visions of his beautiful golden-haired Rosie running into the arms of the man who'd loved her since high school almost destroyed him.

Zach pedaled harder against the wind.

It was God's truth that Nick Armstrong had more right than anyone to return to land of the living and reclaim the wife and child who'd probably been the only reason he hadn't committed suicide in prison.

But it was also God's truth that when her husband had been reported missing in action and presumed dead, Zach and Rosie had been given every right to meet and fall in love, to enjoy a full rich life with Cody.

When his first love had been cruelly taken from him, there had, at least, been a sense of closure, because her death was final, irrevocable.

But there could be no closure if he lost Rosie. Knowing she was living in the same city he was, yet knowing he couldn't see her. Knowing that the woman he loved was affording her husband the pleasure of her company, her sweetness and humor, her intelligence, her sunny smile.

Tonight she'd be sleeping under the same roof with Nick....

Could she forget what she and Zach had shared over the past two years? On the cruise?

Would she turn to Nick tonight and give him the comfort of the beautiful body her husband must have been craving for seven hellish years? The body Zach had yet to possess?

Even if she wasn't physically or emotionally ready to sleep with Nick again, the real possibility that she might make love to him out of the love she'd always

felt for him, out of her compassion for all he'd suffered, ripped Zack apart. Agonizing pictures filled his
mind, blotting out any awareness of his surroundings.

It took the blare of a car horn on the narrow stretch
of curving road to alert him to the drop-off not two
feet from his bike tires. The more he thought about
it, the more he welcomed the idea of a nine-
thousand-foot plunge to certain oblivion.

The only thing holding him back was the sure
knowledge that she'd fallen deeply in love with him,
Zach. So deeply, in fact, that he could never doubt
theirs was the forever kind of love. Rosie was with
him, heart and soul. He had faith in their love. It
wasn't going to go away just because Nick had come
home. Love didn't work like that.

No matter how much she still loved her husband,
the man had been gone seven years. Tremendous
changes had taken place in her, and undoubtedly in
him. She was a different person now, in love with a
different man—and it wasn't Nick!

That was Zach's edge.

By all that was holy, he intended to keep that edge
until Rosie walked down the aisle with him. Unfortunately Cody would fight him every step of the way.

Cody was Nick's edge.

Cody had never liked Zach. He'd made it plain
from day one. Rosie had insisted that, given time,
Cody would come around and get over his initial
resentment of Zach's intrusion into their private
world.

To Zach's chagrin, however, that resentment had
grown into dislike—the major reason he hadn't

brought up the subject of marriage a year earlier.

They'd taken Cody on the cruise, hoping to forge a bond that included the three of them. But when they'd told her son they were planning to get married, Zach saw the hurt in Cody's eyes. Worse, Zach felt the boy's silent brooding anger and realized they had a serious problem on their hands.

Rosie reasoned that Nick's parents, who had a lot of influence over their grandson, had fueled some of his negative response by not accepting Nick's death.

Zach had been encouraged and relieved when he heard Rosie admit that her son could benefit from some counseling. She'd announced that, in spite of Cody's problem, she intended to marry Zach. As soon as they got back from their cruise, she would make an appointment for Cody to see a specialist and get the help he needed.

But with one phone call, everything had changed.

The boy's father's unexpected return from the dead precluded any such appointment. All Cody's problems began and ended there.

That bitter irony brought a sardonic twist to Zach's windburned lips.

He took the next dangerous curve at full speed, surprised and ashamed of his own jealousy over a man who'd been gone seven years in the service of his country. A man who continued to inspire unqualified love and devotion in the hearts of those he'd left behind.

Surprised, because such a destructive emotion was unworthy of him.

Ashamed, because he planned to fight a valiant, honorable, innocent man for Rosie's love—and win!

"GRANDMA! GRANDPA!"

Before Rosie could turn off the ignition and get out of their compact car, Cody had jumped from the passenger seat to greet Nick's parents. Rosie locked the door and started toward them. The wind seemed stronger than ever, molding her slim silk coat-dress to her body.

Cody was so excited his hostility over her engagement to Zach might never have been. The fear that he would bring up the subject before she'd had a chance to tell her in-laws in private was momentarily abated.

"Dad's alive! He's coming home!" His voice cracked; it was changing and came out half an octave lower than it used to. "I can't believe it!" he shouted. His cries of joy mingled with theirs as he ran into their outstretched arms, the tears streaming down his happy face.

I can't believe it, either. I can't. Something must be wrong with me. Nick's supposed to be arriving in a few minutes. I'm afraid it isn't true, that none of this is real....

"Rosie?" Janet rushed up to her and gave her a welcoming hug. "It's a good thing you got back from the cruise when you did. After all he's suffered, can you imagine how Nicky would feel if his own wife wasn't here to welcome him home?"

No. She couldn't.

There was more than a hint of accusation in her

mother-in-law's tone. Though she'd practiced restraint by not voicing her opinion about that cruise with Zach, her disapproval had been simmering beneath the surface.

"This has all happened so fast George and I are still in a state of shock."

"So am I," Rosie whispered. But shock didn't begin to cover it.

"Do you think that's his plane, Grandpa?" This from Cody as they proceeded toward the hangar. All four of them turned to the north to watch the plane's approach.

Rosie's heart leapt into her throat. Could Nick really be on that plane coming in at such a sharp angle?

George had his camera ready, then lowered it. "Nope. That's a C-130. Your dad's coming in on a C-141. Come on. Let's keep going."

"Are you sure this is the right place?"

"I'm sure." His grandpa chuckled before throwing an affectionate arm around Cody's shoulders. "This is the Base Ops terminal, where all the transports come in."

"But there aren't very many people around here. Maybe we got the wrong time."

"Maybe your dad's the only one flying in. After all, he's a war hero, and that makes him a VIP," he added with great pride. "When the Days of '47 comes around in July, he'll have to ride in the parade, and I know he'll want you right there with him."

"Cool."

While they watched the sky, Rosie half listened to

Cody's excited chatter followed by his grandparents' patient responses.

They were wonderful people. The two of them had been making the five-hour drive from their home in St. George to Salt Lake City every other weekend since Nick had left for the Middle East. When they weren't in town, they phoned Cody several times a week to stay in close touch. They'd always doted on their grandson, but when Nick was missing in action and presumed killed during the Desert Shield phase of the war, Cody had become their raison d'être.

Rosie had never known her own parents, who'd died in a car-bus collision soon after she was born. The grandparents on her mother's side had stepped in to raise her. Not long after she'd married Nick, they'd died within a year of each other. Yet she considered herself a fortunate woman to be loved by Nick's parents.

She owed George and Janet Armstrong everything for making her feel an integral part of their family, for loving Cody like their own. Without their support during that black period when Nick was first reported missing after an enemy attack near the Saudi border town of Khafji, she had no idea how she and Cody would have survived the ordeal.

Because they'd been so close to her over the years, it never occurred to her that they might be upset when Zach unexpectedly came into her life.

Throughout the first six months of their tenuous relationship, Rosie had kept it very low-key. He was either working at his business or off winning bicycle races. When he was in town, she urged him to date other women, since she had no plans to remarry and didn't want to lead him on.

Rosie explained all this to Janet and George when they began asking questions about Zach. To her surprise, they admitted they were hurt that she would even consider dating. Not until then did Rosie realize that Nick's parents still held out hope he was alive. Their reaction made her feel guilty, because she was more physically and emotionally attracted to Zach than she was willing to acknowledge. But like her in-laws, she'd never been completely able to accept Nick's death. The conflict between those emotions tortured her.

She had decided to put Zach off, but she'd underestimated his determination to have a relationship with her. He demanded to know why she was avoiding him. When she finally told him the truth, he pointed out that even if Nick had been taken prisoner, all of them had been released and accounted for years earlier. The Gulf War wasn't like Vietnam.

His argument made sense, and she recognized that she couldn't go on living in limbo. It wasn't fair to her *or* Cody. It definitely wasn't fair to Zach, who'd confessed he'd fallen in love with her and was willing to wait as long as it took to get a commitment from her.

Since Rosie couldn't deny the strong feelings between them, they dated each other exclusively when he was in town, despite the senior Armstrongs' reservations.

But in doing this, she not only incurred her in-laws' displeasure, she brought out an ugly side of

Cody she hadn't known existed. All because they could sense the growing bond between her and Za—

"There's a plane, Grandpa!"

"Where?"

"Right there." Cody pointed toward the southern sky.

George shook his head. "Wrong direction."

"You don't think it's Dad's?" The disappointment in his voice spoke volumes.

"I don't know. We'll just have to wait and see."

Rosie stared at the four-engine transport, which had started its descent. The ground crew was scrambling in preparation for its arrival.

For a moment it felt like déjà vu. Only, the last time she'd seen that type of aircraft, her eyes had been swollen shut from crying, and the plane had been headed into the blue, carrying away the husband she adored.

Suddenly she was twenty-four years old. The excruciating pain of that moment exploded inside her all over again.

She gasped for breath as pure revelation flowed through her.

Nick was on that plane.

Its wheels came down. In another minute it touched ground and taxied along the runway before making a U-turn toward them.

"Do you think it's Dad?"

"George?" Janet cried, her excitement almost tangible.

"It's your father's plane." Rosie's voice shook with conviction. "Come on, Cody." Galvanized into action, she grabbed her son's hand, and they began running against the wind. George and Janet weren't far behind.

As the plane pulled to a stop and the engines were cut, the ground crew stood ready to help lower the steps to the ground.

A couple of dark-haired airmen started down. Adrenaline had Rosie almost jumping out of her skin.

"Mom?"

She knew what Cody was asking and shook her head. Her gaze fastened compulsively on the door opening.

A painfully thin man with reddish-brown hair and gaunt cheeks, possibly mid-to late twenties, appeared at the threshold carrying a duffel bag. He was wearing the pine green full-dress army uniform and garrison cap.

Rosie watched him watching them before he took his first step down the stairs. The look of disappointment on his face haunted her.

"Where's Dad?"

"There he is!" both grandparents shouted at the same time.

Rosie's breath caught as a lean pale man emerged slowly from the interior, half a head taller than the soldier preceding him down the steps. He wore the same green uniform, but was carrying his cap along with a duffel bag in his right hand. His black hair was cut in a buzz.

She'd already made her first mistake. She was looking for her dashing, twenty-five-year-old husband, who'd worn his hair a little long. Who'd always been tanned and fit. The man who'd been her entire world from the first second she'd laid eyes on him.

The soldier she was staring at now bore a superficial resemblance to that husband. But this man was obviously older—thirty-two—and thinner. It was like looking at a drawing of someone as the artist might have imagined that person appearing over the passage of time and altered by circumstance.

Seven years had gone by. *Seven!* The realization clutched at her heart.

"Nicky!"

"Son! Over here!"

Nick waved.

"Oh, George—" Janet broke down "—he's lost so much weight!"

"None of that, honey. Give him a couple months of Rosie's home-cooked meals and he'll put it all back on. Except for that, he looks great," George muttered gruffly.

"Dad!"

Cody broke free of Rosie's hand and sprinted toward his father. In the next instant, they were embracing. Cody's initial tears eventually were replaced by joyous barks of laughter as they began inspecting each other. Already that strong father-son bond established during the first six years of Cody's life was back in full effect.

How strange to see the two of them together, yet how…*right* they looked. Cody had inherited his father's build and coloring. Even certain mannerisms were the same.

Still, Rosie checked her steps. Like a faulty imprint on a coin, Nick's image appeared blurry, while Cody's stood out in stark relief, dear and familiar.

Just then Nick raised his head, and a pair of black-lashed, flame-blue eyes no length of time could ever change sought hers over Cody's shoulder. The secret smile he'd always reserved for her alone shone from his face.

His remembered smile conjured up a myriad emotions from their frozen prison, and now they nearly overwhelmed her.

"Nick..." she cried, reaching blindly for him.

He met her halfway, clutching her to him so hard she could feel his ribs through his uniform—graphic evidence of the inhuman treatment he'd received in captivity.

His body quaked. "If you hadn't been here waiting for me, I would have died before my feet touched the tarmac."

That solemn pronouncement of truth shook her to the core. *If she and Zach had extended their trip one more day—*

"Rosie..." His deep voice broke. On a low moan, his mouth closed over hers.

How many times had she known her husband's possessive kiss? How many times had she been swept away by his passion, brought to tears by his tenderness? Who could count all the ways his mouth had brought her infinite pleasure, the times he'd made her feel immortal, no matter the hour, mood or situation?

Yet this kiss was different from the others.

His soul was searching for hers, seeking to ascertain that it still belonged to him, that there were no secrets, no shadows.

Not completely satisfied, he deepened their kiss. When Nick went in pursuit, his instincts never failed him.

Her body, that tangible conduit to the soul, started to tremble.

His body went perfectly still before he relinquished her mouth. In his eyes she glimpsed unspeakable pain, and had to look away.

He knows, her heart groaned.

CHAPTER TWO

"NICKY—WHAT HAPPENED to your hand?"

The undisguised horror in Janet's voice, coupled with a muffled cry from George, filled Rosie with unnamed dread.

She eased herself far enough away from Nick's chest to see his hands. He glanced down. Out of the others' hearing, he said, "It appears we've both mislaid our wedding rings."

Staggering guilt and pain knifed through her body before she saw what the others had seen—there was a bandage where his left hand had been. In the next instant, graphic pictures of combat scenarios flashed through her mind.

She started to weave.

Don't scream out loud, Rosie.

Through narrowed eyes, Nick registered her horrified reaction before she felt him shut her out and turn to Cody.

"As I told my boy—" he tousled the dark hair with his right hand "—I've gotten along just fine without my other hand, but I'll check out the latest hardware to see about making some improvements."

The mocking tone, perfectly gauged to alleviate their son's fears, devastated her. In desperation Rosie put an arm around Cody's shoulders, as much out of a need for his physical support as the desire to reassure her son. He was fighting a losing battle to hold back the tears; obviously, fresh shock over his father's loss had begun to settle in.

Her in-laws fared no better. George was ashen-faced and Janet had broken down sobbing. All Rosie and Cody could do was stand by helplessly and watch the reunion between Nick and his parents, two of the most devoted generous people in the world. People who'd steadfastly refused to believe their only son was dead.

Her heart underwent another convulsion. She couldn't get over the cruel irony that after seven years of unutterable suffering to both body and soul, *Nick* had to be the one comforting all of them.

In that regard, he hadn't changed. Her husband had always been a take-charge kind of man, watching out for everyone else, never worrying about his own needs.

Early in their relationship, she'd come to cherish that unselfishness in him; she'd considered herself blessed to be his wife.

She still did, didn't she?

He hadn't died. He was alive. His flesh-and-blood body was here, just two feet away. His spirit animated his body.

Then why did it seem as if they were standing on opposite sides of a transparent glass wall, able to see each other but unable to break through and make contact?

"There's someone I want you to meet."

Nick had gently disengaged himself from his mother's clinging arms to beckon the thin soldier Rosie had seen leaving the plane first. He'd been standing a good distance away. She hadn't even realized he was still waiting at the airfield.

"R.T.? Come here and let me introduce you."

R.T.? Rosie vaguely remembered the name from Nick's early days in the army reserve, the seemingly safe route he'd chosen to help pay for his undergraduate schooling.

The other man shook his head. "I don't want to intrude, Sergeant."

Rosie saw Nick's jaw harden. "You're not intruding, and the days of calling me Sergeant are over. We're civilians now," he asserted in an authoritative voice. "Everybody, say hello to R. T. Ellis. He was named Rutherford Topham for his grandfather, but nobody knows that except me." Nick grinned.

"He lost an eye when our truck hit a land mine, but that didn't stop R.T. We managed to walk a good fifty miles and give an Iraqi patrol fits before they picked us up and moved us to an underground bunker. The rest is…history."

R.T. gave a solemn nod to everyone. "The sarge lost his hand in the same explosion. Since the Iraqis don't give medical care to prisoners, we were lucky the blast burned us, because it cauterized our wounds so there wasn't any infection. The doctors in Denver cleaned us up with a little surgery before sending us home."

Nick nodded. "Our superiors at the base told us there'd been word that a few isolated soldiers had

been taken prisoner for negotiation purposes in case
Saddam Hussein wanted to start another war later on
down the road. Our incarceration just lasted a little
longer than we'd expected," Nick joked. "You
could say we've adopted each other. Since his wife
and aunt don't know he's back yet, I've invited him
to stay with us." As he spoke, Nick's eyes focused
on Rosie. The message was clear and unmistakable.

*Whatever's wrong between us, for the love of God,
don't let me down in this.*

She started shaking and couldn't stop. The fact
that R.T.'s wife—let alone other members of his
family—hadn't shown up could mean anything. But
Rosie couldn't help fearing the worst; she sensed the
same was true for Nick.

Galvanized into action, she threw her arms around
R.T. and hugged his stiff form. "Welcome home,
soldier. Thank heaven you and Nick had each other."
She kissed his wooden lips in salute.

"Thank heaven is right," he whispered. His body
suddenly relaxed and he hugged her back. "As far
as I'm concerned, your husband walks on water. He
thinks you do, too, but I guess you already know
that."

"I do." She couldn't dislodge the boulder in her
throat. "Apparently he feels that way about you,
too."

Following her lead, Nick's parents took turns hugging the soldier, showering him with genuine affection because he and Nick had helped each other stay
alive. That made him family, and it was good enough
for them.

R.T. shook hands with Cody and put his garrison cap on him, easing any awkwardness there might have been. "You and your dad are spitting images of each other, you know that?"

"Yeah." Cody's smile wreathed his whole face as he stared at his father with open worship. He'd attached himself to Nick's side once more; Rosie guessed he'd stay there for the duration.

"Why aren't you boys wearing your Purple Hearts?" George wanted to know.

A trace of a smile curved R.T.'s lips. "We're no heroes. We should've looked where we were going."

"You can say that again," Nick added with a rueful grin.

George shook his graying head, which had been as dark as Nick's and Cody's, his eyes suspiciously bright. "That's a matter of opinion, R.T."

"Do you have a Purple Heart, Dad?" Cody asked.

"We both do. It's given to all soldiers wounded in the line of duty. When we get home, you can go through our stuff all you like. How about that?"

"Awesome. I'm going to take everything to school and show my friends."

"By the way, where is home?"

Again his gaze shot straight to Rosie, his eyes asking more of her than his words. No doubt he'd tried to reach her at their old apartment in the Sugar House area and found it no longer existed....

Telling Nick about the changes in their lives was like teaching a child about the world. But it was an infinitely more difficult task because Nick wasn't a child eager to explore his new world for the first time. He was a thirty-two-year-old man whose memories were being tainted, one by one.

She couldn't bear to add to his pain, but she knew it was inevitable. None of them had been given a choice, another brutal side effect of war.

"With money from a couple of excellent investments you made as a stockbroker, plus your monthly government stipend, I was able to get into a house up by the Hogle Zoo," she explained. "It's in a neighborhood with a lot of boys Cody's age."

Nick blinked, his keen mind assessing every piece of information. "That means Clayton Junior High and East High. Was their football any good last year?"

This from a former all-state linebacker for Skyline High, one of East High's arch rivals. Nick's old yearbooks showing his football feats sat in Cody's room and were pored over on a regular basis.

"Yeah, they had a great season. They've rebuilt East so it won't collapse if there's an earthquake. You should see the brand-new football field. Lights, bleachers, everything—" Cody rattled on.

"He's the first-string center for the Eastside junior team over at Sunnyside," George interjected with grandfatherly pride.

"Center, huh? That's one tough position. I'm proud of you. We'll have to rustle up a game."

"How about this afternoon? I'll call the team as soon as they get home from school!"

"Cody!" Rosie and Janet cried at the same time. His naïveté at such a fragile precarious moment in their lives stunned them both, but Nick paid no attention.

"You took the words right out of my mouth. There's nothing I want more than to meet your football buddies."

Suddenly Cody gave his father a fierce hug. "I love you, Dad. I'm so glad you're back. Don't ever go away again."

Nick put a consoling arm around his son, allowing him to shed tears of sheer happiness.

No matter how much Rosie had heard or read about a boy needing his father, no matter how well she thought she'd understood the importance of a male role model, it didn't hit home until now.

No wonder Zach hadn't been able to get anyplace with Cody.

While she stood marveling at the indestructible bond between father and son, she caught sight of the private look Nick flashed R.T. In that brief glance, she read *need*. Obviously they'd grown so close in prison they were in the habit of turning to each other for emotional support.

Like the harbinger of bad news, Nick's silent exchange with R.T. seemed to warn her there was more grief on the way.

To think there was a time when Nick had shared everything with *her*.

Nick answered his son. "We're not going anywhere, Cody. Are we, R.T.?"

R.T. picked up his hat, which had been blown to the ground by the wind. "Hey, Cody?"

The boy lifted his head.

"You know the song, 'Oh, Give Me a Home'?"

"Yeah?" He wiped his eyes with the back of his arm.

"Well, your dad and I kind of rewrote it. His part goes like this—'Oh, give me a home, where my Cody can roam/where the Jazz and the Trappers do play/where the wife I adore, feeds me barbecue galore/and the sky isn't cloudy all day.'"

At that point Nick had joined in, his voice as off-key as R.T.'s "'Home, home to the West/where the parents I love still reside/Among mountains so high, that's the place where I'll die/my beloved close by my side.'"

While the words drove another shaft through Rosie's heart, George cleared his throat and clapped. "Change the name of our city baseball team from the Trappers to the Buzz, and you've got it."

"The *Buzz?*"

"The team got sold, so they gave it a new name, Dad. You know—'cause we're the Beehive State! 'Cause the Pioneers brought bees here." All of this was said on one breath.

Both men smiled.

Janet made a nervous gesture with her hands. "I think it's time we left for Salt Lake. What would you like to do first, son? Are you hungry? Shall we stop for breakfast on the way?"

Rosie nursed another hurt when she detected the invisible line of signals running between Nick and R.T.

"I think we'd like to go straight home. Did you all drive up in one car?"

"No." Rosie shook her head. "Cody and I met your mom and dad here."

Nick eyed his parents. "If you'll let R.T. ride with you, I'll drive my family home."

"But you haven't driven for so long! And you don't have—"

"Good plan," George interrupted his wife, who hadn't recovered from seeing her son minus a hand. In this circumstance, however, she'd voiced one of Rosie's concerns, yet had been overruled.

She and Janet shared a legitimate fear. George probably felt it, too. Nick didn't really need both hands to drive an automatic. But he hadn't been behind the wheel of a car for seven years, and the freeway was more crowded than ever. After such a long confinement, she wondered if his nerves could take the stress.

In the past, Nick had always done the driving when they'd gone anywhere together. For the last seven years, Rosie had been getting herself around without his help, but…he was back home now.

Before he'd left for the Middle East, Rosie had never given a thought to such things as who would drive. That had never been important one way or the other, not when their marriage had been based on a solid partnership.

It wasn't important now. Yet all she seemed capable of comprehending were the changes, the differences…

"Come on, R.T." George fought valiantly to maintain a semblance of calm. "As soon as we're on our way, I want to hear *your* version of that song."

"It's lousy, sir."

"Let us decide that." George grabbed R.T.'s duffel bag, and the three of them began walking toward the parking lot.

Cody, strong and tall for his age, paced his stride to match Nick's, determined to carry his dad's bag to the car without help. Judging by the struggle, it had to be heavy.

Their son was trying hard to prove he'd become a man in Nick's absence. It was a wise father who knew better than to interfere. Rosie could only stare at Nick in wonder for knowing exactly how to handle Cody's feelings.

Needing to do something before the feelings inside her exploded, she hurried ahead of them to unlock the doors of her Nissan with the automatic device, then open the trunk with her key.

"Rosie?" Nick prompted. He was standing right behind her once Cody had tossed the bag inside.

Her head jerked around. Their eyes met. In those blue depths she saw anger, bewilderment, disillusionment. She saw pain. Oh, yes. Excruciating pain.

They stared at each other almost as if they were adversaries locked in a strange room, reluctant to begin engagement because they didn't know the rules. Every question of his, every comment of hers, seemed to turn into a weapon capable of inflicting more pain, more confusion.

I'm not your adversary, Nick. I love you. I've always loved you.

"Do you want to give me the keys?"

"O-of course."

He put out his left arm to reach for them, but at the last second, put out his right.

Was it an unconscious gesture on his part, or was this his idea of forcing her to face what had happened to him and deal with it?

Either way, she couldn't stand the sight of his bad arm. Not because of its physical reality. She was grateful the explosion hadn't taken the whole limb.

The loss of his hand could never rob Nick of his appeal. If he'd come home with no arms or legs, he would still be that handsome man, exuding a powerful masculinity undiminished by the cut of his hair, his weight loss, his pallor or the severing of one of his extremities.

If anything, the years had brought him new stature, a new wisdom and maturity, all of which she was discovering made him attractive in ways she'd never been obliged to consider.

No. She hated his bad arm because of the horror it must represent to Nick.

How could he ever rid his mind of the blackness of those years when he had to live with such a reminder for the rest of his life?

He'd been in combat and been taken as a prisoner of war. He would suffer post-traumatic stress disorder until the day he died. So would R.T., she mused heavily. It was every soldier's nightmare, every wife's.

Now it was hers.

Rosie needed someone to talk to. Ironically her first instinct was to turn to Zach, which was out of the question. Yet he'd been her rock for so long....

Darling Zach. The pain he had to be in…

But all their pain combined would never match Nick's. Only someone like Linda Beams, head of the family support group for the Ninety-sixth Regional Support Command at Fort Douglas, would be able to help Rosie understand what her husband was going through. Linda had been there for Rosie when the news had come that Nick was missing in action.

Rosie needed her right now.

NICK LOVED the feel of the steering wheel in his hand. He loved the sensation of speed, and the power that came from being in control of his life again. To be able to go where he wanted, when he wanted, was something he'd never take for granted again.

"The car's a little beauty, Rosie." A gleaming white exterior of classic style and clean rounded lines, with an interior that, thanks to the sunroof, felt airy and unconfined. After being forced to live in darkness for so many years, he craved the light. "I like it. I like it a lot."

The choice of car was a reflection on Rosie herself. That thought put him in mind of the golden-haired, eighteen-year-old girl he'd made his wife fourteen years ago. Her lilting smile and extraordinary leaf green eyes had worked their magic straight into his heart.

Where was that girl who'd sworn she'd wait for him till the end of time?

The composed elegant woman occupying the front passenger seat, gleaming hair caught in a large tortoiseshell clip at the back of her head, was a far cry from his loving, passionate young wife. The day he'd left, Rosie had clung to him at the base airport, refusing to let him get on that plane because they both knew it might be a year before they held each other again.

As it was, they'd made love all night long, not willing to waste a second of the precious time left to them, never dreaming it would have to last seven years.

There'd be no night like that tonight. Perhaps never again.

He'd known that much when he'd kissed her, trying to get something from her she couldn't give. Her mouth had always been like a spring of fresh water to him, but when he went to drink, he discovered that the source had stopped giving freely. He'd only caught a trickle.

After glimpsing his injured arm, she'd attempted to cover up her repulsion, but it didn't work. When her initial horror had fled, he saw only a sorrowing pity in her eyes, the one emotion he couldn't tolerate from her. Not his Rosie.

But she isn't your Rosie. Not anymore.

Who was the man? How much did he mean to her?

She's taken off your rings, Armstrong. That's how much the guy means to her.

How many times has he held you? Touched you?

How long have you been going to bed with him, Rosie?

A cold sweat broke out on Nick's body. He knew he was going to be sick like R.T., so he took the

Bountiful turnoff, searching frantically for the nearest gas station.

After pulling to a stop alongside a set of pumps, he got quickly out of the car. "I'll be right back."

He barely made it to the rest room in time to empty his stomach. While his hand still clutched the wall to support his weakened body, Cody walked in and shut the door.

"Dad? Mom was worried about you and sent me to see if you're okay. How come you're sick? Do you have one of those Gulf War diseases they talk about on Channel One?"

Before the war, if he'd been sick she would have followed him to find out for herself that he was all right.

As soon as the sickness passed, Nick rinsed out his mouth, then turned to Cody, anxious to take away the panic.

His hand went to Cody's left shoulder. "What's Channel One?"

"It's a news channel we have to watch at school. They've had all these stories about vets from Desert Storm who have unexplained diseases. Even their wives and kids are getting them. Do you have one?" The tears trickled down his cheeks.

Nick sucked in his breath. "Have you ever thrown up just before a football game?" His son nodded.

"Well, getting bumped around in that transport over the Rockies and then being reunited with my family after seven years kind of made me feel the same way I used to feel before a game against the Highland Rams."

"Honest?" Cody's eyes were hopeful.

"I wouldn't lie to you, son. The fact that R.T. and I were held in semi-isolation below ground throughout our imprisonment probably protected us from a lot of things, including disease. Our unit had hardly arrived before R.T. and I went out hunting for land mines and were captured."

At those words, relief broke out on Cody's face.

"There's nothing wrong with either of us that a weight gain of forty pounds won't fix. I dreamed about double-thick chocolate marshmallow malts the whole time I was captured, figured you and I would make a stop at Snelgrove's our nightly ritual for a while. In fact, I'm craving one right now. What kind do you like?"

"Chocolate-chip cookie dough."

"Are you putting me on?"

"No. Honest."

"I've loved chocolate-chip cookie dough since I was a little kid. You're my son, all right."

Cody grinned. "What about R.T.?"

"He likes butterscotch. We'll pick one up for him, too."

"He doesn't look very good, Dad."

"That's because he hasn't been able to get in touch with his family yet. We'll let him hang around with us until he can find out what happened to his wife and aunt."

"Does he have kids?"

"No. But after six and a half years of hearing me talk about how terrific you are, he can't wait to have a Cody of his own."

"Dad…"

Pleased to see the light back in his son's blue-green eyes, Nick decided it was time to prepare him for certain new realities. "You'll probably hear me and R.T. talking in our sleep," he began. "We might even scream and act strange. Don't let it scare you and don't be afraid to ask us questions. It won't last forever. But it'll happen for a while because our minds will be working overtime, remembering things we don't want to remember. We're going to hate certain things now."

"Like what?"

"Oh, going into the basement, being in a dark room, being enclosed in a crowded place where we can't get out."

"Will it bother you to be at a stadium?"

He could see where this conversation was headed and ruffled Cody's hair. "No. That's different. That's outdoors in the fresh air and sunshine. Being confined so many years has taught me a lot of things about myself.

"I know I don't want to work behind a desk as a stockbroker anymore. If I had my way, I'd buy some property up in the mountains near Heber and do a little farming. Keep some horses. Grow a garden."

"Hey—they're selling property up there right now! A whole bunch of my friends' dads have already built places near the Jordanelle Dam. They boat in summer and ice-fish in winter."

Ignited by Cody's enthusiasm, Nick's heart started to pick up speed. "The Jordanelle Dam?"

"Yeah. They've built this dam and made a huge

lake—it's just before you get to Heber. It's fantastic. I've already been waterskiing there. Could we do that?'' Cody's eyes were shining like stars at the mere possibility.

"Well, I don't see why we couldn't check into it. Of course, your mom's going to have something to say about it.''

Now would be a perfect opportunity to ask Cody about the man in Rosie's life, but he couldn't do that. It had to come from Rosie.

Cody hadn't said a word. Neither had Nick's parents. Either everyone was keeping quiet to protect Nick from being hurt or none of them knew how deeply Rosie was involved with the other man. But that didn't seem possible, not when she wasn't wearing Nick's rings.

No. The family was guarding the big secret. In any event, it didn't matter. Nick would confront his wife before the day was over.

"Mom won't mind. She could drive to the university every day. Everyone commutes.''

Nick blinked. "Is she still in school?''

"No. She's a teacher on the faculty.''

Stunned by the news, Nick opened the rest-room door and headed for the counter to buy some gum. She'd once talked about getting her elementary-teaching certificate....

He offered Cody a piece before they went out to the car. "What does she teach?''

"Chemistry. She got her doctorate last year.'' Nick heard the love and pride in his voice. "Mom has her own office. Her students call her Dr. Armstrong. Isn't that neat?''

Chemistry? Dr. Armstrong? Nick remembered what a whiz she was at chemistry and physics in high school. All the kids used to ask her for help. Certainly, teaching at the university would pay fairly well and promise her a challenging career.

Was that where she'd met the new man in her life? Was he a professor, too?

As Nick got back in the driver's seat, he studied his wife's features. Her anxious face might have given him a glimmer of hope that she wasn't indifferent to him, *if* it hadn't been for the pitying look in her eyes.

Their leaf green color hadn't changed.

Everything else had.

''You're so pale, Nick. Are you feeling ill?'' she whispered. ''Please stay here for a while if you need to.''

''I'm fine. We're just hungry for some ice cream, aren't we, Cody?''

''Yeah.''

''If it's all right with you, Rosie, we're going to stop at Snelgrove's on the way home.''

''Of course it's all right.'' Her voice actually shook.

She sounded hurt. He hadn't meant anything by the comment. He was just trying to be polite. Hell.

While they got back on the freeway, his thoughts digested the new information about his wife.

He had to admit she looked the epitome of the successful career woman. Earlier he hadn't quite known how to describe her to himself, how to describe the difference in her. Now everything made perfect sense.

"Nick, I've been thinking about the sleeping arrangements for R.T. Since your parents always stay in the guest room upstairs, he could sleep in the spare room down in the base—"

"I want him to sleep with me, Mom," Cody broke in before Nick could suggest the living-room couch.

Cody, Cody. You're not only wonderful, you're a quick study.

"My room has two beds. It'll be cool to talk to him about stuff."

Nick felt Rosie stir restlessly. Her gaze kept swerving to his hand on the wheel; she was obviously still in shock that he was minus the other. "He might not like to be questioned, Cody."

"He'll love it," Nick intervened. "Once you get him going, he won't know when to stop. The biggest mistake a person can make with a vet, particularly a POW, is to clam up on him. He needs to talk everything out, to validate what happened to him."

Do you hear what I'm saying, Rosie?

CHAPTER THREE

"W-WERE YOU AND R.T. put in the same cell?" she asked quietly, breaking the tension-filled silence.

That's a start, Rosie.

"No. Sometimes we were on the other side of the same wall. Other times we were separated by several walls. When the guards were lax, we could talk out loud. Otherwise we spoke to each other in Morse code by tapping on the wall."

"Do they still use that, Dad?"

"Some parts of the military do. But R.T. taught it to me in prison. It's a good communication system if all else fails."

"*Neat!* Do you think R.T. would teach me?"

"Of course. In fact, we'll demonstrate as soon as we get home. You can teach your friends. It's easy. I wish your mom and I had known how to use it in high school. We wouldn't have gotten into so much trouble passing notes in class."

That comment brought a bark of laughter from Cody. More importantly, Rosie's lips softened into a smile reminiscent of the old happy Rosie.

"What do you mean *notes?*" she challenged. "I hate to admit it, but we were terrible, Cody. We had three classes together our senior year, and I didn't learn a single thing in any of them because your father wrote me these long letters I had to return.''

''Yours were longer, and nobody *forced* you to do it, sweetheart.''

Suddenly Rosie went silent and turned her head away.

For a moment they'd met on equal ground, enjoying a memory together.

Until the endearment had slipped out, triggering something so distressing his own wife couldn't face him.

Did the new man in her life call her ''sweetheart,'' too? Was that the reason for her reaction?

''Tell me about your friends, Cody. I want to know their names and hear about the things you guys do when you mess around.''

As he'd hoped, Cody kept up a running commentary until they reached Snelgrove's, in the heart of town. Nick learned that Jeff Taylor was his best friend and that you didn't say ''mess around'' anymore. You were supposed to say ''hang out together.''

''I guess you and R.T. know a lot about that, huh, Dad?''

Nick chuckled, in spite of his pain over Rosie's silence. ''Yup. And you know what? We're still not sick of each other.''

''Yeah, that's how it is with Jeff. We like the same things, and we never fight about anything. Did you have a best friend growing up, Dad?''

''Not the same way you do, Cody. I had a bunch of guys I spent most of my time with. I liked all of them for different reasons. But it was your mom who became my best friend.''

"Really?"

That brought Rosie's head around. Nick could feel her eyes on him.

"You were my best friend, too," she whispered. *But no longer, Rosie?*

"That's why we married out of high school, Cody. It's not for everybody, but it was for us. I was making investments in the stock market, so we struggled to make ends meet. Still, it was fun. I joined the army reserve to pay for college. Your mom worked part-time, and took night classes at the university. Then we found out you were on the way. That was one pretty terrific day.''

"For me, too," Cody said.

Nick laughed again and was pleased to see the faint smile back on Rosie's face.

"I'll run in," Cody offered as they pulled to a stop in one of the parking spaces.

Rosie started to reach for her purse. It shouldn't have upset Nick, but it did. He forestalled her by taking out his wallet. Again he felt her eyeing him as he laid it across his thigh and propped it open with his bandaged arm, while he extracted some bills with his right hand. Then she hastily looked away. *Was the sight so abhorrent to her?*

"Is there anything you'd like, Rosie?"

She shook her head nervously. "But maybe you should buy some rainbow sherbert for your grandparents, Cody."

"Okay. I'll hurry."

He was out of the car like a shot, leaving Nick alone with his wife for the first time since the plane had landed.

Because he didn't know when they'd have this opportunity again before bedtime, he decided to face his worst nightmare right now.

"I've had years to think about what our reunion would be like, Rosie. How much would be the same. How much would be different. Seven years is too long to ask of any man or wom—"

"*Nick!*"

"Let me finish this, Rosie. I don't need details. To be honest, I don't think I could handle them right now. What I need is the simple truth."

A long silence. "I—I thought your parents or C-Cody would have told you by now."

So, there really is someone else in your life. Like a fool, I've been praying I was wrong.

"They didn't breathe a word about it, and our son has told me nothing, hasn't so much as hinted," Nick muttered, exhaling a painful breath. "You've raised a terrific boy who's sensitive enough, and intelligent enough, to leave that up to the mother he adores."

"He adores *you*, Nick." Her voice was full of tears.

His hand had been tapping Morse code on the steering wheel, but he hadn't even noticed until he saw her watching him. She could have no idea he'd been rapping out the same words over and over again, like a litany— "Is there a way out? Are the guards looking?" Old habits died hard. He stopped tapping.

"Who is he, Rosie? What's his name?"

Her body was trembling. Despite the distance separating them, he could feel it.

"He moved here from California two years ago."

Two years? They'd known each other that long?

"His name is Zach Wilde."

"Are you in love with him?"

She buried her face in her hands. "Please don't ask me that question."

Oh, Lord. He'd thought he could deal with this. But he was wrong.

"When I tried to reach you, Mom and Dad said you were on your way back from a Caribbean cruise with Cody. Was Zach with you?"

"Yes," came the muffled answer.

His teeth ground together. "If you've known each other two years, I'm surprised you're not married by now."

Slowly she lifted her head, but she wouldn't look at him. "W-we got engaged on the cruise. Not even your parents know about it yet."

His eyes closed tightly. "When were you planning to be married?"

"June twelfth."

You wanted the truth, Armstrong. Well, you just got it.

"Is Cody crazy about him, too?"

"No." Her voice shook with conviction.

"How come?"

"He didn't want another father if he couldn't have you. Your parents haven't been happy about it, either. They never believed you'd died in that explosion with the others,'' she explained in an emotional outburst, talking faster and faster, more like the old Rosie.

"I didn't want to believe it, either, but after this many years without mention of one POW still being held, I decided I couldn't live with false hope any longer.''

So everyone remained loyal but you.

"Is Cody the reason you haven't married before now?''

She didn't say anything.

"Rosie?'' He wanted the whole truth now, so there'd be no more shocks.

"He's…part of it.''

"And the other part?''

"I couldn't let you go.''

That's something, anyway.

"When did you change your mind?'' he persisted, needing to hear it all.

She sucked in her breath. "Even though Cody couldn't accept Zach, I—I had a wonderful time on the trip. I never dreamed it would be possible to love anyone again after you, Nick.'' Her voice cracked. "But it happened, and I told him I'd marry him.''

Nick felt the way he did after the first week of his captivity, when a select group of Saddam's henchmen took turns roughing him up every two hours for seven consecutive days because he refused to give them any information.

"I'll sleep on the couch tonight.'' He didn't want to think about tomorrow night.

"No!'' she cried. "You can't, Nick. You deserve

to sleep in your own bed. As if I'd let you sleep anywhere else!'' Her cheeks had gone a fiery red.

That's your pity talking, Rosie.

"It doesn't matter where I sleep. I just don't feel like getting into the same bed you've shared with Zach.''

"I've never been to bed with him.''

Nick's head flew back in shock. *What did you just say?*

"After I'd been seeing Zach for a time, I made the decision that I wouldn't sleep with him, because I didn't want sex to complicate my feelings for him, whatever they were.''

"And he's loved you enough to wait?''

She nodded. "Yes. H-he's a wonderful man.''

Nick had been prepared to hate his guts. But he'd found out during the war that it wasn't possible to hate an honorable man.

Rosie might be in love with him, but she hadn't slept with him yet. There might still be a slim chance of winning her back. He'd have to start from scratch. Zach Wilde had two years' head start on him—and he'd won Rosie's love without Cody's cooperation, which meant he was the worthiest of adversaries.

Nick reminded himself that he had another advantage. He'd learned patience.

"Hi!'' Cody climbed into the back seat and shut the door. "Sorry it took so long, but there was a group of tourists from that bus over there up ahead of me. Here's your malt, Dad.''

"Thanks, son.''

He reached for it, no longer worried that he'd have

to throw it out when Cody wasn't watching because he was too sick to eat.

"Does it look good?"

Nick took several large spoonfuls, then couldn't stop. It was sheer ambrosia. "What I'd have given for one of these..."

While his wife and child looked on in wonder, he devoured the whole thing in a matter of seconds.

"Whoa, Dad!"

Nick flashed Cody a smile. "Does that answer your question?"

"I'd get a brain freeze if I ate mine that fast!"

"The trick is to eat it superfast so your brain doesn't have time to get frozen." He deposited his cup in the sack Rosie held open for him.

"Nick, don't tell Cody that!" she chastised. "In high school you used to pull that stunt on people all the time, and they'd imitate you—to their peril."

Rosie was pretending to be disgusted, but he saw that she was struggling not to laugh. Another tiny moment to cherish.

"Dad? You're awesome. I can't wait for my friends to meet you."

"I love you, too, Cody. Let's go home, shall we? R.T.'s been dying for one of these. It would be a sin to let it melt."

He backed the car out of the parking space, then merged with the traffic going east. Within minutes they'd reached Sunnyside Avenue, which ran past the zoo and into Emigration Canyon.

"You'll have to direct me now."

"Turn right on Twenty-second," Rosie murmured. "We're the fourth house on the left."

"This is a nice neighborhood." *Close to the university. Close to Zach?*

"There's Grandpa's car."

The redbrick home with white trim was a moderate-size, one-story rambler with a well-groomed yard and several large shade trees.

Out of nowhere came a deep fierce pride in his wife for making a solid life for herself and Cody. Though Nick knew his parents had lent Rosie their support, she'd had to live through these difficult years alone.

She'd been the one responsible for all the decisions, all the choices that had brought her and Cody to this point.

She'd been the one raising their son, making sacrifices to give him the best life possible. Nick felt profoundly grateful that such a woman was their son's mother.

The next time he got Rosie alone, he'd tell her as much.

"Come on, Dad! Let's find R.T. I want to show you the house and the backyard."

"I'm coming."

Nick got out of the car and went around to help Rosie, but she'd already alighted from the passenger side and had gone to the trunk to get his duffel bag. Was it because she felt sorry for him? Or because she'd grown accustomed to doing everything herself.

To Nick's mind, she'd become more independent. Though it was a great reminder of how much time they'd lost together, he admired this new facet of her personality. He was also frightened of it.

"I'll take that." He pulled out his bag before she could, then shut the trunk.

Once again he faced the sophisticated-looking woman he couldn't quite reconcile with the wife he'd left behind seven years ago. Their gazes locked. She was getting better at masking her pity. Now he saw a hint of pleading in those lush green irises.

"Cody and I just got back from our trip last night, and there's literally no food in the refrigerator. Since we have a full house, I'd better run to the store at Foothill and get some groceries. I'll only buy what we need to get us through to tomorrow. What do you think R.T. would like for snacks? For dinner? What would *you* like?"

Her errand was a legitimate one, yet he could sense her eagerness to get away. She was going to call Zach, maybe even meet him, and there wasn't one damn thing Nick could do about it.

"Orange juice, whole milk—gallons of it. Eggs, fruit, corn on the cob, cauliflower, cheese, potato chips, cashews, bacon, sausage, ham, peanut butter, jam, French bread. A big Hershey bar, a Krackle. Any or all of the above will do for starters."

With every item he mentioned, her eyes filled a little more until the tears overflowed and ran down her cheeks.

On a half sob she cried, *"What did they do to you in there?"*

The old Rosie had come out of hiding for a minute. If he could just find a way to keep her there long enough to make a real connection.

"I want to tell you. I need to tell you, but only when you're ready to hear it."

Her eyes closed tightly. "I'd be a liar if I said I wanted to hear what your life's been like for the last seven years. Ever since I heard the news that you'd been held prisoner all this time, I haven't allowed myself to think about the horror of it. But that's the coward in me talking. No one ever had a greater right to be listened to than you."

That's not the answer I want, Rosie. We're not talking about rights here! This is about love between a husband and wife. How far you've gone away from me, sweetheart.

"Take all the time you need, Rosie. Don't worry about me—I'll be here. With Cody."

NICK'S WORDS still reverberated in her head. He'd always had an uncanny ability to read her thoughts. If anything, his incarceration had sharpened his instincts.

A few minutes after leaving him, she sat numbly in her car, which she'd parked under the terrace opposite the supermarket. Nick had let her know that he was ready to share his story whenever she could handle it. But he'd said a lot more than that.

He *knew* she needed her privacy to make contact with Zach. In his own way, he'd given his permission.

It's not fair, her heart groaned. For years Nick had been locked in prison, and now that he was released, *she'd* locked him out. Unintentionally, inadvertently, but nonetheless she'd locked him out. There'd been too much change. And there was another man....

As for Zach, she could just imagine his pain. With one phone call, his happiness had been wiped away as if it had never been. She wanted desperately to talk to him, but she needed to call Linda Beams first.

There was a phone booth outside the store. Rosie looked up the number and punched it in. The base receptionist said that Linda wouldn't be in her office until the next day.

Trying to recover from her disappointment, Rosie explained her emergency. The receptionist commiserated with her situation and set up an appointment with Linda at nine the next morning.

Of necessity, Rosie realized she'd have to ask Chow Ping to teach her classes again and decided to make the call now before she forgot.

Finally she was able to phone Zach's office, but to her consternation, his secretary said he'd asked her to cancel all his appointments, that he wouldn't be in until the next day.

Rosie's hand shook as she placed a call to his condo, only a few minutes away on Wasatch Boulevard. All she got was the answering machine.

"Zach, darling? It's one-fifteen. I'm shopping for groceries at Dan's in Foothill. If you're home, or if you get home in time to hear this message, come and find me. I'll be here a half hour, no more. I've parked the car in my usual spot. I don't want you calling the house. If we miss each other, I'll phone you later."

Once inside the store, Rosie lost track of time as she went up and down the aisles in search of the items Nick had mentioned, plus a few he hadn't.

Chocolate-chip cookies. He preferred the dough to the baked cookies. He also loved doughnuts, tuna fish, nachos with cheese and refried beans, apple pie. He needed good food and lots of it. She would make certain he put on the weight he'd lost.

One of the friendly baggers, a young man named Dennis, teased her all the way to her car because he'd never seen her buy so many different kinds of groceries. She told him she had company.

If she'd confided that her husband had returned from Desert Storm, she would have been detained by dozens of questions. Not only couldn't she take the time, she felt a strange reluctance to let the world in on her secret—that Nick was alive and home again. Once people found out, their house would be deluged with visitors and phone calls.

Nick was the kind of man who had so many friends and contacts, you couldn't count them all. Everyone would besiege him. He wouldn't have a quiet moment to himself. This was his first day back. He'd want to spend it with family, no one else.

After stashing all the bags in her trunk, Dennis shook his head. "That must be some company. You practically bought out the whole store!"

It did look that way. Maybe she'd gone overboard, but she wanted Nick to eat to his heart's desire. Anything that appealed to him, she wanted him to have.

As she was opening the door to her car, she felt a pair of strong male arms slip around her waist from behind. *Zach.* She'd been so preoccupied, she'd forgotten he might have heard her message and come to find her.

In automatic response, she turned in his arms, seeking his comfortable, solid, familiar frame. But she'd just come from Nick's arms and would never forget how thin he'd felt beneath his uniform jacket. As for R.T.—

"I don't know about you, but I need *this*—" Suddenly Zach's mouth was on hers, claiming her love without hesitation because she'd given him that right when she accepted his ring.

But everything had changed, just as Zach had prophesied hours earlier.

No matter how hard she tried, she couldn't erase the memory of the experience in Nick's arms this morning. Worse, even though they were in a protected area of the parking lot, there were people around—maybe even friends—who would know soon enough that Nick was back and be shocked by her behavior with Zach.

Why on earth had she asked him to meet her here? Her husband was at home, waiting for her!

Fighting another spasm of guilt, she tore her lips from Zach's, but he refused to relinquish his hold on her shoulders. She knew what was coming next, and she couldn't look at him.

"Does he know about us yet?"

"Yes." She nodded. *Nick knows.* He'd known the truth when he'd conducted a search of her soul and found the one thing she'd been dreading he'd discover.

"Rosie?" Zach gave her a gentle shake.

She could hear the questions he hadn't voiced, questions to which there were no answers yet, certainly not the answers he needed to hear.

His fingers kneaded her shoulders with more insistence. "I know you love him, darling, but you're in love with *me!*"

"I am," she said emotionally, "but it's an impossible situation right now."

"I realize that."

"No. I don't think you do." She stared up at him, dry-eyed. "Nick lost his left hand in the war, Zach. The buddy he brought home with him is blind in one eye from the same explosion. When they got off that transport plane, there was no family to greet R.T., so he's going to stay with us for a time. The two of them together would make little more than one of you."

"Lord."

In the next instant, Zach's arms provided the refuge she craved. A torrent of fresh pain over what Nick had suffered ripped through her body.

"We have to talk, sweetheart," he whispered into her hair, "but obviously it can't be here. Tell me what you want me to do. I'll meet you anytime, anywhere. Just don't leave me hanging. I couldn't stand that."

She didn't feel she could stand this untenable situation, either, but neither her pain nor Zach's could compare to Nick's and R.T.'s. "I'll call you."

"When?"

"When I can!" she cried. "Please let me go, darling. I should have been home ten minutes ago."

"Rosie…"

As she pulled out of his arms and got in her car, she took in his chiseled features and windburned cheeks. It dawned on her that he'd been out riding his bike to deal with his grief. How much more agony would all of them be called upon to endure?

"I promise I'll phone you before I go to bed tonight." It was a rash promise, but she owed Zach that much. *She loved Zach that much.*

His pain-filled gaze searched hers for endless moments. He didn't ask her if she'd be sleeping alone. She didn't tell him her intentions.

How could she? She wasn't sure of them herself.

Now that her husband was back needing all kinds of physical and emotional help, she could only function from one moment to the next. The future was terrifying to her.

"I love you," he said in a fierce whisper, leaning inside to capture her mouth one more time before she drove away.

CHAPTER FOUR

NICK NOTICED that a lot of the furnishings in the traditionally styled house were new—but she hadn't gotten rid of their king-size bed.

Were the memories of the passion they'd shared there too precious for her to part with?

Or had she been planning to sleep in it with Zach as soon as they were married—

"Hey, Dad?"

Nick heard his son's voice in the hall and turned swiftly toward the bedroom door. His body had gone clammy from another cold sweat; it had broken out at the thought of Rosie loving another man.

"In here, Cody. Where's R.T.?"

"He's out in the yard with Grandma and Grandpa eating his malt."

"Good."

"Mom let me keep your clothes in my closet. Here they are!"

Cody came into the room carrying Nick's black-and-gray parka, his midnight blue gabardine winter dress coat, a half-dozen of his old pullovers and crew-neck shirts, sweaters, khaki trousers and jeans, all of which would hang loosely on him for some time to come.

Unfortunately, in his naïveté Cody had thought that of course his mom and dad would pick right up where they'd left off and begin sharing a room again. Sharing a bed... Before Nick could suggest that he leave everything as it was for the present, Cody had gone off again, coming back minutes later with another armload of clothes.

"I kept all your T-shirts and shorts so I could wear them when I grow up."

Nick's throat swelled with love and gratitude for this son who filled so many of his needs right now.

"I bet you're tired of all that military stuff, Dad. Why don't you put on something else?"

If he'd thought his old clothes would fit, there was nothing Nick would have liked better. But Cody was so anxious to be of help, Nick couldn't disappoint him. He had no desire to see that eagerness disappear from his son's eyes. "Do you have a belt?"

"Sure. I'll get it!"

Once more he raced out of the room, leaving Nick to deal with the thousand and one memories associated with these clothes—especially the thin T-shirts Rosie used to put on after a shower to entice him away from whatever he was doing in the middle of a lazy Saturday afternoon....

One look at her long slender legs, the way her damp curves transformed the shape of the material, and he forgot the world in the wonder of making love to his gorgeous, giving wife.

He'd experienced enough of life, had heard enough male talk among the men in the reserve long before his capture, to know that his and Rosie's marriage had been exceptional.

It had taken Rosie until the cruise to get engaged again. That had to mean something, didn't it?

Deep in thought, he removed his uniform and shrugged into a long-sleeved navy pullover the sleeve of which could hang down over his damaged arm if he wanted. A glance in the mirror above Rosie's dressing table told him he looked like hell. If anything, the folds of the material emphasized his thinness.

Cody came in as Nick zipped up the old jeans Rosie used to like so much.

"Here you go, Dad." He offered him the belt when he could see that the jeans wouldn't stay up. It made Nick more determined than ever to get some flesh back on his bones.

Cody helped him fasten the buckle. "What do you think, son?"

"You look good, Dad."

Nick flashed him a smile, then pulled Cody onto the bed to wrestle with him. "Liar."

When their wrestling eventually had them on the floor, Cody cried out, "You may be skinny, but you're strong! I quit, Dad."

"Yeah?" Nick sat up, grinning.

"Yeah."

"Say it like you mean it."

"I surrender!"

After Nick released him, a broad smile lit Cody's face. "Your arms and legs are like steel bars."

"That's because R.T. and I worked out on a regular basis."

A haunted look crept into Cody's expression. "I heard the Iraqi guards tortured prisoners for doing that."

They did, Cody, in ways you don't want to know about and will never hear from me.

"Yeah, well, R.T. and I were smart and did our exercising at night when they got lazy and couldn't see us very well." It was time to change the subject. "You know, you're pretty tough yourself."

"No, I'm not. But someday I'm going to be just like you."

Nick's emotions were spilling out all over the place. He stood up and grabbed his son in a bear hug. "I love you, Cody. I'm a lucky dad. From now on, we're going to spend a lot of time together." He paused. "For starters, I thought we'd join a gym and work out together in the evenings after you've finished your homework."

"Cool! And when summer comes, we'll go on a whole bunch of backpacking trips."

"I'm planning on it. We'll take some of your pals and camp up by Mirror Lake in the Uintahs."

"Jeff's dad loves to do stuff like that, too. You'll like him a lot. I can't wait for you to meet everybody!"

"I can't wait, either."

"I guess we won't be able to do much in August because I have football practice. Will you come to my games?"

"I'll never miss another one."

"But, Dad, you're still in the reserve, aren't you?"

Nick shook his head. "No, Cody. I'm through with all that. I'm home forever."

"Yippee!" Cody burst out before hugging Nick again.

Catching sight of the messy bed, Nick let go of his son and suggested they clean things up before Rosie got home. "I'll hang what I can in the closet while you stack everything else over there in the corner. I'm sure your mom will have her own ideas about where my stuff's supposed to go."

"She's sure taking a long time," Cody grumbled.

"That's because I was so hungry I gave her a huge list of groceries to buy."

"Dad?" he murmured tentatively.

Here it comes.

Nick finished hanging his coat and parka in the closet next to Rosie's pink quilted robe, the one he'd bought her the last Christmas they were together. "Yes?" he answered without turning around, burying his face in the soft fabric. It smelled of the bath oil she always used and brought back a flood of intimate memories.

He heard Cody expel a troubled sigh. "I forget. Never mind."

"Cody?" Nick closed the closet doors and faced his son. "If you need to talk to me, then I want to hear it. I guess I hate secrets about as much as I hate anything."

"Me, too." Cody bowed his head. Nick realized he was trying hard to find the courage to broach the one subject guaranteed to exacerbate his father's pain. He needed help.

"I understand you just got back from a Caribbean cruise with your mom and Zach Wilde."

At the mention of the other man's name, Cody's dark head reared back. His tanned face reflected astonishment. "You know about him?"

Nick nodded. "Your mom says they're engaged and planning to be married in June."

His son's eyes glittered with unshed tears. "But you're home now, so she *can't* marry him."

My feelings exactly.

"I wish life was that simple, Cody, but it isn't."

"I *hate* war!" Cody shouted unexpectedly, pounding the wall with his fist. "I hate Zach. She's probably over at his condo right now." He broke down, trying to smother his sobs.

Nick had assumed as much, too, and the knowledge was killing him.

"If Mom marries him, I'm never speaking to her again."

It was starting. The thing he'd been dreading had started. Right now, Cody's justifiable anger terrified him. He had to do something to alleviate his son's pain.

"Do you have a bike? And did your mom keep my old one?"

Cody stared at him in bewilderment. "Yes." His shoulders were still heaving. "Both."

"We can't talk here. Let's take a ride down to Sunnyside Park."

With that suggestion, Cody wiped his eyes, which

had begun to look a little less wild. "Okay. I'll get them out of the garage and meet you in front."

"Good. While you do that, I'll let your grandparents know where we're going so they won't worry."

Cody dashed from the room. Nick followed at a slower pace only to discover Rosie in the kitchen, her arms loaded with groceries.

Their eyes met. She was the first to look away, guilt written all over her face as she started emptying the bags. He studied her mouth, wondering if Zach's kiss had blotted out the memory of the one he'd given her at the base earlier in the day.

"Are there more of those?" He nodded to the bags she'd put on the counter.

"Yes."

"I'll get them."

In the space of a heartbeat, her glance flicked to his left arm, then she averted her eyes. "Nick... please... This is your first day home. Let me wait on you."

"I'm not an invalid, Rosie."

She wheeled around to face him, her cheeks on fire. "I know you're not."

"Then don't treat me like one. Where did you park the car?"

She moistened her lips nervously. "It's behind your parents' car."

He stole an apple from one of the sacks and bit into it. "I'll be right back." Finishing it in a few bites, he headed out the door. Cody was waiting in front of the house, straddling his mountain bike. Nick's old bike lay on the lawn beside him.

Nick reached into the trunk of the car for the groceries. "I'm going to run these in to your mother, then we'll go."

"Okay," he answered quietly.

"Hey— Catch!" He tossed a couple of packages of Twinkies at his son, producing the smile he was looking for. "I'll hurry."

When he reentered the kitchen, Rosie was peeling potatoes. She murmured a cordial thank-you, but her rigid back, the set of her beautiful golden head, betrayed the growing tension between them. He put the bags on the counter.

"Cody's going to take me on a little tour of the neighborhood. We'll be back before the food's ready."

She turned to him, a hint of pleading in her shadowed green eyes. "I—I think that's a good idea."

Nick's chest constricted. "I thought it might be," he bit out, hurting like hell.

"Please don't be sarcastic, Nick. I didn't mean it that way. It's just that Cody has wanted his father for so long now...." Her voice trailed off.

"Shall I apologize now for granting him his wish?"

"What are you talking about?" He could see she was fighting tears, but he couldn't control his feelings any longer.

"I thought it was obvious. My unexpected return from the dead has destroyed your dreams."

She flinched as if he'd slapped her. *"Nick!"* Her face lost all its color, and he felt her pain, her confusion and guilt. But the white-hot heat of his own pain had consumed him; he had to get out of there. He left the kitchen on a run, ignoring her pleas for him to come back.

If Cody was surprised at his quick return, he didn't say anything. Instead, he put a Twinkie in his father's mouth. "I bet you haven't had one of these in a *long* time."

After the gut-wrenching scene in the kitchen, Nick didn't think it would be possible for him to smile again, but he did. "I bet I haven't, either," he responded, his mouth full of cake and filling. The taste took him back to his childhood. "It's nice to know that some things never change." He managed another smile.

"Let's take off, Cody. I think I can still remember how to ride one of these contraptions."

Levering himself onto the seat, he grasped hold of the handlebars, almost forgetting that his bad arm wouldn't be of any use on the hand brake.

"You may have to help me when we need to stop."

"Gotcha, Dad."

Once again Nick found himself thanking God for his son. The bond between them was growing stronger with every passing second.

Side by side, they pedaled to the corner and headed down Sunnyside Avenue, picking up speed. After several blocks they had to stop at a semaphore. On cue, Cody's left hand reached out to Nick's brake. While they waited for the light to change, he asked, "Was it okay with Mom?"

After a slight hesitation, Nick answered. "Sure.

She and Grandma won't have our meal ready for an hour at least.''

''Dad?''

There was that tone in his son's voice again. Nick took a deep breath. ''Yes?''

''Are you and Mom going to get a divorce?''

''MRS. ARMSTRONG? Can I be of any help? Peeling vegetables was my strong suit during KP duty.''

Rosie took a shuddering breath. She hadn't heard R.T. come in the back door and prayed he couldn't tell she'd been crying. ''Thank you, R.T. I've already put the scalloped potatoes in the oven. But if you'd like to finish the carrots, I'm going to put on some jeans and a T-shirt. I'll just be a few minutes.''

''There's no hurry.''

She had a feeling he wasn't talking about her change of outfit. Everyone had given her and Nick a wide berth, including his parents. Through the window over the sink she could see them on the porch swing, their heads close together in avid conversation.

They hate me. They hate what I've done to their son.

Who could blame them?

I hate myself.

At the door to the hall Rosie paused and said, ''Please. Consider our house your home. Help yourself to anything that looks good. Day or night.''

''I'm glad you said that. I've been thinking about a peanut-butter-and-honey sandwich for hours now.''

''They're both in the right-hand cupboard, and the

bread is in the fridge. I bought you your own gallon of milk.''

''I'm your slave for life, Mrs. Armstrong.'' He opened the cupboard and took out the two jars.

''Call me Rosie.''

''Deal.''

After another pause, she murmured, ''R.T.? H-how long were you married?''

He'd already made his sandwich and was in the process of devouring the second half.

''A year. I could be wrong, but I'm pretty sure Cynthia's remarried by now and probably has a couple of kids. Even if I could've reached her by phone, I didn't really think she'd be there to meet me. We didn't have that long a history together, not like you and the sar—'' He stopped for a second, then amended, ''Not like some married couples.''

Rosie's eyes closed tightly. R.T. and Nick were as close, emotionally, as two people could be. There were no secrets between them.

''I—I've hurt Nick,'' she confessed on a half sob.

''I know.''

''What am I going to do?'' she whispered in agony.

''What do you *want* to do?''

''I want to set the clock back seven years.''

He made a sound of exasperation and shook his head. ''Rosie, you don't get it. *You're* the only reason he's alive! The only reason he *stayed* alive!

''Because of him, *I'm* still alive. Talk to him, dammit! After six and half years rotting in an Iraqi hellhole, he needs to talk about it. He needs to talk his head off about everything that happened to him. He deserves that much from you—from all of you—but he can't do it with everyone tiptoeing around him, treating him like he's a piece of glass that's going to shatter.

"Good Lord, he was a superman out there! Anyone else would have left me for dead, but not the sarge. Without me, he could have gotten away and been picked up by our own soldiers.

"Instead, he dragged me from the explosion site and carried me through the rest of that minefield. He didn't even know how bad his injury was. His *hand* was blown off." R.T. swallowed several times, convulsively.

"No one expected the reserve units to see action. None of us was adequately prepared to be so rapidly activated and torn from our families. Yet the way your husband stood up to the torture and never broke, you'd have thought he'd been trained for the military all his life." R.T.'s face screwed up as tears fell unashamedly down his pale cheeks. "I wouldn't have made it without him. He's the best of the best.

"Don't you see it's no good wishing to put back the clock? He's done his time, Rosie. If nothing else, he's earned the right to a full hearing from the woman who sent him off to war a whole ma—"

"*Dear God, R.T.—*"

"Hey." He pressed his forehead against the cupboard. "I'm sorry for going off like that."

"You had every right!" she cried, ashamed of her inability to understand. His words had given her a glimpse into the living nightmare of their past. Selfishly, she didn't want to see anymore. What kind of monster *was* she?

"No. You're as much a victim of the war as we are. You might as well know now. I was the one driving the truck when we hit that mine. If it hadn't been for me, and if your husband hadn't stayed with me, hadn't saved my life, he would have returned home to you with the guys who survived the explosion."

"Don't talk about blame, R.T. All I hope is that you don't hate *me* too much."

He shook his head again. "I've stricken that word from my vocabulary."

"Then you're a far better person than I am. Excuse me," she whispered.

She hurried into her bedroom feeling sick to her stomach. The sight of Nick's old clothes stacked in the corner gave her another jolt. Cody hadn't wasted any time. His father was back, and life would resume as if the war had never taken place.

Swallowing the bile rising in her throat, she rushed over to the closet to change clothes. She gasped when she opened the doors and saw more of Nick's things hanging next to hers.

Unconsciously she reached out to touch the clothes she'd thought she'd dealt with for the last time.

Nick had always been physically perfect to her. In his topcoat, he'd looked sophisticated and rakishly handsome. She groaned. If she allowed memories to intrude, she'd never be able to cope.

Stop it, Rosie. This is sick. You're still thinking of him as dead. He's alive! Why can't you believe it?

Because he doesn't look the same? Because he's not physically perfect anymore and you're repulsed?

Because you're in love with Zach and don't want to believe it?

That's what Nick thinks.

Is that what you think, Rosie? Do you even know what you think?

If you're this shallow and insensitive to another human's suffering, if you're really this cruel and selfish, then you need help, Rosie Armstrong. The kind of professional help not even Linda Beams can give you.

Please, God. Make it possible for me to listen to him tonight. Give me the strength to get through the next twenty-four hours without losing my mind....

Rosie stood there on shaky legs trying to gather the courage to phone Zach and tell him she couldn't see him or talk to him for a couple of days.

Now was the time to call him, while Nick was out of the house. Then maybe she'd be able to concentrate long enough to put dinner on the table. *Nick's first home-cooked meal in seven years.*

Quickly, before any more time was lost, she changed out of her suit into jeans and a cotton top. After exchanging her high heels for leather sandals, she sat on the edge of the bed, picked up the phone and punched in Zach's number.

When she got his answering machine, she let out the breath she'd been holding. To her horror she recognized it for what it was. Relief.

Relief because she wasn't ready for the kind of

pressure she knew Zach would apply when she told him her plans.

He would try to break down her resolve, change her mind. And because of her love for him, she was too vulnerable right now to withstand all the emotional arguments he'd use.

"Zach?" She couldn't prevent her voice from shaking. "I'm keeping my promise by phoning you now. There won't be a chance later.

"I've had a little time to think and I've come to a decision. I—I'm not going to see you for a while. Please don't ask me for a timetable, because I can't give you one. I owe Nick my undivided attention while he adjusts. Cody's emotional state is fragile. So is mi—"

"And what about mine?" an angry male voice broke in, one she hardly recognized as Zach's. He was at the condo, after all.

She jumped to her feet, trembling from head to toe.

"You can't do this to us, Rosie. You shut me out for too damn long as it is. I'm not trying to be unreasonable. All I ask is that you fit me in for at least a few minutes every day so you don't forget what I look like!"

She gripped the receiver more tightly. "That can't happen and you know it. I love you, darling. But think— Nick's been deprived of his life for seven years. *Seven years.* Now I have to spend a few days helping him to put some of the pieces back together. I'm the only one who can do that—but it'll be impossible if I allow myself to see you."

She heard a deep groan.

"No one told him, but I'm positive he knows we were together today. I can't hurt him like that again, Zach. I can't!"

There was a dreadful silence. "But you can hurt *me*."

Her face went hot. "That's not fair, darling. I'm trying to do the right thing. But to sneak behind his back would be cowardly. It's not worthy of either one of us."

"I thought you told him about us!"

"I—I have."

"Then he knows the situation and he'll have to understand that you and I need time together, too."

"You're asking for understanding from a man who was left to rot in underground prisons for six and a half years?" she asked. "Have you forgotten I'm still his wife?"

"That's funny," he lashed out. "Until this morning, I thought you were my fiancée."

"Zach...you know what I meant."

"I'm afraid I do," he muttered. "If you ever figure out who you are, let me know. See you around."

"No, Zach. Don't hang up! Please—"

But the line was dead.

"Rosie?"

No...

She whirled around, the phone still in her hand. "Nick—"

"I didn't mean to eavesdrop."

She swallowed hard. "I'm sure you didn't. I—I

was calling Zach to tell him I couldn't see him for a while."

"It's okay," he murmured, still standing in the doorway. "You don't owe me any explanations. If I were in his shoes, I probably would've charged my way over here long before now."

Knowing the old Nick, he probably would have, she admitted to herself, not wanting to acknowledge the ghost of a smile hovering at the corner of his mouth. For a fraction of a moment she could remember other times when he'd smiled like that. It made her feel light-headed.

"From my standpoint, Zach's self-restraint is highly commendable. According to Cody, he's 'pretty cool, a great guy. I just don't want Mom to marry him.'"

That was quite a heart-to-heart they'd had during their bike ride.

Tears stung her eyes and she looked away.

"Rosie, now that I'm back home to father our son, Cody isn't going to be as difficult. Do you hear what I'm saying?"

She could hear what he *wasn't* saying, and it confused her.

Nick was being so understanding it had caught her off guard. On the other hand, Zach was acting so completely out of character she couldn't explain it.

"Mom and Dad have taken over in the kitchen. We'll all get along fine if you want to use this time to drive to Zach's condo and make peace with him. Judging by your end of the conversation, the man's going through hell. He has a right to be put out of his misery.''

A slow burning anger held her in place. ''Don't say any more, Nick.''

He frowned. ''Say what?'' he demanded.

She dropped the receiver back on the cradle. ''You know what I mean.''

''I think you're going to have to tell me.''

Shades of the old Nick were surfacing faster than she could assimilate them. She whirled around to face him. ''Hell is the place you've just come from. To use the word in any other context is ludicrous, and you know it.''

His eyes narrowed. ''Hell is a place. I agree. But it's also a state of mind.''

''Stop it, Nick!'' she practically shouted at him. ''You can't compare what you've lived through to my state of mind or anyone else's. If you're trying to destroy me, you're doing a stellar job.''

He moved away from the doorjamb and stepped closer. ''Anything but, Rosie. You have to understand that I took a calculated risk in coming home without giving you advance warning.

''My superiors in Germany cautioned me that it would be better if we had our first reunion over there, to give everyone some time to come to grips with the fact that I didn't die in the war.''

Rosie shuddered in renewed pain to hear him say those words so matter-of-factly.

''I thought I knew better.'' His voice sounded gruff. ''I was so anxious to get home to you and Cody I refused to listen to professionals who knew what they were talking about. Poor R.T. thinks he owes me his life because he has some misguided idea that I saved his, so he was willing to do whatever I wanted.

"The poor devil deserved to know his fate long before he got off that plane this morning. That's the other regret I'm going to have to live with." There were tears in his voice. "Not one damn person was there to let him know he'd been missed, to acknowledge that he'd ever fought for his country…"

"Oh, Nick." She moved toward him. But his body had gone rigid. She sensed he'd reject any comfort she tried to offer.

"The timing couldn't have been better, could it?" he asked with evident self-loathing. "If I'd done the right thing, you and Zach would have heard the news about me several weeks ago and you could've had time to talk things out and come up with some kind of strategy before you had to face me again.

"Instead, I burst in on what was probably one of the happiest times of your life. We both know Cody would've eventually accepted Zach as his stepfa—"

"There is no wrong or right time!" She interrupted him before he could say another damning word. "Three weeks or nine hours could make no difference to the fact that you're alive and you've come home! That's all that matters. All that's important!"

One dark brow lifted. "Not true, Rosie. We all need time to get our bearings. After dinner, R.T. and I will move to a hotel for a week or two, maybe the University Plaza Hotel. Cody and I passed it on our bikes. It's two minutes from the house. That close, I'll be accessible to him after school—''

"No!" In the next breath she'd closed the distance between them and grasped his shoulders. "Don't you dare talk about moving out! *This is your home, Nick. I want you here!*" She shook him.

His eyes took on a faintly glacial sheen. "But not in your bed."

"*Yes,* I want you in *our* bed," she fired back.

The cord in his neck throbbed. "Tonight?"

His question pulsed in the air like a live wire. Their gazes collided.

One wrong word and Nick would leave. She could see it in the savagery of his expression.

If she let him walk away now, something told her the painful consequences of that action would haunt her for the rest of her life.

Forgive me, Zach, but this is something I have to do.

"Yes," she whispered. "Tonight. Please, Nick. Promise me you won't move out."

CHAPTER FIVE

THE FEAR IN THOSE pleading green eyes wasn't something Rosie could fake. No doubt their son's welfare figured heavily in her panic-driven petition.

Cody was one terrific kid. But he was fragile right now, and there was a limit to his ability to cope with their hellish situation. Having just heard his son spill his guts, Nick shared Rosie's concern.

Her fear, rather than the touch of her hands on his shoulders or the words she'd felt compelled to say for decency's sake if nothing else, made Nick reconsider his decision to move out.

"There have been enough shocks for one day. I have no desire to create another crisis for Cody. He's already torn apart by conflicting loyalties. I'll stay."

"Thank you," she said quietly. She seemed unaware that her fingers dug into his skin through the pullover as her eyelids fluttered closed. They drew his attention to the faint purple smudges beneath her lashes, evidence of her trauma, the lack of sleep.

New lines radiated from the corners of her eyes and around her generous mouth. The shape of her facial features was a little more pronounced, giving her a more womanly aspect, evidence of the passage of years he'd missed. Years they could never recapture as a joint memory of living together and loving.

To resolve your grief, you must accept the fact that what was will never be again. Then you must give yourself permission to grieve over your grief.

Those words—reiterated by the hospital staff on a daily basis—were so easy to say. So impossible to act on, Nick moaned inwardly.

How do I accept the fact that the stranger in my arms was once blood of my blood, flesh of my flesh, soul of my soul?

How can I bear it that she loves another? How do I stand that?

"Mom? Dad? Grandma says dinner's ready."

"We'll be right there," they both answered at the same time.

As Rosie pulled away from him, her wan little smile came and went too fast for Nick to believe they'd shared a moment of spontaneous humor.

He followed her out of the room and down the hall. Though she was a good fifteen pounds thinner than he remembered her, the shape of her body had grown more svelte and womanly. She looked toned. *She looked terrific.* No doubt Zach was her match in all the ways that counted.

Nick had thought he'd want to see his successor. But certain images of Rosie with the man Nick's mind had conjured up brought on such an intense spasm of jealousy it made him think again.

"I hope you still love ham and scalloped potatoes," she called over her shoulder.

"Why would that have changed?"

At his question, she faltered in her stride and turned to him. "I don't know. I was just trying to make pleasant conversation."

"Hell, Rosie. You know I didn't mean it the way it sounded."

The pinched look on her face told him he'd really hurt her. "Then why did you ask it?"

That's a good question, Armstrong.

"Maybe because once upon a time you would never have felt forced to 'make' conversation with me. Maybe because it was a too-painful reminder of the years we've missed, and for a little while I wanted to forget the past. Maybe because you made me feel like a long-lost uncle, instead of your husband. Maybe because I'm aware you'd rather be with Zach right now than here with me. Is that enough truth for you?"

Her eyes filled, but not one tear fell. "I'm sorry. In the future I'll try to be more careful."

"That's the point, Rosie. I don't want you to *try* to do anything. I'm the one who should apologize for being so damn touchy." He expelled a deep sigh. "Just ignore me and be yourself."

Her gaze didn't quite meet his. "I don't know who 'myself' is anymore."

"That makes two of us. Aside from Cody, it appears to be the only common ground between us. Perhaps because this is brand-new territory for both of us, we can agree to forgive each other ahead of time for any unintentional slings and arrows that find their mark."

Her face crumpled in despair. "You talk as if we're enemies."

"No, Rosie. The exact opposite, I think. An enemy desires to harm. You and I, on the other hand, keep making wider circles to avoid hurting each other. But somewhere in that process, we continue to alienate all the same."

She averted her head. "How are we going to get through the rest of this day without doing more damage?"

"I suppose by accepting the fact that we're both painfully aware of how easily our psyches can be bruised with one wrong word or glance."

"I don't want to hurt you, Nick." Her voice sounded tormented.

"I don't want to hurt you, either." He gestured toward her with his good arm. "Come on, let's go eat."

Unaccountably relieved that they'd survived the latest skirmish, he trailed her into the small formal dining room off the kitchen.

"There you two are," his father said. Nick detected satisfaction in his tone, as if seeing Nick and Rosie together meant everything was getting back to normal in a hurry, and they could proceed with life as it used to be.

His mother fussed around R.T., but Nick recognized the approving gleam in her eyes as he and Rosie emerged from the hallway. That gleam revealed all her hopes and dreams for a happy future.

Nick stood in awe of his parents' incredible optimism. When everyone else had given up, *even Rosie,* they, along with Cody, hadn't believed in their hearts that Nick had been killed in the war.

Was it any wonder they assumed he and his estranged wife would have little difficulty weathering this final storm before ending up in the sunshine again?

When Nick had called them from Germany, there was no mention of Zach. Not until Rosie's kiss did he realize another man had entered the picture.

At first he'd thought his parents had purposely left Zach's name out of the conversation because they didn't want to deliver any blows that might mar his homecoming. But since this morning, he'd had time to reflect on his parents' silence about Rosie's fiancé, and he'd come to a different conclusion.

They hadn't said a word to him about Zach because they refused to face the fact that Rosie could love anyone except their son. Period.

Probably because he was an only child, Nick's parents had a fatal blind spot where he was concerned. If they chose to believe that something was so, then no power on earth could change their belief.

Nick loved them for that astounding quality—for loving him without qualification—but he also wept for them because in their denial, they were going to reap the proverbial whirlwind.

"Sit up here, Dad," Cody said excitedly.

The head of the table. How many times in the past seven years had he dreamed of moments like this?

Stop it, Armstrong. The past is over.

"Don't mind if I do." He tousled Cody's hair,

then pulled out the chair on the left, next to his own. His gaze darted to his wife. "Rosie?"

"Thank you."

As he guided her, he knew his hand rested a little too long on her shoulder, but her warmth and softness had seeped through his palm, grounding it.

She was so alive. Her energy infiltrated his starving body, reminding him how much he craved her touch. *Lord help me.*

Somehow he'd thought he was prepared for this moment, with all his family gathered around the table anticipating this most special of thanksgiving feasts. But as he took in each beloved face, he felt his throat close up. His heart hammered so painfully in his chest he couldn't breathe.

"If you don't mind, I'd like to say grace," R.T. said, intervening at the precise moment Nick thought he'd have to excuse himself from the table.

During their years of captivity, R.T. and Nick had become extensions of each other. When one cut himself, the other bled. Right now R.T.'s steady brown gaze was focused on Rosie, seeking her permission.

Her face softened as she responded in a tremulous voice, "I wish you would."

"Let's all join hands."

Cody grabbed Nick's right hand and clung. It was purely accidental that Rosie was sitting at Nick's left, which meant that she'd have to hold on to his bad arm, above the wrist. He had to admit she hid her revulsion well. So well, in fact, that he could almost believe she wasn't aware of it. No doubt shock had settled in and she wasn't feeling much of anything.

"Dear Father, we thank you..." Nick heard the crack in R.T.'s voice, then a pause. "We thank you for life itself. For the beautiful circumstances in which we find ourselves this day. For the many prayers offered in our behalf, which led to our being freed. Help us find the strength to use this freedom in wise ways, meaningful ways, which might help others.

"Bless this house with every needful thing. Bless the hands that prepared this food, that it will nourish—" his voice trembled "—and strengthen our bodies.

"At this time, Father," he continued, his voice dropping to a lower register, "I wish to thank you for my buddy, Nick, Sergeant Armstrong. He was your servant, your instrument. If it weren't for him—"

Nick felt Rosie's hand slide up his forearm and squeeze it hard before R.T. whispered, "Amen."

"Amen," Nick's father pronounced in a suspiciously thick tone. He picked up the carving knife and began to cut large slices of ham. "Let's eat. You first, R.T."

"Amen," Rosie murmured, staring straight into Nick's eyes before she allowed her hand to fall away. At this moment, he could read admiration in those green depths. The kind of respect one would have for an exceptional human being, whether male or female.

But definitely *not* the look of the impassioned lover he'd left behind seven years ago, the besotted wife who'd once worshiped the ground he'd walked on, just as he'd worshiped everything about her and still did.

No. These days Zach Wilde was the person upon whom she lavished her desire.

Nick's stomach churned.

In his haste to reach his drink, he knocked over the glass, sending the milk splashing all over himself and Cody, not to mention the attractive paisley tablecloth he'd never seen before.

While Cody dashed to the kitchen for paper towels, Nick got to his feet in time to see his mother come rushing toward him with an anxious face, napkin in hand. "What's the matter, Nicky? If you didn't feel well, you should have told us."

"No need to get alarmed, Mom. I'm just clumsy." He walked her back to her chair, then returned to his place to help Cody clean up.

"That was one of the pluses of living in a cell," R.T. piped up. "If we spilled our food, it didn't matter."

Cody looked at R.T. "What kind of food did they give you?"

R.T. paused before taking a bite of ham. "I never did figure it out. Did you?" He switched his gaze to Nick who could never thank R.T. enough for defusing another unpleasant moment.

"Nope. In fact I'm not sure that's what you'd call it."

Neither his parents nor Rosie, especially Rosie, seemed to find his comment funny. R.T. and Cody, however, laughed out loud.

"Forget all that, son," George muttered. "Now here's a real meal you can sink your teeth into."

Nick shook his head at the heaping plate of food set in front of him. If he got through a third of it, he'd be surprised. He and R.T. shared an amused glance. No matter how good everything looked, their stomachs had shrunk. The doctors had told them to eat lots of small meals throughout the day.

"Grandma makes the best biscuits in the whole world, R.T. You can't stop with just one."

"I'm finding that out, Cody."

For a few minutes there was a lull in the conversation while everyone ate. Throughout his marriage to Rosie, Nick had been served this same meal many times. But he'd never appreciated it in quite the same way, especially the scalloped potatoes. He was glad she'd made enough for an army because he had trouble sleeping at night and planned to raid the refrigerator.

Suddenly the sound of a high-pitched siren rent the air. Both Nick and R.T. covered their ears and leapt to their feet. In the process, Nick's cob of corn dropped to the plate with a thud and his chair fell backward on the carpet. But until the din finally subsided, he was rooted to the spot.

"Dad? It was just a car alarm...."

Cody's anxious expression was superseded only by the horrified look in Rosie's eyes.

Slowly Nick lowered his hand. "Sorry," he murmured, then righted the chair and sat down again. "We didn't mean to scare you. I'm afraid R.T. and

I are going to be doing a lot of strange things for a while.''

His mother started to cry, but his father patted her hand and she caught herself. Looking around, he said, ''Who wants more ham?''

R.T. was still on his feet. ''I don't think I could, sir. If you'll excuse me for a minute, I'm going to try to find out if someone knows where my aunt is. But I'll be back for dessert. Since I heard we're having strawberry shortcake, I haven't been able to think about anything else.''

Nick flashed him a private signal. *Get out of here, R.T., before you jump through the ceiling.*

His gaze followed R.T.'s progress from the dining room before he realized that Rosie's complexion had paled to alabaster. She sat rigidly in her chair. ''What just happened, Nick? And don't make light of it.''

For the first time all day, he felt that maybe he had her attention.

After a brief hesitation, in which he weighed the wisdom of letting Cody hear this, he said, ''All right. Part of our harassment in the bunkers was to be awakened in the dead of night by a long blaring siren set at decibels high enough to puncture an eardrum. That only happened once before we learned to stuff our ears with whatever was available, because you never knew when they were going to pull one of their stunts.''

Just reliving the memory, Nick felt sweat break out on his forehead. ''It happened to us on the fourth night of our incarceration. Up to that point they hadn't fed us, given us water or let us go to sleep.

We'd been put in cages too small for us to stand or lie down. There was nothing we could do but sit or stand in a bent position.''

"No, Nicky!" his mother wailed. "I can't bear it." She ran from the room, sobbing.

"Janet?" Nick's father pushed himself away from the table and hurried after her.

By now Cody's pallor matched his mother's. His eyes filled his whole face. "They were trying to break you down so you'd give them information, huh, Dad?"

"That's right, son. But R.T. and I kept our mouths shut. After four days and nights of torture, we didn't care what they did to us. We were too exhausted and just passed out where we were. That's when they used the siren on us.

"As I said, the first time it went off, I woke up thinking the bunker had been bombed. Because we couldn't get out of our cages, we figured we were goners. But we soon learned that it was a routine tactic to make us talk. When that didn't work, they roughed us up on a fairly regular basis, but between sessions, we were at least given cells large enough to lie down in.

"I'm afraid the siren we heard a few minutes ago triggered a reaction that's going to be hard to change. Our nerves have been shot to hell, but give us time. One day we'll be able to sit as calmly as you did."

Which was probably a lie. But it sounded good and seemed to satisfy Cody for the moment.

Rosie's state of mind was another matter. She

looked ill. So ill, in fact, that Nick thought she might faint.

"I—I'm going to fix the dessert. Cody? Will you start clearing the table?"

He nodded.

"We'll both help," Nick offered.

"No!"

Her pleading eyes belied the sharpness of her tone. "I'm worried about R.T. Go to him. He mustn't be alone right now and you'll know how to comfort him. After what you've just told us, I don't think anyone else could."

Maybe he'd gotten through to her a little.

"He'll be all right. If anything, he's embarrassed. I'll talk to him, and then we'll be back in for dessert."

"Your mom's going to need help, too."

But not you, Rosie?

A helpless anger raged inside him. "She's got Dad. That's what a husband's for."

Rosie turned away.

In an instant, he'd destroyed the ephemeral rapport between them. *Another sling, another arrow. More regrets. Hell.*

"MOM?" CODY HAD JUST walked into the kitchen with a load of plates. "Are you okay?"

No. I'm not. I don't think I ever will be again.

"Not really." Her voice shook. "I'm sorry you had to hear those things." Appalled was more like it. Didn't Nick care that those graphic details of his torture would give their son nightmares?

"Jeez, Mom, I'm not a baby. We've learned about a lot of horrible things in my world-history class. Dad's so cool not to break. I love him, even if *you* don't!'

"Cody—"

"It's true!" he blurted, tears gushing from his eyes. "Dad figured out where you went today. He's not dumb."

Before she could demand he apologize, Cody dashed into the dining room for another load of dishes. The violence of his emotions almost immobilized her. She swayed against the counter where she'd been putting whipped cream on the strawberries. Her chest pains felt real.

"I'll tell you one thing," Cody began in that aggressive tone the second he came back in with the ham platter and biscuit tray. "I hate Zach. I *hate* him. If you marry him, plan on me living with Dad."

Rosie felt as though she was going to die. "Cody…Cody…" In despair she reached for him, desperate to prevent the fissure from cracking wide open. But for the first time in their lives, he jerked his body away from her and flew out of the kitchen.

She didn't have to wonder where he'd run. Suddenly her home had turned into an armed camp, and Cody had chosen sides. In less than twenty-four hours she'd managed to alienate everyone she loved….

Rosie hid her tear-wet face in the nearest dish towel. There shouldn't have to be a division. Life wasn't supposed to be like this!

"Rosie, honey?" George said gently. She hadn't heard him enter the kitchen.

"Dad... How's Mom?" she asked in a dull voice.

"Pretty bad. She's lying down. Nicky's in with her. I guess you didn't hear the doorbell. Do you want me to get it?"

Zach? With the circumstances so precarious, he wouldn't come over here now. *Or would he?* Was that what her father-in-law thought?

Nick had said that if he'd been in Zach's position, he wouldn't have let anything stop him. Had she underestimated Zach's pain? His desperation? If he *was* at the door, she didn't want anyone else answering it.

"No," she said, wiping her eyes. "I'll go. Thank you."

He touched her arm to detain her. "Honey..." he began, then seemed to think better of it and fell silent.

It didn't matter. Rosie knew exactly what he wanted to say. *Don't hurt my boy. You mustn't hurt him. How can you hurt Janet and me this way?*

The bell rang again. Her heart had dropped to her feet before she reached the foyer and opened the front door, expecting to see Zach.

Instead, a slender petite brunette with short hair and a pretty face stood anxiously on the porch. Her blue-gray eyes seemed to be searching past Rosie.

"Yes?" Rosie said. "May I help you?"

"I hope so," came the fervent reply. "I'm Cynthia Ellis, R.T.'s wife. I heard he was here," she said in a trembling voice. "R.T.'s aunt phoned with the news a little while ago. I drove up from Orem as fast as I could.'' She sounded completely out of breath. ''Is it true? Is he really alive and home?''

There were no shadows here. No conflicts. This woman radiated a fullness of joy. Her eyes shone like stars.

At a glance Rosie saw what Nick had expected to see—what he had deserved to see—when he'd gotten off the plane this morning.

It couldn't have been just this morning, could it?

Confronted by the immensity of her own betrayal, she felt as though another dagger had pierced her heart. In loving Zach, she'd deprived Nick of a pearl beyond price at the most crucial point in his life.

She could only imagine what seeing Cynthia's shining face would mean to R.T.

''Yes. I'm Rosie Armstrong. My husband was in prison with him.''

''I know. His aunt told me. It's unbelievable, isn't it?''

Yes. Unbelievable.

''Come in. Please.''

The other woman stepped over the threshold and Rosie shut the door. ''Wait right here and I'll go get him.''

''All right.'' Cynthia nodded. ''But I'm so excited I'm sick. I still can't believe he's alive, that he's here!''

''He's not going to believe you're here, either,'' Rosie murmured. ''Just a minute.''

Rosie turned and flew down the hall to Cody's

room. When she entered, she saw R.T. and Cody sitting on the twin beds facing each other.

She was pretty sure R.T. was demonstrating Morse code to her son. Cody avoided looking at her, but R.T. got to his feet.

"Sorry I ran out of the dining—"

"No one blames you," she interrupted him gently. "R.T., you have a visitor. She's in the front hall."

Obviously her news stunned him. "Aunt Laura?"

"Why don't you go find out?"

Immediately his face paled. She saw his hands begin to shake.

Out of pure compassion she moved to his side and put her arm around his shoulders. "Everything's going to be fine. Come on. I'll walk with you." He flashed her a look of gratitude, and they made their way out of the room.

The second they stepped into the front hallway, Cynthia Ellis's cry of love reverberated throughout the entire house. R.T. flew into her arms. They clung to each other with a fierce desperation that was too private, too beautiful to watch, but Rosie couldn't look anywhere else.

Nick, what have I done to you?

It might have been five minutes before either R.T. or his wife spoke. "You've come back to me," Cynthia Ellis said. "I can't believe it. It's a miracle. Oh, R.T, I love you!" she cried over and over again.

"I don't see how. Half of me is gone, and I—I've lost one eye, Cyn," he sobbed into her neck.

"Do you think I care about that? You're home, and I'm going to take care of you, soldier."

"I can't believe you're not married."

His words crucified Rosie; whether R.T. knew it or not, the reception she'd given Nick had convinced R.T. that his wife would never have held on this long.

Like rocks thrown in a still pool, the ripples continued to spread, doing their damage.

"I *am* married, you goof. To *you*. You know you're my guy, don't you?"

"Ah, Cyn, you don't want an old wreck like me."

"How about me, R.T? I'm a much worse wreck. After seven years, I've got the battle scars to prove it. We'll compare wounds all night, shall we? And we'll kiss every one better, okay? Unless I'm not your girl anymore. Did you find someone else over there?" Her voice caught, revealing the depth of her emotions.

"Ah, Cyn," was all R.T. could answer, he was drowning in so much happiness.

"Go on home with her, soldier. Go home *now!* That's an order."

At the sound of Nick's authoritative voice, Rosie wheeled around in shock. She'd no idea he'd been standing there all this time.

A beautiful smile meant for R.T. alone illuminated his face. He moved past Rosie and put his arms around both of them. She saw him tousle Cynthia's dark curly locks—and felt the hairs on the back of her neck prickle.

"In case you didn't hear him say it yet, he loves you, Cyn. I know because he called out your name in his sleep every night for six and a half years. Maybe tonight *I'll* finally get some sleep.''

There was more laughter, more tears of joy as they all hugged. Their own private fraternity to which no one else belonged. Rosie hadn't given the proper password, so she couldn't enter.

She'd never felt so bereft in her life. She had to do something fast, or she was going to lose it in front of all of them.

''Cody?'' she called to her son, hurrying down to his room. When she entered, he looked up with accusing eyes. If an expression could wither, she'd be shriveled. ''R.T.'s wife has come to take him home. Would you help me pack his things and carry them out to her car?''

He blinked. Obviously such an eventuality hadn't occurred to him. ''But he thought she was married to someone else by now!''

''I know.''

''So she *did* wait for him, like he prayed.''

Another blow. Any more, and Rosie wondered if she'd still be alive come morning.

''Yes.''

Cody's face clouded in pain before he jumped to his feet. ''He didn't unpack anything. I'll bring his duffel bag.''

''Thank you, honey.''

''I'm doing it for R.T. Not you.'' He grabbed it from the corner and lugged it out of the room. Rosie followed him down the hall on unsteady legs, wishing the mountains would collapse on her to bury her pain.

By the time she reached the foyer, Cody was being introduced; then they all started out the front door. Suddenly R.T. looked around, and his searching gaze found Rosie's.

He left the group and hurried toward her. But he seemed to be having trouble finding the words. Finally he gave up trying and they hugged.

"Thanks for everything, Rosie."

"There's no reason to thank me, R.T. I'm just so happy for you."

He embraced her harder. "I'll pray for you and the Sergeant."

Her body shook. "I—I'm afraid we're going to need those prayers. So will Cody. Come and see us soon? You're only forty-five minutes away. Nick won't know what to do without you."

"Yeah. We're both going to have problems for a while."

She smiled sadly. "Take care, R.T."

"For what it's worth, your husband's the greatest. I know you know that, or you wouldn't have married him in the first place." He paused. "I guess that means your fiancé's pretty exceptional, too."

"He is," she whispered, dying a little more.

"Please remember one thing. If you need help, if you need to talk, you'll always have a friend in me."

"I don't deserve that kind of loyalty, but I'll probably take you up on it just the same," she murmured with tears in her voice. "Bless you, R.T."

CHAPTER SIX

FOR A MONDAY EVENING the Alpine Club was relatively empty, Zach noted, as he entered the dimly lit bar and sat at the nearest vacant table.

"Hi, there," one of the cocktail waitresses greeted him, a warm smile evident. "What'll it be?"

With a grimace Zach put a ten-dollar bill on the table. Then he took a piece of paper from his trouser pocket and handed it to her. "All I need is for you to dial that number for me and ask for Rosie. If they want to know who's calling, tell them it's Fran. If and when Rosie comes to the phone, tell her just a minute, then hand the receiver to me. Can you do that?" he asked with barely controlled intensity.

She eyed him speculatively. "Sure I can. Follow me."

Pocketing the money, she headed for the phone booth next to the rest rooms. He fed a quarter into the slot and waited while she punched in the numbers. The unrelenting throb at his temple was finally playing havoc with his stomach.

After about ten seconds had passed he saw her straighten. "Hi. May I please speak to Rosie?" There was a pause, then, "Yes, it's Fran."

Zach swallowed hard. This probably wasn't going

to work. If by any chance Rosie's husband had answered the phone, he'd want to know all about Fran. Rosie would have to think fast since Zach had pulled that name out of thin air. Surely she'd realize what was happening and play along until he could talk to her.

"Just a minute, please," the waitress murmured. She handed the phone to Zach, giving him the victory sign as she walked away.

"Rosie—"

"Yes?" came a troubled voice. It didn't sound like his Rosie.

"Don't say anything. Just listen. I'm taking a Delta flight to California tonight—I'm on my way to the airport now. If and when you decide you want to get in touch with me, call Barb at the office and she'll know how to find me. Until later, sweetheart."

Before he could change his mind and beg her to talk to him, he jammed the receiver back on the hook and left the bar in a few swift strides. Once outside, he got quickly into the Passat, one of his company cars, and headed for the freeway.

Reaching for his cellular phone, he called his assistant manager, Mitch Riley. They talked business until Zach reached the huge airport parking lot, from which he could take a shuttle to the terminal.

Mitch would have to handle things until Zach got back. Unfortunately he had no idea when that would be. It was killing him to leave, but it would kill him to stay. But putting a thousand miles between him and Rosie ensured that he couldn't go storming over to her house in the middle of the night demanding her time regardless of her husband's feelings.

Zach's own feelings bordered on the primitive. He could all too easily imagine dragging Rosie off someplace—someplace they'd be alone.

After he'd parked the car, he grabbed his suitcase and climbed into the shuttle van. The flight to L.A. wouldn't be leaving for an hour. He'd purposely told Rosie which airline he was using on the outside chance she'd drive out to the airport to see him off.

But as he checked his bag and made his way to the departure lounge, he realized that such hope existed only in his most delusional fantasies. No matter how much Rosie wanted to be with Zach—and he *knew* she wanted to be with him—she couldn't and wouldn't leave her husband on his first day home from the war.

Zach's rational mind agreed that such an act would be an inhuman thing to do to anyone.

That was why he had to get out of there. His last spark of humanity had been extinguished the moment Rosie said she wouldn't be seeing him for a while.

Since he wasn't fit company for anyone, he'd take out his sailboat. Once at sea, no one would be able to reach him or disturb him, not even his family. Until he'd made contact with Barb, that was the way he wanted it.

"HEY, YOU TWO. In bed already?"

"Nicky!" both his parents said at the same time.

"Come in, son." His father beckoned with his hand, while Janet gave him a faint smile.

Nick approached the foot of their double bed, trying not to think about the agonized look on Rosie's face after Cody had called her to the phone a few minutes ago. It had been a one-sided conversation. Whatever Zach Wilde had said to her, it was enough to drain the color from her cheeks and convince Nick that his wife was in dire pain.

"Mother? I'm sure you've conjured up some horrible images about my imprisonment, but just remember that I survived it, and I've come home."

"To what?" she cried angrily. "I'll never forgive Rosie for what she's done to you."

He gritted his teeth. "Don't blame Rosie. The war changed all our lives."

Ignoring Nick's comment, George patted his wife's arm. "This business with Zach will soon pass. Now that Nicky's back, our Rosie wil—"

"No, Dad," Nick broke in. If he didn't get through to them now, they might never face reality. And maybe saying the words would help *him* chart the precarious course ahead.

"To be honest, I have no idea where Rosie and I are going. We've lost seven years. We're like babes in the woods, floundering around, trying to make sense of everything.

"If Rosie was the cruel insensitive creature your anger is making her out to be, she wouldn't have come to Hill this morning to face me, let alone to tell me the truth about Zach. But she did, and under the circumstances, that kind of integrity is as much as I could've hoped for."

His mother sat up straight in the bed, her eyes red-rimmed. "How can you stand there and defend her?"

Nick expelled a long sigh. "How can I not when she's made such a wonderful home for Cody, not to mention an impressive career for herself?"

"She couldn't have done it without *our* help!" His mother's sharp words rang through the room.

"Your mother's right, son."

"Has she ever shown either of you anything but the profoundest gratitude for all you've done?" Nick fired back, feeling the heat of anger sweep over him.

Neither of them met his gaze.

"When she heard I was MIA and presumed dead, a lesser woman might've gone to pieces and never succeeded, no matter how much help she'd received."

"She gave up on *you!* We *never* did."

The truth of his mother's words hit him like the second shock wave of a bomb blast. Then she was sobbing.

He moved to the side of the bed and embraced her. "That's because you're such wonderful parents, and I love you for that. But the fact remains Rosie has done a fantastic job with Cody. For that I will always be grateful."

His father stirred restlessly. "I think what we all need is a vacation together. Why don't we pack up the Buick in the morning and head for Yellowstone country?"

Grim-faced, Nick got up from the bed, realizing his arguments had made no impact on his parents.

"Good as that sounds, Dad, I can't go anywhere

until I see about getting a prosthesis of some kind. As for Rosie and Cody, they've still got school. I'm afraid that for a while we're going to have to take things a day at a time.''

Most likely there are going to be many changes you'll fight, but it can't be helped.

His mother lay back against the pillows. In the soft light of the bedside lamp, Nick could see how much his parents had aged, though they were still a very handsome couple. He loved them and always would, but he was painfully aware that their single-minded devotion to him had created a breach with Rosie, one he wasn't sure could be mended.

Suddenly there was a knock on the door, and Cody poked his head inside. "Hey, you guys? Can I come in?"

"Of course you can." George chuckled and extended his hands to Cody, who ran toward him. They hugged joyfully while Nick looked on. "This has to be the happiest night of our lives, having your dad back."

"It sure is!" Cody exclaimed, then ran around the other side of the bed to kiss his grandmother goodnight.

Nick noted that the three of them were exceptionally close. Because of his parents' love and Rosie's, Cody seemed to be in the best emotional shape of any of them. Again he sent up a silent prayer of thanksgiving that, in his absence, his son had been blessed with such a strong supportive mother and grandparents.

In a few minutes, he'd be alone with his wife for

the rest of the night. Before they hurt each other any more—which would happen inevitably, despite their most compassionate intentions—he'd offer Rosie his gratitude.

"Come on, Cody. Time to let your grandparents get their rest."

Nick gave his parents each another hug and said he'd see them in the morning, then ushered Cody from the room, his arm around the boy's shoulders. "You need to get to bed, too. School's going to come early in the morning."

"I don't want to go school tomorrow, Dad. Please let me stay home with you one more day."

"That's for your mom to decide," he murmured as they entered his bedroom.

Right now Cody had a serious case of hero worship where Nick was concerned; he felt so hurt and angry about Zach he was taking it out on Rosie. It would be very easy for Nick to play on his son's vulnerability and make it impossible for Rosie to wield any influence. *The last thing he wanted to do...*

Cody scuffed his toe against the carpet. "Mom'll make me go."

"It's probably for the best, son. I'm going to be at the Veterans' Hospital most of the day seeing about a new hand. But I'll tell you what. I'll pick you up after school. Bring some of your friends along. We'll get a malt together and talk football."

Cody's eyes lit up. "All right!"

Relieved that his son hadn't objected, Nick added, "Maybe after dinner we can find a gym where we can work out."

"There's one in Foothill!"

"Really?"

"Yeah. I go there sometimes with my friends."

"Okay. We'll do it. Now, have you said good-night to your mom?"

A sheepish expression crossed Cody's face. "No."

"I'll bet she's waiting. Why don't you go give her a kiss, then come on back to bed."

Cody's eyes clouded. "I'm so glad you're home, Dad."

Again Nick felt that thickening in his throat. "Ditto, son."

Cody wiped his eyes with his arm. "I'll be right back. If you want, you can look at my junior-high yearbook from last year. Here. I was showing it to R.T. I'm in three pictures, but they're kind of dumb. I've grown a couple more inches since then."

Nick took the yearbook. "You've grown about five more *feet* since I last saw you." He winked at his son. "I'm anxious to look at every picture taken while I was away so I can fill in the blanks. When you and your mom saw me off, you were this little curly-headed guy who liked to ride on my shoulders."

Cody made a face. "I looked like a girl."

Nick chuckled. "Did you ever see pictures of me at five years of age?"

"Yeah." Cody grinned. "Grandma has a zillion of them. You had a whole bunch of curls and looked like a girl, too."

"Well, nobody would ever take us for females now."

Their eyes met in mutual understanding and they hugged. "I'll be right back, Dad."

"While you're at it, you might thank your mom for being such a great mother all these years without any help from me."

Cody's grin faded and he looked away. Nick knew his son wanted to say something negative, but at the last second had thought better of it.

As soon as he'd left, Nick flipped through the pages, painfully aware of the years when he hadn't been part of Cody's life. *Or Rosie's.*

For so long, R.T. had been Nick's only link with reality. It seemed strange to think that the man who was closer to him than a brother no longer lived on the other side of the wall, and never would again.

All that time, R.T. had been Nick's immediate concern. On their flight from Germany, Nick hadn't really believed Cynthia would still be there, waiting for her husband. A marriage of only one year and no children... But by some miracle, Cynthia hadn't met—or worse, married—anyone else.

Happy as he was for R.T., it was hard to see him drive off with his wife, who was obviously still very much in love with him.

Nick set the book on Cody's desk and stood up. His palms had gone clammy. He started getting the shakes.

You miss him, Armstrong. You miss him like hell. And you're afraid to be alone with Rosie.

"Dad? I'm back. Did you see the picture of me during the assembly?"

"You mean the one where you're all in grass skirts and bikini tops?"

"Yeah." Cody grinned.

Nick grinned back. "Did you borrow your mother's bathing suit?"

"Yeah."

"Well, I have to say she looks a lot better in it than you do. In fact, I bet your mom's still the best-looking of all your friends' moms."

There was a long silence before Cody nodded. "You love her a lot, Dad, don't you?"

Nick sucked in his breath. "I fell hopelessly in love with her when I was eighteen and that's never changed. We had a wonderful marriage, closer than most."

"Then…"

"Then how come she fell for Zach?"

Cody nodded again.

"For one thing, she thought I'd been killed in the war. For another, you said yourself he's a great guy. For a third…well, it's my opinion that people who've been in a bad marriage are often frightened to repeat the experience for fear they'll make the same mistakes.

"Since she'd been so happy in our marriage, she probably wanted to have that experience again and decided Zach could enrich her life. In a way, it's a compliment to what she and I had shared. Can you understand what I'm telling you?"

I'm not sure even I understand it, Cody, but it's the only explanation I have for the moment.

"But n-nobody's like you, Dad," the boy said brokenly, tears gushing down his cheeks. "Mom always used to say that. How come she can't feel that way now?"

Cody, Cody. If I had the answer to that question...

"The heart's a funny thing, son. You can't order it to feel a certain way. It does what it wants. You can't get mad at it."

Cody blinked and stared across at Nick. "You mean you're not mad at Mom?"

"I was this morning," Nick confessed quietly. "I won't lie to you about that. The truth is, I'm in a lot of pain, just like you. Just like your mom. There's a great deal to work out, and today is only the first day. We're going to have to be patient."

ROSIE THOUGHT she was going to jump out of her skin with anxiety as she waited for Nick to come to bed. She'd busied herself cleaning the house, locking all the doors, turning out the lights.

While he was with Cody and his parents, she'd emptied his duffel bag and made room for his things in her closets and drawers. A clean pair of pajamas they'd given him in Germany lay across the foot of the bed. After showering, she'd put on a nightgown she hadn't worn since before he'd left for the war, then slipped into the pink robe Nick had given her eight Christmases ago.

Finally she'd gone to bed, forcing herself not to think about Zach flying to California. His terse communication had created a sense of loss that made her feel as if her only friend on earth had suddenly deserted her.

But in another sense, she was glad he'd gone to be with his family. He was particularly fond of his older brother, Richard, who could provide needed comfort right now.

Rosie had never had brothers or sisters and could only imagine what a luxury it would be to run to a sibling in a crisis. For that matter, Nick had been an only child, as well. Throughout their marriage, they'd been each other's best friend, had relied on each other for everything.

She and Nick had married right out of high school, their passion too flammable to endure a lengthy engagement. Nick had been her one and only lover. To Rosie, the physical side of their marriage had been pure ecstasy. But when she thought of making love to him now, she couldn't summon any actual memory of what those feelings were like.

It was like looking back thirteen years to Cody's birth—forty-eight long hours of labor. She had an almost abstract awareness that there had been intense physical pain; at the time, she'd thought she would never forget it. But she *had* forgotten those pains, and until she had another baby, there was no way she could ever relive them.

When Zach entered her life, everything was different. Her feelings had taken a long time to get to the point that she wanted him in her bed. She'd heard too many stories of widows and divorced women who'd remarried and then discovered that after their physical needs had been satisfied, there was little else holding the marriage together.

Rosie had been determined to build a rock-solid relationship before she allowed herself to respond sexually to Zach. She'd never felt out of control with him the way she had with Nick. In all likelihood it was because she was much older and because she'd gone through a long period of mourning. Not only that, there were Cody's feelings to consider. The combination of circumstances had made her cautious. Fortunately Zach had loved her enough to wait until they were married before they consummated their relationship.

Bothered by a headache that had begun during dinner, she got up and padded to the kitchen for some painkillers. While she was putting the bottle back on the shelf, the phone rang, startling her.

The only person she could think of who'd be calling this late was Zach. Was it possible he'd changed his mind and hadn't gone to California, after all?

She was afraid to pick up the phone, afraid they'd go through another excruciating emotional battle. But the continued ringing would wake the whole house. After another moment's hesitation, she answered.

"Hello?"

"Rosie? It's R.T."

She blinked. "R.T.? Are you all right?"

"Yes. Could I speak to Nick?"

He wasn't all right at all.

"Of course. I'll get him. Hold on."

Laying the receiver on the counter, she ran to find Nick, who was just coming out of Cody's bedroom.

In the near darkness, his tall body was little more than a silhouette.

For an instant, it reminded her of other times when he'd come from the shower toward their bed, a shadowy figure intent on making love to her. She reeled from the impact of such a deeply buried memory that suddenly, unexpectedly surfaced.

"R.T.'s on the phone."

"I thought he might be calling."

"If you want privacy, take it in the kitchen."

"Thank you," he murmured and strode past her.

Rosie hurried to the bedroom, still disturbed by the strange experience outside Cody's door. She suspected Nick would be talking to R.T. for a while and decided she'd try to reach Zach on the phone line hooked up to the computer downstairs in her office.

He would be with his family by now, and it was an hour earlier in California. She felt as if she'd lived ten lifetimes in one day; she needed to hear his voice again, if only to say good-night.

Without any further hesitation she darted into the hall and flew down the stairs to the basement. She kept a directory of her personal numbers in her desk drawer.

But a call to his family's home revealed that they had no idea he was coming to California. He hadn't phoned them. Maybe he was still on his way home from the airport.

With the assurance that they'd have him call as soon as he arrived, his mother hung up. Rosie replaced the receiver with the awful premonition that Zach didn't want his family to know any of this. In fact, she was pretty sure he hadn't told them about the engagement yet.

Maybe he hadn't gone to California. Maybe at the last minute he'd changed his mind. He could be anywhere. Only his secretary was privy to that information, but it was too late to disturb her. Rosie would have to wait until tomorrow.

On the slight chance that he'd decided not to leave Salt Lake, after all, she phoned his condo, but all she got was the answering machine.

Was it possible he'd gone off somewhere on his racing bike? Whenever he was upset or needed to think, he usually went cycling for a few hours. He'd been training for the Tour de France in Park City when she'd first met him. At the time she'd been unaware that he'd been grieving over the loss of his fiancée.

Rosie, along with Cody and a couple of his friends, had rented bikes to wheel around the restored mining town high in the Wasatch Mountains. It was early in the morning, and they'd come to an unused stretch of road, or so they'd thought. As they rounded a sharp curve, there was Zach, headed toward them with the speed of a torpedo.

Only his expertise prevented a serious accident. Instead of being angry at having to skid to a stop to avoid collision when it was their fault for being all over the road, he graciously apologized and struck up a conversation. Once they found out he was in training, Cody and his friends were in awe of him, besieging him with questions.

What began as a chance meeting turned into an

all-day excursion. Zach led them on an eventful ride to Bridal Veil Falls, where they hiked and picnicked. No one wanted the fun to end, so they ended up having dinner together, as well.

It was the first time Rosie had been in another man's company—outside of school and work—since Nick's death. When Zach asked if he could take her and Cody out to dinner the next time he drove down to Salt Lake, she found herself saying yes.

Cody thought it was cool, and the three of them had a lovely evening out. But then it became clear that Zach was attracted to his mom, that he wanted to start seeing her on a regular basis, and Cody became difficult. The problems began.

He'd been difficult ever since. Right up until tonight. Now, suddenly, he was a different child. After the explosion in the kitchen earlier, she hadn't expected him to come near her, let alone say good-night and give her a hug.

Nick's influence, surely.

Nick. By now he'd probably be off the phone.

With a guilty start, she replaced the receiver and ran up the stairs to the bedroom. The door stood ajar. She could see him in the middle of the room, tying the ends of his old striped bathrobe around his waist. His pajamas still lay at the foot of the bed.

There was an odd fluttering in her chest as she made her entrance.

His enigmatic gaze swerved to hers and narrowed. "Obviously, the prospect of sleeping with me was a little too daunting, after all. If you want me to stay on the couch, just say so. No lies, Rosie. At this point, all we've got going for us is the truth.''

Nick, I'm not trying to hurt you.

''I was taking advantage of the time you were on the phone with R.T. to call Zach. He left for California in a lot of pain, but it seems I can't locate him. Is that enough truth for you?''

''It's a start,'' he muttered, drying his hair with a towel.

He must have just come from the shower. She could smell the scent of her soap on his skin. Another flood of memories unexpectedly assailed her, confusing her.

She scrambled into bed and pulled up the covers. ''H-how's R.T.?''

''He's terrified.''

''Of what exactly?''

''Cynthia wants to make love and he doesn't.''

''Why? They adore each other.''

''That's why,'' he ground out, tossing the towel onto the nearest chair. Then he turned off the light. ''He's afraid he won't be able to perform as he once did. He's afraid she'll be turned off by his skinny body. He doesn't look like he used to, and he's afraid she's only pretending to love him out of pity.''

''She sees past that,'' Rosie said with conviction. ''You saw, you heard her joy when R.T. appeared in the foyer. Pity was the last thing on her mind.''

''It doesn't matter what we know.'' She felt his side of the bed dip as he slid beneath the covers. ''R.T. isn't convinced.''

Nick's tone of voice haunted Rosie. "What advice did you give him?"

"To ask her if it would be all right if they just held each other all night because he needed time to realize that this is real, not a dream."

Hot tears squeezed out of her eyes. "Do you think he'll take your advice?"

"He always does. I'm figuring Cynthia's a smart woman. I imagine ten or fifteen minutes is all she'll need to convince him of her love…as only a wife who has known her husband intimately can do."

A tight band constricted her breathing. "D-do you want to hold me, Nick?"

"No. The idea of a sacrificial lamb has never appealed."

She winced in pain at the swift retort. It didn't seem possible that they could be saying such hurtful things to each other, not after the kind of marriage they'd once shared.

"The next time I hold a woman, it will be because our love is mutual."

A woman? What did he mean?

"I still love you, Nick," she whispered. "I always will."

"I believe that. It's the only reason I'm lying here right now. But the difference is I'm still in love with the Rosie I left behind. The new Rosie is a stranger— one, furthermore, who's in love with another man. I've had all day and night for the dream to die.

"Tomorrow morning, after I've been to the hospital, I plan to consult a good divorce attorney."

"Divorce?"

She cringed, her heart pounding. She hadn't even considered such a thing. She hadn't been able to think beyond the moment.

"It was the first question Cody asked me on our bike ride today. He wanted to know if we were getting a divorce. When I thought about it, I realized it was a perfectly natural question. You can't marry Zach while you're still married to me." A long silence ensued. "Rosie?" he prodded. "Did you hear what I said?"

"Y-yes," came her ragged whisper. He hadn't been home twenty-four hours. Could he really be discussing divorce—and discussing it so...so unemotionally?

"Then we need to get it under way as soon as possible. I can't promise you'll be free by the wedding date you've chosen, but I'll do everything in my power to get our divorce through quickly. I should think that seven years of no history between us will speed up the process.

"As for our son, gut instinct tells me it might be better if I stay here for a while longer. It will give Cody a little time to accept our situation. But I'll leave that decision up to you."

Cody'll never accept it.

I don't accept it.

All at once a terrible anger caused her to throw back the covers and jump to her feet. "Nick, why are you talking about this on your first night home?"

"Why do you think?" he responded blandly. "You should know me by now. At least, you *used* to know me. I've always been a realist. In that regard,

I haven't changed. You're engaged to be married, and I came back from the dead. Two irreconcilable facts."

Rosie started to shake and couldn't stop. "It's too soon to talk about…about these things. Y-you need time…therapy…"

"I agree we can all benefit from therapy, but I'm not in the mood right now." He got to his feet and they faced each other across the bed in the darkness.

"As for time, I've had seven years to think. What I want at this point is to build a new life for myself. Since I've lost my wife, naturally I'm eager to start dating other women with the hope of remarriage and more children down the road. Can you understand that?"

Oh, yes, she could understand that. It sounded like he couldn't wait! And there wasn't a woman alive who'd be immune to his charm.

Hardly able to breathe, she murmured, "Of course."

"There's just one problem, Rosie. The kind of woman I want to end up with wouldn't dream of dating a married man. Therefore, like you, I need to be free first. In both our cases, there's no time to lose."

She couldn't fault his reasoning or his needs.
They made perfect sense.
He had every right!
She had absolutely no right.
She was devastated.

CHAPTER SEVEN

THE SILENCE FROM ROSIE told him he'd hit a nerve. But after weighing the situation carefully, he'd decided there was only one way to stop his pain. His marriage to Rosie had been too wonderful to consider enduring anything less. It was all or nothing.

"Rosie? There's something else I want to make clear right now. I have no hard feelings against Zach. On the contrary. Since he's going to be the other man in Cody's life, I'd like to meet him sometime. You can tell the poor devil he doesn't have to tiptoe around me. The more civilized we all are, the better it'll be for our son, whom I firmly believe should live with you after the divorce.

"Speaking of Cody, will it be all right if I pick him up after school tomorrow? Don't worry. I know you have classes to teach and you'll need your car. Mom and Dad will be here for a few more days, and I'll use theirs."

"*Nick—stop it!*" she blurted, her cheeks fiery hot. "Tonight isn't the night to talk about the future. I'm not going to work tomorrow. I want to hear about your life. I want to help you."

"I know you do. But I told you pretty much everything at the dinner table. Anything else isn't fit for human consumption. The ways people have figured out to torture one another aren't worthy of remembering. I promised myself that if I ever got out of that cell, I'd embrace life and never look back."

"How *did* you get out?"

Pleased she'd thawed enough to be curious, he said, "I suppose when the United Nations inspection teams started snooping around Saddam Hussein's installations after the war, word got out that he'd kept some prisoners no one knew about. R.T. and I were two of the lucky ones released."

"You mean there could be more?" she said, aghast.

"Maybe."

"Oh, Nick! That's so horrible, so awful!" He couldn't see her face, but she sounded as if she was crying.

For a moment, the old Rosie was back in the room, her compassionate heart bleeding all over the place.

"It could drive me mad if I ever really thought about it, which I'm not going to do. Instead, I plan to raid the refrigerator. Do you mind?"

"No," came her pain-filled whisper. "This is your house, too. Bought and paid for with money you earned for us.

"Nick, instead of consulting an attorney tomorrow, why don't you call Jerry Moore and see about getting your old job back at the brokerage house? You were their whiz kid before. I'm sure that with a little refresher course you'd work your way to the top again."

"I appreciate your confidence in me, sweetheart.

If that was what I wanted to do for the rest of my life—if Salt Lake was where I intended to put down new roots,'' he said, taking an enormous plunge, ''it's possible that would all work out.''

Another long silence. Another curve ball she hadn't seen coming. This was one time, he reflected, that her keen mathematical mind was of little use to her. But he had to move on with his life. *So did she.* Her life had been a living hell, too. It was time for all the pain to end.

''Are you thinking of moving?'' She couldn't have feigned the alarm in that question. It was something to cherish.

''That's right.''

''But St. George wouldn't give you the broad base of clients you need.''

''Who said anything about St. George?''

She sounded at a total loss for words. ''I—I just assumed that if you were going to relocate, you'd probably want to be near your parents.''

''St. George is too close a reminder of the desert. In the last seven years I've lost my taste for it.''

''I'm sorry,'' she rushed to apologize. ''I didn't think— Forgive me, Nick.''

''There's nothing to forgive. Are you hungry for some scalloped potatoes?''

''No.'' The word sounded abrupt, as if she'd lost patience with him.

''I could eat the whole pan.''

''Wait—''

Nick paused at the door. She sounded almost frantic, a sign that he was still rocking her foundations.

"What do you plan to do for a living? Where will you go?"

"I want to work in the out-of-doors."

Quiet again. Then, "You're kidding."

"Not at all."

She made a sound of exasperation. "Doing what?"

"Maybe working a small ranch somewhere in the mountains. I have several ideas, but that's all they are right now."

"But you know the market like the back of your hand! Be serious, Nick!"

"My days of sitting in a claustrophobic office watching stocks fluctuate on my computer are over. That's not living, Rosie.

"Before I say good-night, there's something else I have to tell you." He paused, gathering his resolve. "I may have only spent one day with Cody, but it was enough to realize what a superb mother you've been to our son."

His voice was shaking, but he had to finish saying what was in his heart.

"I'm proud of you, Rosie. Proud of what you've accomplished and become, proud of the beautiful home you've made. I love you for keeping close family ties with my parents, for giving them the opportunity to stay in your life. I'm sorry everyone has fought you so hard where Zach is concerned.

"Now that I'm home, all that's going to change. Don't worry about Mom and Dad or Cody. Just give me a little more time with them, and everything will be fine.

"Since I have trouble sleeping, I'll probably stay up half the night watching TV in the living room. Ignore any weird noises coming from there. R.T. tells me my dreams get pretty wild, but I doubt they're any worse than his. I suppose Cynthia is going to go through her initiation tonight. At least I can spare you the worst of it. See you in the morning."

"GOOD MORNING. I'm Rosie Armstrong. I have an appointment with Linda Beams."

"She's expecting you, but she's with someone else at the moment. She asked me to give you this to read while you wait."

Rosie thanked the uniformed officer at the front desk and sat down with the small leaflet. Her eyes were swollen almost shut from crying. At first she had to squint to make out all the letters.

FOR FAMILIES OF LOVED ONES COMING HOME FROM WAR.
STRATEGIES FOR HELPING MY LOVED ONES AND MYSELF.

1. Educate yourself on what to expect when your loved one returns home. Acknowledge your fears that he or she may come home as someone who is "different" in certain ways.

2. Recognize the veteran for participating honorably in the war.

3. Communicate an attitude of "I care," and "I am here for you."

4. Be an empathetic listener. Sometimes the

individual may not feel the full impact of what has happened for days, weeks, months or sometimes years. When your loved one is ready to talk or "debrief," listen without making judgments, moralizing or trying to "make it better."

At times, loved ones will prefer to debrief with professionals or other veterans, instead. This is often necessary because they fear what may happen if they open their hearts too fully to the pain. They may also want to protect their loves ones from this pain.

5. Allow the returnee to adjust and reenter at his or her own pace.

Recognize that change comes slowly. Be supportive, but don't push.

6. Become involved in support groups as quickly as possible.

7. Some common questions and responses you can pose to returnees include:

"What are you feeling?" vs "Are you okay?"

"You must be experiencing all kinds of emotions now."

"I know this is hard to talk about, but it's important to talk."

"What was the hardest part of everything for you?"

Many returnees will find it hard to respond to these questions, and many will avoid such discussions sometimes. Yet, the process of debriefing on some level—whether with family, friends or in a structured support setting—is crucial to a healthy reentry and healing process.

9. Become aware of the many emotions you yourself are experiencing and find healing ways to release these feelings. Prepare your family in advance for what they may experience with the returning veteran.

10. Keep a daily journal of your thoughts and feelings.

11. Pray. Talk to your clergy if you find it comforting.

12. Seek professional assistance whenever you feel overwhelmed and debilitated by the stress and emotional impact of the changes you are experiencing.

13. Observe children and adolescents carefully for signs of emotional distress. They may feel guilt, confusion, anger and a sense of helplessness around the returning veteran. They may feel loneliness and a sense of emotional abandonment.

14. Exerci—

"Hi, Rosie. It's been a long time."

At the sound of Linda's voice, she lifted her head.

"Thanks for seeing me on such short notice."

"Anytime. Come on in."

She followed the older woman into her office and sat down opposite her desk. Linda eyed her frankly.

"Your message was bittersweet. Out of the blue your husband has miraculously returned—minus a hand. And at the same time you're on the brink of being married again. I'd say that the stress in your lives has been magnified a thousandfold overnight.''

Rosie nodded, rocking back and forth on the hard chair, her hands clasped around her knees. "According to the leaflet, I've committed almost every major sin in the lot, including one not even mentioned."

Linda's brows lifted expressively. "The leaflet addresses the issues facing a returning vet, not necessarily a POW. There are some differences.

"In your case you had no advance warning that he was alive, no time to prepare for his arrival. You need to forgive yourself for any mistakes you feel you've made, and learn from them. You also need to forgive yourself for falling in love with another man.

"If that becomes impossible to do, then I suggest you seek psychiatric help. Though I'm here for general support, my work as a thanatologist deals mainly with grieving veterans and their families. You need a specialist to help you cope with your new situation. But let's put those considerations aside and discuss where you are emotionally and mentally at this moment."

"I wish I knew, Linda."

"How is your fiancé reacting?"

"He's in agony. He left for California yesterday. I need to phone him, but..."

"But you don't know what to say," Linda finished for her. "At this stage, you can't possibly have answers since you don't even know the questions."

"Exactly."

"Some time apart won't hurt your relationship, and it will give all of you space to think. Let's talk about PTSD—post-traumatic stress disorder. Turn to the back of the leaflet and read the list of symptoms. Then we'll discuss them in terms of your husband.''

Rosie took five minutes and did as she suggested, then shook her head. ''Except for a few points, Nick doesn't seem to be showing these signs. If you'd heard the things he said last night, you would never have known he'd been a POW for six and half years.''

''Tell me.''

Again Rosie found herself revealing some of the pertinent dialogue.

''Now can you understand why I'm so shaken? He's shown no anger over my engagement to Zach. In fact, he's reconciled to it. He has no confusion of identity, no loss of self-esteem. I see no signs of helplessness or confusion.

''He's very open about having disturbing dreams, but isn't preoccupied over the loss of his hand. He eats constantly. There's no diminished enjoyment of life or activities, no alienation from his parents or Cody. He has plans. He...'' Rosie faltered. ''A-all I can say is, his emotional health is far better than mine.''

''Wait a minute. Let's back up. Tell me what you were going to say after you said, 'He has plans.'''

Rosie averted her eyes. ''He wants to start divorce proceedings as soon as possible. He wants to get on with his life. He used to be a stockbroker. Now he wants to be a rancher!''

Linda sat back in her chair, tapping the pencil

against the desktop. "How does that make you feel?"

"I—I know how I should feel," she muttered. "He has every right."

"We're not talking about 'shoulds' and 'rights' here. I'm asking you point-blank, what's going on inside that psyche of yours?"

"I guess I'm feeling hurt."

"And?"

"And angry."

"And?

She sucked in her breath. "And betrayed."

"Interesting. I would say that's a good place to start. Getting in touch with your own feelings. Once you understand them, then you'll know how to proceed."

"But what about Nick?"

"He's obviously a survivor. Yet, war has reminded him that he's mortal. It's forced him to consider his own 'unfinished business.' He's feeling incomplete and he wants the wholeness and peace marriage once gave him. Thus the mention of divorce—to facilitate the possibility of marrying again, of putting his life in order."

Rosie stared at Linda. "I hadn't thought of it that way."

"It appears to me he's a strong, intelligent, mature human being who has a sound grip on life and an indomitable will. But don't be deceived. He's going to suffer many of those listed symptoms. You just haven't seen them yet."

"You're right. Not enough time has passed. The

trouble is, if we do divorce and he moves out, I never will see behind the facade.''

''Is that important to you?''

Rosie ran unsteady fingers through her hair. ''Yes. Very.''

''Why?''

''*Why?*''

''Another question you need to answer as honestly as you can.''

''I already know the answer,'' she retorted. ''Who will help him if I don't?''

''Another woman?''

Rosie's head flew back. ''Another woman doesn't know him like I do.''

''Ahh…''

''He's so gallant and take-charge, you tend to forget he's lost his hand. He doesn't act like someone who's lost seven years of life!'' Suddenly Rosie broke down in sobs.

''But you're engaged to another man, so you can't do what you might have done for him. That's the dilemma, right?''

''Yes,'' she whispered, trying to get her emotions under control.

Linda sat forward and handed her a tissue. ''When he's ready, there are support groups he can join. You mentioned his parents and your son. I understand he also bonded with the other soldier imprisoned with him. Those are all terrific resources.''

''I know. Especially Cody. They're extremely close already.''

"That's good. Now let's talk about you and this other man. How long have you been together?"

"Two years."

"Then a great deal of energy and emotion has already been invested. As I said earlier, you need to get in touch with your true feelings toward you husband *and* your fiancé."

"How do I do that?"

"At all times be honest and open in your communication with both men. They deserve nothing less. No matter how much you think it might hurt them, don't lie about your feelings and don't hide them. That would be the worst thing you could do. In time, you'll begin to understand yourself. When that day arrives, you'll know what to do."

"That kind of honesty would take a very strong person."

"You *are* a very strong person. Don't forget that you survived the war, too!"

Rosie's head was bowed. "Thank you for that, Linda." Slowly she got to her feet. "You've given me a lot to think about."

"I hope it's helped. Remember, I'm always here. Come again soon."

"Depending on how today goes, you might hear from me tomorrow."

"Then I'll be waiting. Good luck."

By the time Rosie had gone out to her car, she'd made the decision to get in touch with Zach and find out when he was coming home. They needed to talk. Since her conversation with Linda, Rosie felt maybe she could handle it.

With Nick's folks in the house, she thought it would be better if she used a pay phone, so she drove to the nearest convenience store and called his office. Zach's secretary said he hadn't phoned in yet, but when he did, she'd give him Rosie's message.

Relieved to have taken that step, she was able to concentrate on Nick. In her mind she'd been cataloguing the things he'd need. The first order of business was to drive downtown and pick up some sweats and casual clothes for him in one of the local department stores.

"I DON'T LIKE the idea of a fake hand," Nick murmured, gazing at several varieties and colors to match a person's skin.

The technician nodded. "A lot of you vets don't. There's little dexterity. Some people want them for cosmetic reasons."

"I'd better get one for the odd occasion when I have to be out in public for any length of time. When I'm not wearing it, I'd rather keep my arm in my pocket or covered up. But I'd better get fitted with a hook to do work when I'm by myself."

A hook would increase his ability to perform many tasks, but the feel of straps around his upper body would take some getting used to. Though the experience was growing less frequent, he had moments when it felt like his hand was still there balled into a fist, driving his nails into his palm.

The doctor had told him it was called phantom sensation. The nerve impulses to the brain didn't detect the loss. That was why the thought of moving his shoulders to operate the hook seemed so odd.

"What kind of work do you do?"

"I'm thinking of buying a small ranch."

"Then you'll want this." He lifted the larger hook for Nick's inspection. "It's called a farm hook. Some people refer to it as a work hook. You can accomplish a great deal with it. For example, when you're driving a nail, you hold your hook like this to fix the nail in place—" he demonstrated "—then pound with the other hand. If you're using a shovel, you can adjust the space to accommodate the handle."

"That's the idea." Nick nodded.

"All right. We'll start you out with the regular hook to get used to it, then graduate to the farm hook. Plan on coming in here three days a week for a couple of weeks for some occupational therapy. Then you can operate both hooks without problem. Have the receptionist make you an appointment for two weeks from today."

Nick frowned. "You can't get started any sooner?"

"No. The orthopedic surgeon at Fitzsimmons who did the surgery would tell you your arm needs to heal a little longer. It looks clean and dry, but to be safe, let's give it another fourteen days."

Nick nodded again.

The other man patted him on the shoulder. "I know you're anxious to get on with life. I would be, too. Still, you're safely back home."

"Amen," Nick said, then shook the technician's hand and left.

A few minutes later, he was once more behind the wheel of his parents' Buick.

You're home all right, Armstrong, and you're on your way to see a divorce attorney. The counselors in Germany told you to put the past behind you and resume your life. That's what you're going to do because any more time spent with Rosie—knowing she's in love with Zach—is killing you. And her!

BY THE TIME Rosie finished her shopping, she was amazed to discover it was almost four o'clock. She needed to get home and start dinner. But when she finally reached Sunnyside Avenue and turned onto her street, she slowed to a crawl, marveling at the scene before her.

Cars were lined bumper to bumper on both sides beneath the shade trees growing along the street. Their new spring foliage had been tied with hundreds of yellow ribbons. Dozens of yellow balloons had been attached to the wrought-iron stair railing leading to the front porch of her house.

Someone had erected a huge banner, which stretched across the front lawn from the driveway to the opposite boundary of her property. Rosie could read the letters all the way from the corner of Sunnyside.

Our Own Desert Storm Hero! Welcome home, Sergeant Nick Armstrong! We love you!

Her vision blurred. It could only mean one thing: one of her neighbors must have found out about Nick from his parents and organized everyone on the block.

Rosie had always loved her friendly neighborhood, but *this*…this went beyond anything she could have imagined.

A plethora of emotions swamped her, devastating her with a brand-new anguish. As thrilled as she was about their kindness and what it would mean to Nick, a part of her was dying inside because *she* hadn't thought of it.

His own wife hadn't thought of it!

His own wife hadn't breathed the joyful news to a single soul, not even the bagger at the grocery store.

You're a fraud, Rosie. While you were trying to reach Zach, your neighbors were organizing to give your husband a hero's welcome!

What had the brochure said? Let your vet know you're proud of him for serving in the war?

She buried her face in her hands, convulsed, tears streaming down her face.

What would this do to Nick? He'd told her he was seeing a divorce attorney today. The Buick was nowhere in sight. Had he been home yet? Did he know what was here waiting for him?

When he realized all this was for him, would he think she'd been the one responsible—and then find out she'd had nothing to do with it?

Would it tear him apart as it was tearing her?

Was he ready to deal with all these people, thoughtful and generous as they were?

When she'd recovered enough to see, she moved

forward and pulled into the driveway. Once out of the car with her packages, she heard the din of voices coming from the backyard.

"Martha!" she cried when she hurried around the back and saw Jeff Taylor's mom, of all people, supervising an enormous picnic barbecue. There were at least fifty or sixty people gathered, dressed in light jackets and sweaters, some of them in conversation with Nick's parents. Enough food covered the picnic tables to feed at least that many more.

"Rosie!" Martha screamed for joy and came running, her face glowing with excitement. She hugged Rosie so hard she could scarcely breathe. "Cody told Jeff the news, and he called me from school this morning. You must be the happiest woman in the world! We're all so ecstatic for you we can't stand it!

"I'm afraid once we got started, we invited practically the whole city. This party will go on until morning. The boys have kept your husband out with them, but they should be arriving any second."

Help me. Help me, Rosie's heart groaned in fresh agony. "How can I ever thank you?" she finally managed to whisper.

"Hey, this was one party I didn't have to plan. Once people knew the reason, it organized itself. Chip LeChimenant's mother will be here within the hour to film it for Channel Three news."

Overwhelmed by the turn of events, Rosie hugged her friends and neighbors, but she was soon feeling light-headed and excused herself to take her packages inside.

She looked in the bathroom mirror, moaning at her washed-out appearance. For the next few minutes she redid her hair in its tortoiseshell clip, then washed her face and put on fresh makeup.

Searching in her closet, she found tailored gray wool slacks and a red sweater, then quickly slipped them on. Seconds before she left the bedroom, she heard the crowd break into a deafening roar with piercing whistles, car honking, shouts and clapping.

Nick had come home.

She raced through the house and out the back door. Everyone had surrounded him. They all carried American flags. Cody stood crushed at his father's side, his grin idiotic. Nick shook hands as fast as he could, answering questions, receiving continual pats on the back. Friends Rosie hadn't seen for years appeared as if out of nowhere, hugging him long and hard. Someone with a trumpet started to play, "For He's a Jolly Good Fellow," and everyone sang.

Rosie stayed, mesmerized, on the back porch step, watching Cody and Nick make their way through the lineup of well-wishers. An old high-school buddy of his, John Seballa, whispered something in his ear. Nick's dark head reared back. He laughed that deep rich laughter, just the way he used to when he teased Rosie, driving her to fever pitch, as a prelude to making love.

A sudden ache passed through her body—an ache so intense she gasped. Almost as if Nick had heard her, his head swiveled in her direction and he met her gaze. Emotion had turned his eyes a dazzling blue, but their enigmatic expression checked her impulse to run over to him.

And do what, Rosie?

CHAPTER EIGHT

ZACH ENTERED the building that housed the Chemistry Department and stood outside the door of the room where Rosie lectured, his body wired. Four days ago Barb had given him Rosie's message—simply "I need to talk to you." He had no idea what that meant, but he'd decided to stay away a whole week so there'd be no more excuses, no chance for her to tell him she needed time to help her husband adjust to being home.

He glanced at his watch. Almost two o'clock. One more minute and her class would be over. He'd been the nice guy long enough and relished the idea of catching her off guard. *This time the element of surprise is on my side, Rosie.*

At precisely two, the class broke up and the students came pouring out of the amphitheater. Through the open door he could see her standing there in her stylish green suit, explaining something on the blackboard to a male student. Zach could only remember two female professors during his undergraduate studies at UCLA. If any of them had looked like Rosie, he would've found an excuse to hang around all day.

Nick Armstrong now had the privilege of being

with Rosie all day—every day—for the rest of his life. He'd earned that right....

Zach's body stiffened. How naïve he'd been to believe that Cody was Nick's only edge.

The man is partially disabled.

His impairment would bring out Rosie's nurturing instincts as nothing else could.

Another hurdle more daunting than Cody.

Zach waited behind the door until she came out, then followed her down the hall to her office. So far she hadn't seen him, but her sober expression convinced him she was anything but happy.

Have you even thought about me, Rosie?

She paused outside her office and searched in her bag for her keys. As soon as Zach saw their glint, he approached her and took them from her hand.

She looked up in surprise.

"*Zach...*" Her voice shook when she realized who it was.

The urge to take her in his arms was all-consuming, but they were in a public place. He put the key in the lock and opened the door, ushering them inside. To make certain they weren't disturbed, he shut it behind them just as quickly and locked it.

"Miss me?" he demanded before crushing her in his arms. "*Lord,* Rosie. One week—it's been a lifetime—"

He cupped her face in his hands and began devouring her mouth, reveling in the taste and feel of her. He'd dreamed of this moment on the sailboat, needed this physical release as much as he needed air to breathe.

Caught up in his own desire, he didn't realize that the elusive something that had made their Caribbean trip so magical wasn't there for Rosie.

Desperate to recapture it, he instinctively turned them around in the still dark room, moving her against the door, so he could drive home his need of her. But he got the distinct impression she wasn't with him, that instead, she was *allowing* him to love her. Nothing could have cooled his blood faster.

In an abrupt move, he tore himself away and switched on the light.

Zach had been a lifeguard throughout his late teens and into college. He'd pulled numerous drowning victims from the violent California surf, hoping that it wasn't too late, that he could resuscitate them.

Rosie's face reminded him of those faces. Victims in the throes of deep shock.

Her moist green eyes frantically searched his, begging for something.

What?

Forgiveness?

Oh, Lord. She was going to tell him she had to break off their engagement.

Her eyes—they held so much pain....

He stared down at her. "You said you had something to tell me." Zach didn't recognize his own voice.

The sound coming out of her reminded him of rushing waters.

"I do." She clasped her hands to her chest. He noted the absence of any ring on her finger, but that told him nothing. "So much, I hardly know where to begin."

He raked a sun-bronzed hand through his hair. "Just say it, Rosie."

"It isn't that simple. Please—sit down."

"I can't."

"Then I will."

She sank into the chair at her desk, a rigid figure, looking like she'd crack at the slightest vibration.

His hands had formed into fists. *Somebody had to say it.* "You've decided to stay with him."

"I haven't decided to do anything," she returned in a dull voice, sending *him* into euphoric shock.

"Thank God!"

In the next instant he'd caught her up in his arms once more and rocked her the way he would a child. She began to cry.

"What is it, sweetheart?" he whispered urgently against her wet cheek. "Talk to me. You can tell me anything."

"I know. That's what makes this so hard. You're so wonderful. I'd never want to hurt you, but my life is out of c-control. I don't know where I am or what I feel. She said I had to get in touch with my feelin—"

"She?"

"The counselor at Fort Douglas."

Zach frowned. Had Rosie already gone for professional help?

"She told me that no matter how much everything hurt, I needed to be honest with you, and with Nick. Otherwise I'd never be able to take charge of my life."

"She's right," Zach said fiercely. "Terrified as I am right now, I couldn't handle it if you lied to me."

"I won't, but some of the things you hear, you're not going to like."

"You're not going to like everything I have to say, either, sweetheart." With reluctance, he released her so they could both sit down. "Your husband has been my nemesis since the first day we met. His memory had such a stranglehold on you I wondered where I found the strength to keep on persisting.

"That cruise was it, Rosie. If you hadn't reached out to me with your whole heart and soul, I would have walked away and never looked back."

"Don't you think I realized that?" she blurted. "I loved you too much to let you go."

A shudder racked his body. "But not anymore? Is that what you need to tell me?" He had to ask the question.

She stared at him with wounded eyes. "My feelings for you haven't changed. How could they?" Her words reverberated in the tiny room.

"But something else has." He kept on relentlessly, because he sensed there was more to come. "Has he made demands? Does he want six months— a year—to try to put your marriage back together?"

That's what I would have demanded, Rosie. One year to make you fall in love with me all over again. No interference!

She was quiet too long. Her eyes refused to meet his. Suddenly she reached into her purse and handed him what looked like a letter.

Had she written down what she couldn't say?

Puzzled, he opened it, noticing immediately that it was a summons of some kind. Two names appeared. Nicholas Marchant Armstrong and Rosie Gardner Armstrong. It had been served yesterday. He turned to the next page.

It was a standard complaint for divorce brought by Nicholas Armstrong, plaintiff, against Rosie Armstrong, defendant, for alienation of affection due to a seven-year absence because of uncontrollable circumstances created by war.

The plaintiff wishes that minor child, Cody, aged 13, remain in the custody of his mother.

The plaintiff asks for full and liberal visitation rights which will require some travel time for minor child, as plaintiff will be residing outside Salt Lake County, but within the State of Utah.

The plaintiff stipulates that he will pay all insurance, medical and educational costs for said child throughout the duration of his lifetime.

The plaintiff further stipulates that an inheritance fund for said child has been established and will come due on said child's thirtieth birthday.

The plaintiff asks that any funds or investments accrued prior to his leaving for war, which were used to pay for the purchase of current home, be considered as partial alimony to the defendant. Any investments still outstanding are to be continued and used at the discretion of the defendant.

The plaintiff states that until such time as circumstances change and defendant remarries, a monthly alimony payment of $2500.00 will be deposited in defendant's checking account.

The plaintiff asks for no property since all purchases were made after he was MIA and considered dead.

Zach dropped the papers on the desk. His eyes closed tightly.

Nick Armstrong was amazing. Only a man who loved his wife more than himself would be willing to do this, to put her happiness first.

The man had expected to come home to a loving wife, a wife who still waited for him. Since that hadn't happened, he was trying to get out of their lives and make this as easy as possible on everyone. Zach admired him more than any man he'd ever known.

But one look at Rosie, and Zach could see the divorce summons had torn her into little pieces. Every word played on her guilt. Nick's gesture—though meant to give Rosie her freedom—had robbed her of all inherent joy. This was the reason she couldn't respond fully to him a few minutes ago.

What woman worth her salt could walk away from a marriage so fast, from a husband as remarkable as Nick Armstrong—a decorated war hero—without suffering the tortures of the damned?

He gazed at her through veiled lashes and answered his own question. *Only a woman who had fallen out of love.*

Zach had been so sure of her until Nick appeared on the scene. Now that he was back, Zach could sense her torment. *Who could blame her?* Certainly not Zach.

But her reaction to the summons changed the situation drastically. He stood up, surprising Rosie who'd been sitting there in a stuporlike trance.

Reaching for her hands, he drew her to her feet. "All right. About this divorce. How do you feel?"

She fought to keep back the tears. "Honestly?"

He nodded.

"I think it's horrible. All of it. I still love him and the memories we've shared. He's done nothing wrong!"

"I know," Zach murmured, hating to hear the truth. "This isn't a case of right or wrong. The man is trying to do the decent honorable thing so we can get married, but I can see you're not ready for that."

"I'm not."

Zach's heart plummeted. "Does Nick know you've been served yet?"

"H-he wasn't home when the officer came to the door. After his parents left for St. George yesterday morning, he and Cody decided to go camping with a bunch of Cody's friends and their parents. It's spring vacation. They haven't come home yet."

"That's good. Rosie?"

Lord. He couldn't believe what he was about to say.

"I think you need time to see if your marriage

will work again. It's the last thing I want. But on the other hand, I couldn't marry you if you weren't totally in love with me. I'm going to bow out for a while."

"What?" The horror on her face told him how much she cared. She began shaking her head, as if in a daze. "Have I hurt you so badly?"

"No...but while I was out sailing, I had a lot of time to think."

"So that's where you were!"

He nodded. "Nick deserves a fighting chance to make you fall in love with him again. I want you to give him that chance."

His words had obviously baffled her. "But why?"

"Because I don't want to win if I can only have part of you. I'm a greedy man, Rosie. I want the whole damn thing. I want your love, free and clear. No regrets. No what-ifs."

She blinked. "I want that, too."

"All right. If you're agreed, then I'm going to put Mitch in charge of the company and move to Park City for the summer where I can train for the Tour de France."

"No, Zach!" she cried, rushing headlong into his arms. "There has to be another way."

"There is no other way, Rosie, and we both know it." *All I can do now is leave our fate to destiny and hope you love me enough.* "Three months, Rosie. That gives you and Nick enough time to decide if you're going to stay married."

She looked panicked. "But I can't bear to let you go! And...and it's not fair to you."

He seized on those words she'd thrown out like a lifeline. His response, though, was calm and measured. "If you haven't noticed, I'm a big boy. I can take care of myself. I'd be happier if I could be with you, but he was there first. If he hasn't ignited that old fire by the time the summer's over, then I'll know you're all mine."

She lifted her hands to his cheeks, her eyes tender and adoring. "You're so wonderful. I love you with all my heart, Zach. How will I stand it without you?"

You took the words right out of my mouth, Rosie.

"I'm counting on your not being able to stand it. Now, before I forget all my noble intentions, let's get out of here."

"Wait." She moistened her lips nervously. "If I'm really going to go through with this, then I should give you back your ring."

A wave of pain staggered Zach. "You're right. I'll follow you home. He knows it's sitting in your jewelry box. He'll never believe you're serious if you keep it there. When it's gone, he'll call off the divorce. That's what you want him to do."

That's what I want him to do. No pressure. Then you'll have a chance to find out you're in love with me, Rosie Armstrong. And the sooner you do that, the better.

"Hold me for a minute," she begged, burrowing into him. "I'm so frightened. What if you meet someone else in the meantime?"

"Do you honestly believe that could happen?"

Oh, Rosie. You don't have a clue about the depth of my feelings.

"Mom?"

Rosie jumped as Cody walked into the foyer from the back of the house. "I—I didn't know you were home, honey. Did you have a good time?"

"The best!"

She frantically tried to brush the tears from her eyes. Zach had barely walked out the front door. Did Cody and Nick see him in passing?

"We saw Zach getting in his car."

There's your answer, Rosie.

"How come you're crying? Did you two have a fight?"

Oh, Cody. You're so transparent. You'd give anything to hear me tell you yes.

"No. But we did reach a decision about something. Come in the bedroom and I'll tell you."

She had no idea if Cody knew of Nick's intentions to divorce her, but decided that Nick wouldn't have burdened his son that way. At least not yet.

When they reached her room, she shut the door and asked Cody to sit on the bed with her. "Today Zach and I decided to break our engagement."

His shout of joy filled the room, as she'd known it would.

"I asked him to come in the house so I could give him back his ring."

"Then you're not going to marry him?"

Her body shivered in reaction. "No. Your father has come home. I want the three of us to be a family again." *I don't know if it's possible, but I'm going to give it a try for all our sakes. Including Zach's.*

"Oh, Mom!"

For the first time in two years she could honestly say her son sounded completely happy. Those were joyous sobs shaking his body.

"I can't wait till you tell Dad."

"W-where is your father?"

"I think he's still outside talking to Jeff's dad. We had so much fun, but it would've been neater if you'd come. All the guys' moms were there."

"I'm sorry about that, honey, but I had classes and I had to prepare my end-of-term grades."

"I know."

"I'll come with you next time."

He jumped up, too excited to keep still. "Can I tell Dad?"

"If you don't mind, Cody, that's something I need to tell your father myself, when we're alone."

"Tell me what?"

Rosie wheeled around in stunned surprise. Nick had walked in on them unannounced.

If anyone had told her that a week of eating lots of good food could drastically alter a person's appearance, she wouldn't have believed it. But Nick was living proof.

His face seemed fuller. She saw a luster to his hair, which was looking a little longer. In fact, she sensed a general improvement in his overall well-being. He'd picked up some sun on their trip to the mountains, erasing the sallowness of his skin when he'd first gotten off the plane.

Cody eyed both of them intently, then gave Rosie

a significant look. A private message. "I'll put my gear away."

Just like that, she was back in her son's good graces.

"What was that all about?" Nick muttered as soon as Cody had disappeared out the door.

"If you're worried that I told him about the summons, I didn't say anything. I don't want a divorce."

"Since when?"

He rarely relied on sarcasm. It stunned her.

"Nick, we have to talk."

"I'm all ears."

She hated it when his voice took on that aloof wintry tone. Clearing her throat nervously, she said, "Cody mentioned you saw Zach leaving the house."

"That's right."

"I'd like to explain why he was here."

His dark brows furrowed. "I thought I made it clear that you and Zach can do whatever you want. It doesn't matter to me."

Nick, darling. Stop being so damn noble.

Her heart hammered, and she summoned her courage to ask, "Would it matter if I told you I gave him back his ring?"

He started emptying his pockets on the dresser they now shared. "Whose idea was that? Yours or Zach's?"

She'd expected any reaction except that. Linda had told her to tell the truth, no matter how much it might hurt the other person. But *she* seemed to be the only one getting hurt!

"Zach came back from California today and I

showed him the divorce complaint. We both agreed that everything's happening way too fast. We've broken our engagement.''

NICK STARED AT HER in silence. Poor Rosie. Guilt was eating her alive and Zach had had no choice but to go along with her wishes.

She'd gone on talking. ''This idea of divorce is too premature, Nick.''

He should have been elated that she didn't want the divorce, but he knew what was motivating her response. *Guilt. Pity.* And marriage with a wife who stayed out of guilt and pity was not his idea of happiness.

Nick grabbed some clean clothes and headed for the bathroom. Over his shoulder he said, ''Let me grab a quick shower and then we'll talk.''

The hurt look on her face crushed him, but he needed to get away from her before he listened to her pleas and called off the divorce. No, he *had* to continue with it to preserve his sanity and hers.

It didn't matter that she and Zach had ended their engagement. That didn't change the love the two of them shared. Nick knew damn well that if she stayed with him, she'd never be able to fully concentrate on their marriage when Zach was standing in the wings, just waiting for it to fail so he could claim her.

In a few swift strides Nick reached the bathroom and adjusted the taps until the spray was the right temperature. He tried to blot the grief from his mind and enjoy the luxury of a hot shower, something he'd been deprived of for so many years.

But then, there'd been so many things he'd missed. So many people—and one above all. *Oh, Rosie! How am I ever going to let you go?*

The way he figured it, going through with the divorce was, ironically enough, the only hope their marriage had. Because unless Rosie was free to choose—which meant free to choose *Zach* if she wanted—staying together would mean all the wrong things. Be for all the wrong reasons.

A half hour later he found her in the kitchen making hamburgers for dinner. Amazing what a shower and shave could do for a man. Every day he was feeling a little more normal. A little closer to his former life. If only the part with Rosie was right...

"Where's our son?"

Rosie paused in her task of slicing purple onions and turned to glance at him. "I wanted time to talk to you first, so I told him to go play basketball for a while." Nick felt her eyes travel over him. This evening she didn't seem to mind what she saw. Most likely the shock had worn off and she was starting to accept the fact that he was minus a hand.

"Those sweats look good on you, Nick."

"They're comfortable, too. Thanks for getting them for me."

"You're welcome."

"Does Cody know you've broken up with Zach?"

"Yes."

Biding his time, Nick opened the refrigerator to get a pint of milk. "I don't think I'll ever be able to get enough of this stuff." Her eyes rounded as he drank it without stopping to breathe, then tossed the empty carton into the waste basket.

"I realize you're starving, so I've made you nachos." She pulled them out of the oven and set them on the kitchen table.

Nick didn't need a second invitation. He straddled the back of a chair and munched to his heart's content, watching her as she put the meat in the broiler. Then she sat down opposite him, her expression anxious.

"You haven't said anything, Nick. What are you thinking?"

"What a great cook you are."

She actually flushed, a small sign of the old Rosie. "I appreciate that, but you know what I'm talking about."

He eyed her narrowly. *This is going to hurt both of us, but it has to be this way.*

"I'm going through with the divorce, Rosie."

"You can't!" The blood all but drained from her face.

He reached for another cheese nacho. "It's only a piece of paper, Rosie, but it represents freedom for both of us. A chance for all concerned to start fresh."

"A fresh start for *you,* maybe!" she cried. "But what about Cody? He'll be in agony."

"He's no stranger to it."

She shoved herself away from the table. "How can you be so callous?"

"That's your word, Rosie. I prefer realistic."

"You've grown so...cold."

He finished off the last nacho. "Sometimes those bunkers got cold in the middle of the night."

A groan escaped her lips. "I'm sorry. I shouldn't have said that. Forgive me." She rushed over to the broiler to turn the hamburger patties.

Finish it now, Armstrong. You may not have the courage later. "Since you know I'm going ahead with the divorce, do you want me to move out? All you have to do is say the word."

Her back looked as rigid as a telephone pole. "Why don't we let Cody decide? Since you're the one filing, you might as well be the one to tell him."

"He's coming through the back door right now. I guess there's no time like the present."

"No, Nick…" she pleaded with him.

Rosie, Rosie. The pain has got to stop!

Cody proceeded into the kitchen cautiously, staring at the two of them, his eyes shiny with hope. "Is it all right?"

"Of course." Nick motioned for him to sit down. "There's something I have to say, and I want you to hear it, be part of the ultimate decision."

"Sure, Dad." Cody tossed his head to get the hair out of his eyes.

Nick sat forward and grasped his son's right hand. "Cody? Have you ever had someone do you a big favor?"

"Yeah. Jeff kept my aquarium clean and fed my fish while I went down to St. George for a few days."

"Fine. That's a good example. Now, how would

you have felt if you'd learned that deep down, he hadn't wanted to do it, but he felt like he *had* to?''

He hunched his shoulders. "Bad."

"Why?"

"I guess because I don't want anyone doing me any favors unless they really want to."

"Exactly. Now I'm going ask you another question. It's important. Do you think your mom *really* wanted to return Zach's ring when they only got engaged three weeks ago?''

"Nick!"

"Remember what we were just talking about," he said, ignoring Rosie's cry.

Cody bent his head. "No," came the quiet reply. "She didn't...."

Nick squeezed his hand hard, then let it go. "Thanks for your honesty, son. Perhaps now you'll understand that I don't want anyone doing any favors for me, either."

At those words, Cody's head flew back. "Does that mean you and Mom are getting a divorce?"

Nick felt the crack in his son's voice clear to his bones.

"Yes. You'll be living with your mom, but you can visit me whenever it's all right with her."

I'm doing this for all of us, Cody. Trust me, son.

He heard another muffled sound from Rosie.

Nick thought there would be tears, but Cody sat there frozen.

"Your mother and I are good friends, Cody. That hasn't changed and it never will. The point is, we both love you more than life itself. That'll never change, either.

"I don't know how long the divorce will take, but barring any complications, the attorney estimates six weeks. Under the circumstances, I can go on living here, just as we are, until it's final, which should be around the time your school lets out.

"Or I can live in that hotel by the university until my therapy's over, and then make a permanent move."

"Where?" Rosie asked, her tone brittle. When Nick looked over, she was clinging to the counter with both hands.

Cody darted a glance at his father. "Doesn't Mom know?"

"Know what?"

"You tell her, Cody."

"Dad's going to live in Heber."

"Heber?"

"It's not exactly a fait accompli, Rosie. I told you I wanted to live in the mountains. There were a couple of properties for sale in Heber. If you recall, when we were dating, we used to drive up there a lot and talk about retiring there one day."

"I remember. It's heavenly up there," she whispered, still sounding dazed.

It *was* heavenly. But at the time, he and Rosie had been concentrating so hard on each other they scarcely knew what was going on around them.

"One of the ranches for sale seemed the perfect size and it's got a great house on it. So I've put down earnest money. The old couple will be moving out by midsummer. But Cody and I want *you* to see it before I actually buy it.''

''Yeah. It's really neat, Mom. We'll be able to waterski up there with all my friends' families. We're going to have horses and a boat.''

''You really meant it about leaving Salt Lake.'' Her voice was quiet. Haunted.

''That's right. I knew if I didn't at least put a hold on the place, someone else would. Of course, no decision's going to be made until you've seen it and approved.''

Rosie didn't say anything. Just stood there looking shocked.

''So, Cody,'' Nick said, picking up where they'd left off, ''in the meantime, shall I stay here or go to the hotel? What would make you happier in the long run?''

His head swerved to Rosie. ''What do you want, Mom?''

Rosie looked on the verge of fainting. ''As your father said, it's up to you, honey.''

''Then I think you should move out, Dad. Jeff says you have a right to find a new girlfriend, too. Mom? Can we eat now? I'm hungry.''

Oh, Cody. Somehow I was hoping you'd give me an argument. Now I have to follow through, which means this will be my last night under the same roof with you and your mother....

CHAPTER NINE

ROSIE AWOKE from her restless sleep with a jolt. Something had disturbed her. Probably a nightmare, but she couldn't remember it. The scene in the kitchen before dinner had been enough of a nightmare to last a lifetime.

Yet Cody and his father had consumed their hamburgers with enjoyment, not missing a bite as they bantered back and forth. You would never have known anything was wrong. Afterward, they'd helped her with the dishes, then left for the gym.

Rosie couldn't stand her own company, but was strangely reluctant to call Zach. Since they'd already said their painful goodbyes, she hated the idea of calling him and starting everything all over again—when she firmly believed that Nick hadn't meant what he said.

She couldn't imagine that he'd really go through with the divorce. Of course she couldn't stop him from moving out in the next few days, but she didn't think it'd be permanent. His pride and anger had gotten in the way. When he cooled off, he'd see that Cody needed him at home.

The fact that he was waiting for her to see the

property in Heber before he bought it told her that he really didn't plan to end their marriage.

There was that noise again.

Occasionally Cody talked in his sleep. It didn't surprise her that tonight was one of those times. He'd acted so brave at the table, but she knew he was heartbroken over the turn of events.

How could you do it, Nick? How could you shatter our son's dreams like that?

She tried to fall back to sleep, then shot straight up in bed as the sounds grew louder.

Without wasting another second, she climbed out of bed and hurried out of the room to see what was wrong with Cody. But when she reached the hall, she realized the sounds were coming from the front of the house.

Nick!

He must have fallen asleep with the TV on. He insisted it was the only way he could relax; he usually dropped off sometime during the wee hours. She'd tried to persuade him to at least lie down in the guest bedroom, but he always refused, saying he preferred the couch.

She shut Cody's door, then walked quickly toward the living room. But with every step the sounds became clearer. First she'd hear groans, then a voice talking at a frantic pace.

When she entered the living room and saw that the TV was off, she knew the almost inhuman noises had to be coming from Nick.

In the moonlight spilling through the windows she

could see her husband crouched on the floor, wearing only his track pants, his body glistening with sweat.

To her horror his head was moving back and forth as if he were using it as a battering ram. He kept clawing at his injured arm with his right hand.

"Got to get these shackles off. Got to get out the doors, R.T. We need transportation. Got to hijack some kind of bus, going to need some weapons, need someone who speaks Arabic. Got to get out of here, R.T. Got to find out where we are. Here they come. Don't tell them anything, R.T. Oh, God. Don't let us die. Get us out of here. Please God, Please, God. Please, God. Please, God."

Rosie stood transfixed as Nick repeated the same litany over and over again. When she couldn't stand it any longer, she threw her body down next to his and gathered him in her arms.

Even when she held him against her, he continued the rocking motion. Despite his weight loss, he was in amazingly good shape. His strength terrified her because he was in a deep sleep and had no control over his movements.

"Nick...wake up, darling! It's Rosie. Wake up!"

She took an elbow in the jaw before she managed to roll him onto his back. Now she lay on top of him, using both hands to smooth the moisture from his face and forehead. His heart was racing; his breath came in pants.

"Wake up, Nick. You're dreaming. It's Rosie. Wake up, my love. Come on."

She began shaking his shoulders.

"Don't do it, don't do it, don't do it..." he cried,

trying to cover his ear with his arm, flinching repeatedly as if someone was beating him. His motions had thrown her down hard on her side, but she clung to him, wrapping her arms around his head, so that he was butting her chest.

Rosie was terrified because nothing was working, nothing was bringing him out of it. Years ago, when Cody was in the hospital dangerously ill with croup, the only thing that had calmed him was her singing. She'd sat on the side of his hospital bed and sung nonstop to him all night long.

Out of sheer instinct, she began singing to her husband.

"'Away in a manger, no crib for a bed, the little Lord Jesus lay down his sweet head. The stars in the bright sky looked down where he lay, the little Lord Jesus asleep on the hay. Asleep, asleep. Asleep, asleep. Asleep...'"

Miraculously his agitation began to subside. The screams, the mutterings, faded.

Sending up a prayer of gratitude, she sang every Christmas carol she could think of until his body relaxed and he slept in her arms.

For the rest of the night Rosie kept a vigil over her husband. She didn't dare sleep in case his nightmares returned.

Around eight, she eased away from him and staggered to her feet. Every muscle in her body felt cramped. The throbbing in her jaw was bad enough to need a painkiller.

Nick lay stretched out on his side, looking peaceful. For a few moments she studied the familiar profile, the natural male grace of his long lean body. Throughout their marriage, she'd kissed every inch of it, thrilled to every inch of it. They'd shared every thought and dream. Now, seven years later, through no fault of their own, they shared something else.

She had no name for it.

There was no name for it.

Only Cynthia Ellis knew what Rosie was feeling right now because she must be living through the same kind of experience with R.T.

Rosie reached for the down comforter and carefully covered him, then tiptoed from the room to call R.T.'s wife.

"WELL, CODY? What do you think? The black Pathfinder or the green Land Rover? They're both good for four-wheeling, and both can pull a twenty-three-foot boat."

Nick already knew his choice, but he was curious to see if his son had the same taste in cars.

"I don't know, Dad. They're both awesome."

"You're right about that. Of course, we don't have to decide today."

Cody's face fell. "But, Dad, I thought we were going to drive it off the lot."

"First we have to make a choice. Then they have to get it ready and do all the paperwork. That doesn't give me much time to get to my therapy session. As it is, I'll have to drive the rental car back to Hertz and ask them to drop me off at one of the dealerships."

"Okay. Then I say we get the Land Rover. But only if you like it."

Nick grinned and gave Cody a hug. "Like father, like son. The Rover was my choice, too." He liked the comfort of it and the way it handled on the road. "Let's see if they can work us a fast deal."

When Cody repeated Nick's remark to the car salesman, the man said, "Since your dad's a war hero, I'll cut you another couple of thousand off the factory price. Not only that, I'll have one of the guys in the garage take your rental car back for you."

That brought a smile to Cody's face.

Nick murmured something appropriate, but he wasn't so thrilled. Not that he didn't appreciate a few breaks once in a while. But in the five weeks since he'd come home, he'd been singled out every time he appeared in public. The TV spot on him had aired on the ten-o'clock news the night of the neighborhood welcome-home party. Now it seemed he was a minor celebrity.

People meant well, but he didn't think he would ever get used to the unsolicited attention. As for children, it stung every time he saw one hiding behind a mother's skirts, staring at his bad arm. You never knew what questions or comments would suddenly pour forth from their mouths. Adults weren't much different.

"Oh, man. This is a beaut, Dad!" Cody said a half hour later, his voice rising with excitement. "I can't wait to drive it." He'd opened all the windows and turned the car radio to the K-Bear station, acting like any other teenager—enthusiastic and slightly out of control.

Nick chuckled. He could remember telling his father the same thing when he was the same age as Cody. "If your mom approves and the sale of that ranch goes through, we'll go up to the property and I'll teach you how to drive."

"I want to live with you, Dad," he said urgently.

What else is new?

"We've been over that ground before. You belong with your mother, but the arrangement we've worked out is good, isn't it?"

"Yeah. I guess. But it seems kind of dumb. Mom and me alone in the house, and you over at the hotel."

"That was the best decision, to give your mom her privacy."

"But Zach never comes over!"

"Maybe that's because you haven't tried hard enough to make him feel welcome." The thought horrified him clear through—this other man, welcome in Rosie's house—but Nick said the words, anyway, knowing she had a right to the life and the man, she'd chosen.

"I don't care anymore."

Cody, boy. If only you could hear yourself.

"Then you need to tell your mother it's okay, so she'll start letting him come over."

Cody looked genuinely troubled. "Do you really think I'm the reason he stays away?"

Nick nodded. "Now that you know, it would be cruel not to help your mom."

Cody thought about it for a minute. "Okay. I'll talk to her when I get home. Can I come over tonight?"

"I'm afraid not, son. I'm getting together with R.T. But tomorrow, after your class, I'll take you and Jeff up to Heber with me. We'll test this baby out."

"Cool!"

The therapy lasted until six; Cody read magazines in the waiting room while Nick worked with the therapist. It was almost six-thirty by the time they got to the house, and Nick wasn't surprised that Rosie came down the front porch steps as soon as she saw them pull into the driveway.

"Nick? Don't drive off. I have to talk to you!" she called.

Cody jumped down and ran toward her, regaling her with a blow-by-blow account of the afternoon's activities. His rapture over the new car was evident in the running commentary he kept up.

Though she appeared to be listening to their son, Nick could tell there was something vital on her mind. She started toward the Rover, determination in every step.

When she reached the driver's side, she told Cody to go inside and get washed up for dinner.

Cody waved. "See you tomorrow, Dad."

Nick waved back, then turned in Rosie's direction. *Lord, what a sight.* The sunset bathed her in golden light. It was the first time since he'd come back from the war that he'd seen her hair loose like she used to wear it. The strands glistened like cornsilk and fell halfway down her slender back.

He knew what she looked like—what she *felt* like—under that navy-trimmed white suit she was wearing. He knew every singing line and curve. An ache passed through his body. It was so intense he had to stifle a groan.

"How are you, Rosie?"

Her chin lifted defiantly. "Not good."

He frowned. "What's wrong?"

Those gorgeous angry green eyes looked as if they might shoot sparks at any minute. "A warrant was just served on me for my arrest!"

The situation wasn't funny, but Nick fought not to smile. "Why?"

"Because I didn't respond to the summons."

"Why didn't you?"

"You know why, Nick Armstrong."

The blood pounded in his ears. *Oh, Rosie, sweetheart. You're sounding more and more like your old self. If only you wanted me the way I want you...*

"Because I honestly didn't think you'd go through with the divorce. Obviously I was wrong." Her voice trembled, although he knew she was doing her best to cover it up.

"All you have to do is get an attorney of your own, and you won't have anything to worry about. I'm paying the court costs, remember."

"You can be as smug as you want," she snapped. "But you won't feel the same way when I slap a countersuit against you to stop the divorce."

His heart leapt. "On what grounds?"

"Temporary insanity due to your long imprisonment."

Nick threw back his head and laughed till his ribs hurt. He couldn't help it. She was so adorable. *Dear God. How he loved her.*

"You think I won't do it?"

By now her eyes were smoldering. Her fury was something to behold.

"That would require a psychiatric evaluation."

"That's right. You have special needs and require special help."

All I need is to spend the rest of my nights in bed with you, my beloved. But…it's never going to happen.

"Dammit, Nick. Look at me when I'm talking to you!"

"I *am* looking." *I can't look anywhere else. That's my problem. That's why I need to get a divorce as soon as possible. You and Zach need it, too!*

"I'm serious. I want you to get some counseling and support. The last thing you should be thinking about is a divorce."

"I had no idea you felt this strongly on the subject. May I ask what brought it on?"

"Isn't the fact that you were a POW reason enough?" she fired back, but he had the distinct impression there was something else behind her vehemence.

"Much as I'd love to explore this more thoroughly with you, I have other plans tonight and I'm afraid I'm already late.

"Rosie," he said on a more sober note, "tomorrow I'm planning to drive Cody up to Heber after school for a few hours. If you want, we'll swing by

your office and take you with us so you can see
where I have hopes of living. He's been anxious for
you to come, so I can make a decision about buying
the place."

"I wish I could, but I have a chemistry lab on
Tuesday afternoons."

"How long does it last?"

"Till five."

"We can wait until then to go. We could have
dinner at the Wagon Wheel. That'll give Cody time
to get his homework done. Think about it. Tomorrow
he can tell me what you decide. Good night."

Her face closed up, and he couldn't tell what she
was thinking. "Good night."

All the way back to the hotel, Nick reflected on
the subtle changes in his wife since he'd arrived at
Hill. From shock and a distanced pity to...what? Intensity, unselfishness, determination. Just now she'd
seemed more like the Rosie he'd left behind. But he
understood all too well that it was because she felt
sorry for him and didn't want to hurt him.

*I can't hang on to you knowing deep down that
you're in love with Zach, Rosie. I can't!*

Nick spotted R.T. in the lobby talking to one of
the clerks at the reception desk. Even from this distance, he could see that his friend seemed to be putting on weight as fast as he was.

"Rutherford Topham, I presume? My, my, what
civilization has wrought. Chinos and a polo shirt, no
less."

R.T. turned around, a wry smile lifting the corner

of his mouth. *What a wonder was a woman's love.*
Nick hardly recognized the guy.

"Sergeant Armstrong, *sir.*"

Nick's ears picked up the subtle tap-tap of R.T.'s
knuckles on the counter. He was telling Nick the
denim shirt and jeans looked "awesome," one of
Cody's favorite words.

Chuckling, Nick tapped out a response that said,
*You should see me in the sweats Rosie bought. Cen-
terfold stuff.*

R.T. tapped, *We're attracting attention.*

It's my bad arm, Nick tapped back.

*I don't think so. The clerk hasn't been able to look
at anything but my glass eye since I came in. See?
He's still watching.*

*At least you didn't have a little girl scream that
there was a monster with no hand running loose in
the grocery store.*

I need to talk to you. Let's get out of here.

Amen. Nick gave one more emphatic tap and they
headed across the foyer to the guest parking lot.

R.T. whistled as they climbed into Nick's new
Land Rover.

Both of them already knew where they wanted to
go. The choice had been made years ago. Five
minutes later they'd pulled into Hires Drive-In on
Seventh East and gave their order: two frosted root
beers, two hamburgers and two cartons of french-
fried onion rings.

"Where's Cynthia tonight?"

"She's staying at my aunt's till I pick her up
later."

"I don't have to ask you how it's going."

R.T. blushed furiously.

"Come on, now. How long did it take her to make you her husband again?"

"That's classified…sir."

"That fast, huh?" Nick grinned.

"She wants a baby."

"Did you tell her you're going to have a whole football team, and that the first one—boy or girl—is going to be named after me?"

"Yeah. I did. She's planning on it." Suddenly he was sobbing. "I just can't believe she loves me. I mean, look at me. Old one-eye."

"Old one-eye has all the parts that count. And you've got both your hands. You know how important that is, if you follow my meaning."

R.T. sniffed hard. "One hand gets the job done, Sergeant."

Nick sucked in his breath. "I wouldn't know."

"Why the hell not? You had your chance the other night."

A tap on the car window announced that their meal had arrived. Nick paid the waitress, then distributed the food.

"What are you talking about?" he demanded when they were alone again.

"You mean, *who*. Rosie's been down to our place a couple of times already."

Nick almost dropped his mug in surprise.

"How come you're divorcing her, Sarge?"

"She can't marry Zach Wilde if I don't do the honorable thing."

"She's not engaged anymore."

"A mere technicality, Watson."

"I'm not so sure. Perhaps you ought to know that a couple of weeks back, while you were putting on one of your more colorful productions of the late, late show, as Cyn calls them, your wife wrestled you to the ground and held on to you for dear life until morning."

R.T.'s words hit him like a boulder dropping from a mountain. His appetite ceased to exist. "I don't believe you."

"Did you ever ask her about that big purple bruise on her jaw?"

His body went rigid. "She said she ran into a cupboard door."

"Well, for what it's worth, that cupboard did enough blabbing to provide a carbon copy of one of *my* nights. Just thought you'd like to be informed."

"She held me all night?"

How could that have happened and you didn't know about it, Armstrong?

"I guess she sang to you, too. That's when you calmed down. Cyn's going to try it on me next time. The point I'm attempting to make is, what's she doing holding you when she's got a perfectly good fiancé ready to take her off your hands?"

"Hand, R.T., hand."

"You know what I mean, Sarge."

Is that why you're fighting me on the divorce, Rosie? Because the mother in you has bonded with the terrified child in me?

"Did it ever occur to you she might've wanted an excuse to hold you?"

"No."

Rosie had always felt sorry if an ant got crushed. He could just imagine how sorry she'd feel after witnessing his madman performance.

"I know what you're thinking, Sarge, but it isn't that way. For one thing, Cyn said that Rosie was so happy to finally connect with you she practically went to pieces for a while. According to my wife, Rosie said some stuff that kind of puts a different slant on things."

"I don't want to hear it."

"Well, you're going to," R.T. persisted doggedly. "Rosie told Cyn that she'd been cheated out of seven years with you, and now she's jealous of me because I know things about you that *she* doesn't know. When you had that bad night, she felt like she was right there in that cell with you, sharing it. She said it made her feel close to you again, like she used to feel before the war when she knew things about you nobody else did. She said—and this is a quote—'It was like I was given a little present, one I'll treasure forever.'"

She said that?

Nick couldn't talk, couldn't think.

"Sure as hell doesn't sound like pity to me. Sure as hell doesn't sound like Zach Wilde could've squeezed his way in between you two." After a long pause, R.T. muttered, "She said something else, but I guess you don't want to hear that, either."

"Go ahead," Nick half grunted.

"Is that an order, *sir?*"

"What do you think?"

"Just checking. Well, according to Cyn, Rosie's terrified you're going to divorce her and share those seven lost years with some blond bimbo who's only out for your body and won't connect with you on any other level."

Nick's mouth quirked, despite his pain.

"She has one more secret fear."

"Go on."

"Just checking to see if you're still with me. What Cyn says is that Rosie's afraid you'll find the bimbo's, uh, performance better than hers. Apparently she's nervous about being able to make all the right moves after seven years of abstinence. She's afraid you're dying to experiment now, and Zach has given you the excuse you've been looking for."

Quiet reigned.

"Could she be right, Sarge? Have you been holding out on me all this time?"

More quiet.

"I wasn't supposed to tell you all that. It was top secret. Classified. You never heard it from me."

"I never heard it from you," Nick repeated.

R.T. turned his head and stared at him. "What's eating you?"

"She's been in love with another man for two years."

"Correction. She's been *seeing* another man for two years and couldn't commit to him until the eleventh hour. And we know why, don't we, Sarge? Because she was in love with another man for seven years before that.''

Nick gritted his teeth. "She's in love with Zach now!"

"You were there first, Sarge. She still loves you, yet you're practically throwing her at him."

"Because Zach's the man she wants to marry."

"Maybe. Maybe not. All I know is, you're not giving this thing half a chance. If I thought for one minute that Cyn was hanging on to me out of pity, I'd be long gone, so I can understand your reasoning. But I'll tell you, what Cyn heard coming out of Rosie's mouth the other night—that wasn't pity or anything close to it."

Nick groaned. "You think I don't want to believe you?"

"I think maybe you ought to visit a shrink at the Veterans' Hospital."

"Rosie told me the same thing earlier today."

"Maybe you ought to take her advice."

"Maybe. But it won't solve a damn thing if in the end she'd still rather be Mrs. Zach Wilde."

"Excuse me, sir, but you don't sound like the same man who kept me alive all those years and wouldn't let me give up!"

"That man died the morning we flew into Hill, R.T."

"CODY?"

It was a couple of hours since Nick had dropped Cody off. They'd finished supper, and Cody had settled down to his homework at the kitchen table.

"Yeah, Mom?"

Rosie rushed through the kitchen and grabbed her purse. "While you finish your math, I've got to run to the drugstore."

"If you're meeting Zach there, why don't you just tell him to come over to our house, instead?"

Rosie came to a complete standstill and turned around. She'd never imagined the day she'd hear something like that from Cody.

"What makes you think I'm meeting Zach?"

"Well, aren't you?"

Rosie expelled a deep sigh. "No. But I was going to phone him."

"Then phone him from here."

"Cody, I know you don't like him. I've tried not to bring him around, because the last thing I've wanted to do is upset you."

"I know. I've been a jerk."

She blinked. "Does your father have something to do with this complete turnaround?"

His guilty face spoke volumes. "Yeah. But Dad's right. I've been really mean to you. I'm sorry, Mom. I love you." Crying, he got up from the table to hug her.

She wrapped her arms around him and held him tight. "I love you, too, honey."

"If you want to marry Zach, it's okay. I'll be nice to him. I promise. Now that Dad's home, it doesn't matter anymore. Like Dad said, you couldn't help loving another man. He says it's natural for you to want to get married. He said that you and he were really happy once, more than other people, and that's why you want to try it again.''

We were happy, Cody. Happier than you could possibly comprehend.

"What else did he say?" she prodded quietly, shaken by everything she was hearing.

"While we were waiting for him to start his therapy, he said that you're not getting any younger and you probably want to have a baby with Zach right away 'cause that's what real joy is all about. And I'll be its brother and baby-sit and teach it things—you know, stuff like that.''

Nick...

"Dad asked me about the saxophone in my closet. I told him Zach was a really good musician, that he'd bought it for me and had tried to teach me to play it. Dad got really mad when he found out I wouldn't take Zach up on those lessons. He says he would've given anything to be blessed with musical talent and thinks I'm lucky to have someone like Zach to teach me.''

Rosie eased herself away from Cody so he couldn't tell how badly she was shaking.

He wiped his eyes on his arm. "Maybe if Zach's not too mad at me, he'll start teaching me after you get married. What do you think?''

I don't know what I think, Cody. I don't know anything anymore.

"Oh, honey, I love and admire you more than ever for telling me all these things! And as long as you've been this honest with me, I'm going to be honest back.

"I haven't seen Zach for a while and I need to talk to him. If he's home, I'm driving over to his condo. You have the phone number. If I'm going to be late, I'll call you. All right?"

He nodded. "If you're worried, Dad can always come over."

"Not tonight, I'm afraid. I think he had a— I think he had other plans."

"Yeah. He and R.T. are hanging out."

Nick's with R.T., not another woman. It shouldn't matter to you one way or the other, Rosie Armstrong, but somehow it does.

"They need time together," she murmured.

"I know. Dad's crazy about R.T. They talk on the phone every night now."

Rosie had imagined as much. "R.T. feels very close to your father."

"R.T. and Cyn want to move up to Heber, too. He's thinking of buying that other property for sale, the one next to ours, so he and Dad can ranch together."

"I—I didn't know that." She reached blindly for the back-door handle.

"I just found that out when Dad was driving me home. They're even talking about writing a book about their experience. Cyn does word processing, and she'll help them get the book ready to send to a publishing company. Dad said that while they were in prison they kind of wrote it in their minds. They're even thinking of going around the country someday to talk to other vets who've been disabled, to try to help them. Isn't that neat?"

"It is, Cody, and it sounds just like your father. He's a fantastic human being."

"Yeah. I just wish that you and he—" Cody stopped midsentence. "Oh, forget it," he mumbled before running out of the kitchen.

CHAPTER TEN

"Zach?"

"*Rosie!* It's lucky you caught me before I left for Park City. I've been hoping against hope to hear from you. I know I told you I'd keep strictly away, but now that I hear your voice, I can't take this separation any longer. I'm coming to get you, wherever you are."

"I'm downstairs in the foyer of your condo."

She heard his gasp. "You wouldn't tease me..."

"No, Zach. I'm here. I need to talk to you."

"Whenever you get that tone in your voice, I know it's serious. I'll give you the code to the inner door so you can come up."

"I'll be right there," she assured him.

Zach was waiting for her the second the elevator doors opened to the fourth-floor foyer. He was in his blue sweats—he must have just come back from cycling. It reminded her of the first time she'd met him. He'd looked like a Norse god then, too.

"Come here," he murmured huskily, pulling her across the hall to his apartment. He shoved the door closed, then picked her up in his arms and carried her to the couch.

When she was nestled in his lap, he covered her

mouth with smothering force. Rosie let go of a long sigh and kissed him back, deeply, fully. She needed to blot out the world, to experience the rapture she'd felt in his arms during their cruise, when she'd begged him to ask her one more time to marry him.

"I don't care why you're here or what you have to say. All I know at this moment is that I want you," he whispered, raining kisses on her face, her hair. "I want you so much, it's agony. Come to bed with me tonight. I can't wait any longer."

"In six weeks, maybe less, my divorce will be final," she murmured against his lips. "We can fly to Las Vegas and be married, then honeymoon anywhere you say for as long as you want. How's that sound?"

His body stilled, then he gently removed her from his lap and stood up, raking a hand through his dark blond hair. "I thought the divorce was called off."

She averted her eyes, stirring restlessly. "I thought Nick would call it off when I told him I wanted to try and make our marriage work. But he said he didn't want me to do him any favors."

"When did this conversation take place?"

Oh, Rosie. You're going to hurt him again.

"The night I gave you back the ring. He moved to a hotel after that."

Zach's face went ashen. "And it took you this long to tell me?"

His voice grated, bringing her to her feet.

She wrung her hands unconsciously. "Zach... I thought he was bluffing. I couldn't believe he really meant to go ahead with the divorce, that he'd disappoint Cody like that. So I waited before saying anything to you. Surely you can understand.''

He stood there unmoving, totally unapproachable. She'd never seen Zach like this. It frightened her.

''Tell me what he did that's suddenly convinced you he means business.''

''I didn't respond to the first summons. This morning I was served a second. Apparently I owe a fine to the court. Nick is dead serious about this, so I had to retain an attorney today. Mr. Reynolds informed me that because of the unusual nature of the grounds, the divorce should go through quickly.''

''So nothing's been resolved.''

''Of course it has,'' she protested. ''We can go ahead and make our wedding plans.''

''What about the three-month waiting period we agreed on?''

''Nick changed all that when he chose to divorce me!'' No matter how hard she tried, she couldn't disguise the tremor in her voice.

Something about his remote demeanor made her heart sink. ''Zach, why are you being like this?''

He lifted his head, staring at her as if he didn't know her. ''Why do I get the feeling this all sounds too easy?''

''Maybe because I've made you wait such a long time, you're looking for complications where there aren't any. Would it help if I told you that Cody gave me his permission to marry you? He told me tonight…''

Zach's lips thinned to an angry white line. ''Then

we have your husband to thank for that miraculous change of heart.''

"Don't be this way, Zach," she pleaded. "Of course Nick has a huge influence on Cody's behavior these days."

"So if I were to move in with you before the wedding, Cody wouldn't mind?"

Her eyes closed tightly. Zach wanted the ultimate proof that she loved him. If she put him off again after all they'd been through...

"Does this mean you won't move to Park City, after all?"

Zach gave a deep agonizing groan. "Sweetheart? Do you honestly think I'd go anywhere if I thought we could be together from tonight on?"

Her mouth went dry. "Y-you want to move in with me tonight?"

"Well..." His body relaxed and she saw the ghost of a smile soften his stern expression. "Not everything in the condo. How about just me for starters? To give Cody a chance to get used to having me around the house. Every day we'll move a little more of my stuff over, so he hardly notices."

"I—I hope you understand that I haven't changed my mind about making love before marriage."

His mouth quirked. "If anyone knows about that, *I* do. But there's no law that says we can't hold each other all night long, is there?"

A picture of Nick thrashing about in her arms flashed into her mind, haunting her with its clarity and poignancy. That spot on her jaw was still tender, but a little makeup had concealed the worst of the bruise.

"*Rosie.* I asked you a question."

Her head came up sharply. "I know. Of course we can hold each other at night. I was just thinking I should go home before you do—to prepare Cody."

He studied her through shuttered lids. "That's probably the best idea. I need to get a few things together and lock up here. But before I do anything else, there's something I want to give you."

He pulled the engagement ring from his pocket. "Hold up your left hand, sweetheart. I'm putting this back on your finger where it belongs."

She stared at the exquisite two-carat, princess-cut diamond. She simply couldn't hurt him again. If she showed any hesitation, any at all, Nick would notice it immediately. He'd—

No. Not Nick. Zach!

"Until the divorce is final, I can't legally wear your ring," she began in a low voice. "But if you want to give it to me when we get home, I'll wear it on a chain around my neck."

A satisfied gleam entered his eyes. He repocketed the ring and reached for her again. "Tonight, Rosie, you've made me the happiest man alive."

THE NEXT AFTERNOON, Nick was just getting ready to leave his hotel room and drive over to the house to get Cody when he heard his son knocking on the door, calling out to him in an urgent voice.

He crossed the room in a few swift strides and let him in, then gave him a bear hug. "Where's Jeff?"

"He had to go cut his grandma's lawn."

"So how come you didn't wait for me at home?"

"Because there's been a change in plans."

His spirits plummeted. Rosie had probably decided not to go with them.

"That's okay. Your mom can join us another time."

"She and Zach are going to meet us at the Wagon Wheel around six."

Zach? Nick gazed at his son. "You must have done a great job of patching things up with your mom where Zach is concerned."

"Yeah. Everything's fine. He even slept over last night."

Nick felt as if a grenade had just blown up his gut.

"Excuse me a minute, Cody. I think I left my wallet in the other room. Why don't you go out and wait for me in the car? It's not locked."

"Okay, Dad."

Nick raced to the bathroom in time to lose his lunch. R.T. had warned him about precipitating events too quickly.

"Dad?" Cody murmured cautiously, opening the bathroom door a crack.

"I thought I told you to go outside."

"You looked sick. I didn't want to leave you. It's 'cause of what I said, huh? About Zach. 'Cause you love mom."

His son was too astute for his own good. "Don't worry about it." He put the cap back on the toothpaste and left the bathroom, his arm around Cody.

"Thanks for always being there for me, bud. I love you."

"Love you, too, Dad."

Nick suddenly needed to get away. On impulse he asked, "How would you like to sleep under the stars tonight?"

"Could we?"

"I don't see why not. The people selling the ranch told me I can have the run of the place. There's a beautiful meadow over by the stream. We can put our sleeping bags there. First thing in the morning, I'll get you back down in time for school."

"That'll be awesome. But, Dad, you don't have a sleeping bag, and mine's kind of wimpy."

"On the way out of town we'll stop at a sporting-goods store and pick up a couple. In fact, we'll buy a bunch of camping things while we're at it."

"Oh, man, I need a lot of stuff. Can we get one of those flashlight lanterns?"

"Sure," Nick replied, eager to grant his son his slightest wish. Especially after what he'd learned to-night. It was going to be just the two of them....

Forty-five minutes later, they were loading gear into the Rover. "Wow! Dad, I think we bought out the whole store."

"Looks that way, doesn't it? When you camp with me, you do it right. Let's head over to the grocery store and load the cooler. Then we'll take off for the canyon."

With Cody discussing the instructions for their new Coleman lantern and stove, time passed quickly, and they arrived at the Wagon Wheel before Rosie.

"Heck. Mom's not here yet."

"While we're waiting, let's sit on the grass over there and I'll show you how to play cards. We'll start with twenty-one."

"Mom doesn't like card games."

"I suspect your mom doesn't want you to know how good she used to be at twenty-one and five-card stud. Of course, she could never beat me, but she came close a couple of times."

"*Mom?*"

"Your mom was one exciting woman, Cody."

He'd loved their midnight poker games after the baby was down for the night. She'd lose her concentration and he'd wipe her out of all her money. Then she'd have to divvy up whatever she was wearing. And then…

On a sharp intake of breath, Nick pulled the pack of cards he'd bought out of his shirt pocket. After placing one of the lantern boxes between them for a table, he started shuffling.

"Cool, Dad. How'd you learn to do that with one hand?"

"Have you ever heard the expression 'Necessity is the mother of invention'?"

"Yeah." They grinned at each other.

"All right. I'm going to deal each of us a card facedown, and one faceup. You want both cards to add up to twenty-one, or as close to it as possible, but you don't want to go over. Take a peek at your bottom card and decide if you want another card, or if you want to stay as is. If you want a card, say, 'Hit me.'"

Cody had a quick mind. It didn't take him long to catch on and start trying to outsmart his old man. They must have played at least fifteen hands before a shadow fell over them. It was Rosie. He'd know her perfume anywhere.

"What are you two doing?" Her voice sounded half-amused, half-exasperated.

He turned his head, taking in the gold-and-blue vision that blinded him to everything else. "Nothing you and I haven't done on innumerable occasions. Of course the stakes were a little different then," Nick added before he could catch himself.

A becoming flush filled her cheeks. *She remembers.*

Cody was still figuring his numbers and could hardly stop long enough to greet his mother.

"D-do you want to eat first?" She seemed to have trouble meeting his gaze.

Rosie, sweetheart…you're acting just like you did when we first met. All breathless and nervous. Why?

"It's getting darker. Maybe you'd better follow me and Cody to the property while we can still see."

She nodded jerkily, then walked back to the Passat parked three cars down. Nick couldn't stop staring at her. That was when he unexpectedly met Zach Wilde's cool gray eyes. The other man had been watching him, sizing him up.

Nick nodded in acknowledgment. Zach reciprocated.

Because of blindfolds and the darkness of the underground bunkers, he never saw his enemy in Iraq.

Coming face-to-face with the enemy in Heber,

Utah—as benign a setting as anywhere in the world—was a whole new experience.

"We'll continue our game before bed, Cody," he announced, then turned on the ignition.

"Okay, but let's hurry. This is a lot more fun than video games."

"Now you're showing some real maturity."

Five minutes later they'd left the small town and were driving along a country lane toward the snow-capped mountains to the west. Reaching elevations of eleven thousand feet, they towered majestically over the Swiss-like landscape of the lower hillsides.

"Ah, Cody, this is the life. Everything in this valley is so green and fresh. Smell that air."

His son made a face. "Yeah. Manure. Someone's been fertilizing."

Nick threw back his head and laughed.

Every now and then he glanced at the rearview mirror. Zach maintained several car lengths' distance.

"We're here!"

"We are."

Pulling to the side of the road, he turned off the engine and jumped out of the Rover. He had decided to wear the black T-shirt and Levi's jacket Rosie had picked out for him the other day to let her know he appreciated her doing some shopping for him.

Not pausing in his stride, he headed for the Passat and walked right up to the driver's side as Zach levered himself from the car. Cody had joined Rosie, who stood nearby, looking anxious.

Nick could tell at a glance that he and Zach were

the same height. This close, he was forced to admit Rosie had found herself a good-looking man.

"Hello, Zach. I've wanted to meet you for some time. From all I've heard, you've been wonderful to Cody. I appreciate everything you've done for him." He extended his right hand.

Zach gave it a firm shake. "Nick. It's an honor to meet you. Congratulations on surviving an ordeal few men will ever have to go through. Welcome home."

He nodded. "It's good to be home." His gaze switched to Rosie. "If you'll look to the west over here—" he gestured "—that Swiss-style chalet and barn, all the property going to the foothills, is going to be my ranch in a month or so, but only if you like it and approve of the whole idea."

Her voice sounded faraway when she said, "It's beautiful, Nick. There isn't anything not to like. How about you, Cody?"

"I love it up here, Mom, and it's not that far from home."

"No, you're right. Of course I approve."

"I'm glad." Nick managed to find the words, then once again addressed Zach. "The property due south, with the ranchstyle house is still for sale. My friend, R.T., and his wife, would like to move up here, too. We plan to ranch the land together, and I think we can make a go of it."

"I don't doubt it," Zach replied. "I've lived near the ocean most of my life and it's a part of me, but I have to admit it's beautiful up here. If I'd been in prison as long as you, I'd head for the mountains, too. Being in the outdoors makes all the difference."

"Cody told me you're quite the cyclist, which means you're outdoors a lot."

"I'm not the nine-to-five office type, either."

Nick nodded, then looked around at the pink-frosted peaks. "I dreamed about retiring to this place long before I went to war. If I do live here, Cody will be spending a lot of time with me.

"As I told Rosie, since you're going to be the other man in my son's life, I want us to be able to communicate so that we all get along and do what's best for him."

"I couldn't agree more."

The man's sincere. I can't fault your choice, Rosie.

"You'll be joining us for dinner at the Wagon Wheel, Nick?"

"Thanks, but no. Maybe another time."

"Yeah," Cody piped up. "Dad and I decided to camp out tonight."

Rosie seemed astounded. "Where?"

"Here, on the property."

"But, Cody, you have school in the morning."

"It's all right, Rosie," Nick intervened. "I'll have him down in time. Tonight we're going to count stars and tell Big Foot stories."

"Do you have anything to eat?" she blurted, her troubled gaze passing from Cody to Nick. *Worried about me, sweetheart? Won't the mother in you let go?*

"We've got everything, Mom. T-bone steaks, hash browns, alligator jaws."

"Alligator jaws? Those pastries with the whipped cream inside? I didn't think anyone made them anymore. Nick, those were your very favorite snacks after school. I can remember the filling getting all over your—" She stopped abruptly.

Another memory, Rosie. We share so many it's going to be hard not to be haunted by them.

"Are you going to be warm enough?" She recovered in time to ask a question on a completely different subject.

"We bought all new gear," Cody said. "Do you want to see it?"

"I think Zach and your mom are anxious to go back to town for dinner. As for us, bud, we've got a camp to set up before we get lost in our own cow pasture."

Cody seemed to find the remark funny and laughed. Rosie's expression remained unaccountably sober.

"Are you all right about this, Rosie? If you'd prefer that I take Cody home, I will."

"N-no," she stammered. "It's fine." Her gaze fused with his. "Just take good care of yourselves."

Are you worried about my having another nightmare? Afraid Cody will see it?

"Cody and I will watch over each other," he reassured her. "Zach, it was nice meeting you."

"My pleasure." They shook hands.

"Let's go, son. See you two later." He nodded to Rosie, then turned and headed for the Rover.

Cody followed suit and jumped into the car. Nick

started the engine and drove past the chalet, forcing himself not to look through the rearview mirror.

Don't think about them. Just don't think.

He gave two brief honks to let the Olsons know they were there. The houselights blinked twice in response.

"Hey, is that the secret code you worked out with them?"

"That's right."

"I want to learn Morse code."

"I'll give you a couple of lessons tonight, and you can practice."

"This is so awesome. I wish Mom—" He stopped himself, embarrassed.

"So do I, son. But I'm afraid it's going to be just you and me from here on out."

ROSIE GOT BACK in the Passat, trying not to stare at the Land Rover driving off through the meadow.

"I've hated his guts since the day you first told me you had a husband named Nick who died in the war. When you phoned me and said he was coming home, I prayed his transport plane would crash. Now I wish to God I'd never met him."

She shivered at the vehemence in his tone. "I'm sorry, Zach."

"Rosie, let's go back to Salt Lake for dinner."

"I—I was just going to suggest it."

"Why don't we pick up some Chinese and a video? We'll spend a relaxing, low-key evening, since we've got the house to ourselves."

"That sounds lovely."

He reached for her hand. She clung to his, even when he had to shift gears, and tried hard not to think about anything. What she really wanted was to attain that glorious state of oblivion where there was no hurt, no pain, no guilt. Just *nothing*.

"Hey, sleepyhead. We're home."

"So fast?" Rosie lifted her head to look around. "I can't believe I passed out on you like that."

"I can. You've been under a lot of stress."

He leaned over to caress her hair. "You go on in and I'll run over to Charlie Chow's. Any movie preferences?"

"Something happy."

He came around to her side of the car and helped her out. "I'll see what I can come up with." After giving her a swift hard kiss on the mouth, he left.

Rosie hurried into the house and locked the door, relieved that he hadn't insisted she go with him. This was one time she couldn't burden Zach. Her emotions were in such a chaotic state that she couldn't explain them to herself, let alone to him.

Why wasn't she jumping up and down with excitement at finding herself truly alone with Zach— her husband-to-be? It didn't make sense. They'd been given a whole night of privacy, to talk without interruption, to hold each other, to make definite plans for the future.

Shaking her head as if to ward off the guilt, she made her way to the bathroom to freshen up and replace the clothes she'd worn to work with her quilted robe and slippers.

As she walked toward the living room, it struck

her as odd that the house felt so empty. Heavens, she'd been alone many times. Cody often slept over with friends or spent a few nights in St. George with his grandparents.

Why did the emptiness seem different tonight?

You know why, Rosie. Because you're feeling lonely. Because Cody's not in any of his usual places. He's in paradise. He's with Nick.

She could see them now, the lanterns lit, fierce looks of concentration on their faces as they tried to beat each other at poker and outdo each other with scary stories. When the lights went out, they'd place their sleeping bags side by side, then climb in and gaze up at the heavens.

They'd philosophize a little, chat about nonessentials. Eventually Cody would ask questions about the war. How did Nick keep himself alive in prison? What did he think about? What frightened him? What did it feel like not to have a hand anymore?

Nick would answer some of Cody's questions with a watered-down version of his experiences, then change the subject to something more on Cody's level, like friends, sports, girls. They'd talk about all kinds of things, all kinds of people—except one. Cody's mother, Nick's wife.

A sharp pain pierced Rosie's heart. She cried out in the oppressive stillness of her empty home.

Face it, Rosie. You wish you were there with them. You feel left out.

Terrified at the direction of her thoughts, she rushed over to the couch and began rearranging the pillows. She tried not to think about Nick using it as a bed. She fought the memory of his hunched body, fallen to the floor as he relived his imprisonment.

When the divorce was final, what lucky woman would have the privilege of holding him at night, of sharing his future? Who else knew how to scratch his back in just the right way, rub the ache out of his legs when the muscles tightened up?

Who else knew he was his most amorous at four o'clock in the morning? Who else knew how ticklish he was behind his knees? That if you kissed him there, he was putty in your hands? Your slave for the night?

What woman would be the recipient of that secret smile of his that said, *I've got you where I want you. There's no one to save you. You're all mine. Come here, little girl. You know when your number is up.*

The memories of Nick chasing her around their old apartment making ridiculous hooting sounds like a gorilla were so real she found herself giggling out of fear and excitement.

"Sweetheart?"

"Nick!" she screamed laughingly in automatic response, whirling around.

Too late she realized her error. Zach had stopped dead in his tracks, the bag of food in one hand, a video in the other.

Like an automaton, he put the things on the coffee table, then straightened, his expression grim.

"Do you want to tell me what that was all about?"

Remember. To get in touch with your feelings, you have to be honest. Always tell the truth, no matter how much it hurts.

She gazed into his eyes without flinching. "I was reliving a memory of life with Nick before he went to war. I didn't mean for it to happen. I'm sorry if it hurt you. I love you, Zach. I think you know that."

The muscles twitched along the side of his jaw. "Has this been happening a lot?"

"No," she answered with conviction because it was true. "In fact tonight is truly the first time I've entertained any intimate thoughts of him."

"*How* intimate?" he fired back.

She couldn't sustain his glance and looked away. "Intimate," she whispered.

She could tell he was struggling for breath. "I swore I wasn't going to ask you this question—"

"I haven't slept with him!" She cut him off before he could say another word.

"But you want to."

At all times be honest, no matter how much you think it might hurt. In time you'll begin to understand yourself. When that day arrives, you'll know what to do.

"I—I don't honestly know."

"*Rosie!*"

"Zach," she cried, "make love to me tonight. It's long past time for us to create our own intimate memories. That's what's wrong here. All this time I've asked you to wait. I've asked too much of you, of myself. I made a mistake!" She took a deep, shuddering breath. "Forgive me. I've loved you so long. Let me show you how much."

"You think I don't want that?" His voice shook.

"I know you do. Come on, darling." She lifted her hand, willing him to take it.

"If I make love to you tonight, Rosie, there's no going back."

"No going back."

"Be sure, my love."

I'm going through with the divorce, Rosie. It's only a piece of paper, but it represents freedom for both of us. A chance for all concerned to start fresh.

"I'm sure."

Finally he took her hand and she led him through the house to the guest room, where he'd taken some of his clothes and personal articles.

When they entered, she grasped his other hand and held on to both as she looked up at him. "I'd take you to my room. But that's the bed Nick and I slept in."

His features tautened. "Nick won't be in this one," he vowed fiercely.

Relinquishing her hands, he unclasped the chain around her neck. Within seconds, the ring was back on her finger.

"The first thing I want to do, Mrs. Wilde-about-you," he murmured with a half smile playing around his mouth, "is take a shower with you. Since the day we met, I've had this fantasy of shampooing your hair and rubbing soap into your skin and…"

The world tilted as he lifted her in his arms. With his mouth fastened to hers, he carried her out of the bedroom to the bathroom across the hall.

"Yoo-hoo, Rosie!" a familiar voice called from the front foyer. "It's Grandpa and Grandma. Are you here? Rosie? Cody?"

CHAPTER ELEVEN

"JUST A MINUTE!"

Rosie was absolutely horrified. "Darling…" Her eyes darted to Zach's.

"Go!" he whispered against her lips. "I'll be in the kitchen."

She fairly leapt out of his arms and tore off her robe on the way to her room. Once there, she pulled on jeans and a sweatshirt. Then she ran through the house to greet her in-laws, totally out of breath. "I didn't know you were coming!" She gave both of them a hug.

Janet patted her hair in the hall mirror. "We called and left a message."

Rosie urged them into the living room, where they sat down. "Zach and I just got back from Heber. Nick and Cody wanted to show me where he plans to live."

Her in-laws would have seen Zach's car in the driveway, so she didn't dare lie about it.

Might as well take the bull by the horns.

When nothing was forthcoming, she continued, "Cody and Nick are camping out on the property tonight. They'll be back early because Cody has to go to school in the morning. Zach and I were just about ready to eat some Chinese food. I think he bought enough to feed an army.'' She walked to the doorway and called to him.

"Zach, bring plates and cutlery for four, will you?"

"What's that ring on your finger, Rosie?" Janet demanded.

Oh, no!

"Rosie and I are officially engaged, Mrs. Armstrong.'' The announcement came from Zach, who entered the living room loaded down with dishes and containers of food. "We're going to be married as soon as the divorce is final."

Nick's father sat there attempting to pacify his wife. He kept clearing his throat.

"We heard you'd become engaged on the cruise, but we thought of course you'd call it off now that Nicky's back home." Janet's voice had grown cold and stiff.

Rosie's hands shook as she dished the food onto four plates. "I returned Zach's ring and told Nick I'd like to try to make our marriage work again. But he said no, Mom. He's filed for divorce. I received the complaint yesterday. He wants to get on with his life.

"In a few weeks he'll own a ranch in Heber. He's doing everything possible to carve out a new future."

Janet's eyes glittered a hostile blue. "He's only doing this because you think you're in love with Zach. It isn't what he *wants* to do. I can assure you of that!"

This time Nick's mother was too angry for tears. She turned her venom on Zach. "How does it feel to move into another man's house and steal another man's wife, Mr. Wilde?''

Rosie shook her head at Zach to indicate that he shouldn't respond. This confrontation had been coming for some time. With Cody out of the house, tonight was as good a time as any to set Nick's parents straight.

''Mom, I know you're hurting terribly. I know you are too, Dad. But we can't change what's happened. We've all got to move forward. Nick's doing better than any of us. This evening he and Zach met and shook hands. They're both behaving like civilized human beings because they know what it means to Cody.''

Now that she'd started, she couldn't stop. ''I wish this decision didn't have to cause you and Dad so much pain. You know how much I love you, how grateful I am for everything you've done for me over the years. I want your love and friendship to continue forever. But the fact remains that Nick has made his choice.''

''And you can't even wait until the divorce is final to put that man's ring back on?'' Janet lashed out.

''I'm in love with Rosie, Mrs. Armstrong,'' Zach inserted in a calm tone. ''She's in love with me. We've known each other two years, and we're ready to have a life together.''

''What kind of life can it be when *she*—Nicky's wife—took an oath before God to love him through the good times and bad, in sickness and health, to comfort and keep him until…until *death*…?''

Zach's lips had thinned, a ready sign that he was

barely containing his rage. Rosie was feeling really frightened and tried to hold him back, but it was like trying to single-handedly change the course of a rushing river.

"Your son was presumed dead for more than six years, Mrs. Armstrong. Did you expect your daughter-in-law to stay in mourning for the rest of her life? Do those vows reach beyond the grave?" he asked furiously.

Janet got to her feet. "There was no grave, Mr. Wilde. My son is very much alive. He fought for his country. Did you? I don't see any hands or eyes missing on you." She drove the point home.

Rosie flinched, sick to her stomach. "Mom...don't say another word!"

But Janet was too far gone to listen. "He spent six and a half years in a prison underground where they tortured him, beat him up repeatedly, day in and day out. They put a gun to his head every morning, threatening to kill his wife and child if he didn't talk. Every time they pulled the trigger, he didn't know if he'd be dead or not." She broke down sobbing hysterically.

"They did *that?*" Rosie weaved and would have fallen if Zach hadn't been there to hold her. *I can't bear it. I can't bear it.* She clapped a hand over her mouth, trying to stifle her pain.

"They did that and more. But they didn't destroy him. We all know who did that, don't we, Mr. Wilde? I've heard of kicking a man while he's down, but I never dreamed you could stoop that low."

Rosie couldn't look at Zach. "Stop it!" she

shouted, half sobbing. "Zach doesn't deserve any of this. If you're going to start placing blame, then blame me." She pounded her chest. "I'm the one who didn't believe Nick was still alive. I'm the one who let Zach think he had a chance. It's not his fault! I want you to apologize to him. If you don't, you're not welcome in this house anymore."

"Rosie…" Zach whispered with compassion.

"I mean it, Mom."

When he could see that his wife wasn't about to speak, George got tiredly to his feet. "We'll go, Rosie. Janet and I will stay over at the University Plaza Hotel tonight. Then we can meet up with Nick tomorrow."

"Dad?" She swung around. "Surely you don't blame Zach for this."

He stood there and shook his head. Tears ran down his pale cheeks. "No. War is an evil thing. It's the handiwork of the devil."

Rosie watched them leave. Even when the front door closed, she stayed frozen to the spot.

Zach didn't say a word. He simply picked her up in his arms and carried her to the couch. She burrowed her face in his neck and sobbed.

"WERE YOUR BUNKERS ever bombed, Dad?"

Nick took a deep breath and turned on his side to face his son. He'd thought the time would come when he'd want to talk about the past, but thoughts of Rosie alone with Zach were tearing him apart.

"Several times, near the beginning of our captivity."

"What did it feel like?"

"Well...I can remember one night. I knew it was night because they'd just transferred us from one bunker to another. It was cold. No sun. Even blindfolded, you knew it had to be night. Anyway, they'd just shoved us inside when the air-raid sirens went off. Suddenly I heard the front end of a low-altitude fighter coming in.

"It's easy to determine when a fighter's pointed at you. There's this very distinct sound, kind of a crackling noise, then there's the concussion of the bunker.

"I can't describe it very well, but you kind of feel like you're floating in air while the bunker's being hit. It's an unbelievably strange feeling. The bunker vibrates and there's this popping in your ears, but it's more than a pop. You wonder if you're dead or alive. And then you hear the second fighter, so you know you're not dead yet and you wait for a third then a fourth.

"Since most formations fly in fours, that wait for the fourth one seems extra-long. By now the whole bunker's in chaos. Everyone's shouting and yelling. The Iraqi guards scream at each other, at us.

"That one time I kept thinking if R.T. and I could run out the doors, we'd get transportation by hijacking a local bus, and we'd steal some weapons and find somebody who spoke English.

"But then the fighters stopped coming and we were shoved in a cell, and any chance for escape was gone."

"Whoa! Dad!" Cody audibly gulped back sobs.

"Whoa is right."

"I don't see how you lived through all that." After his tears were spent, he said, "Dad…"

Here it comes. "Yes?"

"I wish Mom were here."

"So do I," Nick said softly.

"I wish Zach would die."

"Don't ever say that again, Cody!"

"I'm sorry."

Nick put his arm around his son and hugged him close. "Even if he was dead, your mother would still love him. Death wouldn't change a thing. You kept loving me, right?"

"Yeah."

"Go to sleep, son. We've got to be up early in the morning. Listen—just in case I have a nightmare, I'm going to move my bag a couple of yards away from yours. Sometimes I fling around. I'd never hurt you, but if you try to touch me, I might hit you thinking I'm trying to protect myself from one of the guards. Do you understand what I'm saying?"

"Yeah."

Nick was tempted to tell Cody about his mother's bruise, but thought the better of it for fear Cody might read more into that night than was there. *Hell.* Nick sighed. If only he'd been aware of Rosie's arms around him.…

"Are you scared, bud? If so, you can sleep in the car."

"I'm kind of nervous. But I figure if you survived all that torture, I ought to be able to survive one of your bad dreams."

"Like father, like son, eh? You know what? Your mother not only raised a wonderful boy, she raised an honest one. You're terrific, Cody."

"You're the best!"

"Tell me that in the morning and I'll believe you."

"I love you, Dad."

"Love you, too. Good night."

Fortunately for Cody, Nick couldn't sleep, not when his thoughts were filled with visions of Rosie in Zach's arms.

As soon as Nick knew his son had fallen off, he got out of his bag and walked around for hours, making plans for his ranch, thinking about the innovations he and R.T. could make. Together they would be successful. He was determined about that.

Whatever the future held, he wanted to build something solid for his son. Right now he couldn't imagine marrying again, having more children. He supposed it was possible. One day he'd try dating, but he wasn't going to hold his breath that anything would come of it.

Thanks to his father, who'd watched over an investment of Nick's no one else knew about, he had enough income to keep him going until he made the ranch profitable.

As early as his senior year in high school, Nick's business teacher had taught the students how to make money through rollovers on stock options. It was risky, but if you knew how to play it right, your success could be impressive. Nick had applied the theory and begun seeing results.

That led to his working for a brokerage, which in turn led to his making some good money, which he kept putting into investments. With the army paying for his education, he didn't have to touch them. He had no doubt that in today's market, he could make a lot of money in very little time if he wanted to.

However, all those years in prison had taught him that other things were more important. Family topped the list. Helping those less fortunate came a close second. The next time he went for his therapy, he wanted to talk to the sixteen-year-old foot amputee who was also getting fitted for a prosthesis and having a hard go of it.

By the time the sun's rays were sending pink and gold shafts slanting across the valley, Nick realized he should begin making breakfast. Cody's school would be starting in a little over an hour. They'd have to hustle to arrive on time.

It was no news that Cody wasn't a morning person, especially after their late night. He ate with his eyes closed and had no idea what he was doing when he helped Nick load the Rover. The minute they were off, he fell asleep and was out for the count during the forty-minute drive down the canyon to his school.

Nick pulled the car up in front and had to practically shove his son out the door. Cody muttered something incoherent but managed to give his dad a hug before he disappeared into the building with the other kids. Nick watched the scene with pure pleasure. *This was the stuff of life, what he'd missed out on. Never again.*

Eager to clean up, Nick headed to the hotel. The

temptation to drive by Rosie's and see if the Passat was there was overpowering. But Nick figured that, if he was reduced to spying on the enemy, he'd lost more than his hand in this war.

The minute he entered his hotel room, he saw the light flashing on the phone. Someone was trying to reach him. He wanted the message to be from Rosie, but it was probably R.T. To his surprise, the desk informed him that his parents were staying at the hotel.

Though pleased that they'd driven up from St. George to see him, he wondered why they hadn't slept at Rosie's. When he called their room, his father answered. Apparently his mother was still asleep, but George would be over in a few minutes. He had something serious to discuss with Nick.

The somber tone of his voice didn't bode well. Nick felt a sense of dread as he showered and dressed. His worries that something was wrong were borne out when his father appeared at the door looking pale and drawn. Nick had the distinct impression Rosie was involved in some way.

Nick drew his father into the room, then ushered him to the small dining table, where they could sit down.

"Nicky—" George leaned forward with his hands on his knees "—I hardly know where to begin. It's about your mother..."

Nick was sitting back in the other chair, his long legs extended in front of him, ankles crossed. "I'm aware that Mom hasn't been herself. She probably needs some counseling, Dad."

His father nodded his head sadly. "If you'd seen her in action last night, you wouldn't have recognized her."

"This has to do with Rosie, doesn't it?"

"Yes. Your mom hurt her deeply. Maybe irrevocably."

A jolt like a current of electricity passed through Nick. "Tell me what happened."

Listening to his father relate the incident of the previous night, Nick felt as if his insides had exploded. He couldn't sit still any longer. The thing he'd been dreading had happened. He'd lost Rosie, finally and completely, and now his family was reacting.

"I couldn't get your mom to apologize. I'm hoping you can influence her. She refuses to face reality. When we heard you were MIA, we couldn't believe it. We *wouldn't* believe it. We never gave up hope. Your mom was the strongest of us all, and I love her for it.

"But Rosie and Zach are another matter. They're planning to be married, and that's a fact your mom simply has to face or I don't know what'll happen. Janet's unreachable right now...."

Face it, Armstrong. The world has blown up in your face. Now you're going to have to put up the bravest front of your life.

"Tell you what, Dad. After my therapy today, we'll take off for Yellowstone for a while. Just the three of us. Since I got home, Cody and I have been pretty much inseparable. I think he'll be able to handle my being gone for a week or so.

"Mom needs to understand that I'm going to make it without Rosie. Maybe by the time our vacation's over, she'll believe it."

Even if I don't.

"Thank you, son. You don't know how good that sounds. We've wanted to be able to spend time with you. This will be the best therapy Janet could have."

"I agree. So it's settled. Why don't you go on back to your room and tell Mom what's up? I'm going to take care of some last-minute business concerning the sale of the ranch—I want to make sure everything goes through while I'm gone. So, let's plan to leave here about two."

His father stood up. "Ah, Nicky." He hugged him hard. "It's so wonderful to have you back home."

"I feel the same way, Dad. It's what I longed for, too. All that time."

"…HAVE ONE S ORBITAL. The P orbitals have a more specific orientation of charge distribution. One of you asked about the hourglass distribution. This refers to the P orbital. For any one P orbital, the region of high-charge distribution is oriented with respect to an atom passing through the nucleus.

"This phase correctly implies the orientation as far as an axis is concerned, but it incorrectly implies that the electrons are confined to a specific volume.

"For a given principal quantum number of two or higher, there may be a maximum of three orbitals."

A movement out of the corner of her eye made Rosie pause in her lecture. She saw a tall dark male figure enter the auditorium and take a seat near the back.

Nick!

Her body started to tremble. *He knows what happened last night.*

Since his return from the war, he'd never made an appearance in her classroom. He'd never shown a modicum of interest. She could think of only one reason he was here.... Class would be over in a few minutes. She dreaded being alone with him, but his presence ensured that she had no other choice.

Clearing her throat, she tried to remember where she'd left off. "There may be a maximum of three P orbitals, Px, Py and Pz, oriented at right angles to each other along the x-axis, the y-axis and the z-axis, with the nucleus and constricted portions of the hourglasses at the origin."

Taking an unsteady breath because she couldn't withstand Nick's scrutiny another second, she announced that class was dismissed. Immediately the students began filing out of the hall.

Needing some way of channeling her nervous energy, she wiped off the equations she'd written on the portable blackboard.

"While I was sitting there—" his deep familiar voice said, "I had to keep telling myself that the impressive and attractive Dr. Armstrong was once Rosie Gardner, the fun-loving, carefree girl who used to skip math and physics classes with me to go for a ride in my old Jeep. You've come a long way, baby."

Despite her fear about the outcome of this confrontation, his words brought a smile to her lips. She hesitated turning around to face him. She felt a reluctance to mar a shared memory that represented a time of pure bliss for her. In those days she would have done anything to be with Nick.

"All you had to do was flash that sunny smile and I thought I'd died and gone to heaven."

At least she turned to meet his gaze. "Nick Armstrong was the big man on campus. Captain of the football team and financial wizard all rolled into one. Every guy's friend. Every girl's secret fantasy. All *you* had to do was beckon me with those famous Armstrong eyes and I forgot who I was and what I was doing."

Nick's smile devastated her. It came to her then that he was starting to look more and more like the Nick she remembered. An older version, of course, but in all honesty, better-looking. She'd married a boy.

Now he was a man. An amazing man who'd come back from the dead a true hero. He was bigger than life. Bigger than death...

"We had our time in the sun, didn't we, sweetheart?"

She averted her eyes. It pained her to hear him say that. His use of the past tense had the effect of dashing every dream.

What dream, Rosie? You're marrying Zach. It's all settled.

"H-how was your camp-out with Cody?"

"Honestly?"

Her heart skipped a beat and her head came up abruptly. "What happened?"

"I think it's more a case of what didn't happen."

She shook her head. "I don't understand."

"Cody missed you. In his words, you're a totally awesome mom."

Don't tell me that, Nick. The things you say clutch at my heart. Every time we talk, I bleed a little more.

"I missed him, too. I always miss him when he's gone. The house feels so empty."

"Until my mother showed up and a bomb exploded."

She looked away. "I imagined that was the reason you came to see me. I love your mom as if she were my own, but…"

"You were right to demand an apology from her. I'm sorry she caused you so much grief. Mom's got a problem right now. Dad and I both agree she needs professional help. The trick is to get her to see a psychiatrist. That's why I'm going away with them for a while."

Going away? Her heart started to pound out of control. "Where? For how long?"

"You know how much the folks love Yellowstone. We'll be gone for a week or ten days."

That would sound like an eternity to Cody. Unless…

"Did you want to take Cody with you?"

"Much as I'd love to, it wouldn't be a good idea. I need to spend some time alone with my parents. Maybe it's what Mother needs."

"Are you going today?"

He nodded his dark head. Rosie could see that his hair was getting longer and starting to curl around his neck. When he was asleep, she used to love playing with those curls until she roused him enough to kiss her. That was all it took to get his total attention. Those kisses would set off a conflagration that brought both of them rapture for the rest of the night and gave Rosie a thrilling reason to greet the day.

"One of the reasons I came here was to ask your advice on how to tell him. Dad wants us to leave around two. It's twelve-fifteen now. Do you think it would be better if I just left and you told Cody after he gets home from school?"

"No!" she cried. She felt an immediate sense of panic because she walked a shaky line with Cody these days. "I think you should go over to his school and get him out of class. Explain to him that your mom isn't very well and you're going to spend a week or so with her.

"Even knowing that, Cody's going to have a hard time. Maybe you can reassure him that you'll phone him at night so he won't feel abandoned."

"I'll do that. I was also thinking it might be a good idea if you came with me to see Cody. When's your next lecture?"

"I'm through for today."

"Then let's talk to him together. If we present a united front, he'll be more accepting."

You always did put me first. You're always thinking of me, always smoothing my path with Cody. How do I thank you? Any other man might have tried

*to create a wedge. Not you, Nick Armstrong. Maybe
it's time I returned the favor and thought of you.*

"I agree. I'll come with you," she murmured.
"Let me grab my purse from the office."

As they walked through the auditorium, a memory
came back so strongly she found herself expressing
it to him. "Do you know that the first time I ever
taught a chemistry class in here I wondered if you
could see me from the other side."

"Of the grave?" he quipped, clasping her elbow
as they went out the door.

She smiled. "Yes."

"Frankly, my dear, I don't give a damn about the
other side. I much prefer seeing you in the flesh."

"Why, Rhett, how you do turn a girl's head,"
Rosie couldn't resist responding in an exaggerated
Southern accent before breaking into laughter.

She loved his old imitation of Clark Gable in *Gone
with the Wind*. Sometimes when he used to call her
from the brokerage, he'd ask for Scarlett. It had been
a silly private joke between them and was as amusing
to her now as it was then.

As she let herself into the office to retrieve her
purse, Nick flashed her an answering smile that made
her heart turn over, exactly the way it had when
they'd first met during a school-sponsored carnival.

There'd been a pie-throwing contest—the football
team got to throw pies at the pep-club girls. All the
girls' faces were covered in whipped cream. Everyone looked like the characters in her favorite childhood storybook, *Snipp, Snapp and Snurr*, about the
little boys who fell into a gingerbread vat.

When it was Rosie's turn, there was Nick, towering, virile and holding a pie in his hands. She'd started to scream—and that was when he'd laughed. Then he'd thrown the pie at her. Through it all, his white smile and brilliant blue eyes became the focus of her world. She'd never been the same again.

"Rosie?" Nick's voice brought her back to the present. "Zach's out in the hall."

"Oh, dear. I forgot we were going to have lunch together. Stay here for a minute and I'll talk to him."

Nick put a detaining hand on her arm. "Don't break your lunch date. I'll go to the school without you."

The touch of his hand on her arm was electric. Stunned, she pulled away from him. "No. Seeing Cody is much more important. Why don't you go out to the car? I'll join you in a minute."

He nodded and left her office. She gave him a minute's head start, then locked her door and went in search of Zach.

She didn't have to look for long. An arm slid around her shoulders and for a moment she was crushed tightly against Zach's lean body. They began walking toward the entrance of the building.

"What was Nick doing here?"

Without stopping for breath, Rosie explained what had happened. "I'm so sorry, darling. Do you mind?"

"Not at all. In fact, I don't envy you your job. Cody's just been reunited with his father. If this isn't handled right, it could set him off again."

"Thank you for being so understanding, Zach."

They'd reached the outside steps. "I'll see you at six." Nick's Land Rover was in her line of vision.

How many times had she seen his Jeep in front of the high school with him in it, waiting for her? Again her heart gave a curious kick.

"Maybe earlier." Zach swooped down to brush her mouth with his before loping off in the opposite direction.

Though the kiss was an automatic gesture with him, she wished he hadn't done it, on the off chance that Nick had seen it.

Rosie felt a strange lingering guilt as she made her way toward the Rover. Never in their lives had either Rosie or Nick tried purposely to make the other jealous. Theirs hadn't been that kind of relationship.

It felt like a betrayal of the great trust they'd shared to know that Nick might have seen her being kissed by another man. Then she chastised herself for criticizing Zach. They were engaged. What could be more natural? Everything was out in the open, understood.

Still, when she got into the Rover and they drove off, the disquieting premonition that Nick had been witness to that small intimacy hurt her.

Because you know it hurt him, Rosie.

CHAPTER TWELVE

"I'LL RUN IN and get him out of class."

Before Rosie could respond, Nick had leapt out of the Rover. She watched him sprint across the concrete and up the stairs with that familiar male grace of his.

A tense disturbing silence had prevailed during their five-minute drive from the university to Cody's school. She lamented the loss of the rapport they'd shared for those brief moments in the building where she taught.

While she waited, she glanced around the car's interior, noting the gear that had been stashed in the back. Despite her absence last night, she had no doubt Cody had been in a state of ecstasy. Part of Nick's charm lay in his ability to make every moment count, to turn even a routine activity into an event.

There'd never been a man as exciting to her as Nick. He made things happen, lit his own fires.

"Hey, Mom?" Cody jumped into the back seat of the car as his father came around the front. "Dad says we're all going to have lunch together."

Her eyes read the message in Nick's as he slid

behind the wheel. "We thought it would be fun, honey."

"This is so cool."

Cody's face glowed. Obviously he approved of this simple outing, just the three of them.

"Tell me about your camp-out," she asked as they drove off. Had Nick had a nightmare? Would Cody mention it? How many secrets did they share that she'd never know about?

"Dad told me what it was like when his bunker got bombed. I told my class about it during Channel One. Mrs. Clegg thinks it would be neat to have an assembly at school so you and R.T. could come and talk to everybody, Dad. Do you think you could? Do you think R.T. would do it?"

Nick didn't bat an eyelash. "Of course. You just tell us the day and we'll be there. In fact, I'll promise to do that favor for you if you'll do one for me."

Rosie could feel it coming.

"Sure, Dad."

"Your grandma got upset at your mom last night and really hurt her feelings."

Cody blinked. "Grandma did?"

"That's right. It's because I'm her son and because of what happened to me. You know how she cries all the time and just keeps wanting to hold me. Stuff like that."

"Yeah. I know."

Rosie closed her eyes. *Nick's a master father, a master psychologist.*

"*Well,* she wants me all to herself for a little while. Your grandfather told me that when I was born, she had to count my fingers and toes to make sure they were all there. Now that I've lost a hand, I guess she wants to find out if anything else is missing. Of course, nothing is. But do you know what I mean?''

"Yeah."

"The thing is, your mom's all upset, too, and now she wants *her* son to herself for a little while. Fair is fair."

Cody sat forward and put his arms around Rosie's neck. "I'm sorry, Mom."

"It's okay, Cody. I'll get over it—especially if you're with me and we can do some fun things together."

"You mean just the two of us? No one else?"

Rosie had to make a split-second decision. *Forgive me, Zach.* "No one else, honey."

"Great!"

"So how about us working out a deal, son? You take care of your mom for a week and I'll take care of mine."

"It's a deal."

"Where do you suppose your grandma would rather go than anyplace else in the whole world?"

"Yellowstone Lake."

"You think if I took her up there and we did a little fishing, it would calm her down?"

"Yeah. She and Grandpa love to fish."

"Suppose I call you every night, and we all get on the phone and tell you who caught the biggest fish."

Cody giggled. "Grandpa always gets the biggest."

"No matter what, right?"

"Right!" Cody laughed.

"So, how about you and Jeff flying up to West Yellowstone a week from Saturday morning? I'll meet you two guys at the airport and we'll go horseback riding on Ferron's Dude Ranch. Then we'll drive back after a couple of days. Is that all right with you, Rosie?"

Rosie couldn't talk.

They'd spent part of their honeymoon at Ferron's in a tiny cabin hidden away in the forest. It was a time of such love, such ecstasy, Rosie could hardly breathe, remembering it.

"It sounds wonderful." Her voice quavered a little.

"Why don't you come, too, Mom?"

"You know why she can't, Cody," his father intervened.

"Yeah. I know. I was just asking. Where are we going to have lunch?"

"Hires."

"They have good onion rings."

"I know. I dreamed about them for seven years."

"This morning in English, Jeff and I made a list of the things we'd miss if we were in prison for seven years. Mr. Magleby caught us, but when he found out what we were doing, he made it a class project. Do you want to see it?"

Nick's deep rich laughter was so contagious Rosie started giggling, too. Then laughing—she laughed until her sides ached. She couldn't recall enjoying a moment this much…in seven years. Before Nick's reserve unit was called up for Desert Storm.

Be honest, Rosie. You haven't known this kind of happiness for so long you've forgotten until just now what it feels like.

Their lunch turned out to be a lighthearted affair, with Cody doing ninety-nine percent of the talking, never noticing his parents' silence. Rosie smiled and laughed frequently, but hardly spoke, savoring the feeling of closeness and contentment. But it was a bittersweet emotion, tinged with regret.

Later Nick dropped her off at the university and took Cody back to school. Rosie went to her office and prepared for the next day's lecture, then drove to Zach's office in North Salt Lake. At four o'clock she entered the parking area; he'd indicated he might leave work early and she wanted to surprise him. To her chagrin, his Passat wasn't there. His secretary, Barbara, said he'd already left for the day.

Frustrated, she called Zach's condo from the office, but got his answering machine. There was nothing to do but leave a message that she was coming out to his place and asking that he wait for her there. Then she thanked Barbara, and returned to her car.

Last night, or rather early this morning—when Rosie had finally stirred from Zach's comforting arms, where she'd sobbed half the night—she'd gotten up from the couch to make coffee. They'd talked everything over and had decided that Zach's moving in would only add fuel to the fire. So, until their wedding, they would live apart as they'd been doing for two years.

Secretly Rosie had been relieved by that decision; she'd only agreed to his living with her before their marriage as a way of proving her love to him. Circumstances—set in motion by the arrival of Nick's parents—prevented her from following through on that decision.

Neither of them had counted on Janet's vitriol. And though they hadn't discussed it, Zach knew Rosie had been devastated by the revelations concerning Nick's torture in prison. It was an ugly moment. Rosie sensed that Zach had been affected by it, as well.

It was better to forget the incident and simply maintain the status quo.

With one difference.

They were now making plans for their wedding. Zach wanted to build a home for them farther south and east in the valley. But he acknowledged that uprooting Cody would be the wrong thing to do.

They both hoped that by the time her son graduated from high school, they could build their dream house together, and Cody would play an active part in that project.

As soon as exam week at the university was over, Zach wanted Rosie to fly to California with him for a round of family parties and wedding showers. When the divorce was final, they would be married in Newport in Zach's family church. Afterward, there would be a reception at the Newport Beach Club and another one in Salt Lake at the Colonial House on the Avenues.

Rosie had picked the Avenues area of Salt Lake because it wasn't linked to any memories of Nick or their life together. She needed to start her new life without shadows. Without regrets.

She reached Zach's condo and once again saw that his Passat was missing. Letting out a sigh, she turned around and headed home.

No doubt she'd hear from him before dinnertime. Twenty minutes later, when she got home, she listened to her messages and heard Zach's voice.

"Sweetheart? After I left the office, Mitch called me on the mobile unit. There's a problem I have to see about. I hope it's all right if we give dinner a miss. I'll call you later tonight. I love you."

Rosie was sorry she'd have to put off talking to Zach about Cody. On the other hand, there was no time like the present to prove to her son that she wanted to spend some quality time with him alone. He loved her homemade pizza. She'd fix that and have it ready by the time he walked through the door.

Though Cody had taken the news about Nick's going away better than she could have hoped, he would start missing him once dinner was over. That was when he and his dad went to the gym—their special time together. Maybe she could distract Cody by playing poker with him. He'd find out his mother wasn't in her dotage yet!

She'd never played poker with anyone but Nick, which was an experience too personal to talk about to anyone else. Somehow he beat her every time and exacted payment in ways that still had the power to make her blush.

I've learned a lot since my days of being a blushing bride, Nick Armstrong. Just once, I'd love to have the opportunity to beat the pants off you. Literally. Just once I'd love to make you blush!

"Mom?"

"Hi, honey."

"I'm home. Has Dad left yet?"

"I think he has. Why?"

"I stopped at Jeff's on the way home. His mom said he could go to West Yellowstone with me. I just wanted Dad to know."

"He'll be calling you tonight. You can tell him then."

"I can't wait!"

It was going to be a long ten days.

ZACH SHOULDERED his way through the throngs of people at the L.A. airport, anxious to meet his brother, who was picking him up in front of the terminal.

"Richard!" he shouted when he saw the blue Oldsmobile. He sprinted over to the car. "I owe you for this, especially when you had to battle five-o'clock traffic."

"Hey, bro, it isn't like I don't want to see you or anything, but it would be nice to get a little more notice. Do you mind if I ask what in the heck is going on with you?"

Zach couldn't answer him. Since the scene in Rosie's living room last night, his world had exploded in his face. He had a sickness in his gut that wasn't about to go away.

"The last time you flew down here, you didn't tell anybody. Today at lunch my secretary informs me that I'm to pick you up at six o'clock, but no one else is supposed to know. The folks would come unglued if they found out you were in town again and didn't phone them. As it is, I had to make up some story to Bev about working late tonight.''

"Like I said, I owe you. Big time.''

Richard sighed. "Where do you want to go?''

"Anywhere, but not too far from the airport. I have to get back to Salt Lake tonight.''

"How about we just pull off at the first exit and sit at a Stop sign?''

"Fine.''

"Whoa. You *are* in bad shape." As they wound in and out of traffic leaving the terminal, Richard kept looking over at him. "Did you and Rosie have a fight?''

"No. Last night we got engaged for the second time.'' *Last night showed him a whole new meaning of the word "terror."*

"*Second* time?''

"It's a long story.''

"Spill it!''

"Hell, Richard. Her husband didn't die in the war. After seven years as a POW, he's back home in Salt Lake.''

"*What?*''

Richard pulled off the road and braked in front of an elementary school.

"I saw a clip about that on the news a while back! But I never would've associated him with Rosie. Zach—look me in the eye and tell me you're putting me on.''

Zach turned his head and faced his brother.

"*Oh, Lord*—you're *not!*" He reached across the seat to give him a brotherly hug. "No wonder you couldn't just tell me this on the phone."

Zach raked a hand through his hair. "I think I'm going to lose her, Richard. If that happ—"

"Shut up, Zach. Just start talking to me!"

"She loved me, Richard. She really did. We were making it. On that cruise she finally agreed to marry me. The first night out at sea, the band was playing requests. Suddenly the lead singer asked if there was a Zachery Wilde in the room. Naturally I wondered what Rosie was up to.

"When I stood up, he announced that the next song was dedicated to me. Then he called Rosie to the microphone. She whispered something in his ear, and he said into the mike, 'She's expecting a marriage proposal when the song is over. Are you ready, Zach?' They played Eric Clapton's 'Wonderful Tonight.'" The words of that song would be forever impressed in Zach's memory.

"Before she'd even sat down, I had that ring on her finger. At the end of the cruise, I drove her and Cody to her door, knowing that the rest of my life was going to be pure happiness because Rosie and I were getting married in June.

"Six hours later I got a phone call. Her husband, Sergeant Nick Armstrong, had been freed from captivity and was on his way home to Hill Air Force Base. Rosie had to go. She'd call me later."

Richard groaned, then suddenly leaned across the seat to grasp Zach's shoulder. "Tell me the rest.

Don't stop until I've heard every damn thing that's eating you alive!''

Zach heard the love in his brother's voice. Richard had been at his side when Zach's former fiancée died in the hospital. There wasn't another human being who understood him the way Richard did. Zach had repressed his feelings for so long it served as a catharsis to be able to confide in his brother.

Once he'd begun, he didn't stop until he'd told him every detail and had admitted his deepest fear. ''I have the gut feeling Rosie's falling in love with her husband all over again.''

''But that's crazy, Zach! Last night she agreed to wear your ring. You made specific wedding plans.''

''I know. I know,'' Zach said. ''But you didn't hear what I heard in Rosie's voice when her mother-in-law started in about the tortures Nick had been subjected to. What I heard came straight from Rosie's soul. It sounded like love.''

''Does that really surprise you? He was her husband all those years. But they're getting a divorce and she loves *you*, wants a life with you now.''

''I know Rosie loves me. But you didn't see what I saw today at the university.''

''Okay. What did you see?''

''She was talking to Nick. They didn't know I was standing there watching. Have you ever been near a couple who are so involved with each other they have no awareness of anything else around them?''

''Zach, you're paranoid. Not without good reason, but I honestly think you're looking for trouble where there isn't any.''

"No. I know what I saw. This was different. There was a...light shining in Rosie's eyes. I never saw anything like it. She even *acted* different. I could hardly believe it was her."

"What you saw is the way Rosie responds to the man she married. If he saw you and Rosie together, he'd say the same thing—that she doesn't seem like the same Rosie to him—because you bring out certain things in her that he doesn't.

"Those two had a particular chemistry together. They made a child. You and she have another kind of chemistry. You'll create your own child one day."

His brother had a lot of wisdom. "What you're saying makes perfect sense. But I've got this awful feeling that one day after we're married, Rosie will wake up and wish she was with Nick. He's never going to go away! They share a son. Cody will be around as a constant reminder of their marriage. For the past two years I've done everything but stand on my head trying to erase his shadow. Now he's back—in the flesh!"

"Zach, thousands of couples are in second marriages and they work beautifully. Once you and Rosie are living together as husband and wife, you'll forge bonds so strong nothing will threaten your love."

"Those thousands of women weren't married to Nick Armstrong first."

"Aside from the fact that he was a victim of war, which turned him into a hero, why is he such a threat to you? I don't get it."

Zach looked over at his brother. "The truth?"

He nodded. "Is there any other way?"

Zach squeezed his arm. "Her husband reminds me of a man I pretty well idolize."

"In other words, if you didn't hate Nick Armstrong's guts, you and he would probably be friends."

"He's got many of *your* qualities, Richard."

Richard eyed him soulfully for a minute, then patted his shoulder. "I appreciate those kind words, bro. But if what you say is true, you've got something even more remarkable going for you. Despite the fact that her husband's a paragon—" he gave a self-deprecating grin "she's picked *you* for her husband."

"Maybe. Then again, the fact that Nick filed for divorce may have made me the winner through default, and you're looking at Rosie's consolation prize. I don't doubt she'd go through with our wedding. With her noble little heart, she wouldn't dream of hurting me again. She'd be a real trooper and try not to let on. But something deep inside tells me Nick would always be in bed with us. I couldn't handle that." His voice was harsh with pain.

Richard had no ready comeback. His expression grew solemn. "Zach, if you're really that unsure of Rosie's feelings, if your gut's telling you something's wrong, then you need to have it out with her. I mean a knock-down, drag-out, bottom-line session. No holds barred. You know what I'm saying?"

Zach nodded.

Oh yes, Richard. I know exactly what you're saying. Rosie might have had a legitimate excuse to go off with Nick and Cody today. But something tells me she wanted to be with them.

He sucked in his breath. ''That's why I came down here to see you, Richard. Before I left Salt Lake, I'd half made up my mind to confront her—to get inside her heart and soul, even if I had to fight my way past every defense. I just needed to hear you confirm it.''

WHEN ROSIE HEARD the front doorbell ring at eleven o'clock, she knew it had to be Zach. Cody had gone to bed an hour ago, but he wasn't asleep. Nick hadn't phoned yet. Something must have detained him. The waiting was killing both of them, for different reasons.

Zach hadn't called, either. All evening she'd been expecting word from him, yet she'd been dreading that conversation because she'd made a promise to Cody. Spending all her free time with her son meant she wouldn't be seeing anyone else. Including Zach. *Especially* Zach. She could just imagine his reaction.

It wasn't fair to him. Nothing had ever been fair to him. They'd just gotten engaged for the second time. Now she'd have to ask for his understanding about not seeing him in the evenings until Cody flew to West Yellowstone to be with his father. Even a man as marvelous as Zach had his limits. She knew this would be pushing them, but Cody had to be her first priority. Keeping her son emotionally stable with Nick away translated as cruelty to Zach, a no-win situation. Rosie honestly didn't know how much more stress she could take. As for Zach…

With a mixture of reluctance and trepidation, she walked to the door and called out, asking who it was.

"It's Zach."

Something was wrong. He didn't say, "It's me, sweetheart. I've missed you."

She opened the door, expecting him to reach for her the way he always did. It threw her when he remained in place, almost aloof. "I'd almost given up on you tonight. Come in, darling."

After closing the door, she headed for the living room, waiting for his arms to slide around her waist and pull her against him. To her surprise, he came to a standstill just inside the entry to the room, his hands on his hips.

"Has something serious happened at work? Is there trouble?" She was starting to feel anxious.

"No."

The one-syllable answer filled her with a new form of dread. "So you got everything straightened out with Mitch?"

"I lied to you, Rosie. I needed some time to think, so I made up an excuse for not having dinner with you."

She shook her head sadly. "Why did you have to lie to me? Why didn't you just tell me you wanted to be alone? I would've understood."

"I know you would've. But I didn't want to alarm you, not when you're dealing with so much here at home."

"Zach, I realize everything is precarious right now." Her voice trembled slightly, despite herself. "In fact, there's another favor I have to ask of you, and I'm afraid to ask it. But I know we'll eventually get past all this, because we love each other.''

"What favor?'' he demanded, his features taut.

"Nick left for Yellowstone today with his parents. He'll be gone ten days and he's worried about Cody's reaction. That's why he came to see me at the university, to decide how best to tell Cody.''

She moistened her lips nervously when she realized Zach wasn't going to help her out. "Nick told Cody his grandmother needed her son, just as I needed Cody. So they made a deal. Nick would spend time with his mother. Cody would spend time with me.''

"And nobody else.'' Zach filled in the blanks. "So I'm to get lost for ten days while you fulfill your part of the bargain.''

"Don't put it that way, Zach. He was only thinking of Cody. It worked. There were no hysterics.''

"But there will be if I step foot in this house before the ten days are up. Under the circumstances, I'm surprised you bothered to let me in.'' By now his face was completely drained of color. "It looks to me as if from now on I'd better check with Nick before I make plans with my future wife.''

He was out of the room and the front door so fast she had to run to catch up with him. She'd just managed to slide into the passenger seat as he got behind the wheel and started the ignition.

"Get out of the car, Rosie.''

"No! Not until we talk.''

"I'm off-limits, remember?''

"I know it sounds horrible. It's just that Cody's

been a different boy since Nick came home. If everything can stay on an even keel until Nick returns from vacation with his folks, you and I won't have to worry about Cody as much anymore.''

"Until the next time," he ground out.

"What do you mean?"

Zach's hands tightened on the steering wheel. "There will always be a next time where Cody's concerned, Rosie. You're his mother. For the duration of our lives, you will always put him first. And he will always resent me. He'll pit us against each other to test your love for him. He'll try to make you choose between us. I'm not saying that to be cruel. I'm saying it because it's true.

"Today you made a promise to him. I realize you have to keep it. In fact, you're breaking it by being out here in the car with me.''

"Zach, I need to talk to you, darling. Please, will you take time off tomorrow to be with me while Cody's at school? As soon as he walks out the door, I'll drive over to your condo.'' She paused, then added, "I can always go to the University later to work on my grading.''

Zach hesitated for a moment, then nodded. "I'll expect you at nine.''

She waited for him to take her in his arms. "A-aren't you even going to kiss me good-night?''

"No. If I start kissing you, I won't be able to stop. Go in the house. Now!''

With tears blinding her, she got out of the car and raced up the lawn to the front porch. She heard a screech of tires as Zach drove away. The sound had a kind of desperate finality about it.

She had expected way too much of Zach. He was the one who felt fragile right now. She had to do something, quickly. Tomorrow they'd talk, and she'd try to reassure him... But while she stood there in a quandary, the phone rang. She dashed over and picked up the receiver.

Nick.

"Hello?"

"Rosie?" came the deep voice. Her heart began to race. "I'm sorry it's so late."

To hear Nick over the phone sounding so natural and familiar made it feel as though they'd never suffered a seven-year separation.

"Are you all right?" she asked anxiously.

"I'm fine." There was a pause. "If you're worrying that this is something war-related, then stop."

"Thank heaven! When I think what you've lived through... I wish I had a magic pill I could give you to make it all go away. I can't—"

"Rosie—"

She was so choked up she could hardly talk. "I can't get the things your mom told me out of my mind. Oh, Nick... Nick... When you flew off on that plane, I suffered a thousand fears, but the reality is so much worse. I wish there were something..."

By now she was sobbing.

"It's over, Rosie," he murmured. "The only problem facing me now is a broken thermostat on Dad's car."

She sniffed. "You didn't take yours?"

"No. Dad had the Buick all packed, and he wanted to drive. You know how much he loves that car."

"I do know." She managed a quiet laugh. "You probably could have fixed it if you'd had a replacement."

"True. Instead, I had to flag down a motorist with a cellular phone. Remind me to get one when I return."

"Dad has one."

"He left it in St. George."

"Every time they come up here, they forget something."

"It's kind of touching to know they've stayed true to form."

But I didn't. I didn't.

"Rosie, I didn't say that to upset you."

He could read her thoughts. He always could. "I know you didn't. Oh, Nick... I've always loved you. So much. I never wanted to hurt you. I'm so sorry for what you've had to endure and so proud of you at the same time. I'm...I'm in awe of you, Nick. It's such a helpless feeling to know what happened to you, and not be able to do one thing about it."

Another silence.

"You can do something for me now."

"What's that? Anything."

"Get on with the rest of your life and be happy. Don't look back."

Another paroxysm of tears threatened. "Where do you find the strength to say that to me?"

"In prison I discovered many things. That God lives, that life is fleeting and precious. I plan to make the most of the time I have left. That's what you need to do, too, sweetheart.''

But you're going to do it without me. I won't be there. I can't bear it.

''Mom? Is that Dad?'' Cody came bounding up to her. When he saw her wet face, his crumpled, too. ''What's wrong? Has something happened to Dad?'' He started to cry.

''Just a minute, Nick,'' she said in a gravelly tone. ''Here's Cody.''

CHAPTER THIRTEEN

THE BLARING SOUND of the test pattern on the TV brought Rosie awake. Six in the morning. She sat up on the couch with a tension headache and cramps in her stomach. *Today she had to face Zach.*

When she hadn't been able to get to sleep last night, she lay on the couch to watch TV, hoping it would relax her, get her mind off things. Cody had wandered in to say good-night again, his peace of mind restored after talking to Nick for half an hour.

Once he'd left the room, she turned on the classics channel to watch a movie. It was *Random Harvest*. She hadn't seen it since she was a girl. Rosie had been too young then to really understand the story of the man who'd lost his memory and the wife who loved him so much she stayed in his life as a stranger rather than let him go.

Rosie knew she should have turned it off. Instead, she felt a compulsion to watch it. The ending, in particular, tortured her—the husband got his memory back and the wife got her husband back, while Rosie's story…

She honestly didn't know how her story was going to end. In the movie, the hero's amnesia made things simpler, more straightforward. There was nothing remotely simple or straightforward about Rosie's life.

After staggering to her feet, she left the living room, bleary-eyed, in search of Cody. He needed to get up and take a bath. She needed one, too. Long and hot.

"Cody?" She opened the door to his room. "Time to wake up, honey. I'll start your tub."

"I'm sick, Mom. I can't go to school."

Her eyes closed tightly. No, this just couldn't be happening. Not this morning. Not to Zach. Not again.

Taking a determined breath, she marched into his room and over to his bed. He didn't look sick. But after reading the brochure Linda Beams had given her, she realized that Cody had his own ways of dealing with grief and confusion. Psychosomatic illness was just one of the manifestations.

He'd caught her in tears last night. No doubt that had created new monsters, new fears, in his mind. She had to put them to rest, whatever they were.

She sank onto the side of the bed and smoothed the hair out of his eyes. "Where do you feel sick, honey?"

"I don't know. I just don't feel good. Do you have to go to work today?"

"Yes," she lied. "For a little while. If you want, I'll ask Mrs. Larson across the street to look in on you while I'm gone."

"I'm not a baby, Mom. I don't need a sitter. I just wish Dad was here."

"I know. But since he isn't, we'll make the best of it. Do you just want to stay in bed?"

"I think I'll get up."

"You can watch TV in the living room or play video games when I go."

"Okay. How long are you going to be gone?"

"Two hours," she improvised.

He climbed out of bed and followed her into her bedroom. "Why were you crying last night?"

I knew it.

"I was just talking to your dad about the war."

"He loves you, Mom."

"I know. I love him, too."

"But I mean he *really* loves you."

She couldn't endure another minute of this. "Honey...I have to get ready."

He waited outside the bathroom door. "Mom?" he called.

She turned on the shower, preparing to step inside. But she couldn't ignore him completely. "What is it, honey?"

"I know you love Zach, but do you *really* love him?"

Oh, Cody, my darling boy. You've asked the question I've been skirting all night. This morning I believe I know the answer.

"Let me finish my shower and then we'll talk."

"Okay," he said in a grumpy tone. She heard him stomp off down the hall.

She purposely took a long time to wash and blow-dry her hair, hoping he'd be engrossed in something once she was dressed and ready to drive to Zach's.

No such luck. He was waiting for her when she went to the kitchen to find some painkiller for her headache. The huge bowl of cereal he'd poured testified to the state of his physical health.

"You know I'm running late? I've got things to do at the office before I teach class." She bent to give him a kiss on the cheek. "We'll talk when I get home. I'll call you in a little while and see how you're doing. And don't forget—you can always phone Mrs. Larson."

"Okay. But hurry!"

"I will."

Zach would be shocked to see her on his doorstep at eight, but there was no help for it. She waved to Cody as she backed the car down the drive. *Two hours*. That was all she had to give Zach. But she might not need that long when he heard what she had to tell him.

SOMEONE WAS TRYING to get him on the phone. Whoever it was had rung three separate times in succession. Zach rolled over and glanced at his clock through bloodshot eyes. Five to eight. He rolled back onto his stomach.

There was only one person he wanted to talk to, and she wouldn't be here until nine.

The ringing started again. *Damn the phone.*

He put the pillow over his head, but nothing deadened the sound. The person on the other end wasn't about to give up.

Muttering a curse, he reached blindly for the receiver. "Yes?"

"Hello? Is this Zach?"

Zach tried sitting a little straighter. "Rosie?"

"It didn't sound like you. I'm down in the lobby. Can I come up?"

"What do you think? Hell, Rosie, I'm sorry. I wasn't expecting you for another hour. I'm a mess."

"I'm afraid there was an unavoidable change in plans. Cody didn't want to go to school this morning. I've left him at home alone."

He shook his head to clear it. "You know the code. I'll leave the door open."

He levered himself from the bed with difficulty. Last night he'd had a few too many at the Alpine Club. This morning he was paying the price.

Throwing on his robe, he hurried through to the front door. When he'd unfastened the bolt and opened it a crack, he took off for the bathroom. A quick shower and shave would help restore him. By the time he'd dressed in a clean T-shirt and jeans, he felt he could face Rosie without totally revolting her.

Normally Zach didn't drink much. But he'd wanted everything about yesterday and last night to be obliterated from his consciousness. Unfortunately the memories were back this morning, and his heart felt so heavy he knew he couldn't go on like this any longer.

Rosie wasn't a drinker, either, but judging by her haggard appearance, she looked as if she needed something a lot stronger than coffee to sustain her.

With painful clarity it came to him then that they weren't the same two people who'd danced the night away on the cruise.

Gone were the carefree lovers. Gone were the whispers in the night about a honeymoon.

Gone was all talk of the baby they were going to make together. All gone.

When she didn't rush into his arms, he called her name.

One tear, then another, coursed down her pale cheeks. Her shoulders started to shake. "Zach?"

With that one word, a groan escaped his throat. He shook his head, sensing a burst of adrenaline that was making him feel like a crazy man.

He took several deep breaths, attempting to hold on to his sanity. "Rosie…" he began.

"Yes?"

She was facing him as bravely as she would a firing squad. His adorable Rosie, noble to the bitter end.

"Can you look me in the eye and tell me you want to live the rest of your life with me?"

The energy radiating between them could have lit up a small city.

"You know how much I adore you, Zach. You know it," she whispered fiercely.

"That's not the answer." He folded his arms to keep from touching her. "I'll ask it again a different way.…

"Knowing that your husband's alive, that you'll be seeing him coming and going in Cody's life, that you'll be talking to him from time to time, consulting him on occasion, being at functions where he'll be, standing with him in Cody's wedding-reception line one day, seeing him at the hospital when Cody's wife has a baby, or two or three… Knowing all that…

"Do you, Rosie Armstrong, take me, Zach Wilde,

to be your lawfully wedded husband, do you promise to cling only to me, to want only me, to dream only of me, to have children with me, to forsake all others—to put Nick Armstrong completely away—until death do us part?''

I know what your answer is, Rosie. But I have to hear you say it.

"Take your time. This day had to come. This question had to be asked. I'm asking it now.''

"I know,'' she whispered. "That's why I'm here.''

The quiet grew more ominous. His mouth had gone dry. "I'll ask it a third way. Will it tear you apart when Nick marries another woman and starts a new life in Heber?''

She buried her face in her hands.

"Will it tear you apart to think of him on a honeymoon with another woman? Making love to her as only you can imagine? Giving her a baby like the one he gave you?''

A knock-down, drag-out, bottom-line session. No holds barred.

"Will it tear you apart that he comes home to *her* every night, instead of to you? Will it tear you apart that he's living out the future with someone else when it should have been *your* future?''

After an eternity she lifted a ravaged face. "It's already tearing me apart that I've hurt you so deeply.''

"Say it, Rosie,'' Zach demanded. "Get it over with. Say, *'I'm in love with Nick.'*''

He heard the sob. Then, "I'm in love with Nick.''

Zach reeled. "Thank you."

Unable to hold back any longer, he reached for her and caught her in his arms, crushing her to him. "Rosie, Rosie...I'm dying now, but if I'd heard those words after we were married... I don't even want to think about it."

"If Nick hadn't come back..."

"I know. We would have had a fantastic life together."

She raised her head and grasped his face between her palms. "We would have. You're the most wonderful man, Zach. I'll always love you."

"And I'll always love you, my darling Rosie. But Nick's so deep in your heart, so deep and tight, there's no room for anyone else. That's the kind of love I want, Rosie. So deep and tight it's forever."

I'm telling you these lies because you want to hear them.

"I pray to God you find it."

I won't. I've had my quota of lost loves.

"It's time to take back my ring," he said.

A new pain shattered him when she thrust a hand in her purse and handed the ring to him. She'd come over early to give it to him....

"I'd let you keep it, but Nick's as possessive a man as I am. You don't want a major fight on your hands before you've settled down to loving each other again."

That won a smile from Rosie, whose drenched green eyes lit up at the very thought of her husband.

Nick's seven-year nightmare is over. Mine's just beginning.

"What will you do, Zach?"

"Mitch is going to be put in charge of the company here. I'm moving back to California."

Another lie, but it'll make you happier to think of me there....

She squeezed him hard. "I'm so thankful you have family. I know they'll help you."

No one will be helping me. I'm going to finish what I set out to do when I came to Utah and got sidetracked by you, Rosie. After that, it doesn't matter.

"I'm going to miss you," she said with an ache in her voice.

"Maybe until Nick gets back from Yellowstone."

The tears were starting again. "If there'd been any way to know that he was still alive... You've spent two years of your life on me... It isn't fair, Zach—"

"Shh. I don't regret one single second of what we had together. I'll treasure it all my life." He kissed her forehead. "Now, go home to Cody. His happiness is going to make all of this worth it."

With their arms around each other he propelled her to the door. She looked up at him, searching his eyes. "Zach, how can I leave you like this?"

He put a finger to her lips. "Make it easy for me and go."

The second she was out the door, he dashed to the kitchen and phoned his brother. His nephew answered. Luckily Richard hadn't gone to work yet.

"Go get your dad out of the shower for me, Richie."

"Okay, Uncle Zach. Just a sec."

Come on...

"Hey, Zach?"

"I confronted her, Richard. No holds barred. Now I'm a free man."

"*Zach...* I'm flying to Salt Lake. I'll be there as soon as I can."

"I may not be here."

"Just stay put till I get there."

"I thought I could handle it."

"You'll handle it."

"You want to make a bet?"

"Zach? We've both been through a lot together. We'll get through this, too. For the love of God, hang tight till I get there."

"HI, CODY. I'm home! How're you feeling?"

"Not good." He wandered into the kitchen still dressed in the sweats he liked to use for pajamas. They matched Nick's. "You've been crying again, huh?"

She nodded. "Yes. I've been crying hard." *Forgive me, Zach, darling. Please, God, let him find happiness again soon. Please—*

"Over Dad?"

She set her purse on the counter. "Over a lot of things. Come here." She held out her arms and they hugged. "I think you and I could use a little cheering up about now. Are you too sick to drive down to Orem with me?"

"You mean to see R.T.? Heck, no!"

"Of course to see R.T. Who else do we know in Orem?"

"How soon can we go?"

"As soon as you get dressed."

"Does he know we're coming?" he called minutes later from the other part of the house.

"Yes. I just phoned him. Cynthia's at work and he'd love the company."

"He's the coolest guy."

"He is."

When Rosie had told R.T. she needed a friend to talk to, he didn't ask any questions. He just told her to come and stay as long as she wanted.

Forty-five minutes later, R.T. had Cody ensconced in their study, teaching him the fundamentals of a new computer game. With his quick mind, Cody didn't take long to catch on. Soon he was too engrossed to talk to either of them.

She and R.T. shared a secret smile and left her son entertained while they made their way to the living room of the small home.

R.T. gave her a long thorough appraisal. "You're so sad. It makes me feel guilty."

"For you to say something like that tells me you and Cynthia must be getting along terrifically."

His shy smile touched her heart. "To be honest I'm so happy it scares me. Only one thing could make me happier."

"What's that? The news that she's pregnant?"

"Well, that, too, of course." He grinned, then sobered. "To see you at peace."

Rosie sat foward on the chair. "R.T., this morning Zach and I said goodbye to each other forever. He took back his ring. It's over."

R.T. had been sitting with his head bowed, but at her words he looked up quickly, astonishment written on his face. "Are you putting me on?"

"No. That's why I look this terrible. Zach's a wonderful man and I'm hurting for him. He's in a lot of pain."

"Ah, Rosie..." R.T. lunged for her from the couch. She had no idea his hug could be so powerful. "I know you loved him, but there's no one like the sarge. No one."

She hugged him harder because they were both crying. "You're right, R.T. Nick's one of a kind. I've always been in love with him. I always will be.

"If he'd never come home, Zach and I would have had a marvelous marriage. But Nick *did* come back, and I want to live with him again. Forever."

R.T. just hung on to her, weeping. Pretty soon that got Rosie's tears going again.

"How come you guys are always crying?"

R.T. let go of her and turned to Cody. "We're just happy."

Cody scratched his head. "Mom? You're both acting kind of weird."

"I know. Why don't you sit down, honey? I've got something important to tell you."

Immediately alert to the inflection in her voice, he perched himself on the arm of the couch, his expression anxious.

"The thing is, I have a problem only the two of you can help me solve. That's because your father loves you and R.T. more than anyone in the world."

"What's wrong?" By now Cody was starting to look ill.

"Cody? Do you remember the question you asked me early this morning and I told you we'd talk later?"

"Yeah?"

"Well, now I'm ready to answer you."

"You are?" He sounded scared.

"Zach and I have said goodbye to each other because I *really* love your father."

It took a moment for her message to get through. When it did, even she wasn't prepared for her son's ear-piercing whoop. Cody practically levitated from the couch and knocked her over in his eagerness to show his joy.

"How come you're always jumping around and yelling, Cody?" R.T. baited him. That brought an hysterical giggle from Cody.

"Have you told Dad yet?"

"No," Rosie replied. "That's what I need to talk to the two of you about. I thought if we put our heads together, we could come up with a plan. Right now he's in the process of divorcing me."

"One phone call to your attorney telling him you and Nick are back together again ought to fix that in a big hurry."

She clasped her hands together. "Therein lies my dilemma, R.T. Nick might not want me back. He'll think I'm doing it out of pity."

R.T. didn't deny it.

"Hey, you guys?" Cody said. "I've got an idea. You know that religious ad on TV about the family that kidnaps their dad because he doesn't spend enough time with them?''

Rosie nodded while R.T. looked blank.

''Well, we could kidnap Dad and you guys could get married again or something. Dad would go for that big time!''

R.T. jumped to his feet. ''You know something, Cody? I think you're on to a great idea. I've been thinking about doing something special for Cyn, to let her know how happy she makes me. I even had this idea we'd get married again.''

''A double ceremony?'' Rosie interjected.

''A *surprise* double-wedding ceremony,'' R.T. muttered. ''One the sarge won't know about until it happens. I'll get him to the church on the pretext of coming to my wedding. Then we'll have the pastor say something like, 'We're all gathered here to witness the marriage of R.T. and Cyn, and Nick and Rosie. Will the two couples step forward?''

''He won't be able to say no, will he?'' she cried. ''Not when everyone's there watching and waiting? Not if he loves me.''

R.T. shook his head. ''He won't say no. Trust me on this one, Rosie.''

''I want to trust you. I want to believe it. The thing is, I hate going behind Nick's back. Maybe I shouldn't.''

R.T. looked her in the eye. ''Has the sarge told you he's still in love with you?''

Rosie took a deep breath. ''He told me he was in love with the Rosie he left behind.''

A smile lit up R.T.'s face. ''Then you've got nothing to worry about. Go ahead and plan to your heart's content.''

"You think so?'' she almost squealed.

"I know so,'' he pronounced firmly.

"Dad told me he wished you were with us on the camp-out, Mom.''

"Really?''

"He didn't sleep all night. He just walked around and around. Oh, Mom, you're going to make him so happy! When's all this going to happen, anyway? Jeez, why did Dad have to go to Yellowstone in the first place?'' he grumbled.

Now Rosie was on her feet as another idea came to mind, an idea so exciting she could hardly stand it. ''There's this little Chapel of the Pines in West Yellowstone. Your father and I commented on how quaint it was when we were up there on our honeymoon.''

"And his parents are already up there with him...'' R.T. had immediately picked up on her train of thought.

"That gives us about one week to get everything ready.'' If she called old Mr. Ferron and arranged for that little cabin in the forest...

"Can Jeff still come?''

"Of course, darling. Grandma and Grandpa will be happy to take care of you. The four of you can have fun on the dude ranch while R.T. and his wife and your father and I enjoy a short honeymoon.''

In fact, Janet and George are going to be so happy they'll become the people they used to be—before Nick went missing in action.

"Cody, when your dad calls tonight, you've got to act perfectly natural and not give anything away. Remember how smart he is. Nothing ever gets by him."

"Don't worry, Mom. This is one time I'll outsmart him. You can count on me."

"Sure we can." R.T. tousled Cody's hair. "When your dad calls me tonight, I'll start setting him up."

Rosie's gaze swerved to his. "Has he been calling you a lot?"

He gave her a serious look. "We talk every day. Did I ever tell you about this funny thing that happened on the way to the minefield?" Rosie smiled through the tears. "We can't seem to break the habit."

"Don't ever break it!" she murmured fervently. Her love for R.T. was growing deeper and deeper.

"So that means we have to wait a whole week?" Obviously Cody couldn't comprehend keeping a secret that long.

"Honey, I've got a lot of preparation to do so I can go up to West Yellowstone early and get everything ready. I'll take the car."

"Jeff's mom will let me stay with them until we fly up with R.T. I'll tell Dad he has to call me over at Jeff's. If he asks to talk to you, I'll tell him you're out with Zach."

At the mention of Zach, she felt another stab of pain. "I think it'll work. I'll show up at the airport in the car and tell Nick that it was a last-minute decision on my part to drive up and see R.T. and Cyn get married."

Cody beamed. "Yeah, and I'll say that I'm going to be the guy who gives the ring during the ceremony."

My rings! "That's right, Cody. You can carry them."

"Do we have to get dressed up and stuff?"

R.T. answered him. "No. Up until the last second, while he's sitting in that pew watching the pastor, we have to fool your dad." A huge smile broke out on his face. A face that was fuller and looked more handsome every day. "The sarge isn't going to know what hit him!"

"R.T.—" CYN CAME running into the study where he was working "—it's Nick on the phone," she whispered. "Can I sit here and listen?"

He pulled his wife onto his lap and kissed her hard. "If you can keep from squealing with excitement, I'll let you. You think you can do that?"

"I promise I'll be good. I want this to work as much as you do," she murmured with tears of happiness in her voice.

"Okay. Here goes."

He picked up the receiver and sat back on the couch with Cyn still curled in his lap. "Hey, Sarge? What's up?"

"I've got Mom busy thinking about how to help me redecorate the chalet in Heber. While she was poring over some *Better Homes and Gardens* this evening, ten German brown trout sprang for my fly before it even touched the water."

"Oh, come on."

"I swear it. Dad's caught and thrown back at least a dozen fish that were fifteen inches long. He's waiting for a trophy."

"Sounds like quite the life! I haven't been fishing in years."

There was a pause. "To be honest, I'd rather be doing what you're doing. It's been a hell of a long time. You know what I mean?"

Just you wait, Sarge. Just you wait.

"Yeah, I know. Just remember, all good things come to those who wait."

"I believe that. But seven years?"

R.T. chuckled, then gave his wife a kiss. "Speaking of that particular subject, I was thinking of getting married."

Silence.

"Run that by me again?"

"You know, Cyn and I taking our vows over. Maybe going on a little honeymoon." Her hand entwined with his and she kissed it.

"Sounds great. You two ought to be up here, instead of me." R.T. could hear the despair hidden under Nick's light tone.

"Are there any churches in the park?"

"I don't know about that, but there are several in West Yellowstone."

R.T. squeezed her hand tighter. "Maybe I'll check it out. When did you say you were going to be there?"

"Barring anything else happening to the Buick, we should arrive there next Saturday morning in time to meet Cody's plane from Salt Lake."

"Maybe Cyn and I could fly up with him."

After a pause, "If you did that, you'd make me a very happy man."

R.T. sobered. The sarge was in pain. *It was bad.*

"You'd make me even happier if you'd agree to be my best man."

"I wouldn't let you get married without me."

"If I had known you way back when, I would have asked you to be my best man the first time."

"Yeah, well, you know what they say. It's better the second time around. At least it's going to be for you."

You're going to believe it, too, Sarge. And that day can't come soon enough.

"Well, I'm thinking seriously of looking into it. As your son always says, it would be kind of *cool* to go on a second honeymoon and then carry my wife over the threshold of our new home in Heber."

"You've got that right." Nick's voice sounded like it had come from a great distance. "I say go for it, R.T. Make every second count from here on out."

That's exactly what we're all going to do, Sarge. Just hang on seven more days.

"I guess I'd better sign off. I still have to talk to Cody."

"Right, Sarge. Over and out till tomorrow."

"Till tomorrow."

CHAPTER FOURTEEN

FRIDAY EVENING Nick packed all their fishing gear and suitcases in the trunk. It was only an hour to West Yellowstone from Old Faithful, but he wanted to be sure they were on the road in plenty of time to get to town before the plane arrived.

Much as he adored his parents, he missed Cody and R.T. like crazy. As for Rosie, she was never home at night anymore. In fact, for the past three nights he'd had to phone Cody over at Jeff's house. The pain of not hearing her voice, of not discussing their son, was getting to be more than he could stand.

Thoughts of her and Zach alone together, planning their life, were ripping him to shreds. Her name never came up in his conversations with Cody, who'd apparently accepted the situation without question.

The sooner he moved to Heber, the better. The sooner he met another woman, the better. Actually he'd met a couple of extremely attractive women who worked at the lodge. They'd be willing, *if* he'd given them as much as a smile. But he couldn't even consider it. Neither of them had green eyes and golden hair. Neither of them had a smile like sunshine.

At least for tonight, he had R.T.'s wedding to think

about. It was kind of exciting to imagine them renewing their vows. When he thought of those empty years in the bunkers…

Don't dwell on the past, Armstrong. Don't look back.

R.T. and Cynthia deserved a special present. Nick couldn't think of anything better than getting checked in at the dude ranch as fast as possible so he could arrange for that little cabin in the forest. It was the perfect place for their second honeymoon. Maybe they'd find the same joy there that he and Rosie had fourteen years ago.

Since he hadn't brought a suit and tie with him, he thought he'd buy a Western suit and some cowboy boots for the occasion. Maybe he'd get a matching one for Cody, do R.T. proud.

Speaking of Cody, it was time for their nightly phone call.

It's Friday night. Rosie and Zach have the weekend ahead of them and no Cody.

Feeling sick, Nick headed for the lodge on a run. Sometimes he just wanted to take off and keep running until he'd left every crucifying thought behind.

He reached his room out of breath, but it wasn't from exertion. Rosie'd had a stranglehold on his heart since the first time he'd seen her, when she'd cried in terror because he was going to throw a pie in her face.

After he'd hit his target, all he could see was a bewitching smile and jewel-toned green eyes pleading with him to be kind, not to rub the cream in her face. He'd started toward her with another pie, then stopped, unable to move while his heart performed maneuvers he'd never before experienced. That was when it happened. That was when he fell in love with Rosie Gardner.

What if he never got over her?

The terrifying thought drove him to the phone. He needed distraction. He needed his son. It was ten. Their arranged time.

"Hi, Dad." Cody picked up on the first ring.

"It sounds like you're as excited as I am about tomorrow."

"You can say that again. Jeff's folks said he could stay up there as long as we wanted."

"That's great. I was hoping we could do a little fishing, as well as riding."

"Mr. Taylor bought us some new flies to try."

"I'll let you in on a secret, Cody. The fish are biting just about anything that moves."

"Awesome! I can't wait!"

"How's your mom?" *I swore I wasn't going to ask, but I have to know.*

"She's okay."

"You're not giving her any more trouble about Zach?"

"No, Dad. I promised you I'd be good."

Nothing else was forthcoming. *What did you expect, Armstrong?*

"Dad? You'll be sure to meet us? Ten-thirty exactly."

"Yup. I'll be there."

"How's Grandma?"

"Better."

Mother will be fine until the next time she sees Rosie with Zach. Then the tears and recriminations will start all over again.

"I can't wait to see you," Cody said.

"Ditto, son. Until tomorrow."

"Bye, Dad."

THE LANTERN had been lit. Rosie looked around the little cabin on Ferron's Dude Ranch, just outside Yellowstone Park. She felt slightly feverish. Luckily the indoor and outdoor snapshots of their honeymoon trip had helped her recreate that halcyon time, down to the clothes they'd worn, the snacks they'd eaten.

She'd brought Cody's portable tape player. In order to provide the music they'd listened to, she'd asked Jeff's older brother, Mike, to tape songs from the early to mid-eighties.

The only thing left was to arrange her hair as she'd worn it at the church on their wedding day.

Her eyes darted to her wedding dress, hanging on a peg. She'd had it cleaned, along with the veil. She couldn't wait to wear it again to meet her husband.

There'd been one change in plans since that meeting at R.T.'s a week ago. Rosie would stay out of sight until the wedding.

After she'd discussed everything with the pastor, who was delighted to be a part of this unusual ceremony, it was decided that he would give a small speech first.

Nick would already be up in front at R.T.'s side, as his best man. When the wedding march began,

Cynthia would proceed down the aisle, followed by Rosie.

Seeing all of it in her mind, Rosie extinguished the lantern. She slid under the covers of the bed where she'd known rapture with her husband thirteen years ago. Where she would know rapture with him again tomorrow night.

Tomorrow.

There would be two brides, two grooms, one ceremony, two happily married couples.

Please, God. Make it come true.

THE YELLOWSTONE AIRPORT, three miles from the park entrance, was seething with activity. From the observation window inside the lounge Nick could see another plane coming in.

Nick felt again the sensation he'd experienced as he and R.T. approached Hill. The tightness in his gut threatened to cut off his breathing. *This isn't like last time, Armstrong.*

He watched the plane touch down. There was precious cargo inside. He expelled a sigh of relief as he saw it swing around and come toward them.

"Oh, I can't wait to see my grandson!" Nick's mother exclaimed, leading the way to the door where the passengers would be arriving.

Nick followed with his father at his side, fighting disappointment that the little forest cottage had been taken by another honeymoon couple. But Mr. Ferron had said there was a kind of honeymoon suite at the main ranch house, which he was sure R.T. would like, so Nick reserved it. A bottle of champagne on ice and two glasses stood ready.

"Look at your mom, Nicky. She's happier than I've seen her in a long while. Thanks for taking time to be with us."

"You don't have to thank me for something I wanted to do, Dad. I love you both." He gave his father's shoulder a squeeze, then turned to watch the incoming passengers.

As soon as Cody and Jeff burst through the door there was mayhem. R.T. and Cynthia were right behind them. For the next few minutes, everybody hugged everybody. The reunion with loved ones warmed Nick's heart. Only one person was missing, one person who could have turned the occasion to the greatest joy.

Like those seven years in prison, you've got to put Rosie away, Armstrong. You've got to do it, or you won't survive the rest of your life.

They all agreed to head to the dude ranch to get settled in their rooms, then enjoy a prewedding brunch.

Though he realized this would only be a reenactment of the real thing, Nick couldn't shrug off the feeling that everyone was caught up in the kind of nervous excitement that preceded a real wedding.

R.T. was higher than a kite, and Cynthia walked around with stars in her eyes. But the biggest change seemed to have fallen over Cody. Nick had never seen his son so jubilant, almost euphoric. He knew Cody was excited to see him again, but there was something else. Nick couldn't put his finger on it.

In a way it worried him. Had Rosie's love for Zach caused their son to shut off his feelings for his mother? Had her absence at night hurt him too much?

Nick could only praise Rosie's mothering instincts. But Zach was a different matter altogether. Possibly Cody was overcompensating to deal with what he viewed as his mother's defection from the family. Nick thought about this on the drive to the lodge; he was still thinking about it as they prepared for the wedding. Maybe he and Cody should go in for some group counseling after the trip. The army urged vets and their families to participate. Nick hadn't given it much credence until he'd seen Cody's behavior today.

Naturally he was thrilled that his boy seemed so happy. But Cody was overdoing it, and that troubled him a lot.

"Hey, Dad! We match!"

"We sure do." They both stood in front of the mirror in Nick's room. The brown Western-cut suits didn't look half-bad. Nick was back up to 160 pounds. Twenty-five or thirty more pounds to go, but he wasn't complaining. The natural-toned cowboy boots would be great around the ranch.

"Whoa, Dad! That Stetson looks cool on you."

Using his good hand, Nick dipped the brim down level with his eyes, then stared at Cody in the glass. *"Make my day."*

Jeff and Cody shrieked with laughter.

Then it was time to go to the church.

ROSIE HAD ARRIVED at the little Chapel of the Pines two hours before the ceremony to get all the ribbons and flowers arranged. She'd left her car parked behind the forest cabin. One of Mr. Ferron's employees had driven her to the church.

The rings lay inside three tiny pockets on a white satin-and-velvet pillow left on the front pew. Cody's job was to carry the ring pillow and distribute the carnation boutonnieres to all the men and give the gardenia corsage to Nick's mother.

When everything looked as perfect as she could make it, Rosie hurried to one of the little anterooms off the foyer used as changing rooms for bridal parties.

The box of bridal bouquets had been placed on a chair. Fashioned of white roses, baby's breath and fern fronds, they looked exquisite.

Almost sick with excitement, she removed her T-shirt and jeans, then began to put on her wedding dress.

"Most married women can't fit into the gown they wore at their wedding. Yours fits like a dream," Cynthia murmured as she let herself into the room, carrying her wedding finery over her arm.

"Cynthia! You're here!" They hugged. "I'm so relieved. That means everyone's arrived safely. H-how's Nick?"

Cynthia started to change out of her clothes. She eyed Rosie solemnly. "He's putting on a great show for everyone, especially the boys, but Rosie—the man's heart is broken. There's only one thing he wants, and that's to be married to you. R.T. and I agree we would never have forced him to go through with this today if we hadn't known you were going to make his greatest dream come true by the end of the ceremony. It would have been too cruel otherwise.''

''I know.'' Rosie's voice shook. ''Sometimes I wonder if I've done the right thing.''

Cynthia smiled her sweet smile. ''If you could see the way you look, you'd know this is the *perfect* plan. Believe me.''

''It's got to be. Here, Cynthia. Let me help with all those buttons. This dress fits you beautifully. You must be exactly the same size you were the day you got married.''

''Hopefully, eight months from now I won't be able to step into it, let alone pull it all the way up.''

''*Cynthia!* Does R.T. know?''

''No, that's going to be my wedding present to him.''

When she'd finished doing up her dress, Cynthia started on Rosie's. ''It won't be noticeable, but I can tell you're a little thinner than you were thirteen years ago.''

''If all goes well, I'll be in your condition soon. I want our children to grow up together.''

''I think I'm too happy, Rosie.''

''I think I am, too.''

They both looked in the mirror to arrange their veils.

''Cynthia, our dresses are amazingly alike.'' They wore full-length, off-white silk with lace trim. Both dresses had long sleeves with a scooped neck and empire waists. The biggest difference lay in their veils. Cynthia's was shorter and fashioned of nylon tulle. Rosie's matched the lace cutouts on her dress and cascaded to her shoulders.

She turned to Cynthia with tears in her eyes. "We're the two most fortunate women around. Our men came home."

They clasped hands and said a little prayer to remember the men who didn't.

NICK REMOVED his Stetson and entered the chapel, marveling at the beautiful decorations. The scent of flowers produced a flashback of his own wedding. He shook his mind to clear it of the memory and proceeded down the aisle.

Cody darted his father a brilliant smile and was right there to pin a red carnation on his lapel. Once again Nick had the distinct impression that something was wrong with his son.

The pastor came in, followed by the organist, breaking Nick's train of thought. Soon all the introductions were made, and the pastor showed Nick and R.T. where to stand.

Cody was positioned on the other side of the altar. Nick watched his mother give Cody a kiss and hand him the ring pillow. Then she took her place in the first pew with his father and Jeff.

Nick could feel R.T. shifting his weight. "How come you're so nervous? You've done this before."

"How come *you're* nervous?" he fired back. "I heard you doing Morse code through lunch. You're still doing it. *Got to get out of here. Got to get out of here.*"

"I don't know. It doesn't mean anything. It's just a habit."

"Yeah, sure. You're nervous, all right." R.T. grinned. "Maybe it's that new getup you're wearing."

"You don't approve? I bought it in your honor."

"Hey, I approve, Sarge. You look like a hero out of a Western. I hardly recognized you."

"And you look like the smitten bridegroom if ever there was one, all decked out in that fancy suit and white shirt."

"Do you think Cyn will notice?"

"Nope. She's too crazy about you to bother with the details."

Nick loved to tease R.T. about Cynthia because he could always get his buddy to blush.

The pastor began to speak. "Let us first say a prayer."

Nick had been prepared to hear the wedding march. Quickly he bowed his head and closed his eyes.

"We thank you, oh, God, for your bounteous blessings. Two of your servants, Nicholas Armstrong and Rutherford Topham Ellis, are home with family and loved ones after their seven-year exile in a foreign land."

Nick's head jerked back and he stared at the pastor. Slowly his gaze passed over everyone. All heads were bowed except his. He lowered his head again, but his eyes remained open.

"They've served you and their country honorably, and now they wish to repledge their love and devotion to their wives in front of you and these witnesses. Amen."

"Amen," the congregation returned. Immediately the organ broke into the wedding march.

Wives...

"Steady, Sarge," R.T. whispered. "Don't pass out on me."

"What's going on, R.T.? Tell me, dammit!" he whispered back fiercely.

His palms were clammy and the room felt too hot.

"Just keep your eyes focused on the back of the church, and all your questions will be answered."

At R.T.'s injunction, Nick swung his head around.

He saw Cynthia start down the aisle. Her sweet face glowed as she kept her eyes on R.T. Then he saw another bride emerge from the foyer of the chapel. The lacy veil looked familiar.

Out of nowhere he heard his mother cry out in shock. His father looked like he was going to faint.

She drew closer.

Dear God. Rosie?

His heart was racing. "I think I'm sick, R.T." he said in a low aside. "I'm starting to hallucinate. Get me out of here."

"Steady. What do you think you see?"

"It's Rosie! She's wearing the dress she wore at our wedding. I'm telling you, R.T. I'm losing it."

"No, you're not, Sarge. I see her, too. It's no hallucination. But I admit Rosie *looks* as heavenly as a vision."

Nick's whole body began to tremble. *"What the devil...?"*

"You're a smart man, Sarge. You figure it out."

"Rutherford," the pastor said, "if you'll make room for your bride here and clasp hands. And, Nicholas, if you'll do the same and clasp hands with your bride, we'll begin the ceremony."

Like a heat-seeking missile, Rosie's eyes locked on Nick's. The light that had been missing in them at Hill blazed green fire now. She reached boldly for his right hand and squeezed so hard he felt pain. He welcomed it, though, because it proved he wasn't experiencing some kind of weird flashback.

Nick could hear the pastor talking to R.T. and Cynthia, but he wasn't cognizant of anything except the flesh-and-blood woman at his side, pulsating with life, looking at him as if he was her whole world and everything in it.

"For as long as we both shall live." She mouthed the words to him.

Those were the words they'd had inscribed on their wedding bands.

"Rosie Gardner Armstrong, inasmuch as you're already joined in the bonds of holy matrimony to your husband, Nicholas, do you renew your vows before God and these witnesses to love, cherish and honor him, through sickness, through health, clinging only to him and forsaking all others, until death do you part?"

Nick watched breathlessly as Rosie turned, her whole heart reaching out to him.

"I, Rosie Gardner Armstrong, consider it the

greatest privilege to renew before God, before our son, Cody, before our dearest parents and friends, my vows to my beloved—'' her voice shook ''—my beloved husband, Nick, whom I've always loved and adored.

''I ask his forgiveness for any pain I have unintentionally caused, but I vow that from this moment on, I will do everything in my power to bring him nothing but joy all the days of our lives.'' She paused. ''I come to him having forsaken all others.''

Is it true, sweetheart? Zach really has no more claim on your heart? Rosie? Do you know how much I want to believe you?

''I come to him prepared to be all the things I was to him in the past, prepared to be even more in the future. Dearest friend, dearest lover, dearest wife, dearest mother of his children.''

''Nicholas Armstrong?'' the pastor addressed him.

Nick felt as if he were in a dream.

''You've heard your wife's solemn troth. Since you are already husband to Rosie Gardner Armstrong, do you wish to renew your marriage vows before God, family and friends?''

Rosie's body started to shake like a leaf. Fear had robbed her cheeks of color.

Why are you frightened, Rosie? Don't you know this is what I've longed for? Prayed for?

I'm the one who's afraid.

Clearing his throat, he began, ''I, Nicholas Armstrong, in front of God, my family and friends, wish to renew my vows to my beloved wife, Rosie, the mother of my son, Cody, the light of my life whose love has sustained me through thirteen years of marriage, whose love kept me alive through a dark and perilous time."

He felt her body go limp with relief, and he braced her with his hand and arm, holding her close.

"I forgive her for any pain she might have unwittingly caused and ask that she forgive me for any pain I might have inflicted on her. I am the most blessed of men to have the love of such a woman, and swear to do everything in my power to show her what she means to me. I swear I will respect her, watch over her, honor her, keep her in sickness, in health, until death do us part."

Nick heard her cry his name.

Ah, Rosie…can this really be happening to us?

"You may now exchange rings as symbols of your love. First, Mr. and Mrs. Ellis, and then Mr. and Mrs. Armstrong."

Nick couldn't take his eyes off Rosie.

She's going to live with me again. She's going to be my wife!

"Dad! Take the rings," Cody whispered.

Cody. *He'd known all along.* There was nothing wrong with his son. *Joy* had transformed him.

Suitably chastened, Nick flashed the boy a conspiratorial smile, which he returned, then felt in the little pocket for the rings he'd put on Rosie's finger thirteen years earlier.

Rosie lifted her left hand and helped him slide the rings home with his good hand.

To his surprise, she reached in another little pocket

and brought out a ring that looked exactly like the one he'd lost when they'd run into that land mine.

"As long as we both shall live." She read aloud the inscribed words before taking his right hand and pushing it onto his third finger.

"Sweetheart..." His voice caught in his throat.

Suddenly Rosie threw her arms around his neck and pulled his head down, kissing him exactly the way she'd kissed him before he'd gone off to the war.

They might be in a church, but her hunger, her passion, broke all the rules and he felt himself going under. No one had ever loved him the way she had. No one ever could. His Rosie was back where she belonged, burrowing into his arms, into his heart. Her mouth set him on fire.

The war was finally over.

"Hey, Sarge—" Nick felt a nudge in his ribs "—maybe you better take it easy. Another minute of that and this holy house is going to go up in holy smoke."

Rosie must have heard R.T., because she tore her lips from Nick's and hid her face in his shoulder, still clinging to him as if she feared someone would drag him back onto that plane.

Holding her against him with his left arm, Nick fought for the presence of mind to extend his right hand to the pastor. That seemed to signal the cessation of formalities. In the next instant Cody had launched himself at them, laughing and crying at once, jumping up and down. Jeff was right there with him.

Nick saw his mother out of the periphery. She had collapsed in his father's arms. He knew she was overcome with joy. He and his father made eye contact. His father was weeping. They smiled at each other with an understanding that surpassed words.

Behind his back he could hear R.T. sobbing uncontrollably in Cynthia's arms.

With Rosie still molded to his body, not saying a word, he lowered his head to R.T. "Haven't you done enough of that already?"

"I can't help it, Sarge. Cyn just told me I'm going to be a father in January."

Nick knew life didn't get much better than this.

"And you called me up because you were afraid to make love to your wife on your first night home…" He quietly baited him with relish.

"Ah, Sarge!"

He felt Rosie stir. She finally lifted her head, a beguiling smile on her face. "The getaway car for the four of us is outside the chapel."

Without taking his eyes off her, he said, "Did you hear that, R.T.?"

"I'm ready when you are, *sir*."

"Are you ready, sweetheart?"

In answer she pressed her mouth to his. That was all Nick needed before picking her up in his arms and carrying her down the aisle. He didn't have to look back and wonder what R.T. was doing.

Everyone had preceded them outside. Cody and Jeff held the doors open while George took pictures.

Rosie's car stood parked a few yards away. At least he thought it was her car, but it was covered with shaving cream. Just like his old Jeep that his friends had gotten hold of thirteen years ago. There were cans and streamers tied to it, writing all over it.

JUST MARRIED! WAY TO GO, 57. NAUGHTY NICK'S GOING TO CALL ALL THE PLAYS TONIGHT. HAVE FUN! HAVE A ROSIE OLD TIME.

"You remembered!"

Again he felt a sense of wonder that his darling Rosie hadn't forgotten a single detail about that night of nights.

Still holding her in his arms, he walked around the front of the car to the passenger side. There was more writing.

REDHEADS HAVE MORE FUN. THERE'S SIN, AND THEN THERE'S CYN. TONIGHT RUTHERFORD TOPHAM WON'T KNOW THE DIFFERENCE. MORSE CODE'S A LOT OF FUN WHEN YOU DO IT RIGHT!

Nick burst out laughing and shot an amused glance at his buddy. R.T. was helping his wife into the back seat of the Nissan. His face had gone beet red.

"Oh, Rosie. You did it this time. R.T.'s a wreck," he whispered against her delectable neck.

"I love him, Nick. He's so much fun to tease."

I love him, too. I love you for loving him.

He set her down on the seat and helped fit her

gown inside. "Where are you taking us, my adorable wife?" He couldn't resist kissing her again.

"*Sarge,* come on. Let's get out of here!"

Her eyes held his. "I'll give you one guess."

I'm sorry, Mr. Armstrong, but our little forest cottage has already been booked by a honeymoon couple.

Nick felt a swelling in his throat and couldn't talk. Struggling for breath, he straightened, then shut the door.

As he walked back around to get in the driver's seat, he realized they had an audience and rushed over to embrace his parents.

"Nicky, Nicky," his mother murmured. "I'm so happy for you. Tell Rosie I'm sorry."

"I will, Mom. Now, all of you have a wonderful time. I'll see you back in Salt Lake."

"Be happy, son," his father said hoarsely.

"Dad," Cody said as they hugged one more time, "she *really* loves you."

Nick clung to his son. "I think I kind of figured that out, Cody. Be a help to your grandparents. We'll see you soon."

"Thanks for coming, Jeff." He tousled the affable teen's blond head before getting back in the car.

Afraid to look at Rosie for fear he'd lose all sense of time and propriety, he turned on the ignition and headed toward the dude ranch at full speed.

"Go easy on the sarge, Rosie. He almost passed out on me in there. Maybe you ought to have someone at the clinic look him over."

Nick grinned. "No one's looking me over but my wife!" Now Rosie was blushing.

"Do you have our room number extension, Rosie?" R.T. asked.

"Yes." Her voice sounded more like a squeak.

"That's good. When the sarge gets to the part where he doesn't know what to do, call me."

"Dammit, R.T.!"

Cynthia started to laugh.

"You made him blush, R.T." Rosie screamed in delight. *"Finally!"*

Unable to resist, he flicked his wife a probing glance. "What do you mean, *finally?*"

"You know exactly what I mean, Nicholas Armstrong."

He did. *Midnight poker.*

"I'm warning you now, you're in for a *big* surprise."

He shook his head. "You'll never win, sweetheart. Don't even think it."

CHAPTER FIFTEEN

ROSIE HARDLY NOTICED the jack pines along the road that wound through the forest, taking them farther and farther away from the main cluster of cabins. She was so absorbed in her thoughts that she didn't even notice the darkness around them. The late-afternoon sun could scarcely penetrate the green canopy.

Nick had escorted R.T. and Cynthia to their honeymoon suite in the main lodge. Now she and Nick were finally alone.

Last night Rosie had felt slightly feverish. Now she knew she was running a temperature. She'd reached her emotional saturation point while waiting for Nick to respond during the ceremony.

He might not have. Not because he didn't love her, but because she wasn't sure he'd accept that she'd come back to him out of love, not pity. And because he might not believe that she and Zach were through.

The fact that he'd made his vows to her—with no warning, no explanation, and in front of everyone—meant he was going on pure faith. Rosie was humbled by that faith and planned to take away every lingering doubt he hadn't allowed her or anyone to see.

They needed to talk. She would insist that they

talk before she made love to her husband. He'd gone all quiet since coming back to the car.

If God would grant her just one more wish, the intricate preparations she'd made would prove her love to Nick, show that she was wholly his, forever. *Tonight had to set the seal on their marriage.*

As soon as Nick had parked behind the cabin, she turned in her seat so her back was to him.

"Darling? Would you undo me? I need to go inside first and prepare a couple of things. Then I'll signal you."

Still no words. She felt his fingers on her back, releasing each button down the long row. He'd become incredibly adept at managing with one hand.

When he'd finished his task, she felt his hot palm against her skin with a sense of wonder. His hand followed the curve of her spine, then slid compulsively to her waist and around to her hip, as if he couldn't help himself.

She never wanted him to stop. But the time wasn't yet. *Soon, darling, soon. I promise you it will be worth the wait.*

Forcing herself to get out of the car, she disappeared into the cabin and quickly changed out of her dress and veil into the outfit she'd resurrected from the past.

The jeans were new, but they looked exactly like the ones she'd worn here on their honeymoon. More important, she still had Nick's old T-shirt, the one she'd had on when they'd arrived at this cabin the first night.

Reaching for her brush, she caught her hair back

in a ponytail. She'd been practicing so she could do it just right. A few drops of bath oil behind her ears and on her wrists, and she was ready.

The only difference was in the outfit Nick had been wearing that night. The original clothes lay in a brown sack at the foot of the quilted double bed. She knew they'd be a little loose on him now, but she'd added a belt, so it wouldn't matter.

She picked it up and went to the door. Opening it enough to set the bag on the ground, she called to Nick and told him to change outside.

"What are you planning in there? A costume party?"

She smiled. "Don't be embarrassed. The chipmunks will never tell. When you're ready, knock."

"It's a good thing R.T. can't see me now. He'd never let me live it down."

She pressed a hand over her pounding heart. "In a minute you're going to forget R.T. and everything else."

"Is that a promise?"

That voice—the old Nick.

"What the hell?"

She had to stifle her excitement.

"Where did this old shirt come from?"

"Don't ask questions. Just put it on."

"Already she's ordering me around."

"And you love it!"

There was a slight pause. "I love it."

She waited, anticipating the next outburst.

"My Dodgers baseball cap!" Another silence. "Rosie…"

She bit her lip. "Are you ready to come in?"

When there was no answer, she turned on the tape player and started dancing in place to their song.

The sounds of Toto's "Rosanna" resounded in the cool air as the door flew open.

On the night she'd come home from a long miserable vacation with her grandparents—miserable because she was dying to be with Nick—he had played that song on his Jeep's tape deck and had sung along, a little off-key.

When the song was over, he'd leaned across the gearshift and placed his hands on her shoulders. His dark handsome face was within centimeters of hers and he whispered, "You're my Rosanna. You know that, don't you? You know we're in love. Tell me you're in love with me. Tell me now."

She'd stared into the flame-blue eyes, her heart skipping crazily. "I'm in love with you," she'd answered him honestly. It had been no less true all those years ago than it was now.

"That's all I needed to hear. We're getting married," came his fevered response.

Rosie could believe it was that same handsome young man who entered the cabin now and shoved the door closed with his boot. He wore the baseball cap backward, as he had the first time they'd come home.

His chest rose and fell. "You still look eighteen and too beautiful to be real."

"I'm real, Nick. Come here and find out." She held her arms wide.

The smile he'd always reserved for her transformed him. Rosie's senses ignited as he moved toward her and drew her into his arms. He pulled her close against him and they slow-danced to the music, delighting in the feel of each other. She heard his voice, still a little off-key. But he made a few changes in the words. He said "Rosie" in place of "Rosanna." And he changed one line to, "It's been a long time since I went away."

Then he was kissing her. She was kissing him. All the things they hadn't been able to say over the past month they were saying now. They clung together, talking, remembering, laughing, kissing, through a dozen songs.

She could *feel* them healing. It expanded and lifted her to a fullness of ecstasy. Caught up in the same intensity of feeling, he finally raised his head, revealing the eager tremulous face of joy.

In an awestruck voice he whispered, "I have my Rosie back."

"You always had me, darling. Don't you see? Until six weeks ago, I couldn't make a commitment to Zach—because of you." Her eyes clouded over.

"If I'd truly been in love with Zach, I would have—*should* have—married him two years ago. Obviously what I felt for him was never enough. Deep down, a part of me wasn't ready. I was too much in love with you, even when I thought you were dead. Even then, I couldn't—"

"Rosie, you don't have to explain."

"Yes, Nick, I do. When Zach took Cody and me on that cruise, I noticed that most of the other tourists were older couples. I envied them because they had someone to share their lives. It made me think about Cody, that he was growing older and would be gone sooner than I could imagine.

"That's when I broke down and asked Zach to propose to me again. I loved him very much, and inside I wanted a reason to go on living. I didn't want to grow old alone."

Nick's eyes softened. "I would have wanted that for you, Rosie."

She ran her hands lovingly up and down his cheeks. "I know that. Then I got the phone call from your parents telling me you were alive and coming home. Nick...I went into shock!"

He lowered his head and pressed his forehead against hers. "I won't presume to understand how you felt, but there's no doubt that kind of news would have turned your world inside out."

She nodded. "It did. And do you know why? Because it threw me into a morass of confusion and guilt and torn loyalties.

"Last week, my head cleared of that confusion. I realized that no matter what you and I had once meant to each other, if I had truly been in love with Zach—the way I'd been with you—I would have gone up to Hill wearing his ring. It would have killed me to hurt you that way, but I would have done it because I was so certain of my feelings.

"Obviously I *wasn't* certain. That's how I *know* that what Zach and I shared wasn't the profound love I'd had with you."

"We have something extraordinary," he said, his voice husky.

She nodded. "It was an illuminating moment for both of us when Zach asked me if I was going to wear his ring to meet you."

Nick's eyes searched hers intently. "What did you say?"

"I told him I'd put his ring in my jewelry box with yours. Consciously I didn't realize that, in saying this, I'd taken a giant step away from Zach. I'm afraid he recognized what was happening to us long before I did.

"From the time you and I drove down from Hill, things started to degenerate between Zach and me. The more I tried to make it work, the more it didn't work.

"I have no doubt we would've been very happy together, if nothing else had changed. But the second I knew you were alive, the part of me that was your wife wouldn't let me give myself emotionally to Zach.

"I found myself wondering what you were doing, what you were feeling. I was so jealous of the time Cody spent with you. I was jealous of your relationship with R.T. I felt left out at every turn.

"Those weren't the feelings I should have had when I was planning to marry another man! Nick, when you told me you were going to divorce me so you could start fresh—with someone new—I almost died.

"Zach knew I was in agony. Last week I went over to tell him that I couldn't go through with the marriage. He'd come to the same conclusion. I hated hurting him, but it felt so good to finally say the truth out loud—that I was in love with you. That I wanted to stay married to you.''

Nick frowned. ''Where is he now?''

''He's moved back to California.''

''The man must be in hell.''

''I know he is. But as he said to me the last time we were together, he would rather hear those words about my loving you *now* than after we were married. I'm counting on that wisdom to help him recover.''

Nick's eyes narrowed and his right hand tightened on her arm. ''You'd be impossible to replace.''

''Your bias is showing, darling. He'll find a woman who loves and needs him desperately. I'm sure of it. In the meantime, he has an amazing family, and all the support he needs from his brother, Richard. Zach's a strong man. I know that in time he'll end up as happy as I am.''

She pressed a hungry kiss to Nick's lips, needing him as much as she needed water, air, sunlight.

He rocked her back and forth. ''Now that I have you in my arms, I can feel compassion for him. But when I first found myself kissing a stranger, the pain was worse than everything I went through in all those seven years.''

''Nick—''

''Shh. It hurt too much, Rosie. I couldn't stand it. And the other thing is…I wanted you to be happy. So I had to file for divorce. There wasn't any other way.''

''I'm so thankful you did!'' she cried. ''It straightened out my confusion in a big hurry. The thought of you belonging to anyone else… I couldn't let it happen. You were *my* Nick. No one but me was going to hold you during one of your nightmares!"

He ran his finger along her jaw. "R.T. told me about that night. I'm grateful you didn't end up with anything more than a bruise."

Tears gathered in her eyes. "I'm glad it happened. That night I felt like I was a part of you."

A pained look crossed his face. "It could happen tonight."

"Not if I have anything to say about it." She smiled provocatively.

That little comment took the pained look away in a hurry. "Is that right?"

"That's right." She slid her hand into his and drew him over to the bed. "Now, you sit down here. And I'm going to sit here."

"You're too far away from me, sweetheart."

"It's the perfect distance to play poker."

He gave a devilish chuckle. Then grabbed a Snickers bar from the nightstand and tore off the wrapping with his teeth.

Taking a bite, he grinned. "You trying to sweeten me up on the same stuff you fed me the last time we were in this room?" His intent look reminded her he was a fierce competitor. "As I recall, you lost every game. In fact you lost a lot more than that." His piratical half smile sent delicious shivers across her skin.

She sat cross-legged on the bed and pulled out a pack of playing cards. "I learned a few tricks while you were gone."

"Who from?"

"I bought a book."

He reached out and covered one of her hands with his. "You shouldn't believe everything you read."

"You're scared, Armstrong. Admit it."

"You've got that one wrong, sweetheart." He offered her a bite of the candy bar. "Win or lose, I win."

She fluttered her lashes at him. "We'll see about that. You need a handicap so we'll start with twenty-one. Here's hoping your little brush-up session with our son did the job. Winner decides the penalty. I'll deal."

At this point, Nick stretched full-length on his left side, his smile almost wolfish. She felt breathless with anticipation. "Ready when you are," he murmured silkily.

She dealt two cards facedown, then two more face-up. She had an ace. They both checked their cards.

"Hit me."

She gave him a card.

"Hit me again."

With a deadpan face he said, "I'll stay."

"So will I."

"All right, Rosie, baby. Let's see what you've got."

She turned the card over. "A jack. Now let's see yours."

He eyed her suspiciously, then turned everything over.

"Hmm. Nineteen. You lose, Armstrong. Give me your hat."

"You have to come and get it."

"That's not part of the rules."

"What's the matter? Are you scared?"

She felt a quiver of excitement. "No."

"Then come here."

Rosie leaned over the cards to take it from his head.

"Oh!" The next thing she knew, she was flat on her back and he'd rolled on top of her. He pinned both her arms with his injured one.

"The problem with you, sweetheart, is that you never did know when your number was up."

"No, Nick!" She screamed and giggled at the same time because he was feeling in her pockets with his right hand—and taking certain liberties as he did so.

Suddenly he pulled out a bunch of cards. "My, my, my. What have we here? All aces and jacks." He tossed them over his shoulder. "I wonder if there's any more where *they* came from."

A further exploration turned into something else as their mouths fused in passion and Rosie found herself clinging blindly to her husband.

A SERIES OF ODD TAPPING sounds outside the cabin brought Rosie out of a sound sleep. As she started to stretch, she felt the heavy weight of Nick's arm and leg thrown across her body, his right hand tangled in her hair.

Their lovemaking had been so feverish and intense, their desire for each other so insatiable, they couldn't have fallen asleep before six or seven in the morning. Nick had gotten up during the night to close the wooden shutters. There was no way to tell what time it was. She would have to remove his hand from her hair if she wanted to take a look at his watch.

The tapping started again, a little louder. This time Nick stirred. Just feeling him take a breath ignited her desire for him all over again. She kissed her way to his mouth.

He groaned in satisfaction, returning her kiss with shocking ardor for one still groggy with sleep. To her joy he shifted his weight and began to make love to her in earnest. The tapping continued, even more loudly than before.

"I think we have a woodpecker outside our door," she whispered against his lips.

Nick raised himself up on one elbow to listen. "That's no woodpecker, sweetheart. That's R.T."

Intrigued, Rosie asked, "What's he saying?"

His body shook with silent laughter. "He says it's two o'clock in the afternoon, and he and Cyn are getting worried."

"You're kidding! Two?"

He nuzzled her neck. She could feel the rasp of his beard. "After our all-nighter, are you really surprised?"

Heat swept up her body. "What else is he saying?"

"He's afraid we've both suffered cardiac arrest from too much excitement. He wants permission to enter." Nick kissed her in a very sensitive spot. "Sometimes he worries about me. Do you mind?"

"No, of course not. I know exactly how he feels."

For that she was given another passionate kiss. "Put on the robe I gave you."

"I didn't bring it—or a nightgown."

"Did I ever tell you you're every husband's fantasy?"

"Yes. Last night. You told me over and over again."

"No nightmares?"

"Not one."

"Tell you what. You snuggle down in the covers and I'll get the door."

"Okay."

She heard a few grunts and groans as Nick felt his way around in the dark. Suddenly the room filled with dazzling light, outlining his lean physique, which had started gaining mass and muscle. But even thin and haggard, he'd been a beautiful man to Rosie; he always would be.

She watched him pull on jeans and T-shirt. He darted her a quick glance. "Ready?"

She nodded.

He opened the door. "Come on in, R.T."

"Is it all right?"

"Is it all right, Rosie?"

"R.T., you're welcome anytime."

He entered the cabin hesitantly. "I'm sorry to disturb you. Cyn and I were wondering…if you don't have anything else to do, you might like to come horseback riding with us."

Rosie decided to say nothing and let her husband answer for them.

"We have something else to do, R.T. Trust me."

"That's what I figured. I was just checking."

"Go on and find your wife. I'm sure she wants you to herself for a while. We'll see you at the lodge for dinner."

His face lit up. "Thanks, Sarge. See you later."

Nick shut the door.

"It's time for a shower, Scarlett." He tossed the covers aside with his good hand.

Rosie didn't move a muscle. She bestowed a bewitching smile on him, instead. In her phony Southern accent she drawled, "I declare, Rhett Butler, you are no gentleman, sir. Why, I just go pink all over when I think what you were doing to me all nigh—"

"*Hey, Mom? Dad?* R.T. says you're up. Can I come in?"

"Quick, darling. Hand me the comforter."

Nick let out an expletive and threw the quilt over her.

She heard the door creak open.

"Hi!"

"Hi, bud. Where's Jeff?"

"He's over at the corral."

Rosie sat a little straighter in the bed, the covers up to her chin. "Hi, honey! How are you?"

Cody finished hugging his father and ran to the side of the bed to hug her.

"Hey, Mom? How come you're still in bed? Are you sick?"

Over Cody's shoulder she eyed her husband, who was smiling with unholy delight. *The wretch isn't going to help me out of this one.*

"I feel fine. Your dad and I are just taking it easy, but I love you for caring."

If anything, Nick's smile had broadened.

"Are you and Dad...well, you know, are you happy and everything?"

She swallowed hard, realizing how important this was to their son. "We're divinely happy, Cody. Aren't we, darling?" she said to Nick who'd come to sit on the bed next to her.

He pulled Cody onto his lap and gave him a hug. "We didn't know we could be this happy."

"I didn't know I could be this happy, either," Cody confessed. "Are we all going to live on the ranch then?"

"Yes."

"What about Mom's job?"

"She's going to commute from Heber to Salt Lake when she starts teaching again in the fall. That way she can drive you down to school every day so you won't have to be separated from your friends."

"That's great, Dad! I want—"

"Yoo-hoo! Knock, knock!"

Rosie heard Nick's frustrated sigh of resignation, then felt his hand slide around her waist and give it a squeeze.

"Hi, Mom and Dad. Come on in and join the crowd."

"We just wanted to know how the lovebirds were doing today."

"They're doing great, Grandma," Cody answered. "Mom's just relaxing."

"That's good, dear. You need it, Rosie."

George chuckled, then winked at Nick, who'd started laughing. Rosie joined him.

"What's so funny, Dad?"

"I thought they taught you everything there was to know on Channel One."

"I'm going to go ask R.T. He'll tell me."

"You do that, son."

"Come on, Cody," his grandfather urged. "Let's leave your poor mom and dad alone. Come on, Janet. Give them some privacy."

Nick closed the door behind them.

"It's almost three o'clock." Janet's voice carried all too easily. "I mean, there is such a thing as…"

Rosie held out her arms to her husband. When he was back in bed with her, she nestled close to his heart. "There's a lot of love in this family."

"Amen."

"I love you, Nick Armstrong. More than you'll ever know."

He gave her another possessive kiss. "Most men get one shot at life. I was given two, and both times I ended up with you. That's my blessing and my joy."

"Oh, Nick…"

What about Zach Wilde? Does he have another chance at love, at happiness? Find out in
LAURA'S BABY by Rebecca Winters
coming next.

Laura's Baby
REBECCA WINTERS

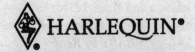

TORONTO • NEW YORK • LONDON
AMSTERDAM • PARIS • SYDNEY • HAMBURG
STOCKHOLM • ATHENS • TOKYO • MILAN • MADRID
PRAGUE • WARSAW • BUDAPEST • AUCKLAND

To Terry, my friend and colleague.
Thanks for sharing your cycling expertise,
which was invaluable.

CHAPTER ONE

TOURISTS AND MEMBERS of the press crowded the reception area of the Hotel Metropole. Only one clerk, his hands gesticulating wildly with frustration, appeared to be manning the front desk.

Laura Donetti was almost dead on her feet as she approached him, thanks to the long crowded L.A.-to-Brussels flight and subsequent drive in a rental car to St. Léger. She fought an oppressive fatigue as she half listened to the cacophony of voices, speaking a dozen different languages, surrounding her. She'd probably caught her little niece's cold.

"Oui, mademoiselle?" the harried clerk said, then no doubt recognizing her as an American, added, "How may I help you?"

"I'm Tony Donetti's wife. He's here with the Ziff team." When the man frowned she explained, "You know, Ziff? It stands for Zindel Foto-Films? They're the Belgian team for the Tour de France." The owners of the Belgian team had been plagued with problems in the past, so they'd gone on a talent search and had found cyclists from several different nations who had gained outstanding reputations in the sport, Tony among them. "Could you tell me which room is his?"

Thank heaven *she* didn't need a room. There wasn't one to be found anywhere. The world's greatest annual biking event had attracted thousands of cycling enthusiasts to the starting point of the race in St. Léger, only a few miles from the Luxembourg border.

After checking in to the smaller Hotel Beaulieu around the corner, where a reservation had been made ahead of time for the team members' families, she'd tried to phone Tony at the Metropole, but kept getting a busy signal. Either he or the teammate he roomed with was holding a lengthy conversation with their coach, or one of them had taken the receiver off the hook.

The exasperated hotel clerk shook his head. "You are the second woman today insisting that she is his wife and must see him. *Je regrette.*"

Groupies. The inevitable result of Tony's rising popularity among the sports crowd. She was sickened by the knowledge that her husband loved that side of his rise to fame.

"Perhaps this will convince you." She whipped out her passport, plus some wallet-size photos of the two of them together. "I'm staying at the Beaulieu. If you wish to ring over there to verify who I am…"

"You think I have time to make a phone call with this crowd?" He threw his hands in the air. "*Très bien.* But it will be on your head, eh? Room twenty-two." She knew it would be futile to ask for a key.

"Thank you."

Laura turned away from the desk and began working her way through the throng of people. When her husband was on the racing circuit, trying to get in touch with him was like trying to speak to the president. And before a race such as this one, well...her only choice had been to walk the short distance through the crowds and stifling late-June heat to the Metropole.

Tony would probably be surprised to see her on the doorstep of his hotel room. The last time they'd been together had been five weeks ago when their two-day reunion had turned into disaster. Too restless to stay in their apartment for five minutes, let alone talk about the sorry state of their marriage, he'd made perfunctory love to her, then told her he needed to get out and talk to his cycling buddies. That had spelled the end of their private time together.

"Look, April!" Laura heard someone whisper in an American accent as she passed a group of people on the stairs. "Isn't that Margo from 'The Way Things Are'? Can you believe it? She's even more beautiful in person!"

Laura groaned and darted up the second flight. Being recognized for her role as the spitfire attorney in a popular soap opera was a daily occurrence back home in California. But somehow she hadn't expected to be spotted quite so easily here. For the international scene was *Tony's* arena.

Speculation that he could win the Tour de France, beating out Ernesto Farramundi, the four-time winner and favorite, had spurred Tony's ambition.

Even if the Ziff team didn't win, she knew that when the Tour de France was over, Tony would want a chance at the Olympics. Obsessed with racing, he'd continue to pursue new heights. Much to the disappointment of his family, not to mention hers, his plans to attend law school had been cast aside.

When she'd accepted his proposal of marriage six years ago, how could she have known his love of cycling would become so all-consuming? She certainly didn't begrudge him his brilliant success. But the compulsive need to win and indulge in every perk that went with that success had taken him down a road that had changed him into someone she didn't know anymore.

Yet Laura's respect for her wedding vows, plus her conscience—which wouldn't have allowed her to be as cruel to him as he'd been to her, especially on the eve of the big race—had brought her to Europe. And in case he lost out tomorrow and made a poor showing during the prologue—the torturous time trials—she didn't want him to use her nonappearance as the reason for his failure. She knew he'd love to do that, because that was how his mind worked. She refused to give him that opportunity. Instead, she planned to be close at hand every kilometer of the race.

Besides, every competitor needed family support. If she didn't show up, no member of the Donetti family would be there cheering him on. Even though the love had gone out of their marriage a long time ago, she didn't want their marital problems to threaten his chances to make a name for himself in the annals of sports history.

She could well imagine what the media would make of her absence. They were always gnawing at the heels of celebrities, especially a rising sports star like Tony. Because she and Tony both had highly visible profiles, it was even more vital they present a united front.

There were other less altruistic considerations, as well, she mused as she approached the room where he'd been staying....

With determination, she lifted her hand and knocked on the door. Until five weeks ago she'd doggedly clung to the faint hope that their marriage could be salvaged. But she didn't believe that anymore and had made the decision to file for divorce. Deep down she knew it was what he'd wanted for a long long time. Now he would get his wish because finally *it was what she wanted, too!*

ZACHERY WILDE had just stepped out of the shower when he heard a knock on the door. He paused in the process of reaching for his shaving kit. Tony was next door in teammate Klaus Waldbillig's room with some young thing he'd met last week.

Maybe Klaus had come back, forcing Tony to return to the room he and Zach shared, and he'd forgotten his key. Then again, it could be another female fan beating down the doors to get to Tony. It was a common enough occurrence.

The knock sounded again.

Grabbing a towel, which he hitched around his hips, Zach strode across the room to answer it.

"Who is it?"

"Laura Donetti."

Tony's wife?

Zach's frown turned to a grimace. He'd never met Mrs. Donetti.

Until he'd come to Belgium in March to train with the team chosen by their sponsor, Zindel Foto-Films, he'd had no idea the arrogant high-living womanizing Tony Donetti even *had* a wife.

Because they were the only Americans on the Belgian-sponsored team, they'd roomed together on and off throughout the spring. Zach had been forced to listen to many uncomplimentary, even scathing remarks about Tony's spouse, most of which Zach wasn't certain he believed, at least not coming from the mouth of such a world-class jerk. If anything, he felt sorry for any woman foolish enough to marry the guy in the first place.

On the other hand, maybe she was Tony's match. Maybe she didn't care what he did out of her presence, so long as she had a trophy husband to brandish before the world. If that was the case, he supposed they deserved each other.

But whatever the situation, Zach couldn't ignore the reality that Tony's wife was at their door, and Tony was in the next room—with another woman.

However much he disliked his roommate and despised his life-style, Zach had no desire for any member of the team to get caught in an ugly situation this close to tomorrow's prologue. Many cycling experts, Zach included, believed that Tony was one of the top contenders for the *maillot jaune,* the coveted yellow jersey proclaiming the winner.

Unfortunately Tony's appetite for women was becoming well-known. If at this point the media got hold of anything salacious, they'd create a scandal that could taint everything the team had been working for.

At thirty-three Zach was probably the oldest competitor in the Tour de France. This was his one shot at the race. He'd needed a challenge to test his mettle after surviving a broken engagement more than a year before. When the Tour de France was over, he would quit the cycling world altogether and take off for parts unknown.

But right now Laura Donetti's unexpected arrival could mean that their most important team member might be in a hell of a lot of trouble. Zach realized it was up to him to avert disaster.

"Just a minute," he called.

He pulled on a T-shirt, shorts and running shoes, then dashed back to the door and opened it. "Sorry about that, Mrs. Donetti," he murmured. "I had to get dressed first. Come in."

"Thank you. I-isn't he here?" she asked in a slightly husky voice. Eyes of dark brown velvet, heavily fringed with black lashes, looked at him in confusion.

Lord. Tony hadn't exaggerated. His soap-opera-star

wife was gorgeous. Zach's gaze moved from her short curly black hair to her face with its smooth olive-toned skin and wide full mouth, then to her voluptuous body, which did wonders for the simple white two-piece suit she was wearing. She was even more striking because of her height. Five foot seven, at least.

Suddenly he had reason to reassess his thinking. A woman as exquisitely beautiful as she was, who made her living as a soap-opera queen, could quite easily be guilty of every sin her husband had accused her of and then some.

More than likely she drew attractive male stars on and off the set. Maybe Tony's flamboyant charm had lost some of its appeal. Particularly when he and his wife led such divergent lives on different continents.

Or maybe Tony was truly in love with her and she'd lost interest. Possibly that was why he seemed driven to act the way he did. An effort to dull the pain of losing her love.

"No," Zach replied. "He just stepped out, but he'll be back soon. I'm Zach Wilde, the guy he's been rooming with."

"I've heard a lot about you, Zach, professionally and otherwise, and all of it good. You're a little taller than I'd imagined. Is that why they call you King of the Mountain?"

Zach smiled, surprised she even knew the term.

"I'm just kidding," she murmured. "I know why they say that about you. Because you're the best on the climbs." She extended her hand.

As they shook, he had to admit she was good. She knew how to make a man feel important, special. It was a trait that was dynamite on and off the set, no doubt, and probably had Tony on his knees the first time he'd met her.

"All I have to offer is warm Perrier water. Would you like some?"

She nodded, looking flushed. "I'd love it, if it's not too much trouble."

"No trouble at all."

While he took the cap off the bottle he'd swiped from the table he and Tony used for their meals and poured the sparkling water into a glass, his eyes followed her progress. With all their racing gear scattered about, the room was a disaster. She had to do a little rearranging to make a place for herself on one of the chairs.

When she crossed those long shapely legs, he could better understand certain offhand remarks Tony had made, such as the thing he had for well-built brunettes.

Apparently he'd met his stunning wife during a publicity shoot after winning the Shopwise Drug Classic Race in California. He'd pursued her relentlessly, and they'd married quickly without ever getting engaged.

Zach had been engaged twice. Once in his early twenties to a young woman who'd died unexpectedly of a brain tumor. Years later in Utah he suffered through a long hellish second engagement, only to lose out in the end.

It had been fourteen months since Zach had left

Utah. In that time he'd come to grips with the fact that Rosie's husband, who'd been presumed dead after he went missing in action during Operation Desert Storm, had suddenly come back to life seven years later and returned home to claim his wife.

Given his own history, Zach could see Tony's point in not wasting time once you found what you wanted. But the racing star seemed to live his life too impulsively. For certainly it seemed something had gone wrong in their marriage.

What was she? All of twenty-seven, twenty-eight? A dangerous age to live so many thousands of miles away from her husband and looking like the embodiment of most men's fantasies.

Even yours, Wilde?

Zach had always appreciated beauty in any form, and he always would. If he was being completely honest, he had to admit that Laura Donetti's looks were exceptional. More than that, her sex appeal reached out to him like a living thing.

How odd. Up until this minute he'd thought he'd lost the ability to respond this strongly to a woman, no matter how gorgeous.

"Here you go." He handed her the glass, then returned to the project he'd begun before his shower—lining the inner sole of his right biking shoe where it rubbed against his heel. He wondered if he should ask her to wait while he went "looking for Tony."

"I assume you've already checked in at the Beaulieu," he said, instead.

She nodded. "Yes. The place is a madhouse."

He flashed her a smile. "You're right. My brother, Richard, and his family are staying there, too. I'll have to introduce you to his wife, Bev. She and the kids are going to be doing some other activities while Richard drives one of the support wagons. How long are you going to be here? Maybe you can do a little shopping and sight-seeing with them. Bev would enjoy the company."

"That's very kind of you to offer, but I arranged for a leave of absence from the set so I can follow Tony around in one of the support vehicles, too. His aunt and uncle don't..." She paused. "His family can't be here."

Zach blinked in surprise. Tony had always been vague about the people who'd raised him, but he *had* said that Laura hated cycling and hadn't been to his last six major races. In one of them, the Paris-Roubaix, he'd set a world record and Laura hadn't even known about it.

"Y-you don't think he'll mind, do you?"

"Of course not," Zach came back forcefully, trying to recover from his surprise.

"That's good. When you didn't say anything, I thought..." She bent her head. "Well, it's not important what I thought."

He put down the shoe he'd been working on and eyed her levelly. "If I seem surprised, it's because he's told me how difficult it is for you to break away from your tapings."

A wry smile animated her features, giving her another dimension, almost an impish appeal. "Not when your parents help produce the show."

Another thing Tony had neglected to mention. One dark blond brow lifted. "Your parents are in showbiz, too?"

She nodded. "So are my sister and her husband. They're screenwriters. I couldn't escape it I guess, but since I'm the only one without any real talent, I act." She laughed lightly.

"According to Tony, you're a famous soap star."

"If I were famous, even *you* would know about me."

"Even *I*?" He smiled back, disarmed by her humility. If it was all a facade, she was a better actor than he'd realized.

"Tony tells me you eat, drink and sleep racing. No women, no alcohol, no distractions. Which probably means you haven't watched television in years."

His smile broadened. "You're right. I haven't."

"Except maybe a special on racing."

"Or the coach's videos on our team's performance to point out our weaknesses," he said wryly.

"You see?" she said. "It only makes sense that you wouldn't know I'm really a two-bit actor playing the part of an outrageous fire-breathing attorney. But they put me in a car crash and now I'm in a coma, so I could come and be with Tony."

Zach chuckled.

"That's what happens when your parents have

clout,'' she confessed. ''Of course, it's a secret—about the accident and coma, I mean—so please don't tell anyone. The viewers won't know it happened for a couple of months because everything's shot so far ahead.''

''And so when you return to the set...''

''Yes. I'll have miraculously come out of the coma.''

His chuckle turned into laughter. Maybe it was contagious, because her face broke out in a full unguarded smile. Zach felt his pulse leap.

''They would have put me in a coma earlier so I could fly over for the Tour of Luxembourg race a while back. But Tony told me not to...'' She halted in midsentence again. A habit of hers. ''Anyway, it doesn't matter, because I'm here now and anxious to be of support to him.''

Zach turned away. This was all news to him, unless everything she'd told him was a lie. He didn't know what he believed and couldn't figure out why it mattered one way or another.

It had nothing to do with him. Their marital problems were none of his business. What concerned him was that the team be psychologically ready for tomorrow.

In a way he worried that when Tony found out that his wife had come and planned to follow the entire race, it might throw him off.

Zach inhaled sharply. Tony reminded him of a high-strung stallion. The last thing the team needed right now was a display of Tony's volatility. It could affect everyone.

"Tell you what," Zach said. "I'm going to go ask around and find out what's keeping your husband. Make yourself at home. I'll be back in a minute."

"No, please don't bother," she said, and rose to her feet. "I appreciate your willingness to look for him, but he could be anywhere and—"

"I'd like to help," he insisted, realizing that the real reason he didn't want her to leave was that he was enjoying her company. Maybe Klaus had a point when he teased Zach about "all work and no play."

"I know you would. You're very kind. But I'm tired and need to lie down for a while, anyway, so I'll go back to the Beaulieu. When you see him, tell him to phone me. I'm in room eight."

Her determination frustrated Zach in ways he couldn't understand. If it was up to him, he wouldn't let her go. "You're sure?" he asked.

"Yes. Thank you."

Behind her poised demeanor, feigned or not, he sensed resignation mixed with a certain degree of agitation. She was, in fact, a mass of contradictions. Right now he didn't know what to make of Laura Donetti, let alone his own troubling reaction to her.

As for Tony, the sooner that idiot knew his wife had arrived, the better. Their team manager, Leon, who also doubled as their psychologist, would need to be informed of the new development, as well. He'd definitely want a chat with their number-one boy before the day was out.

Zach preceded her to the door, opened it and stepped into the hall, hoping to warn Tony should he suddenly emerge from the other room with his latest plaything in tow.

To his relief, all was quiet at their end of the dimly lit hall. "Come on. I'll walk you downstairs," he said, thinking he'd run interference on the way if necessary. "Maybe we'll catch sight of another team member who knows where he is."

"Thank you, but I hate putting you out."

He found himself avidly defending his position. "You're not! I need a new pack of razor blades, and now is as good a time as any to get one."

They walked the length of the hall and started down the stairs. "I brought a bunch of them and some shaving gel in case Tony runs out," she said. "They're the kind he swears give his legs the best shave. Before I met him, I had no idea how important it was to remove the hair so the skin could be cooled by perspiration."

"Little details like that make a big difference," Zach concurred.

"If you'll come to the hotel with me, you can have as many packs as you need."

Once again Zach was struck by her natural down-to-earth attitude, which was at total odds with the picture Tony had painted of a selfish man-eating television star in love with her own image.

Unless this was her way of coming on to a man so he didn't know what hit him until it was too late. But in his gut, Zach felt her offer was a hundred-percent genuine. So, until she showed the side that Tony had talked about, he'd reserve the right to think whatever he wanted.

"Well, if Tony endorses them, then who am I to refuse such a generous offer?"

It might be just as well if he escorted her to her hotel. After seeing her to the door, he could go to his brother's room and ring Klaus. If Tony was still there, he could alert him, and if Klaus answered, he could tell him to search for Tony until he found him.

At the second-floor landing she said, "I also brought a sackful of my homemade packets of granola with the little dark-chocolate morsels he loves. You're welcome to some of those, too." A trace of anxiety lurked in her eyes while she was making the offer. *Why?*

"I'd never turn down a gift like that. Something tells me I've miraculously glommed on to Tony's secret weapon. We've all wondered where he suddenly finds the energy to go on when the rest of us are ready to lie down and die."

She actually blushed. "I—I don't know about that, but I do express-mail him a dozen of them before every race."

Zach had had no idea. "Lucky guy," he murmured before he realized the words had escaped his lips.

More than ever Tony's wife was turning out to be the surprise of the season.

"It's just a little something to remember me by when he...I can't be there."

Zach caught the change in pronouns and continued down the next flight of stairs a little ahead of her, puzzled by the large number of conflicting factors in the Donetti marriage.

The minute the crowded lobby came into view, several cameras flashed in succession, briefly robbing him of his vision. If Tony had made an appearance down here, the press would have been all over him, which meant he was still upstairs...

Suddenly Zach heard people pointing out him and Laura. He cursed under his breath and felt her trembling hand on his arm with a sense of wonder. An actor could fake a lot of things, but not nervousness, which in this case appeared to border on panic.

A member of the international press started to approach them. "Mrs. Donetti, Mr. Wilde...how about an interview before tomorrow's race?"

Damn.

"There'll be a team press conference later tonight." Without conscious thought Zach grasped Laura's hand and whispered, "Come on."

She didn't seem to need any urging. In fact, she ran to keep up with his long strides. Once they were out on the street, she let go of his hand but kept up her pace to stay abreast of him.

"Thanks for getting us out of there."

"Sometimes the paparazzi can be a pain."

She shook her head, drawing his attention to the glistening black curls that framed the perfect oval of her face. "I'll never get used to them. Tony always orders me to smile and says I should tell them what they want to hear. I suppose it's the only way to survive, but I'm afraid it's not me, if you know what I mean."

Zach knew only too well, but she'd surprised him once again. Apparently she was as violently opposed to unsolicited publicity as he was. More and more he was beginning to feel shame for some of the thoughts he'd harbored about her when she'd announced her presence on the other side of his hotel-room door a little while ago.

Klaus and fellow team member Jean-Luc Vadim, both in their early twenties and unmarried, had laid bets that Tony's wife wouldn't show up at all, or if she did, it would have more to do with *her* need than her husband's, to be in the limelight.

They went so far as to speculate that if she should actually make an appearance in St. Léger for the big day, she would probably be motivated by a money-grubbing publicity agent who could smell a red-hot opportunity. "Soap queen unites with cycling king for Tour de France debut." The stuff that sold newspapers and paid six-digit salaries. Any woman married to Tony Donetti had to know exactly what went on when he wasn't burning up the road winning one big race after another. She obviously didn't give a damn.

How wrong could everyone have been?

The Beaulieu was indeed a madhouse. And the minute they stepped into its crowded foyer, an elderly American woman recognized Laura and ran up to her, thrusting a travel map and pen in her face.

"Please, could I have your autograph? And sign it to Dawn from Margo? I watch your show every day when I'm home. You're my favorite character. I always wanted to be an attorney, but in my day women were expected to stay home. My daughter's taping it for me while we're here...."

When her babbling wound down, Laura smiled and said, "Thank you for the compliment, Dawn." She signed the map quickly along the border, then handed it back to her. "Just between you and me, I'd much rather stay home and be a mother like you've been."

The woman looked stunned, but no more so than Zach, who was again obliged to make some readjustments in his thinking about Tony's wife. He admired her grace and dignity with the autograph seeker. He was sure the intrusion was the last thing she wanted or needed.

"You handled that like a pro," he said as they started up the stairs.

"It's easy enough to sign something. Much harder to speak in front of a microphone when you know someone will twist your words and take everything out of context."

"Amen."

When they reached the next floor, she hurried to a door down the corridor and pulled out her key to open it. "Come in. I'll get those things I promised."

Zach had a better idea. "While you do that, I'm going to step across the hall to my brother's room. If they're in, I'd like to introduce you."

She flashed a grateful smile. "That would be nice, Zach. Then, I'll see you in a minute."

With a nod, he turned away and headed for room number ten. *I don't know the whole story yet, Tony,* he thought. *But there's one thing I'd stake my life on— you don't deserve your wife!*

There was no response to his knock. Zach let himself into the empty room with the spare key Richard had given him. He'd have to make introductions later.

After a quick scan of the directory for the number of the Metropole, he dialed the hotel and asked for Klaus's room. He waited a few minutes and was told no one had answered.

Tony was probably still in there and didn't want to be disturbed.

Frustrated, Zach instructed the concierge to ring the team manager's room. Rather than try to hunt Tony down, he would explain the situation to Leon and let *him* shoulder the potential crisis. This one was a beaut. But everyone on the team had a job, and problems were what Leon was getting paid to solve.

A minute later Zach was connected with him. When he told him the situation—that Laura was looking for Tony, who was probably in Klaus's room with some groupie—Leon let loose a stream of invective against Tony and his stupidity. As soon as he'd calmed down, he told Zach he'd get right on it, then hung up.

Zach wrote a note to his brother telling him that Tony's wife was just across the hall and could probably benefit from some company. Then he went out of the room and locked it.

Laura had left the door to her room ajar. Zach gave a couple of raps to announce himself, then entered. She lifted her head and seemed to study him, as if she was seeing him for the first time.

"Hi," she said in a soft voice that sounded somewhat timid. Then, apparently realizing he'd caught her looking at him rather intently, she averted her gaze almost guiltily.

"Hi, yourself. I'm sorry—it looks like my brother's family is out, but there'll be another opportunity to introduce you later tonight."

She paused in the process of unpacking her suitcase, the only one he could see anywhere in the tidy room. Bev had brought several, much to Richard's chagrin. Between the kids and all the paraphernalia, their hotel room looked like a tornado had blown through.

"I'm sure there will. Here you go." She handed him a plastic bag.

He glanced inside. She'd wrapped each granola-and-chocolate square in plastic wrap.

"Mind if I try one now?" he asked.

"If you'd like." Her voice kind of wobbled.

"I *would* like," he said, aware of an odd lack of

confidence in her tone. Every time she opened her mouth, he heard or felt something unexpected.

"Uh-uh-uh-uh," said a familiar male voice. "I was under the impression that those particular treats were meant only for me, darling."

CHAPTER TWO

ZACH WATCHED her face pale as a sun-bronzed Tony breezed through the open door smiling his dashing smile. She appeared anything but happy to see him, which seemed a bit strange, considering she'd been looking for him.

As for Zach, he felt a disgust that bordered on anger. Tony had presented such a false picture of his wife! It prompted Zach to retaliate. To hell with the kid gloves.

"Sorry, old man," he said. "But your secret is finally out."

Tony, Zach knew, had let his pro status go to his head, and he enjoyed dominating the people around him. On more than one occasion Zach had seen him use intimidation to get what he wanted. But it had never worked on Zach, and certainly not now that certain things had come to light.

Without any compunction at all, Zach removed a snack, undid the wrapper and popped the whole bar into his mouth. Laura looked apprehensive, which made him wonder what kind of treatment Tony subjected her to. All the more reason for him, Zach, to want to champion her cause.

With great relish, he reached into the bag for another bar and took a bite. He'd wait and see if his teammate turned nasty. Tony was known for his rapid mood swings.

Unable to resist baiting him, Zach asked, "How come you never told us what a great cook your wife is?"

Tony *was* angry now. "Because I didn't think it was anybody else's damn business!" he fired back.

"Well, it's my business now." Zach flashed her a warm smile. "These are delicious, Laura. I'm saving the rest for the race. Thank you. For the blades and gel, too."

"You're welcome."

She'd barely said the words before her husband's arm went around her shoulders, pulling her close. But Zach could see it was anything but a loving gesture, and the anxious expression on her face spoke volumes.

"Why didn't you tell me you were flying over?" he heard Tony mutter as he brushed her temple with his lips.

"As soon as I was given a leave of absence from the set, I tried phoning you from home, but I couldn't get through. Then I phoned from the airport in Brussels and later from the hotel here, but either there was a busy signal or no answer. When I finally went to your room, Zach was there and he wasn't sure where you were."

Tony gave Zach a murderous look. "So what are you doing over *here?*"

You're worried I've spilled the beans, aren't you, Tony? You should be worried.

Laura must have picked up on her husband's anger because she broke in with, "He needed some blades, and he wanted to introduce me to his family."

"That's right," Zach concurred, munching on the last bite of granola. The bar really was exceptionally tasty. "Some of the other guys' families don't speak English that well. I thought maybe Laura would enjoy Bev's company."

Tony ignored Zach and turned to his wife. "How long are you here for?"

"The whole race. I plan to follow you around the circuit."

If the tautness of his expression was anything to go by, Tony wasn't pleased by the news. This was further borne out when Tony said tightly, "We both know you can't be gone from the show that long."

"Haven't you heard the latest?" Zach preempted her response.

Tony swung back to him, his expression irritated. "What are you talking about?"

"They've killed off her character to accommodate you, Tony. You're a fortunate man to have in-laws who'd allow such a drastic change in the script of a nationally televised program so your wife could be here for you. I envy you that kind of support."

There was a tension-filled pause while Tony eyed Zach narrowly. "Then you'll understand that I'd like some time alone with her."

You're running scared, Donetti.

Zach smiled as pleasantly as he knew how. "No one would understand that more than I. The minute I saw Laura at the door, I realized I'd be minus my roommate tonight. I was just going to say that I'll go back to the hotel and bring all your gear over here so you don't have to spend a single minute away from her." He paused, then added, "I know that if my wife had just arrived, I'd put a Do Not Disturb sign on the door until further notice."

Laura started shaking her head. He caught a pleading look in her eyes that begged him not to taunt Tony any further. "Th-that's very kind of you, Zach, but—"

"No buts. That's what friends are for, right, Tony?" Zach was enjoying this once-in-a-lifetime moment. Tony couldn't make even a token response, because he was well and truly trapped.

Now that his legally wedded wife had shown up, the sleeping arrangements he'd made with his various girlfriends around the circuit would have to be called off for the duration of the Tour de France. With Laura driving a support car for the whole world to see, the Donetti marriage would look to be on solid ground, and the Ziff team would be spared any negative press.

"I'll be back in a little while." As Zach turned to leave, he was aware of the dangerous glitter in Tony's eyes. He felt sorry for Laura, yet for reasons of her own, she still clung to the marriage. But he had a strong suspicion she was just barely holding on.

What really troubled him, though, was why he cared so much.

THE SECOND Zach had disappeared out the door, Tony relinquished his hold of Laura and flung himself into the nearest chair. He stared up at her through hooded eyes. She gazed back dispassionately.

Her husband was definitely good-looking, she thought, with his dark hair and deep tan, attractive enough to play a lead role in a daytime soap. The running shorts and tank top he wore now revealed his superbly fit condition, and she couldn't blame any woman for wanting to be the object of his attention.

In the beginning she'd been blinded by her attraction to him; but it soon wore off when she discovered that beneath the surface, he didn't have the depth of character she'd naively attributed to him. They'd met at a cycling event in California. He'd been attending college at the time and had led Laura to believe he wanted to go to law school. He'd been a different person back then. Raised by his aunt and uncle, who had six children of their own and lived on a very modest income, he'd appeared to be a man who valued family and loved kids. He'd been especially attentive to Laura's two nieces.

He'd fit in so well, in fact, with her own relatives and friends, she'd assumed they would eventually enjoy a solid traditional marriage, that his hobby would take a back seat to the more important role of finishing school and settling down to a career and family.

But after they'd been married only a few months Laura realized that there was always one more race he wanted to win. Little by little the amateur competitions separated him from her and his family. At the end of their first year of marriage, Tony turned pro and admitted that he'd been training for the Tour de France for years. For the past four, he'd been winning important races, stacking up world-ranking cycling points. She no longer knew who he was.

Right now she was somewhat repulsed by him. He smelled strongly of mouthwash. She didn't even want to think what he'd been doing before Zach had accomplished the miracle that had unearthed her husband from wherever. From *whomever*.

"I can't figure out why you came, Laura. You hate what I do, so why did you bother?"

Probably nothing would suit his purposes better if she *hadn't* come to watch him compete in the most important race of his career to date. Then he could lie to himself and everyone around that his wife didn't care about him or their marriage. By placing the blame squarely on her shoulders, he could exonerate himself from all guilt and entrench himself in the life-style she so abhorred.

She sat calmly on the edge of a small love seat, needing to choose her words carefully. For the first time in years maybe, he seemed prepared to have the kind of long serious talk she'd been hoping for.

Ironically the timing couldn't be worse for him.

"Whether you believe it or not, I'm very proud of

your racing accomplishments. Here.'' She reached into a bag next to the love seat and handed him the gift she'd made for him.

''What's this?''

''A scrapbook of all your triumphs.'' The leatherette binder was thick with newspaper articles and photographs from magazines. He leafed through it, but she couldn't tell if it brought him pleasure or not.

''You're an athlete's athlete,'' she said. ''Only a handful of men in the entire world have the talent to win the Tour de France. I'm married to one of them.''

For once he didn't have a ready retort. His silence gave her the impetus to go on.

''Tony…we've never talked about this before, but I'm not unaware that deep down inside you, there's a void—because your own parents aren't here today to see you ride to victory.''

His head flew back in surprise.

''I know it hurts that your uncle George and aunt Ann have never shown up at one of your races. I bet you're thinking that if they really loved you, they would've found a way to come up with the money to see this one.''

''I don't want to talk about them.''

Laura had an idea that his aunt and uncle, seeing Tony's neglect of her, had probably been instrumental in getting him to come home for that short visit five weeks ago.

But as awful as those two days had been, they proved to Laura that Tony wanted out of their marriage. Unfortunately he would never be honest enough with himself or with her to ask for a divorce. He'd also been brought up a Catholic, and while his religion meant little to him, his aunt and uncle were quite devout. It was unlikely he'd want to risk their disapproval. So, what with all that, he hoped *she'd* be the one who forced the issue, which would then free him from all ties and blame. For the past few years he'd become an expert at twisting situations. More often than not she ended up feeling like the culprit.

Surely you understand we can't have a baby right now. Come on. How many men get the chance of a lifetime to really make it big? I have the talent, Laura, and I'm going all the way to the top. We'll talk about starting a family later.

Many times throughout their six-year marriage he'd thrown that argument in her face. Yet never once had he considered that her desire to be a mother might be every bit as important; nor would he have given a thought to the ticking of her biological clock.

If he'd hoped, five weeks ago, that in reasserting his position about this not being the time to start a family she would finally get the point and stop harassing him about it, then he'd succeeded. In fact, he'd written the death sentence of their marriage.

But right now nothing was as important as the race tomorrow. She pulled a second scrapbook from the bag. "Here. Take a look at this." She extended it to him, but he didn't make a move to reach for it. She dropped her arm.

"I went over to see your aunt and uncle before I flew here. Ann was there alone and we had a long talk. I told her I could easily afford to bring the whole family to Europe if they wanted to watch the race."

He rubbed the bridge of his nose. "I can just imagine how that went over."

She shook her head. "Do you know what she told me? Money has never had anything to do with their decision to stay away from your races."

"Tell me something I don't know." The bitterness of his tone broke her heart. "I'm not their kid and was never wanted. I've always realized that."

"Wrong, Tony. They've always loved you. No, that's not the reason for their lack of support." She felt like a parent dealing with a recalcitrant child.

He glared at her. "And you're going to tell me what it is, are you?"

"If you'll just look through this—she tapped the scrapbook—you'll understand a lot of things. I only wish it hadn't taken my going over there and pleading with Ann for an explanation to finally get an answer."

He let out an expletive. "What is it? Another scrapbook?"

"Yes. It's your father's."

Tony looked stunned.

"I want you to know," Laura went on, "that your aunt would have given it to you years ago, but your uncle wouldn't let her. However, she and I both agreed it was long past due for you to have it, so she let me bring it to you."

As Laura had hoped, he shed that armor of belligerent indifference and got to his feet in one lithe movement. He looked pale beneath his tan.

She stood up, as well, and handed it to him. "Consider it a gift from beyond the grave. I hope it inspires you to find that secret weapon of yours that Zach was talking about."

"What secret weapon?" he demanded.

"He said that when the rest of them are ready to quit, you always find the necessary energy to perform the impossible."

She wasn't sure why his eyes slid away from hers so quickly. She'd hoped to ease the antagonism he seemed to feel toward his roommate. She tried again.

"Zach says you're a champion of champions and he's dedicated to helping you win."

As far as Laura was concerned, *Zach* was a champion of champions for bowing to Tony's expertise and working for the good of the whole team rather than only himself. Tony would never do the same thing if their positions were reversed.

"Take a look at those pictures, Tony."

After eyeing her skeptically, he opened the cover. As he thumbed through it, she watched the expression on his face change to amazement.

On the flight to Europe, she'd memorized every page of the book. At an early age, Tony's father, Carl Donetti, had been the best swimmer at his neighborhood pool. Six years older than his brother, George, he excelled in almost every swimming event throughout his years in public school. From there he went on to regional and national meets. In time he made it to the U.S. Olympic swim-team trials. But that was where the scrapbook entries stopped.

When she heard her husband groan, she said, "Your father was a remarkable athlete. Now we know where you get your fantastic athletic ability. In some of the pictures, you and your father look so much alike I can't tell the difference."

Tony's eyes were suspiciously bright. "Why didn't Uncle George ever let me see this?"

She could hear raw anger in his voice, and took a deep breath before continuing, "Your aunt told me that your dad didn't make the Olympic team, and he couldn't get over the failure. Your uncle watched him beat himself up and felt powerless to help him—except by being your dad's greatest fan and never missing a meet, no matter where it was. He worshiped your dad. When your parents were killed in that freeway collision, the only thing that helped George to go on living was to take care of his brother's baby boy and raise him."

Tony's hands curled into fists. "He should have told me."

"Apparently when you started to show an interest in cycling so early in life and could beat everyone on the block, George saw history repeating itself. The pain of what he'd lived through with your dad was too great.

"That's why he moved the family from Thousand

Oaks to Pasadena. He hoped to thwart you by separating you from your cycling friends. He prayed you'd finally lose interest. Instead, you seemed more determined than ever. He knew the Tour de France was your dream, but he couldn't bear to watch you go through all the stages on the way up, only to lose out in the end.''

"But I'm going to win!'' Tony vowed with a fierceness Laura had never heard in his voice before. "Pictures of me holding up the winner's cup are going to be in *my* scrapbook.''

As she'd hoped, the scrapbook she'd brought had focused her husband like nothing else could have. Temporarily, at least, he'd forgotten to be angry with her.

"I *know* you're going to win, Tony. That's why I'm here, why I brought these books with me. They'll bring you luck. No one has worked harder and longer than you have. No one deserves to win more. But just remember that when you pop the cork on that bottle of champagne on the Champs-Elysées, it will be a victory for your dad and your uncle, too.''

His glazed eyes met hers briefly and he nodded, but his thoughts were obviously on that triumphant moment.

"I have every confidence that when you return to Pasadena wearing the yellow jersey, you'll make a new man of George, and he'll be the one pushing you all the way to the Olympics.''

The fire of competition ignited Tony. "That's where

I'm going, Laura. All the way. History isn't going to repeat itself this time, because unlike my dad, I'm going to make those trials!''

''I know you will.''

I'm counting on it. After you've won, you'll be so high our divorce will go through without recriminations.

He dropped the scrapbooks on the table. ''I've got to go talk to the coach.''

Laura felt relief. She couldn't imagine anything worse than being closeted with Tony this close to the race. His restlessness made him difficult to be around at the best of times, but when he was filled with new purpose, there was no holding him.

''Zach said there was supposed to be a press conference later.''

Tony paused midway to the door. ''He's right. There's one scheduled at the Metropole tonight.''

''Do you want me to come over for that?''

''No. I'm going to get it canceled. I've got some new strategies to work out with the team and I'll be late before I get back here. Don't wait up for me.''

He bussed her on the cheek and started for the door. His single-mindedness also made him forgetful.

''Tony?''

He paused in the doorway.

''Take the key. I won't need it.'' She tossed it to him, watched it make a graceful arc and land in his hand.

He flashed her a trouble-free smile, the sort she

rarely saw anymore, then left the room. She said a little prayer of thanks that Ann had finally broken down and told her about Tony's father. The scrapbooks and the knowledge that his family loved him had now become her husband's *other* secret weapon. They would give him that needed edge.

Content that her gifts had produced the desired results, she locked the door behind him and headed for the bathroom. Within minutes she'd taken a shower and had put on a nightgown and robe, wanting nothing more than to lie down.

Dealing with Tony was an exhausting experience. Coupled with travel fatigue, it meant she needed at least twelve hours of uninterrupted sleep so she could be ready for the time trials tomorrow.

No sooner had she turned down the covers than she heard a rap on the door. Who…? It wouldn't be Tony because he had the key. Then she remembered that Zach had been going to come back with Tony's things.

"Just a minute!" she called, and padded to the door.

"Hi again," he murmured as she opened it, a smile curving his wide attractive mouth. His arms were loaded.

Despite her fatigue, clearing the air with Tony must have sharpened her ability to concentrate, because she couldn't stop staring at Zach. As she'd noted earlier, he was taller than her husband, with a larger build and quite a spectacular physique. He didn't resemble a lot of the bikers who, in the main, were small in stature.

In fact, while he wore nineties sportswear and kept

his hair cropped very short—no doubt to help give him minimum wind resistance when he cycled—Zach was a different type altogether. His big well-toned body could make a woman feel incredibly safe, protected. And with his dark blond hair and silvery eyes, she could be forgiven for thinking he had Norse blood running through his veins.

"C-come in," she stammered, suddenly embarrassed. He must have noticed her staring. "You shouldn't have bothered to bring Tony's things over, you know. Tony could have done that later."

He put the bags and paper sacks he was carrying on the floor next to the dresser, then turned to her. "It was no bother. He came back to the room before I left. Apparently there's been a change in our plans tonight and we're meeting with the coach. Tony's all fired up to win those time trials tomorrow."

She nodded. "He told me he was going to cancel the press interview."

"That was music to my ears," he said in his deep vibrant voice. "I'd say the arrival of his wife is just what the doctor ordered."

Laura looked away. "What do you mean?"

"He's a changed boy from an hour ago."

You're right, Zach. He's a boy. A very difficult one at that. But then, Zach, probably more than anyone besides herself, knew the dark side of Tony—his moodiness and compulsive habits. He'd been forced to room with him the past few months, and it couldn't have been easy. She found herself feeling a good deal of sympathy for Zach; he'd probably been subjected to the worst rather than the best of her husband.

Another part of her cringed, because she was certain Tony had made up a lot of half-truths and outright lies about her and their marriage. Long before they'd met today, Zach would have formed his own opinions about her and Tony, none of them good.

It would take an incredibly mature person to deal with Tony's confidences and temperament, and still have any respect for him. Maybe if she told Zach about the scrapbooks, he'd understand Tony a little better and not judge him too harshly.

Moving over to the table, she picked up the books and handed them to him. "These are what made the difference. I hope they bring your whole team luck."

Zach sat down on a chair at the table with Laura seated opposite him. As he leafed through the pages, she proceeded to tell him everything.

"I know Tony can be difficult," she finished. "Obviously he never felt accepted, never mind loved, by his aunt and uncle. That's why he's always had this drive to prove himself. But when he heard that his own father was close to being Olympic material, I think it gave him the sense of identity he's been looking for."

Zach closed both albums and looked up at her, his expression solemn. "You gave him a priceless gift today. He's not the same person who walked in here earlier. Not so...fragmented."

Fragmented. That was the perfect word to describe

Tony. Zach understood things much more than she'd realized.

"I hope he thanked you for them," Zach said.

She moved her head, neither a confirmation or a denial.

"Even if he didn't," Zach went on, his gaze missing nothing, "on behalf of the team, I thank you for doing something for him no else could have done. It's just possible that in turning Tony around, our team has a real shot at the championship. I've said it before and I'll say it again—He's a lucky guy."

She was touched by his kindness. "I think Tony has been very blessed to have had you for a roommate. In case he hasn't thanked *you* yet, then let me say it for him. Thank you."

Again their gazes met in quiet understanding.

"Laura?" he said softly.

She swallowed hard. "Yes?"

"Do you mind if I call you that?"

"I'd prefer it."

"Have you ever driven a support car for your husband?"

"No."

Zach appeared to be pondering something vital. "Would you be interested in driving the circuit with my brother, Richard? He's done it for me many times, but he's going to have to go it alone this time because Bev says she can't take the pressure.

"I know he'd welcome your company. Because you both have a vested interest in me and Tony, I think you two would be good for each other, and definitely good for the team as a whole.''

She blinked. "You're kidding!" His suggestion flooded her with warmth.

"No." He rose to his feet, and she had to look up at him. "I'm being earnest. Following us around can be very grueling. It's nice to know there's another person to rely on. You two could spell each other and use each other for a sounding board. Richard's a great talker. It's hard on him when he doesn't have anyone around to listen."

She ran a shaky hand through her curls. Lately she'd been tired a lot, and nauseated. The opportunity to be able to share the work with someone, not have to do the whole circuit alone, was a godsend.

"He...he might not want to ride with me."

"Actually I've already talked to him about it. I was over in his room just before I came here. He couldn't be happier with the idea and is anxious to meet you. So, what do you say?"

Her gaze swiveled to his once more. *You're such a good man, Zach Wilde. A remarkable man.*

"To be honest—" her voice trembled "—it's like an answer to a prayer." She paused. "It seems all I ever do is thank you."

Something flickered in his eyes. "I think all our prayers were answered when you showed up today."

His remark produced a small smile. "Are you certain your sister-in-law won't mind?"

He smiled back. "She's the one who begged Richard to say yes. Actually it will relieve her of a lot of guilt.''

''Guilt?''

''She wants to help, but I guess she's been to too many of my races and can't take the suspense. To know someone else is there to assist Richard takes a huge load off her mind.'' Now it was his turn to pause. ''If there's anything I'm worried about, it's Tony's reaction.''

She shook her head. ''He'll be relieved I'm driving with someone who's experienced at this sort of thing. I'm afraid he still believes a man is better behind the wheel of a car.''

He smiled. ''Good. Then it's settled. Tony told me you're in for the night, so I've suggested to Richard that the two of you meet tomorrow morning at seven-thirty. We'll all have breakfast in the dining room downstairs.''

''That would be perfect,'' she said.

He studied her for a moment. ''You look a little pale. Are you feeling all right?''

''I'm tired, I confess, but it's jet lag. A good night's sleep will work wonders.''

''You probably need to eat, too.'' He gestured at the paper sacks he'd brought. ''You'll find some cheese, French bread and grape juice in those.''

''Zach…''

''Uh-huh?''

''You're not some kind of guardian angel sent down

here just for me, are you? Should I touch you to see
if you're real?''

She did just that, reaching out and grasping his forearm. It was hard and warm. She quickly removed her
fingers and stepped back.

He smiled again. ''As you've discovered, I'm quite
real and nothing out of the ordinary. Only a teammate
of your husband's who's very thankful you arrived in
time to give Tony the best shot at the title.''

She wrapped her arms around her waist. ''You're
not ordinary at all, you know. Most men would want
the glory for themselves.''

His smile faded. She couldn't fathom it.

''I'm not here for the same reasons as Tony is, and
I know my limitations.'' He headed for the door. ''I'll
see you in the morning.'' In the space of a heartbeat
he'd changed into someone unapproachable and remote.

Laura had the strongest urge to run after him as he
let himself out to ask him what those reasons were.
But she didn't dare. He'd closed up on her. Maybe the
day would come when there'd be enough trust between them that she could ask.

*And maybe you've come down with a full-scale flu,
Laura. Zach Wilde is nothing to you. He can't be!*

CHAPTER THREE

FOR ZACH TO AWAKE to an empty hotel room was not an unusual experience. Over the past few months Tony had slept elsewhere and it had never mattered.

The knowledge that he slept in his wife's bed last night shouldn't have made the slightest difference. In fact, if anything, Zach should have been relieved that for once Tony was exactly where he should be.

Cursing because he'd cut himself twice while shaving, Zach left the bathroom only to stub his big toe on the doorjamb. Then he decided to phone Richard at the Metropole to make sure he was up and ready. All he succeeded in doing was waking Bev, who was still in bed. She muttered something about her husband having gone downstairs already. After apologizing for disturbing her, Zach hung up, his state of mind a mix of self-loathing and befuddlement.

For a moment he was tempted to ring the room across the hall from his brother. But the picture of Tony in bed with his wife filled him with such distaste he squelched the impulse.

You're a mess, Wilde.

Today was the beginning of the race, yet he couldn't get another man's wife out of his mind. His skin still burned where she'd grasped his arm last night. He'd wanted to cover her hand and keep it there. *Be honest. You wanted to feel her hands on you, her mouth beneath yours.*

Donning his sweats, he left the room and headed out of the hotel for the Beaulieu. The minute he stepped outdoors, he could smell rain in the air. He looked up at the sky. The heavy cloud cover didn't bode well for the time trials, which were scheduled to start at noon and would probably go on until well into the evening.

Even at seven-thirty in the morning, the normally quiet streets were alive with activity. It didn't surprise him, not when it was estimated that at least 350,000 people from all over Europe and America had descended on St. Léger to watch the start of the race.

To avoid members of the press, he sprinted around the corner, making it difficult for anyone to pursue him with a TV camera in hand. But he couldn't escape the newsmen completely. One was waiting for him as he entered the crowded dining room of the Beaulieu.

"Here's Zachary Wilde, the Newport Beach American dark horse who was out of the racing circuit for a time, only to come back and win an impressive number of European championships, earning him the title King of the Mountain. So, Mr. Wilde, who do you think will be the first five finishers in the first stage tomorrow?"

Zach could see Richard waving to him from a corner table. No sign of Laura yet. When she did show, she'd be forced to run the media gauntlet, too.

"Donetti, of course, and Farramundi or Poletti of the Italian team, possibly Glatz or Richter of the German team. Vadim maybe."

"I notice you don't put yourself among the top contenders of your own team."

"The sprints are Donetti's long suit. Vadim does well on the flats."

"Do you estimate anyone setting records today?"

"No. The rain will slow everyone down. Now if you'll excuse me..." He shouldered his way through the crush of interested spectators listening to the interview and strode toward his brother.

Richard was only two years older, and when he was seated, many people mistook him for Zach. But in fact, Richard was three inches shorter, and his eyes were blue not gray.

Richard was an excellent swimmer and diver, and over the years he'd shared a love of sailing with Zach. These days, however, his responsibilities as a husband and father to three children, plus the growing outdoor-sign business, which was a Wilde-family enterprise, prevented him from indulging in much sporting activity.

When Richard did have free time, he'd given it to his brother. Zach knew he'd never be able to repay him for all the emotional and physical support he'd provided over the years, the unqualified unstinting love, the steady encouragement—and faith that one day Zach would find ultimate fulfillment with the right woman, despite his thus far poor track record.

At his approach, Richard got up and gave him a hug. "This is your big day, brother. How are you feeling?"

They sat down opposite each other. "Pretty good."

Richard broke off the end of a fresh baguette and handed the rest to Zach, who refused it. He eyed him speculatively. "You could have fooled me. What's eating you?"

"What do you mean?"

"How come you're not hungry?"

"I had a bagel in the room."

"You've nicked up your face."

Richard didn't miss much. Zach rubbed his jaw where he'd been careless with the razor. "Prerace jitters," he lied.

"Come on, Zach. It's *me* you're talking to here. What gives?"

Avoiding his brother's probing stare, he murmured, "I guess the team's holding its breath wondering if Tony's still as focused as he seemed last night."

"Well, he passed through the foyer about ten minutes ago. From the looks of it, he appeared more rested, relaxed and confident than I've ever seen him. He chatted amiably with the TV people, then left. I would say it's the best of signs."

The news should have pleased Zach, but instead, he suddenly felt acutely out of sorts and shoved himself away from the table.

"Hey!"

Zach ignored his brother's protest and got to his feet, glancing at his watch. "It's quarter to eight. I'm going to go see what's keeping Laura."

Richard squinted up at him. Zach didn't like it when he looked at him like that, as if he could see right through him.

"I've got time to kill, Zach. If she just flew in yesterday, then she's suffering jet lag. Give the poor woman a break. Why don't you take off and meet up with your team? If she doesn't come down in a little while, I'll go upstairs and introduce myself."

His brother's suggestion made perfect sense, but Zach wouldn't rest until he'd talked to Laura and found out for himself that she was all right. Tony, he knew, could be an insensitive swine when he felt like it. Yesterday he'd gotten an inkling of Tony's cruelty to her. It had accounted, in all probability, for his restless night.

"No. You stay here and enjoy your breakfast. I'll be right back."

"Have it your way. I'll be waiting."

"Thanks."

Zach gave his brother's shoulder a squeeze, then dodged the crowd and bounded up the foyer stairs two at a time to her floor. No sooner had he reached her door intending to knock, when it opened.

"Oh! Zach!" she said breathlessly, and clung to the doorknob for support. Dressed in a casual pink-and-white-striped top and skirt, she looked good.

Be honest, Wilde. She looks a lot better than good.

"Sorry to have startled you." He smiled. "Good morning, Laura."

"Good morning." She put a well-manicured hand to her throat, a sign of nervousness. "I'm afraid I'm the one who should apologize for keeping you and your brother waiting. Bed felt so wonderful I couldn't bear to get up, but I'm ready now." A faint but enticing flowery fragrance clung to her.

Zach took a deep breath. "I just dropped by to make sure you're all right, and to say that it's fine with us if you want to meet later—you know, if you're still feeling jet-lagged...."

I should have phoned her first. Why in hell didn't I?

"No, no. I wouldn't dream of putting you out more than I already have."

She pulled the door closed behind her and walked down the hall with him. A strange tension hung between them that prevented him from making desultory conversation. Not until they reached the bright lights of the dining room did he notice her pallor and the faint smudges beneath her eyes. Tell-tale signs that all was not well. He supposed crying could have produced them, but then again, so could illness. Either would account for her not being on time for breakfast. Until he knew the truth, it would gnaw at him.

Even if you knew the truth, what is it to you, Wilde?

The minute Richard saw them, he rose from the

table, smiled and extended a hand as they drew close. Zach saw the admiration in his brother's eyes. In fact, he saw the same damn admiration in the eyes of every man in the room.

"I've been looking forward to meeting you for more reasons than one, Laura. My wife is hooked on your soap."

"That's nice to hear, Richard." She laughed gently and shook his hand. "Glad someone in the Wilde family watches TV. Until yesterday, Zach had never heard of the show I'm in, let alone seen it! Anyway, it *is* how I pay the rent."

Zach found himself wondering how much of her paycheck had gone to fund Tony before he'd turned pro and could rely on financial backing from other sources.

Richard's smile broadened. Zach could tell his brother was already captivated. "Now that I've met you, I'm going to have to give work a miss so I can watch an episode or two myself! You're awfully easy on the eyes, if you know what I mean. Just don't tell my wife, Bev, I said that or I'm in serious trouble."

She laughed again. "Your secret is safe with me."

Well, Zach thought, no need for formal introductions here. Their easy camaraderie should have relieved him, but instead, he felt excluded. For no apparent reason everything was irritating the hell out of him this morning. Maybe he *was* having prerace jitters.

"Why don't we all sit down?" He pulled out a chair for her.

"Thank you," she murmured, darting Zach an appreciative glance.

He gave her an answering nod and sat down next to her. "What would you like to eat? I'll call the waiter over."

"Some tea would be nice."

"Nothing else?" Zach asked, realizing it was none of his business what she ate or drank.

"No. I'm afraid I'm too nervous to eat anything."

"Nerves make me *over*eat," Richard said. "I'm starting to get a pot—unlike my little brother."

"Cycling burns every calorie," Zach heard her respond as he gave the waiter her order.

Richard grinned. "Well, I hope you don't mind if I snack while we're driving around in the van. My wife, Bev, bought me enough sweets to last the entire tour."

"That makes me feel better, since I've brought along a rather large assortment of crackers and ginger ale myself."

"You're not pregnant, are you? When Bev's expecting, crackers and soft drinks are her staple diet for the first trimester." He chuckled. "Hey, I'm just kidding." Richard kept up his lively banter, but Laura's lack of response had made Zach feel like someone had just kicked him in the gut.

"How many children do you have, Richard?"

"Three."

"I'd love to meet them."

"You're going to meet the whole family when we drive Tony and Zach over to the stadium for the beginning of the time trials."

"I think I'd better warn both of you now that today will probably be the hardest driving you'll do," Zach inserted, still disturbed by his brother's innocent remark.

Richard was no one's fool and had lived through three pregnancies with Bev. In fact, twice Richard had known Bev was pregnant before *she* did. Zach supposed it was possible Laura was pregnant but didn't want anyone to know about it yet. She was a private person, he'd sensed, and the last thing she would want was for the press to get hold of the news.

Being pregnant could certainly account for her symptoms.

It could also account for the reason she still clings to their marriage.

Maybe the scrapbooks weren't the only gift she'd presented to Tony last night. Perhaps knowing he was going to be a father was the real cause of his good mood after dinner while he'd briefed the team on his new strategies. And it could explain why Richard thought Tony looked so at peace this morning.

A dark thought entered his mind. If she *was* pregnant, how long would the reformed Tony's glow last before he became bored with the whole process of child rearing and resumed his old habits?

Zach's younger brother, Mike, was a new father. It took a tremendous amount of time and work, a huge commitment. Somehow Zach couldn't see Tony in the role, especially not with the Olympics foremost in his mind.

Already Tony was talking about forming a professional cycling "dream team" that would include a triumphant Tony and Farramundi among the select group. Zach wagered that Tony would be a worse absentee father than he'd been an absentee husband. His wife deserved better.

Of course he could be wrong and she wasn't pregnant. Maybe he was getting way ahead of himself. *Maybe you're cracking up, Wilde*.

"I'll tell you what," he said, cutting in on their conversation and rising to his feet. "While you two finish getting acquainted, I'm going to see about some last-minute details and instruct the garage to bring the van around in front of the hotel at eleven-thirty. We'll load up then."

Richard flashed him a puzzled look. "Sounds like a good plan."

"I'll be by your room about eleven-twenty, Laura. If Tony's been held up, I'll bring your things down to the van."

She shook her head and said hesitantly, "I—I appreciate that Zach, but I don't think it'll be necessary."

Still, you don't know for sure, do you? He stared her down till she looked away.

"Talk to you both later," he said.

He left the dining room and then the hotel at a walk,

but broke into a run the moment he hit the street. People seeing him would assume he was giving himself a workout. In a sense he was, but not for the reasons they thought....

"BEV, HONEY?"

"Oh—you're back!" She didn't look up from the suitcase in which she was fiddling madly. If he didn't know better, he would think she was hiding something from him. "The children are in the other room getting dressed. We plan to do a little sight-seeing."

Richard caught his wife around the waist from behind and kissed the nape of her neck where her blond hair fell away. "I'm glad we're alone. We have to talk."

She lifted her head and turned around, instantly alert to that tone in his voice. "What's wrong? Is Zach ill or something?" Her anxious blue eyes searched his.

"Or something."

"Honey—" she cupped his face with her hands and kissed his lips "—stop being mysterious and tell me."

He heaved a sigh. "I wish I knew."

"Is he having second thoughts about the race?"

"To be honest, I don't think his mind is even on cycling."

"What?"

"My little brother is acting very bizarre."

"Since when?"

"Since the moment we came back to the room yesterday and found his note."

"The one asking us to befriend Laura Donetti?"

He nodded.

"Did you meet her? Is she as gorgeous in person as I told you she was on TV?"

"Yes to both questions."

"And?"

"I like her, and I think she'll make a terrific traveling companion."

When nothing else was forthcoming she blurted in exasperation, "Honey, tell me what you're thinking! This is one time I can't read your mind."

He took a deep breath. "I'm thinking that Laura Donetti has happened to my brother."

His wife blinked. "That's impossible!"

"You're right."

"She's married to that heartthrob, Tony Donetti! Zach would never have a thing for a married woman, particularly the wife of a teammate. He wouldn't even consider it."

"You're right."

"He's far too honorable!"

"You're right."

"And furthermore, Zach isn't over Rosie. I'm beginning to wonder if he ever will be."

"You're right about that, too."

"Richard Wilde, stop saying that!"

He grinned and shrugged, then kissed her unsuspecting mouth.

After a moment she pulled away. "Honey?" Astonishing, he thought, how she could ask a loaded question with that one endearment.

"What?"

She frowned. "Richard, you don't really think…" Her voice trailed off.

He decided to relent. Rubbing her arms with his hands, he said, "Tell you what—I'll let you be the judge."

"When?"

"When Zach comes by for us in a little while. The plan is, the Donettis will come in the van with us to the stadium."

"But if we're all together, how will I possibly be able to tell anything?"

"I have no idea."

"Richard…"

WHEN LAURA HEARD the knock on the door, she was having another attack of nausea, worse than the one she'd experienced while Tony was in the shower earlier that morning.

He'd promised to be back by eleven, but over the years she'd learned not to rely on her husband for anything.

Last night she was asleep when he came in, and so had no idea of how late it had been. Around dawn she'd felt him stir. When she asked him how he was feeling, he told her he was ready to take on Superman.

He seemed particularly pleased that one of the members of the favored Italian team would probably draw a fine and even be penalized with a poor starting position. It was because the racer was insisting on wearing red shorts for the prologue when it wasn't the team's officially registered color.

She listened as he told her how he planned to ride the course later in the day, then informed her that he and Klaus had decided to get up early and check it out for any hidden problems.

No doubt they were still out there and had gotten so involved, he'd forgotten his promise. This was one time she could have used his help to run to the local market and get some apples, the only thing that sounded remotely palatable to her.

She glanced at her watch. It was eleven-twenty exactly, which meant Zach Wilde was on the other side of that door. How odd that she'd only met him less than twenty-four hours ago, yet already she knew the man was as good as his word.

Again she experienced an embarrassment that bordered on shame because he knew things about her and her pitiful marriage to Tony she'd rather die than have anyone know.

If she let him in, he'd see that she'd lost her color and was wet with perspiration. He wouldn't leave it alone until he knew the reason why. Instinct told her he was that kind of man.

His brother's chance comment earlier that she could be pregnant had shaken her, particularly since her period was a week late. Of course, she knew that stress and worry could affect her cycle, but the unusual fatigue and nausea were something else again.

The flu was usually accompanied by fever, sore throat, earache—none of which she had.

If Richard were right and Tony had made her pregnant on his last visit home—despite the precautions they'd taken—then it was an accident. She would be one of those statistics that defied all odds.

Under no circumstances could she tell her husband what she suspected.

Until she could get to a pharmacy and give herself a home pregnancy test, this had to remain her secret.

What if she *was* pregnant?

She buried her face in her hands. She would have no choice but to keep it from him. But for how long? *Until I start showing?*

Once Tony found out, he'd tear into her, blame her for ruining his life. She couldn't bear the thought of such an ugly confrontation.

"Laura? Are you in there?" He knocked harder. "Tony's gone on ahead with Klaus."

Well, no surprise there.

She hurried to the door, feeling queasier by the second. "I—I'm here, Zach, but I just got out of the shower," she lied. "Give me a minute after I unlock the door. Everything Tony will need for today's race is right there in the small bag and can be taken down."

If she could buy herself a little time, maybe the nausea would pass and she could prevail on Zach to get some fruit for her without his becoming suspicious.

After she'd dashed into the bathroom, she called out for him to come in, then ran water in the basin and rinsed her face of the perspiration. But still her nausea worsened.

For the longest time she clung to the sink, pretty sure she was going to throw up. The thought of driving to the time trials and being hemmed in by thousands of people made her feel panicky.

Maybe some more ginger ale would help, but she'd have to go into the room, where Zach was, to get it. Besides, she wasn't sure she could walk that far.

Oh, Tony—this is one time I need a husband....

Certain, suddenly, she was about to be sick, she lifted the toilet seat.

"Laura?" Zach called. "Can I do anything for you?"

For the life of her she couldn't answer him.

"Laura?" Now there was alarm in his voice. "Are you all right?"

All at once she lost the bread and cheese she'd consumed earlier, the bread and cheese Zach had been so thoughtful to supply her with.

There was a tap on the bathroom door, then she felt Zach's presence right behind her.

"Good Lord! You *are* sick, just as I thought. What can I do? Tell me!"

Laura had never been so mortified. "I'll be out in a minute," she managed.

He put steadying hands on her shoulders. "Richard was right, wasn't he?" he said, staying right where he was. "You're pregnant."

"I don't see how," she said, mostly to herself. "But if I am, it w-wasn't supposed to happen. Please...you can't tell Tony."

Silence followed, then, "You mean he doesn't know? Doesn't suspect?" Zach sounded incredulous.

"No."

"But surely he'd be thrilled."

"No. Trust me, he wouldn't. I—I'm going to have to find the right time to tell him. Maybe after the Tour de France." She realized that the nausea had made her vulnerable. Now Zach possessed yet another family secret and would be mulling over this latest damning piece of information.

She heard a muttered imprecation before he let go of her with seeming reluctance. "I swear he'll never hear a word from me." His voice was thick with suppressed anger.

Laura went limp in reaction. "Thank you," she whispered.

"Are you through being sick?"

"I think so. At least for the moment."

She wished Zach would go away, but she felt too weak to assert herself. To her amazement, he rinsed out a cloth, then reached down and gently wiped her face and lips. Then he reached for the bottled water on the counter and gave her a moment to rinse her mouth before he put his arm around her waist and helped her out of the bathroom.

She had no idea a man could be this caring and selfless. It was a revelation to her.

When she was settled, he said, "You lie there while I get you what you need. Name it."

Hot tears pricked at her eyes as she looked up at him. "You've done too much already. I feel so guilty, Zach. This is the day you've been living for. I refuse to ruin it for you!"

His eyes had gone a dark pewter. "How could you possibly ruin anything for me? Because of you, Tony's in the best mental shape he's been in all year, and that in turn helps the rest of the team. You're the one we need to concentrate on right now. What can I get for you?"

It was no use arguing with him. "Would it be too much trouble to buy a little fruit—some apples or pears? A roll, maybe?"

"I'm on my way."

"But I'm putting out your entire family!" she cried.

If he'd heard her, she had no way of knowing. He was gone almost before the words left her lips.

From the first moment she'd met him, she'd sensed Zachary Wilde was different from all the other men she knew. After what had just happened, she was convinced there couldn't be too many like him around.

The only information she'd gleaned from Tony, aside from the fact that Zach could beat out just about all their competition on the mountain stretches, was that his California teammate was a confirmed bachelor.

In Laura's mind, a confirmed bachelor was fatally flawed. How could anyone, except perhaps the most selfish of persons, shun marriage, a union that she believed, despite her own unhappy experience, was the ultimate expression of love and intimacy? Yet Zachary Wilde seemed the embodiment of the perfect man and husband.

You're an enigma, Zach. A marvelous unique enigma who'd had the great misfortune of getting involved with the Donettis. Too bad fate had made it impossible for him to wash his hands of her just yet.

CHAPTER FOUR

ALL THE WAY OUT to the van Zach reeled with the knowledge that Laura was probably carrying Tony's baby and was too terrified to tell her husband. If she was this sick already, how in hell was she going to keep from showing it in front of Tony?

Not only did Zach need to get the items she'd requested, he needed some expert advice and thanked providence that Bev was here to talk to. He'd promised Laura he wouldn't say anything to her husband and he wouldn't; but this was an emergency situation that required more than one head to sort out.

Richie, his twelve-year-old nephew and the oldest of Richard's children, was hanging out the back window of the blue van double-parked outside the hotel. When he saw that Zach was alone, he frowned.

"Where is she, Uncle Zach? We wanna get going!"

"Yeah, Uncle Zach," Rachel, their ten-year-old, chimed in. "What's taking so long?"

Robin's voice got mixed up in there, too. She was nine, and Richard called her their little red caboose because she was a strawberry blonde and made up the last of their family.

Richard watched Zach approach through narrowed

eyes. "Is there a problem with Laura?" he asked, too quietly for the others to hear.

Zach nodded. "Tell Bev to come inside with me for a minute."

His brother did a double take before he complied with Zach's wishes.

"I'll be back in a sec, kids," Bev said.

The children moaned as their mother got out of the van and joined Zach. He put his arm around her shoulders and together they walked to the doors of the hotel. He took her aside once they'd reached the empty foyer.

Since the time trials would be starting in another hour, almost everyone had already gone to their spots to view the race. She gazed searchingly at Zach.

"What's wrong?"

"Laura's upstairs throwing up." Bev's eyes rounded in surprise. "She's pretty sure she's pregnant, but she doesn't want anyone to know, least of all her husband. Not yet, anyway. Can you help her out?"

"Actually I think I can." Bev suddenly averted her eyes. "You see…I'm pregnant again."

"What?"

"Yeah." She nodded. "Richard thought Robin was our last but…well, I wanted one more and I'm excited about it. I know he will be, too. I haven't told him yet for fear he wouldn't let me come on this trip.

"So far I've felt better than I usually do. When we get back home, I'll think of a creative way to let him know he's going to be a daddy again. For the last time,'' she added. ''Unless he figures it out before-hand, which he probably will.'' She grinned.

Zach felt a stab of pure envy. Nobody had a better marriage than Richard and Bev.

''Anyway, my obstetrician supplied me with enough Bendectin for a couple of months. It's a new drug for me and it works like a charm. I'll give Laura a box. If she takes a pill tonight, it'll prevent her from being sick in the morning. But for the rest of today, I'm afraid she'll just have to suffer through and try to eat something that'll stay down.''

Zach raked a hand through his hair in amazement. ''She said to bring her back some fruit and rolls.''

''Yeah. That'll help. And some Coke. Celery works for me, too—she might try munching on a stock later. The trick is to eat before the sickness hits. Let's order some food from the dining room and go take care of her.''

Grateful for his sister-in-law, Zach followed Bev's lead. In no time at all they were laden with fruit and rolls and had made their way to the third floor.

When they walked in the door he hadn't locked, Laura was sitting on the side of the bed sipping some gnger ale. She still looked drawn and pale, but her natural beauty was very much in evidence.

''Don't get up,'' he urged. ''Laura Donetti, this is my sister-in-law, Bev Wilde. I had to tell Bev what was going on. You can trust her not to say a word to anyone but Richard, and I trust *him* with my life!''

''It's all right.'' Laura smiled wanly. ''It's nice to

meet you, Bev. I've already met your husband. He's wonderful.''

Bev moved closer to her. "He says the same thing about you. Zach tells me you could be pregnant. So am I! It's a secret I'm keeping from Richard until we fly back to the States.''

"You're kidding,'' Laura said with a giggle.

Thank heaven for you, Bev. Zach thought. *I didn't think it was possible for Laura to smile now, let alone giggle, but you've managed to make both happen.*

"That's why I concocted that business about my nerves not up to taking the drive around the circuit.''

"So *that's* it,'' he murmured.

Bev nodded. "Your race is more important than anything else. Since I knew I'd be a liability if Richard was worried about me, I came up with my master plan to go to Paris and wait with the rest of the family there. Then if I have a few bad days, I can lie around in the hotel room and watch the Tour de France on TV, and he'll be none the wiser.''

Laura gasped. "But if your husband is saddled with me—''

"You're not his wife,'' Bev broke in. "It won't be the same thing at all. Knowing you're pregnant, he'll be distracted just enough to not agonize so much over Zach's performance. Besides, Richard is positively euphoric about driving you around. You know how I can tell?''

Laura eyed Bev in awe and curiosity. Zach was just as curious about the answer.

"He's been very quiet about you. Now I know why. You're absolutely gorgeous and he's already halfway in love with you. Of course he's not going to tell *me* that."

Tony's wife smiled again. Another miracle. Zach felt some of the shackles fall from his body. Bev was the best medicine around, bar none.

"Try a croissant with that drink." She handed Laura the plate.

"Tonight I'll give you a pill to take. If it works for you like it does for me, you'll feel fine in the morning."

Laura shook her head. "I couldn't do that."

"I've got plenty, believe me. And I have another tip, as well. Keep some crackers and juice or soda right by your bed at night and try eating and drinking a little before you lift your head from the pillow in the morning. It stops the sickness from starting and then you're all right for the rest of the day."

"Really?"

"I swear. Just don't tell Richard I gave you the pills."

"My lips are sealed. I'll be indebted to you if I can wake up in the morning and not feel nauseated. Even if I hadn't flown over for the race, I would have had to quit work. It's been awful this past week."

"Now when you go back on the set, you're going to have to be a *pregnant* attorney!"

With a sense of wonder, Zach watched the animation return to Laura's face.

"I suppose both my baby and I could have survived the coma they have me in."

"Coma? And whose baby is it? Cash's or Stone's?"

"Shh, don't tell anyone about the coma. As for the father, I don't know. I slept with both my clients *and* my ex-fiancé."

They chortled merrily. Obviously Laura was starting to feel a little better.

So was he.

"You may have a problem," Bev speculated. "You would probably want an abortion."

"True, but remember, money is what drives me. Silvestro Marchiani has always wanted a baby and none of his wives could have one."

"That's right! You could give him yours for a price, and he could bring it up to head the mob in Sicily."

"I'll let him have it for ten million dollars."

"Oh, you've got to think bigger than that. Make it twenty, and then you can buy out Aurelia's newspaper and get your revenge for her sleeping with your father when you were a little girl and he was in Europe buying horses from the sheikh while your mom was dying in the hospital of that disfiguring disease."

"Perfect!"

That did it for Zach. He burst out laughing.

Both women swung their heads in his direction. Laura's expression turned to horror. "Zach! The time trials!"

"Relax. We've got time to spare. Besides, even if

it *had* made me late, I wouldn't have wanted to miss what I just heard.''

''But you should be over there with the team right now, shouldn't you? Your coach'll have a fit.'' Bev got up from the bed, and Laura followed suit.

Zach studied her upturned face. ''How are you feeling? Honestly.''

She met his gaze without wavering. ''Throwing up helped a lot. I think the croissant I just ate is going to stay down, especially with this drink and apple. I'll bring along an extra supply of everything in case I start to feel really awful again.''

Bev moved toward the door. ''Luckily we'll all be together today, and tonight we can come back here and crash. If worse comes to worst during the trials, we can use the excuse that we're bored and want to do some shopping. Then we'll run behind a tree and Laura can do her thing.''

Zach's mouth quirked. ''The trials are boring, I agree.''

''Except when *you* head down that ramp, brother dear. Then we'll be cheering you to the skies.''

But Zach's thoughts were on Laura. Whatever her husband's faults, Laura would be cheering Tony, which was as it should be.

His jaw hardened. *You don't know how lucky you are, Donetti. You don't begin to have a clue.*

''I'm going to sit in back with Zach and the kids,'' Bev announced as they made their way out of the hotel and headed for the van. ''You sit in the front, Laura.''

"But I don't want to separate you from your husband."

"I'll be right behind him. Besides, you can see the horizon better from the front, and you won't get car sick."

"That's true. When I was little and we were on trips, my dad had me sit in front if I started to feel funny. The odd thing was, I always did feel better, but I thought it was because I got to sit next to him."

"That works with our children, too," Bev said. "Richard's a great dad."

Laura smiled. "I'm sure it works equally well with a mother like you."

Zach couldn't get over how well the two women were getting along. By the time they'd climbed into the van and the introductions had been made, he had the impression that Laura and his brother's entire family would soon be fast friends, and remain so long after the Tour de France was over.

Richard announced they were off, but no one was paying much attention, not when the children learned that Laura was a television celebrity. In awe of her beauty and status, they couldn't stop asking questions.

As Richard plowed and honked his way through the traffic-filled streets of St. Léger, Zach made up his mind that when he returned to California, he would watch her soap. Now that he was getting to know her, he couldn't imagine her as the conniving man-eating Margo.

The more he reflected on the situation, the more he

realized it was Laura's TV personality rather than her own gentle unassuming character that Tony had portrayed to him.

Why?

It didn't make any sense—unless Tony was simply assuaging his guilt by telling himself that her actions were more reprehensible than his. Was Tony one of those people with such deep-seated psychological problems he couldn't distinguish between fact and fiction?

Whatever the explanation, it had to be a hellish situation for Laura to live with such a man, especially now that a baby was on the way.

Richard spoke from the front seat. "Zach, we're here! This is as close as I can get. Your team van is three cars ahead of us. We'll stay put. This is about the best view we'll get of you coming off the ramp."

"You do great work, Richard."

"Yeah, yeah."

"Good luck, Uncle Zach! We love you! We hope you win!"

The whole family gave him hugs and kisses. He sensed Laura's eyes on him, then her hand grasped his forearm over the seat.

"Thank you for everything, Zach. Be careful," she said in a low husky voice. "Don't let anything happen to you."

"Haven't you heard?" Behind his carefree smile he fought the impulse to kiss those lips that had expressed concern for him. "I'm indestructible."

An anxious expression entered her eyes. "I know better."

She *did* know.

Cycling could be extremely dangerous, even deadly. Over the years, two of Zach's racing colleagues had been killed in crashes. Laura lived through that fear every time Tony entered another race. That kind of anxiety couldn't be good for the baby.

"I'll tell Tony you're here," he said, if only to remind himself once again that she was well and truly married to his roommate.

After he'd gotten out of the van and had come around to the window at her side, she said, "In case he can't break away, here's his bag." She handed it to him through the window. "Good luck," she added.

Zach gave her a slight nod before wheeling away. *Don't think about her, Wilde. Just don't think.*

By the time he reached the team van, he felt his first drop of rain.

"What took you so long?"

As head of the Ziff team, Tony had every right to know why Zach was late.

Zach climbed into the oversize vehicle holding his racing buddies and handed Tony the bag Laura had given him. "*This.* Your wife is three cars behind in Richard's van."

Tony took the bag and placed it on the floor. Then he darted Zach an unfathomable glance. Zach had no idea what his roommate was thinking. "Hold down the fort for a minute, guys. I'll be right back."

The second the door closed, Zach looked at Leon. "Is everything all right?"

Their manager nodded. "Tony's up for this like I've never seen him before. Never underestimate female magic."

"With a wife who looks like her, Tony's a fool to waste his time on bimbos," Klaus said, loving to use the American slang he was constantly hearing.

"Yeah, quite a babe," Vadim concurred.

Zach could have done without hearing his teammates' unabridged comments about the breathtaking Mrs. Donetti. He particularly didn't want to think about the farewell send-off she'd be giving Tony.

"Gentlemen," their Belgian-born coach broke in, "shall we get our minds on business? Jacques? You'll be leaving the ramp first."

"THERE'S YOUR HUSBAND! He's coming this way! Cool!"

Laura had been facing the rear of the van chatting with Zach's family. At Richie's exclamation, she turned in her seat.

Wearing the Ziff-team colors of red and yellow, Tony stood out from the crowd. A lean romantic darkhaired figure with a smile that dazzled his fans.

If her baby was a boy, no doubt he would grow up to be every bit as handsome and dashing as Tony. But in her heart of hearts, she hoped her child's *character* would be exactly like another man's, a man she'd met only twenty-four hours before.

Already she thought of Zachary Wilde as her own heroic Viking. He was a *real* man and ought to be giving the world lessons.

How could two men be so different?

Before her husband reached the van, she had to make a split-second decision—step out to greet him or stay put? She decided to stay put. Aside from the fact that it had started raining and her stomach was still a bit upset, this was Tony's greatest moment, and he wouldn't like sharing the spotlight with anyone, especially her.

She rolled down the window and called out to him. When he got to the van, he reached inside and caught her around the back of the neck with his hand, bringing her head forward to give her a hard kiss on the mouth. "Wish me luck, Laura."

Dozens of flashes went off as she'd known they would, as Tony had planned they would. He loved the idea that a picture of him kissing her would make the front pages of a dozen foreign magazines and newspapers.

"You know I do," she whispered against his lips, trying to reassure the insecure little boy inside him, the boy no one but a few realized inhabited his man's body. It was to that little boy she said and could still mean, "I love you, Tony, and I'll be here for you. Please don't take too many chances."

"That's lousy advice, Laura," he whispered back, his eyes alive with the heat of imminent battle.

She was so used to him throwing barbed comments in her face, they didn't faze her anymore.

"In that case I'll pray for you."

"I'll win, anyway."

He gave her one more kiss, then saluted everyone in the van before heading back to join his team.

"Good luck; Tony!" hollered Richard's kids.

"Dad, can we get out and walk around?" Richie asked.

"You'd never find your way back to the van."

"Yes, we will!"

While they bantered good-naturedly, Laura shut the window, her gaze following Tony until he was out of sight.

At Bev's suggestion Richard started the engine to run the air-conditioning. With relief, Laura breathed in the cooler air.

"Oh, no!" Bev cried suddenly. "One of Zach's racing gloves must have fallen out of his pack."

"I'll take it to him," Richie volunteered.

"Oh, sweetie, I don't know about that."

"Jeez, Mom. You sound like I'm a baby!"

"You could be a hundred and still lose your way in this crowd, Richie. I couldn't handle that."

"I'll go with him, honey."

Richard took the glove and got out the driver's side. Richie followed—and so did his two sisters.

"See ya, Mom."

"See ya, guys."

"Good," Bev said once they'd left. She pulled

down the blinds so curiosity seekers couldn't peer in. "Knowing Richard, he'll stay outside with the children for a while. Now that we're alone, come on back here and stretch out."

Laura didn't need any urging. Soon they were both lying down across from each other. "I feel kind of guilty or naughty or something."

Bev chuckled. "I know what you mean. Can you believe we're at the site of the time trials for the Tour de France of all things, and we're lying here exhausted because we're *enceinte,* as the French say, and nobody knows but us. Here—eat another apple."

Laughter bubbled out of Laura as she accepted it and took a bite. Bev was so easy to be with she felt as if they'd been friends for years. "It's an amazing coincidence. How far along are you?"

"Five weeks, I think. What about you?"

"The same."

"I've been going over names. If it's a girl, we'll call her Lisa, after Richard's mother. But if it's a boy, I'd like to call him Zach. I swear if I'd met him first…"

Laura's heart turned over. She hid her face in the crook of her arm. "He's a wonderful man. So's your husband."

"All the Wilde men are. Wait'll you meet the baby brother, Mike. He'll be in Paris for the finish of the race."

"How old is he?"

"Twenty-seven. He and Carrie just had a little girl.

Mike's terrific, just like his brothers. Of course, no one compares in the looks department to the famous Tony Donetti.''

At that comment, Laura stifled a groan.

''Don't let on that you know, but Rachel has a poster of your husband on her closet door. Zach got it for her because she begged him so many times.''

That sounds like Zach. ''How sweet, Bev.''

''I bet there are several thousand girls who have that same poster on their walls.'' A pause. ''Does it bother you?''

Because of the difficulties in her marriage, and the nature of her job, Laura hadn't confided her problems to anyone. But Beverly Wilde was growing on Laura, and she was amazingly easy to talk to.

''It used to, but not anymore.'' *Thank goodness.*

Within a couple of months she and Tony would go their separate ways. She'd raise their baby alone and give it all the love she had to give.

''How does he handle your celebrity status?''

''He's so busy cycling I don't imagine he thinks about it very often.''

''I didn't mean to pry. Forgive me, Laura—I must sound very rude. Chalk it up to my shock over the privilege of getting to know the lovely woman behind the famous Margo facade. I have more questions to ask than my own children.''

''Don't apologize for anything. I'm indebted to you. As you and Zach have found out, I'm awfully human.

Too human, maybe. Poor Zach—he walked in on me while I was throwing up.''

"He came into the bathroom?'' Bev sounded incredulous.

"Yes. He saw what was happening and proceeded to take expert care of me. If he's anything like your husband, then I envy you that kind of devotion and attention.''

"What did he do?''

Laura found herself telling Bev the details. "I've never been so grateful for anyone's help in my life.''

Bev's voice sobered as she confided, "He should have been a father several times over by now, Laura.''

She bit her lip. "Tony says he's a confirmed bachelor.''

"That's Zach's reputation, but no one knows the pain he's been through to bring him to this point.''

I knew there had to be an explanation.

Laura lifted her head, her heart pounding hard. "What happened?''

Laura lost track of the time as Bev told her about Zach's first fiancée who died of a brain tumor. A few years later he met another woman—Rosie Armstrong, a young widow—and got engaged, but the husband who'd been thought dead suddenly came back. Bev didn't think he'd ever gotten over her.

"That's…that's rough,'' Laura's voice shook.

"Honestly, Laura, Zach's the greatest guy. It isn't fair what he's lived through. I'm so scared.''

"What do you mean?" Luckily it was too dim for Bev to see the tears in her eyes.

"Well, Zach's trained for the Tour de France and is competing in it, I think, as a way to get over Rosie. When the Tour's done, though, he's through with cycling. What scares me is that I have no idea what he's going to do with the rest of his life. He says he's not going back home, and he's ruled out the possibility of another romantic relationship. He won't put himself at risk again, you know?"

"I—I don't think I would, either, Bev."

"When I think of all the awful husbands and fathers out there, and then I think of Zach, who's so wonderful, I can hardly stand it."

Laura couldn't agree more. "Tony says he has a very successful outdoor-sign business in partnership with the rest of your family."

"That's true, but I think Zach has gone into a deep depression. After the final ceremonies, we're not going to see him for a long time."

"Honestly?" Laura found she was holding her breath.

"Yes. Richard's sick about it. You see, he and Zach are very close."

Laura shut her eyes tightly. Now she understood what Zach meant when he said he wasn't into racing for the same reasons as Tony. And for just a second she'd seen that aloof cold side of him. She shuddered just remembering it.

"I don't blame you for being scared," she said.

Bev sniffed. "Hey—I didn't mean to burden you with all the Wilde-family problems. I must be insane."

"No. I wanted to hear."

Maybe I'm insane, too, but I want to know everything there is to know about your brother-in-law.

Bev sat up. "Let's change the subject. You didn't tell me yet what you're thinking of naming *your* baby."

My baby. Laura was pretty certain she was pregnant, and in fact would be strangely disappointed if it turned out she wasn't.

"Well, now that you mention it, if I have a boy, I think I'd like to call him Carl, after Tony's father. He and Tony's mom were killed in a freeway collision when Tony was just an infant."

"You're kidding! How tragic."

"It was. But he has this terrific aunt and uncle—they're the ones who have raised him. I found out only recently that his father was a swimming champion, so I guess Tony inherited his athletic ability." She paused. "Anyway, if I have a girl, I'd like to be completely frivolous and call her something like... Astrid."

"Now *that's* a coincidence."

"What do you mean?"

"I've been doing some genealogy on my family and Richard's, and found out there was an Astrid way back in the Wildes' Norse ancestry. It means something like having the beauty of the gods. It's a lovely name. What made you think of it?"

Laura, feeling heat sweep up her neck and over her face, was unable to answer.

"Do *you* have Viking blood somewhere in your ancestry, too?" Bev prodded.

Laura laughed nervously. "None. I'll probably call her Jane."

"I prefer Astrid."

"Well... Tony may have something to say about it. Then again, if we have a girl, he probably won't care and he'll leave the decision to me."

"When do you think you'll tell him?" Bev asked quietly.

Laura ran an agitated hand through her curls. "That's a good question. If I'm really pregnant, then this baby was a complete and total accident. Don't get me wrong—I'm thrilled. In fact, I'm more than thrilled. I'm overjoyed. But we've always taken precautions, because that was what Tony wanted. He'll be in shock when I tell him."

"There's always a risk, no matter what."

"Yes. As I've found out."

Bev made a commiserating sound.

"I guess it's no secret that my marriage to Tony has pretty much failed. Basically I've always wanted a family and he's fought me every step of the way."

"Oh, Laura. I'm so sorry."

"I might as well tell you the whole truth. After the Tour de France, I'm asking him for a divorce."

"Wow. Life gets complicated."

"You're right. Learning I'm pregnant won't make

any difference. In fact, it will probably ease Tony's conscience to know I won't be living alone, that I'll have the baby I always wanted.''

''A baby needs both parents.''

''I wish it were that sim—''

''Hi, Mom. We're back!'' Robin's bright little voice broke in on them as she pulled open the van door.

''Good grief!'' Richard exclaimed, then threw back his head and laughed at the sight of the two of them lounging.

He sounded exactly like Zach just then, and Laura was filled with inexplicable warmth.

''If I didn't know better, Mrs. Wilde,'' he said sotto voce, ''I would think you're in the same condition as Mrs. Donetti.''

''Really, Mr. Wilde.'' She remained poker-faced, but Laura caught the mischievous glance she darted her. ''To talk about such things in front of the children…''

Laura could almost hear the wheels turning in Richard's head.

''Bev?''

''Mmm?''

''Good Lord! You're not…''

''I guess my secret's out now, Laura.''

''You mean you *both*—''

''I've decided there's going to be a change in plans. I think we'll all drive around the circuit, instead of my going to Paris. That way Laura and I can help each other and tend the children at the same time. We'll leave the driving to you.

"It's going to be a lot of togetherness, but that's what being family is all about. Right, darling?"

He shook his head in exasperation, but Laura saw the gleam in his eye. He was delighted to learn he was going to be a father again. He was delighted his wife would be joining him for the tour. Again she thought about Tony, *How could two men be so different?*

"You do pick your times, honey. My brother's going to be heading down that ramp any minute now."

"One day, won't it be fun to tell our little Zach or Lisa that we watched their famous uncle ride in the Tour de France on the same day you found out I was pregnant?"

"There won't be a tale to tell, if you don't hurry."

"We're up, aren't we, Laura?"

"Absolutely." Laura couldn't wait to have a legitimate reason to feast her eyes on Zach. With the binoculars she'd be able to see him clearly, in spite of the drizzle.

Richard grabbed his binoculars from the visor, then helped his wife out of the van. In plain view of everyone he gave her a resounding kiss before they all took their places in front of the van with Richie to watch the start.

Laura wedged between Robin and Rachel and raised her binoculars to focus on the activity at the ramp. There was no sign of Tony. Earlier he'd told her he wouldn't be starting until late afternoon.

Slowly she brought the lens into focus. To her shock, to her *joy,* Zach was staring straight at her. He held up one of the granola bars she'd given him, then put it in his mouth and waved.

Zach.

At this point, her heart was galloping.

She waved back, but the hand holding the glasses was shaking so hard she almost dropped them.

Just before she heard an announcement in French, he flashed her a broad smile. Then he lowered his head and body into position over his bike.

Within seconds, he was off.

Laura followed his progress for about a kilometer, then lost him as he rounded a corner. It looked to her like he was moving with the speed of a torpedo. Not for the first time since she'd met him, she found herself holding her breath.

CHAPTER FIVE

LATER THAT NIGHT, Richard heard the door to their hotel room open. "Honey?"

"I'm back," Bev whispered, coming into their bedroom.

She shut the bedroom door, then scrambled across the room and got under the covers with him. "I just gave Laura a pill and she's gone to bed. What about the kids?"

"They're out like lights. Where's Tony?"

"He hasn't joined her yet."

"The team is probably still planning tomorrow's first stage."

"I don't want to talk about the race. Zach placed seventh and Tony placed third. That's good enough for me. Right now I've got so much I'm dying to tell you, I don't know where to begin."

Richard chuckled and held her close. "Well, for starters I'd like to enjoy a little togetherness and celebrate the coming event."

"Richard...we don't have time for that right now. I need to talk."

He sighed.

"This is really important, honey," she said. "It's about Zach!"

He smoothed the hair off her forehead, loving everything about his adorable wife. "Okay. Was I right about him or what?"

"Oh, boy, were you ever! But guess what?"

"What?"

"Zach Wilde happened to Laura Donetti, too!"

"Tell me something I don't already know."

"All right. Try this on for size. She's asking Tony for a divorce after the Tour de France."

Richard blinked, then raised himself up on one elbow. "That's something I didn't know."

"Amazing, huh?"

"Does Zach have any idea?"

"No. She confided that to me in absolute secrecy when we were in the van. I think their marriage was bad from day one."

"That's a shame."

"It is. Especially if there's a baby on the way. I like her, Richard. I mean, I really like her a lot."

He tickled her nose. "I do, too."

"Are you thinking what I'm thinking?"

"Probably."

"Do you think this might be the miracle we've been praying for?"

"Ordinarily I would say it was way too soon to tell. But I have to admit the chemistry between them is powerful. Not even Rosie had this kind of effect on him in the beginning."

She cuddled into him. "I know. He acts like he's been hit with a hundred-megaton bomb.'

"Do you know what he did at the start today?"

"What? You wouldn't let me look through the binoculars."

"That was because I couldn't believe what I was seeing."

"What do you mean?"

"Zach was smiling and waving, but it was for Laura's benefit, not anyone else's."

"So *he* was the person she was looking at through her binoculars!" Bev exclaimed. "Breathlessly, I might add."

"Zach couldn't have cared less about the race," Richard said. "Neither could she. It's a good thing her husband wasn't around, because I swear she and Zach didn't know anything or anyone else existed. He was so busy eating one of her granola bars I'm surprised he even heard the official tell him to go."

Bev squeezed him. "Oh, Richard. This has got to work! It can't blow up in our faces. Not this time."

"Well, one thing's for sure. If this keeps up, by the end of the Tour de France she and Zach will be so close we won't be able to pry them apart with a crowbar, and he won't be running off someplace where we can't find him."

"I know. But what worries me is that when Tony finds out he's going to be a father, maybe he won't want a divorce."

Richard let out a weary sigh. "I'm worried about

that, too, although my instincts tell me it won't make a difference. If a marriage has gone wrong, a child won't solve the problem.''

"I agree. Am I evil, Richard, wanting them to break up?''

"Don't be silly, honey. Obviously they're both very unhappy and have been for a long time. Otherwise she wouldn't be contemplating such a decision, let alone revealing her deepest thoughts to you. And as far as I can tell, she's been giving out vibes to Zach without even meaning to. The miracle is, he's been picking up on them. Whatever they're both feeling, it appears to be mutual.''

"I have a hunch they'd be really good together.''

"They already *are* good together. I must say my brother has excellent taste. This one is a major, major knockout.''

"Whoa. That's high praise indeed. Well, she's met her match in Zach. Next to you he's the most gorgeous man on the planet.''

"More gorgeous than Donetti? Our daughter would never believe it!''

"Our starry-eyed Rachel is a *girl*. Right now she's crazy about Tony Donetti because he's slick and glamorous. But he's shallow. It takes a *woman* to appreciate Zach, to see that he looks like a Norse god, you know?''

"What?'' Sometimes his wife astounded him.

"I told you that when I was doing the Wilde genealogy, I found out there's a large dose of Viking blood running through your veins because you all descended from Queen Astrid of Kelby.''

Richard's only response was a chuckle.

"Oh—" she made a sound of frustration "—you're a man and wouldn't understand.'' *But Laura does. She already has a Norse name picked out.*

"Let me get this straight." Richard's chest was shaking with laughter. "When you first saw me, you thought I was a Norse god? Is that what you're telling me?"

"Well, maybe a lesser god, because you're a little shorter than Zach and you don't have silver eyes. Yours are more fjord blue and—"

"A lesser god? Silver eyes? Fjord blue?"

"Honey—" she kissed him lingeringly "—don't get your feelings hurt."

"Trust me. They're not hurt."

"Oh, Richard... I'm scared. If the Donettis don't break up, then it means that Zach could be in trouble for the *third* time."

Suddenly Richard didn't feel so jovial. "Don't say that. Don't even think it."

"What are we going to do? How can we protect him?"

"It's too late. The deed is done."

"I couldn't bear it if he got hurt again."

"Neither could I, but these are early days and anything can happen. Let's sleep on it, shall we? We've got a long day of driving ahead of us tomorrow."

"What do you bet Zach is over at Laura's room first thing in the morning to find out if she's okay."

"I'm not going to bet when we both know he'll be there the second her husband is out of the room."

"It sounds positively indecent and here I am condoning it. Honey? You don't think Zach would actually... I mean...she's still married, and—"

"Bev," he interrupted her gently, "in the frame of mind my brother's in, anything is possible, but let's not borrow trouble. Good night."

"Good night."

Richard drew her closer and closed his eyes. But before he fell asleep, the last image his mind conjured up was the look on his brother's face earlier in the evening when he'd told him that Laura had been too ill to join the family for dinner.

Richard's news had extinguished the light in Zach's eyes. They'd suddenly looked as bleak as a winter battlefield after the last body had been counted.

Zach was emotionally involved with Laura Donetti.

That wasn't good. Not when Laura wasn't available yet.

But soon... God willing.

LAURA GLANCED at her watch. Eleven p.m. She'd been asleep four hours.

Tony still wasn't back, but it didn't surprise her. He was running true to form. No strategy meeting would have lasted this long. Everyone on the team would be in bed right now. *Maybe Tony is, too.*

Nothing he did bothered her anymore. How sad, she thought. How tragic.

Their marriage should have lasted forever. Their baby should have had the guarantee of a wonderful caring father. But all the shoulds in the world hadn't made it happen.

Earlier today, when Tony had crossed the finish line with the third-best time of the prologue, fans for the Belgian-sponsored Ziff team had gone wild with excitement. But it had been all she could do to wave to him, because her nausea had flared up again.

At that point everyone in the family had been hungry and exhausted. Richard had driven them all back to the Beaulieu. Laura had gone straight to her room to lie down while the family had dinner, and so she hadn't seen Tony or Zach, who'd been collected in the team's van.

Now she was hungry and threw off the covers to get something to eat. A pear and another croissant sounded good.

As she finished the last of her fruit, the phone rang. *Must be Tony.* Why did he bother to call with an excuse? She had half a mind not to answer it, but the ringing persisted. At the last second she wiped her hands with a cloth and dashed across the room to get it.

"Hello?"

"Laura?"

Stunned because the deep male voice wasn't Tony's, she sank onto the side of the bed. "Zach?"

"Forgive me if I woke you."

"You didn't," she rushed to assure him. It was ridiculous, but every time she heard his voice or got near him, she experienced this fluttery reaction inside.

"I don't know if you heard. The rain was coming down pretty hard when Klaus went around the last curve of the course. He crashed into a concrete divider and was taken to the hospital with a concussion. That's where I'm calling from."

"Oh, no!" she cried. "I had no idea. The poor thing. How is he, Zach?"

"He's going to be okay. They're about to release him. The whole team's here. Since Tony doesn't know about your condition, I thought I'd better call so you wouldn't worry." There was a tension-filled pause. "Do you need anything, Laura?" His voice sounded husky.

She got to her feet, indescribably touched by his concern. "No. Thank you. I'm fine. Between your brother and his wife, I feel pampered and spoiled already. Bev swears by the medicine she gave me earlier. They're terrific people, Zach."

"Yes, they are."

She started pacing to counteract the adrenaline pulsing through her body. "Congratulations on a fantastic finish. I couldn't see it up close because I let the girls watch through my binoculars. But I know that seventh place is remarkable."

"Tony's the man of the hour, but it's nice to hear. For what it's worth, that was my best prologue time to date. I think it must have to do with the granola bar I ate on the ramp.''

She smiled in remembrance. ''There're more where those came from.''

''Good. I'll be over in the morning for a refill.''

Her eyes closed tightly. ''If the pill I took performs the required miracle, I should be able to make it to breakfast with your family.''

''Around eight, I understand.''

She moistened her lips nervously. ''I-if I can't come down, I'll send you a care package via Richie.''

''I just got off the phone with my brother. He says Richie is crazy about you already. Apparently you know more about baseball than any 'girl' he's ever met. Richie doesn't like girls, so you must have made quite an impression on him.''

Laura knew she shouldn't be so thrilled by a simple compliment. ''I never had a little brother, but if I could've picked one, he'd be it.''

''No one else ever had the patience to go through all his baseball cards with him at one sitting.''

''It was fun!'' she asserted. ''Do you realize he can reel off more facts than my own father? Dad's a Yankee fan from way back. Until this afternoon I didn't think anyone else knew more about baseball than he did. Just wait till I get him and Richie together!''

Zach's laughter rumbled over the line and seemed to travel through her, making her feel more alive than she'd felt in years. ''Do *you* like baseball?'' he asked.

''I love it. So does my sister. We wear our baseball

caps and go to every evening game with Dad, help him yell at the referee, throw popcorn, stuff like that. Dad's just waiting for one of us to have a boy so—'' She stopped, shocked to realize she really was going to have a baby.

She didn't need a test to know it. There were other signs that before this morning had seemed unconnected to the nausea. After consulting Bev, she now knew differently.

''So he can go to his Little League games?'' Zach finished for her, but the lighthearted tone had disappeared from his voice.

''Something like that. Yes.''

''Well, in about eight months it looks like he may just get his wish.''

She swallowed hard. ''So far, girls run in our family—my sister's had two. Neither of them shows a penchant for baseball yet.''

''Tony's child might be different.''

Tony may be the biological father, but I have difficulty associating him with my baby.

''Maybe you'll give birth to an Olympic alpine skier,'' he suggested.

''Maybe my baby will turn out to be Jane or John average, like me.''

She heard a sharp intake of breath. ''There's nothing average about you.''

This conversation needed to end, for reasons she didn't dare explore. But perversely she didn't want it to. ''All I care about is that it's healthy,'' she said.

"Amen. On that note, you ought to be in bed. Good night, Laura."

"Good night." She replaced the receiver slowly. *You're reading way too much into this, Laura. Zach Wilde is just a decent human being who would be this kind and thoughtful to any woman in distress.*

He didn't want her worrying that Tony was doing something he shouldn't. He knew she was pregnant, and had simply called to make sure she was all right. Some men in the world were like that.

Besides, she'd heard what Bev had said about Zach's past. So she'd better forget what she felt when she was around him. She must not make this out to be something it wasn't, or she could be headed for the greatest heartache of her life....

"ZACH, *MON AMI!*" Vadim called to him. "*Viens!* They are talking about us."

Zach relinquished the receiver he'd been clutching and turned in Vadim's direction. While they waited for the doctor to release Klaus, the guys had gathered around the TV set in the lounge to watch any late-night specials on the race.

On the screen now, a French sportscaster was interviewing the Belgian-born members of the team in Liège. Next came a film clip of Klaus having dinner with his parents and friends at home in Darmstadt. Then, viewed with a lot of guffaws and good-natured teasing, several segments of the guys answering questions for news commentators several weeks before the Tour de France.

After one clip, which showed Zach in a race in the Italian Dolomite mountains the previous fall breaking away from the peleton—the main group of bikers, the newscaster explained—Jacques poked Zach in the ribs.

"You hear that, Zach? King of the Mountain they call you. The best biker on the hill. You deserve the title."

"Maybe not after Val d'Isère," Tony broke in, his expression intense as his eyes darted to Zach, challenging him.

What's gotten into you, Donetti?

"So, Tony," Jacques inquired in mild amusement "you're the all-round best, but do you really think you can take Zach in the fifth stage, when we hit the mountains?"

"We'll see, Jackie boy. We'll see," came the cocky reply.

Zach ground his teeth. *Since when have you ever been in competition with me, Donetti?* But Zach already knew the answer to that question.

Since your wife showed up at our room.

It wasn't part of the plan, was it, Tony. Despite the priceless treasures she brought you, you're still angry.

Suddenly highlights of the time trials flashed on the screen. The camera zoomed in on the crowds near the ramp. The guys assembled around the TV pointed to

Tony, whom the newsperson had caught walking toward Richard's van before the start of the trials.

Zach's mouth went dry as the camera panned to Laura. She took everyone's breath away, including, it seemed, the newscaster's. Zach had picked up enough French to realize the man was talking about Tony's wife. He used words like *"belle," "fameuse"* and "Hollywood."

The guys started whistling and clapping. Vadim spoke for the team when he said, "Your wife is a real beauty, Tony."

As the tape showed Tony leaning inside the window to kiss Laura, Zach felt as if he'd been kicked in the gut. The other guys, oblivious, cheered Tony on, nudging him in the ribs, making suggestive comments that made him grin.

At the height of all this, however, Tony shot Zach a venomous glance and muttered something about his wife only having eyes for the winner before looking back at the screen.

So, you haven't forgiven me for siccing Leon on you yesterday, spoiling all your fun. Well, that's just too damn bad. You want a fight in the mountains of Val d'Isère? You're on, Donetti.

"I am ready to go home, in case anyone wants to know," Klaus announced, walking into the waiting room. That brought a cheer from the guys. Someone shut off the TV.

Though Zach couldn't have been happier to get

away from Tony, the thought of him going home to Laura's bed made Zach's blood congeal.

"Glad to see you're all right," Zach murmured to Klaus. "Let's get out of here. Leon's waiting in the van out front."

"It has been a long day."

"And longer tomorrow, I'm afraid."

"Yes, I know—209 kilometers."

"Think you'll be up to it?"

"Whether I am or not, I will do it," Klaus said firmly. "I didn't come all this way to watch the race on television." They went out the doors of the hospital ahead of the others. Zach noticed the drizzle hadn't let up.

"Just take an easy pace tomorrow. It'll still be flat."

"I can sleep and let my legs do the work." Out of the range of the others Klaus whispered, "I heard Tony baiting you. Don't listen to him. He's just angry his wife showed up and he's been forced to kiss all his little bimbos *auf Wiedersehen.*"

"He's a fool."

"Let me teach you what to say the next time he attacks." They'd reached the van.

"What's that?"

"Du bist ein Schwein."

Zach's mouth quirked. "I took German in high school, Klaus, so I'm familiar with that."

"Ja? Well, it gets the message across, doesn't it?"

As far as Zach was concerned, Tony was a swine in any language. Unfortunately the fact that everyone on the team held the same opinion didn't help the situation.

Thanks to Laura and the scrapbooks, there'd been a moment of illumination for Tony last night. But it hadn't lasted long. Tonight Tony's dark side had taken over again. They would all have to live with it for the duration of the Tour.

Laura had to live with it on a permanent basis. Even more alarming, when she finally chose to tell her husband they were expecting a baby, the pendulum might swing even *farther* that way.

Zach supposed it was possible Tony would turn into a responsible parent, but his gut feeling was that this wasn't likely; his teammate would probably continue selfishly down the road he'd been headed, wreaking more destruction.

But whatever happened, none of it should have any bearing at all on Zach's life. The wise course would be to take Klaus's advice and ignore Tony's gibes. Wiser still would be to avoid Laura as much as possible from here on out.

Easier said than done, he knew, but as he prepared for bed ten minutes later, he made a vow to himself, one he intended to keep. As of this moment, he was removing himself from the Donettis and the emotionally dangerous situation surrounding them.

Already he'd stepped over that invisible line when he'd called Laura tonight. He could try to rationalize why he'd phoned another man's wife, but no matter what name he gave it, it was a mistake, one of several he'd made within the past thirty-six hours.

No more. He wouldn't make any more.

Tomorrow morning, and every morning for the duration of the Tour, he'd do what he'd been doing for months now. Eat breakfast and ride in the team van with the others to the start of each new stage.

The only difference would be that, at the end of the day, he'd make certain Laura and Tony weren't around when he spent time with Richard and his family. Away from the circuit, the Donettis and the Wildes would lead separate lives.

Resolve hardened, he stretched out in bed and began flipping through a travel magazine Bev had inadvertently left in his room the other day. An article on the Galápagos Islands, off the coast of Ecuador, caught his eye. Interesting area. He decided that when the Tour de France was over, it would be as good a spot as any on earth to explore.

The idea of sailing to the various islands appealed to him. In fact, on the Tour's rest day in Villeneuve, nine days from now, he'd look into making travel arrangements so he could fly there straight from Paris at the end of the Tour.

For a long time he'd been toying with the idea of turning over his part of the outdoor-sign business to the others in the family and buying a larger sailboat, one that could accommodate four to six people at a time. The revenue from operating his own boat commercially for tourists could take him around the world.

If he liked what he saw in the Galápagos, he might just begin there. Why not?

He particularly needed to stay faraway from California and anything to do with television....

ON THE FIFTH DAY of the race, the crowds lining the mountain roads presented a real hazard to the cyclists. Laura couldn't believe how spectators crowded the roadsides, pressing in so far that the road was little more than a narrow path in places.

They'd left Belgium for France four days ago. The heat had become insufferable and was getting worse. What with that, coupled with the crowds and the difficulties of pedaling uphill, it was no wonder several of the entrants had already collided, resulting in minor spills.

One overly exuberant fan had thrown a bucket of water in Farramundi's face with such force it caused him to run into Tony's bike. Fortunately both men were such good racers they didn't fall, but the collision slowed them down. As predicted by the media and his own team members, Zach was still in the lead by a good thirty seconds.

Eight of the cyclists had broken from the peleton, leaving the others behind by a fifty-five-second margin. If Zach kept this up, he would win the polka-dot jersey for the fifth stage. Secretly Laura was rooting for him to triumph in this leg of the Tour, at least.

So far Farramundi was leading overall, with Pieter

De Raet of the Dutch team making a surprising sec-
ond-place showing and Tony coming in third.

"The crowd is terrible, Richard!" Bev cried, trying
to get everything on video.

"It's always like this, honey. Zach's used to it.
They all are."

"Well, I don't see how anyone can win when
they're hemmed in at every turn. There ought to be
police or something."

"No, that isn't how this works."

"Yeah, Mom," Richie interjected. "Uncle Zach
says all's fair in love, war and the Tour de France."

Richard chuckled, but apparently Bev didn't see
anything funny about it. "I hate this. Don't you,
Laura?"

"Yes, especially when Tony didn't stop at the last
feed zone for anything to eat or drink. He's driving
himself too hard!"

"Don't worry. Your husband has never been in better form. That's what everyone on the team's told me.
According to Zach, Tony's pretty well invincible."

If Zach had told Richard that, then he'd not done it
within Laura's hearing. In fact, she'd hardly seen him
the past few days, except during the race itself. He
hadn't come to breakfast with his family since the first
morning, and he was never around at dinnertime. That
phone call from the hospital had been their last conversation.

It looked as if she'd been right about Zach. He'd
shown surprising concern when she'd arrived in Bel-

gium—making her comfortable and locating Tony, arranging for her to ride around the circuit with Richard—simply because he was that kind of man.

But since the pregnancy test she'd bought had turned up positive, and Bev's medicine had helped her morning sickness, Zach apparently assumed she was in good hands. He'd put everything out of his mind except the race.

What a fool she'd been to think for one second that he might have had a more personal interest in her. Zach wasn't the sort to get involved with a married woman, a *pregnant* married woman at that. Besides, Bev's assertion that Zach's emotions were in some kind of deep freeze made nonsense of the notion he might have felt an emotional response to her.

If anyone was emotional, it was she. Chalk it up to her pregnancy. It seemed Tony's callous treatment of her had made her vulnerable to any man who showed her the slightest kindness. It was humiliating.

"Laura?" Bev asked. "Are you all right?"

"Of course."

"Sure? You've gone so quiet I thought maybe you felt a bit nauseated. Why don't we change places? I'll sit in back with the children."

"No, thanks, Bev, I'm fine. Honestly. I guess I worry too much. Tony's a big boy and can take care of himself."

For the past few nights he'd made a habit of returning late to their hotel room. Just when she'd finally manage to drift off, he'd wake her up to listen to him talk about his racing plans for the next day.

He never volunteered where he'd been or with whom, but one thing was perfectly clear. He intended to win the King of the Mountain official title, as well as the Tour de France itself. Even for Tony, he sounded obsessed.

Sometimes she worried that the articles in the scrapbook about his father may have made him overconfident and caused him to take chances he wouldn't ordinarily take.

Richard eyed her through the rearview mirror. "If you noticed, Laura, Farramundi didn't stop, either. They've been pros long enough to know if they need sustenance or not."

"That may be true, but in this heat even they could get dehydrated and not realize it until it was too late."

"Well, it won't be long before they reach the top, then it's downhill to the finish."

"Zach's already over the summit!" Bev shouted, still filming. "I bet he's going to win!" Everyone in the van clapped and cheered.

Laura thrilled to the news, but trembled inside because she could imagine Tony's fury. Lifting the binoculars to her eyes, she saw that her husband had gained the lead over Farramundi and the others.

He was going after Zach.

She marveled at his speed, wondering where that fresh spurt of famous Donetti energy sprang from. Though there'd been rumors of drugs, she dismissed them. After all, the media cast that same suspicion on most famous athletes.

Tony's legs were like pistons as they propelled him to the top. Then, suddenly, everything changed. It looked as if he'd lost control of his steering. She gasped when the bike veered from one side to the other, then fell.

"Tony's down!" Laura's voice shook.

"I think one of his tires blew," Bev said, exchanging the camera for their binoculars. "Hurry and catch up to him, Richard."

"I am, honey."

Through the glasses Laura could see the Ziff-team support wagon draw up alongside Tony carrying all the bikes and spare parts.

"He's still down," Laura whispered as a fresh burst of anxiety swept through her. "I don't think it was the bike."

"Don't assume anything yet, Laura."

Richard's gentle voice was meant to calm her. But Laura knew something no one else knew about her husband—how determined he'd been to beat Zach in this stage. It was obvious to her he'd overextended himself.

Dear God, don't let this be serious.

She jumped out of the van and ran toward the group huddled around Tony's inert body. Jules Massonac, the Ziff-team doctor, took his vital signs, then flashed Laura a compassionate look.

"I believe he's suffering from heat exhaustion, Mrs.

Donetti. We'll take him to the hospital. He'll be all right in no time. Come, you can ride with him.''

"We'll meet you there,'' Richard murmured from behind, pressing a gentle hand to her shoulder.

She wheeled around. "No, Richard. Zach needs you. Please go on and watch him win. We'll all meet at the hotel later.''

"You're sure?'' Bev asked anxiously.

"Yes. You heard the doctor. Tony'll be fine in a little while. Go on, both of you. Please. For me? This is Zach's big moment!''

She saw them exchange glances. "All right. But we'll come to the hospital as soon as it's over.''

Laura nodded and squeezed their hands before climbing into the van where they'd put Tony. As they drove off, the doctor hooked up an IV to get fluids into him. Soon a siren blared; they'd been given a police escort to the hospital.

Laura's gaze fastened on Tony's face and chest, watching for signs that he'd regained consciousness.

When he remained motionless, she asked, "Is it normal to be out this long?''

The team physician's only response was a worried expression.

CHAPTER SIX

ONE KILOMETER TO GO.

Zach never once looked around to see if his opponents were gaining on him. Such a move would cost him one- or two-tenths of a second of precious time, which he couldn't afford if he wanted to beat Tony. Today, more than any other time in his racing career, he wanted to be number one—if only to wipe away that smug Donetti smile for a few minutes.

Val d'Isère was like every town on the circuit, with cheering spectators and cycling enthusiasts congregated on its main street. That made it difficult for him to see the finish line. In case Tony was at his heels, Zach drew on any remaining reserves for the last sprint.

A huge roar went up from the crowd as he crossed it first. Exultant, breathing hard, Zach looked back, eager to see how far ahead he was of Donetti, but well-wishers and cameramen besieged him from all sides, blocking his vision.

As far as he could tell, Pieter De Raet crossed the finish line second, followed by Farramundi. Zach frowned when he couldn't see Tony anywhere. Had he just missed him, or had Tony fallen way behind?

His gaze darted to the peleton coming up on the
finish line. Vadim was among the lead group. Klaus
trailed in the back. The rest of the Ziff team was far
behind. Still no sight of Tony.

"Uncle Zach! You won!" the kids yelled, as they
ran up to him with Bev following.

After much kissing and hugging, Richie took charge
of Zach's bike and fit it on the van's rack. Then they
all moved around to where Richard stood, smiling.

Where's Laura? Zach felt a pit of dread in his gut.
Something was wrong.

"Congratulations, little bro. That was one great
race!" Richard gave him a bear hug, but Zach scarcely
responded.

"Why isn't Laura with you? Where's Tony? What's
going on?"

A shadow crossed Richard's face. "He collapsed at
the summit."

Collapsed? Tony?

"Laura went with him to the hospital in one of the
support vans."

Zach sucked in a breath. "At a time like this, she
shouldn't be alone. Let's get over there." He tried to
move, but Richard blocked his path.

"Hey—you can't leave until the ceremony is over
and you're awarded the polka-dot jersey."

"I'll ask Vadim to accept it for me."

Richard shook his head and placed his hands on
Zach's shoulders. "No, Zach, you're not going to do
that. This is your big day. King of the Mountain!" He

paused. "Tony fainted, that's all. It isn't serious. He was apparently suffering from heat exhaustion—he didn't stop at the last feed zone."

Guilt consumed Zach. "That's because he was determined to beat me," he muttered.

"What are you talking about? Tony was out to beat *everyone!*"

"No." Zach shook his head. "You don't understand." He stared into his brother's eyes. "I—I baited Tony, and this is the result. His chance to win the Tour de France this year is over now."

Zach's guilt deepened when he remembered Laura's eyes pleading with him not to provoke her husband that day before the time trials, but he hadn't been able to resist. Now that he was victorious, Tony's resentment over having lost this stage—coupled with the fact that he would no longer be able to compete in the rest of the race—would turn to a burning hatred. Team morale would plummet to an all-time low.

Worse, Tony would be impossible to live with. Poor Laura.

Before everything fell apart, there had to be something he could do to ameliorate the situation.

"I've got to get to the hospital, Richard."

Finally Richard gave up the fight. "All right. Let's go."

"Let me talk to the guys for a second."

He signaled to Vadim and Klaus. They rode their bikes over to him, their faces wreathed in smiles for his triumph. But when he told them what had happened, their pleasure vanished. This was the first they'd heard about Tony. The news effectively dashed their dreams to be champions.

Zach, of course, wasn't in the race for the same reasons as his teammates. With Tony down, the chances of the Ziff team coming out number one were pretty well shot. Deep in his psyche, Zach knew it was his fault. He felt almost overwhelmed with guilt.

Yet, all he could really think about was Laura. In her condition she would need protection from Tony. So, ignoring an inner voice that reminded him he had no business being around Donetti's wife, he asked Vadim to accept the jersey for him, then assemble the other team members and join him and Tony at the hospital afterward. According to Vadim, it was only three blocks away.

"Let's get out of here," Zach muttered to Richard as he climbed in the van after Bev and the kids.

"MRS. DONETTI?"

At the sound of Dr. Massonac's voice, Laura's head jerked around. She'd just gotten off the phone with her parents and Tony's aunt and uncle—she wanted both families to hear the bad news from her, not the television set—and was standing outside the cubicle in the emergency ward where they'd brought Tony.

Everyone from the Ziff owners and sponsors to the coach were there with her. Hospital security had called in more police to stave off the onslaught of media people anxious to cover the top story of the race so far. Laura realized that with Tony out of the running, the team would have to perform brilliantly throughout the rest of the Tour to finish among the top five or six.

"Doctor? Can I see him now? Has he regained consciousness yet?"

He eyed her solemnly. "No, he hasn't. The attending physician, Dr. Sardis, wants to talk to you." He indicated the older man with him." Please...come in this other room with us."

Her heart was pounding like a trip-hammer, as she followed them in and heard the door close.

"Perhaps you should sit down," Dr. Massonac said.

Her eyes darted from one grim face to the other. "I don't want to. What's wrong? Why isn't Tony conscious yet?"

She heard a deep sigh. "I am afraid we lost him," Dr. Sardis said in his heavily accented English.

She stood there, not comprehending. *"What?"*

"Oui, madame. We did everything possible for Tony, but we couldn't revive him."

The awful words had been spoken, but still nothing computed.

"I don't understand. Are you trying to tell me that Tony's *dead?"*

When neither doctor spoke, she felt the room start to spin. Dr. Massonac put an arm at her waist and guided her to a chair. Shock made her cling to the sleeve of his shirt.

"I thought he fainted from heat exhaustion. How...how could he die from something like that?"

"We don't know the cause of death yet. What we *do* know is that it wasn't from exhaustion or dehydration."

She was incredulous. "His heart, then?"

"Madame Donetti," the older doctor importuned gently, "we are making tests and will know the results shortly."

"What kind of tests?"

Dr. Massonac's expression looked pained before he murmured, "Blood tests."

She paled even further if such a thing were possible. That meant they were searching for— *Oh, Tony*. Tears began to gush down her cheeks. "You think he d-died of a drug overdose or some such thing?"

"It's possible."

"But he's always checked before a race!"

"He may have injected himself with something that doesn't show up right away, but we hesitate to speculate. I'm very sorry."

The finality of Dr. Massonac's tone chilled her. This had to be a bad dream or some kind of ghastly mistake. Tony couldn't be dead!

"Please. I have to see him."

"Of course."

They preceded her out of the room. Dr. Sardis pushed the curtain of the cubicle aside so she could enter.

Beneath the white sheet Tony lay perfectly still on the examining table, all animation gone from his handsome bronzed face and limbs.

In horror she approached his inert body and reached for his hand. She gasped to realize his skin was already cooling.

He really was gone.

It didn't seem possible. She felt like someone functioning in slow motion, her own body lethargic.

"Tony..." A sob escaped her, as she placed her cheek against his. "What happened out there, Tony? This race was supposed to be the supreme moment of your life. You...you were going to win and...and finally be happy."

Suddenly she was convulsed with sobs. She rested her head on his chest to cry out her grief for the little boy inside the man who'd never known his parents. The little boy who'd never thought himself loved.

She grieved, too, over the marriage that seemed to have brought Tony so much unhappiness. And for his aunt and uncle, who would, no doubt, suffer more pain for not being here and blame themselves in some way for his death.

She mourned the loss for the baby growing inside her, the child who would never know its father. And, dear God, that she'd been contemplating a divorce without ever having discussed it with him. It was unforgivable.

"I should never have shown you those scrapbooks," she whispered brokenly. "It was wrong of me. They made you try too hard, want too much, and...and I should've known that. No matter what the tests say, *I'm* the one responsible for your death. I didn't even tell you I was pregnant with your baby. Forgive me for my dishonesty, Tony. Forgive me for everything…'' She sobbed afresh.

After a moment a warm solid hand clasped her shoulder. ''Madame…what can I do to help you?''

Dr. Massonac meant to be kind, but she couldn't be comforted.

''Please. Let me be alone with my husband. I don't want to see anyone.''

''Whatever you say. If you need me, I'll be right outside. The priest who administered the last rites is here if you wish to talk to him.''

''Th-thank you. Maybe later,'' came her pain-filled whisper.

''GOOD GRIEF,'' Richard muttered, seeing the enormous crowd in front of the hospital. ''The police have cordoned off the entrances.''

The pit in Zach's gut grew. ''I'm not surprised. Anything to do with Tony is big news. Let me out here and then go back to the hotel. I'll call you later when I have some news.''

Richard nodded. ''That's probably the best plan. You're one of the few who might get through that line.''

''Thanks for everything.'' Zach embraced both Richard and Bev quickly before climbing out of the van. He was still dressed in his racing jersey and shorts.

''Give Laura our love,'' Bev said.

If Zach was grateful for anything, it was the friendship that had sprung up between Laura and his family. She would need it to get through this black period. For losing today's stage, which meant Tony was no longer a contender in the Tour de France, would put him in the blackest mood of his life.

Zach worked his way through the crowd but was stopped near the hospital entrance by a local gendarme.

"Il ne faut pas entrer, monsieur."

So, he wasn't allowed to go in, but not to be put off, he said, "I'm a member of the Ziff team."

The gendarme didn't budge. *"Je regrette, monsieur."*

Zach cursed under his breath. "That's too bad because I'm going in, anyway."

Stepping around the uniformed officer, Zach ducked under the rope and sprinted toward the double doors, unheeding of the whistle blows and shouts coming from the police.

His speed worked in his favor. He managed to squeeze in the doors before anyone could stop him, then raced down the hall, following the arrows to emergency.

As soon as he saw the sponsors and owners of the Ziff team huddled in the reception area, Zach realized that Tony's problem had to be serious. There was no sign of Laura, but he did spot a familiar head of black hair with distinguishing gray wings. It belonged to the team doctor.

Zach hurried up to him. Without preamble he asked, "How's Tony?"

Dr. Massonac put an arm around his shoulders and led him a short distance from the others.

"We lost him, Zach. He was unconscious before he was put in the wagon and he never came out of it."

Zach's head reared back in shock.

A long time ago he'd heard words like those—when his first fiancée had succumbed to an inoperable brain tumor.

"I don't believe it," he whispered more to himself than anyone else, but the doctor heard him.

"None of us believes it yet. Neither will the racing world."

Zach felt as if a giant hand had just squeezed all the air from his lungs. "Where's his wife, Laura?"

"She's still in the cubicle. I can't get her away from him. She has this crazy idea she killed Tony. She's absolutely inconsolable. I'm worried about her."

Dear God. What have I done?

Zach headed for the only cubicle where the curtain had been fully drawn for privacy. The grief he could hear coming from it clawed at his heart, ripping it to shreds.

He took a deep breath and slipped inside. She was seated next to Tony's body and was rocking back and forth, her head buried in her hands.

The picture of Laura Donetti in abject despair would be permanently etched on his brain.

Zach had reached the end of the line. He had nowhere to go with his pain. Instinctively, he moved toward her. "Laura…"

She lifted her head.

He barely recognized her swollen tear-streaked face. In the next instant she was in his arms.

"Tony's dead, Zach, and I killed him. I should've stayed in California. My coming here has *killed* him!"

Zach crushed her to him, half smothering the self-condemning words pouring from her soul.

He knew exactly how she felt, for he was consumed by the same guilt.

"If anyone's responsible, *I* am," he murmured into the glistening black curls. "I knew Tony wanted to win this stage today." Through gritted teeth he muttered, "I should have let him. But for me, he'd still be alive."

"You're *both* wrong, you know."

At the sound of Dr. Massonac's voice, Laura tried to pull out of Zach's arms, but he refused to let her go completely and kept a supportive hand at her waist.

"What do you mean?" he demanded as Jules and another doctor Zach didn't recognize approached them.

Jules pulled the curtain closed to onlookers. "We just got the test results back. Tony died from blood doping."

Laura's tormented eyes lifted to Zach's in entreaty. "Blood doping?"

The other doctor cleared his throat. "Sometimes athletes inject an extra supply of their own blood that has been treated to enrich it. Dr. Massonac and I believe that your husband probably had someone do this for him, *after* he took the normal drug test, to give him that extra boost.

"But it can have lethal consequences. Today the blood thickened and formed clots—which caused complications and ultimately his death."

"No one's to blame for what happened to Tony but Tony himself." Jules spoke with authority. "He knew better, but chose to take the risk, anyway."

"Zach—" Laura, wild with desperation, grabbed his other arm "—we can't let the press know how Tony died! We *can't!*"

Zach understood only too well why Laura wanted the truth hidden from the world. And right now what she wanted was all that mattered to him. He turned to the team doctor.

"You heard her, Jules. Tell everyone he suffered a fatal heart attack."

The two doctors looked at each other, then back at Zach. They were obviously in a quandary.

"Do it for the sake of Tony's aunt and uncle, who raised him out of love," Zach said in a low quiet voice. "Do it for Laura, who has to face millions of television fans when she returns to the U.S. But especially…do it for the baby she's carrying."

Both doctors gasped in shock and dismay, exactly the reaction Zach wanted.

"Let's at least allow her son or daughter to grow up believing Tony died honorably. Surely a lie like that could be no sin."

Jules's eyes grew hooded before he nodded his assent.

The other doctor said softly, "In this case I agree that the sin of the father should not be passed on to the head of the child, monsieur. I will have a private word with the person who did the lab work before I leave the hospital."

It was just as well Zach was still supporting Laura, for her body went limp with relief.

"No one must ever know the truth," Zach insisted. "Not the sponsors, the owners and certainly not the team. They believed Tony was a winner. Let them keep that belief. Tomorrow we're going to go on with the race and we're going to finish up in Paris—*in Tony's honor*. Do you hear what I'm saying?"

"You don't have to do that, Zach!" Laura cried, but the look of gratitude in those tear-filled brown eyes made him more determined than ever.

"Jules," Zach rapped out, "tell Leon we need his help. As the team manager, he can make a formal announcement to the press so they'll clear out and leave Laura alone. I've got family here who can help take care of her and inform Tony's family of his death."

He paused briefly to glance at Laura. "It'll be up to Laura and her relatives to plan funeral arrangements—those will have to be announced at a later date.

In the meantime, Jules, you can tell the team there's going to be a meeting at the hotel tonight. Nine o'clock. Everyone is to be there so we can plan to-morrow's strategy."

Jules nodded and patted Zach's shoulder. His eyes reflected a mixture of admiration and relief. "It's the best plan."

Zach had been well aware of the fear running through the team doctor's mind. It was everyone's fear. After a tragedy of this magnitude, no one would be surprised if the Ziff team broke up, bringing a pre-mature close to all those years of preparation, of sac-rifice, of money—everything ending up an utter waste.

Zach wasn't about to let that happen.

"One more thing," he added. "Since Laura would prefer to tell her family she's pregnant before it's spread all over the world, please keep that news to yourselves, all right?"

"You have our promise," Jules murmured. He kissed Laura's cheek, offered a few more words of condolence, then left the cubicle to do Zach's bidding.

As for the other doctor, his compassionate eyes fas-tened on Laura and he reached for her hands. "I am very sorry you have lost your husband, Madame Do-netti. If you should require medical assistance, do not hesitate to call me at home. Dr. Massonac has my number."

"Thank you for everything you've done. I'm in-debted to the two of you for keeping this a secret," she murmured through her tears.

"It is a little thing to ask for something as important as the birthright of an innocent child, *n'est-ce pas?*"

"Thank God you understand."

Amen, Zach concurred.

As soon as the doctor had gone, Zach dropped his arm from her waist, then immediately realized he didn't like the feeling of separation.

"Laura, I'll leave you some time alone with Tony while I call Richard to come and get us. Is there anything I can bring you? A drink, maybe?"

She shook her head, not looking at him. "After the grueling race you lived through today, *I* should be the one bringing *you* something."

She turned suddenly to face him. "I hope you won."

Lord. She was the most honest woman he'd ever met.

"I did."

"That's good," she whispered. "Thanks to you, Zachary Wilde, I think I just might get through the rest of this night."

Little did she know that those words were going to help *him* survive the next twelve hours. His gaze wandered to the lifeless body beneath the sheet, the body that had once housed the troubled spirit of Tony Donetti. Though Zach had been his roommate, it saddened him to know that, until Laura had shared some personal insights with him, he'd had no idea what demons had driven her husband.

"Come out to the desk when you're ready."

She nodded. "I won't be long. I need to call his

aunt and uncle, as well as my own parents, but I'd prefer to do that from my hotel room.''

Naturally she craved her privacy. No one understood that better than Zach.

''I'll tell Richard to hurry.''

CHAPTER SEVEN

BEV EYED her husband anxiously. It was getting dark and he was driving a little too fast. Thousands of local inhabitants and racing enthusiasts were out partying, most of them still unaware that only hours ago Tony Donetti's brilliant cycling career had ended in tragedy. When the ten-o'clock news aired, it would be a different story.

The reality of his death still hadn't sunk in. She couldn't even begin to imagine *Laura's* state of mind right now. All she knew was that Zach's phone call had plunged her husband into an abyss. Whatever her brother-in-law had confided, it had caused Richard to close up, which wasn't like him.

After putting the receiver back on the hook, he'd told Richie to mind his younger siblings while he went out with their mother for a bit. On the way out to the van, he'd broken the ghastly news to her.

"Any way you look at it, it's a hellish situation. Zach's convinced that if he hadn't made Tony angry and tried to beat him in today's race, Tony would still be alive."

"How could he have made him angry?"

"You know Tony's reputation with women. Apparently Zach rubbed it in about how lucky Tony was to have such a beautiful wife following him around the circuit. I guess it didn't sit well, and Tony decided to turn the race into some kind of duel.''

''Then that's *Tony's* fault!''

''Try telling that to Zach. His guilt's compounded a hundredfold because of his attraction to Laura.''

''She has feelings for him, too.'' Bev sighed. ''Her guilt is probably just as bad as Zach's.''

''Maybe worse.'' He darted his wife a tortured glance. ''After all, she's carrying Tony's child.''

As usual her husband's insight got to the core of the problem. Bev buried her face in her hands. ''They're both going to need our help.''

''You can say that again. Right now Zach has decided he's directly responsible for Tony's death.''

''That's ridiculous! We saw Tony go down. His body simply gave out!''

''No, honey. Tony died from an illegal drug that clotted his blood.''

She gasped.

''Apparently this wasn't the first time,'' he added.

''Oh, poor Laura. How awful!''

''Zach got the powers that be to issue a statement that Tony suffered a fatal heart attack. The only people who know differently are the doctors, Laura, Zach and the two of us.''

''Thank heaven Zach had the presence of mind to prevent the truth from coming out. It would have created a scandal and ruined Laura's life, not to mention her baby's.''

"Exactly."

"Did she get a chance to talk to Tony before…''

"No." Richard took a shuddering breath. "After he fell, Tony never regained consciousness. According to Zach, he died shortly after the support van reached the hospital.''

"I don't believe this has happened." Her voice trembled. "I wanted…I hoped that one day when Laura was free, she and Zach might really get to know each other. But never at the expense of Tony's life!''

Richard groaned and shook his head. "Let's not start feeling guilty, too.''

"Oh, honey—'' she gave a deep sigh ''—think how devastated the team must be.''

"Zach says they're in pretty bad shape. Later tonight he's going to get them together and urge them to finish the race as a tribute to Tony. He knows how much they were counting on placing among the top finalists. Until this is over, he'll be the glue that holds them all together.''

Bev's eyes filled again with tears. "That sounds like your brother. He's a rock. But how much longer does he have to go on being the giver, Richard? When will it ever be *his* turn to find happiness?'' Her voice throbbed with pain.

"Don't, or you'll get me going.''

"He's doing this for Laura," came her tortured whisper.

"We both know that."

"I can't bear it, Richard. Even if she was going to divorce Tony, she'll still mourn his loss. She cared for him in some ways."

"You're right. And I can tell you one thing—" he cleared his throat "—Zach won't be interested in consoling the grief-stricken widow this time. He wasted two years praying Rosie would lay her dead husband's memory to rest, and look what happened!"

"But Rosie's husband wasn't dead. Laura's *is*. He won't be coming back. So don't you think there's a chance—"

"No. Not for Zach. I know him." The veins stood out in Richard's neck. "When this race is over, he'll be long gone—burdened by needless guilt he'll probably never throw off."

She shook her head. "We've got to do something—maybe call in professional help?"

"He'd never agree to that. Before Zach's phone call, I would have said Laura Donetti was the one person who might have been able to save him. But it's too late now. Tony's death has cast a pall over what might have been. When Zach's duty is done, there'll be no holding him."

"Don't say that."

"It's the truth, Bev. It's something I need to face."

Bev looked over at her husband. *If Zach leaves, you'll be in mourning. The one shadow on our marriage.*

"It would have been a lot kinder to Zach if *he* had been the one to die out there today," he muttered.

"*Richard!* You don't mean that. It's just your pain talking."

"You didn't hear him on the phone a little while ago. He couldn't feel guiltier if he'd held a gun to Tony's head and pulled the trigger. There's no reaching him. Honey…" He groped blindly for her hand.

She grasped his and held on tight, feeling the fragility of his emotions to the depth of her being. In that instant her protective instincts came rushing to the fore.

"We'll find a way." *I promise you that, my love.*

"MADAME DONETTI? Just sign these papers and we'll take care of everything until you decide when and where you wish to have your husband's remains transported."

The hospital administrator couldn't have been kinder. Neither could Zach, who stood nearby, ready to fulfill her slightest wish.

For the last little while he'd been running interference, smoothing her path. Without his masterly yet sensitive way of dealing with the press and the crowds, she didn't know how she could have handled any of it.

She sighed and murmured, "I'll let you know tomorrow."

"That will be fine."

She felt a familiar hand at her elbow. "Richard's here."

It would be easy to pretend that the shock of Tony's death, coupled with her pregnancy, caused her body to react to Zach's touch and deep voice.

But the real reason was Zach himself, this wonderful caring man who had appeared so unexpectedly in her life, teaching her about the things she'd been starving for, about the things of which she'd been deprived throughout her marriage, had she but known it.

She knew it now.

And if ever she needed proof that her wifely love for Tony had died years ago, she had the proof tonight. When she reflected on the past, it stunned her how blindly, how innocently, she'd entered into marriage. Tony had presented a dashing exciting figure. Her young heart had been in love with love, and he'd come along just as those new feelings were burgeoning.

She'd been too naive to ask the right questions. She hadn't known enough about life to realize she should have taken more time to find out who Tony really was.

She took a moment again to stare down at his inert body. She knew who he was *now*. Coming to France had been an education she'd never forget.

Suddenly a great calm descended, and her tears dried. One thing had become perfectly clear to her. It would be foolish to go on blaming herself for a situation that had always been out of her hands.

She knew as surely as she knew anything that her husband, who had been, in a way, on a tortured quest for the meaning of his life, had finally found peace. She believed that Tony was with his parents now, that he was getting his answers. Armed with this conviction, Laura was determined to make sure her baby knew its place in the world and would be happy there.

But alongside this verification lay a new form of torment, even more profound and disturbing. She veiled her eyes to prevent Zach from discovering her sinful, guilty secret. "I'm ready to go."

In silence they walked out of the hospital, Zach's hand at the small of her back, their hips occasionally brushing. Laura's breath caught sharply at the sweetness of the honeysuckle in the warm evening air.

Concentrate on Tony. Be thankful he's in a place where he's no longer hurting.

Tonight when she called George and Ann, she'd urge them to overcome the guilt she was sure they'd feel. Perhaps if she explained some of what she was feeling, they could find peace. If she wasn't successful, she'd ask them if they wanted to go with her to seek professional help. *Heaven knows I need to talk to someone about my wicked thoughts.*

Several times on the way to the van, she felt Zach's all-seeing gaze studying her profile, trying to gauge the depth of her pain. *If you knew what I was thinking, Zach, you'd be repulsed.*

"Laura?" Richard was the first one out of the van. His heartfelt embrace said it all. So did Bev's. *Where did these wonderful people come from? What is it they say about true friends? Those who are willing to mourn with those who mourn, to comfort those who need comforting?*

The tears Laura shed now were tears of gratitude— to the Wildes and their genuine outpouring of love.

"We're at your disposal, you know, Laura," Bev said after they'd all climbed into the van.

"That's right. Tell us how we can help," Richard called over his shoulder as they drove off.

Zach sat across from her in the back of the van, his powerful legs extended, his eyes on her face while he waited for her to speak. He had to be beyond exhaustion, especially after winning today's race, but it didn't show. The faint shadow of beard only enhanced those rugged features.

She, on the other hand, knew she must look as dreadful as she felt. "A-after I make some phone calls home, I plan to get a good night's sleep so I'll be ready to travel with your family in the van tomorrow."

With that unexpected announcement Zach sat forward, his expression disbelieving. "You're not planning to fly back to California?"

"No," she replied. "If you don't mind, I'd like to follow you around the circuit as we'd originally planned and hold a memorial service for Tony in Paris after the Tour is over. It's what he would have wanted. With this much lead time, his family and mine will be able to join us."

A long tension-filled silence ensued. Zach stared at her, his gaze still disbelieving. "But the baby..."

"Thanks to Bev, I'm fine. Zach, I want to do my

part to honor Tony's memory, too. I couldn't handle going home right now, not when all his racing buddies are here." *Not when* you're *here.* "But if it's a problem, I'll rent my own—"

"What in hell are you talking about?" he broke in with uncustomary harshness. "You honestly think I'd let you drive the circuit alone?"

She moistened her lips nervously. "No. I didn't think that. But Tony's death has changed everything, and it's possible Richie and the girls might be uncomfortable riding in the car with me."

"Don't be absurd. They're crazy about you. If anything, they'll get on *your* nerves trying too hard to make you feel better. Richie'll probably offer you his entire baseball-card collection."

Laura smiled softly at that, and he reciprocated.

"I'm going to let you two out here, then look for a parking place," Richard announced.

Laura had been so immersed in her conversation with Zach she hadn't realized they'd reached the hotel where they'd be staying for the night.

Without comment, Zach got out of his seat and opened the back door of the van, then helped Laura down. Immediately there were cameras in her face, reporters bombarding her with questions.

"Will there be funeral services in California?"

"Did you know your husband had a preexisting heart condition?"

"How soon are you going back on your television show?"

"There've been rumors your husband was on drugs. Would you comment on that?"

Then to Zach— "With Donetti out of the running, Mr. Wilde, can we assume that as King of the Mountain, you're now the number-one hopeful to take home the yellow jersey for the Ziff team?"

Laura had never liked the insensitivity of the news media, but tonight she felt a particular aversion to them. Zach's arm went around her shoulders protectively, an eloquent expression of his own disgust at their callousness.

"The team manager has already given the press a statement," he said firmly as he led her through the throng of reporters congregated around the entrance.

She slowed. "It's all right, Zach. Let me deal with this now, then maybe they won't hound us so much tomorrow."

He stiffened. "You're sure?" The fierce expression on his face would have frightened off any normal person. But Tony's death during the Tour de France had provided the kind of news that produced three-inch headlines and created millions of dollars in revenue. There was no stopping them.

"Yes. Just keep holding on to me," she begged softly.

His answer was to draw her closer to his side. She heard his sharp intake of breath before he said, "Despite her grief, Mrs. Donetti is willing to say a few words. Would it be possible for you to give her a little space?"

Something in Zach's tone had a sobering effect on the crowd, and they backed off a few paces.

Swallowing hard, she began, "No one is ever prepared for the death of a loved one. But if Tony could have chosen his time to go, it would have been during this race. He'd planned and dreamed of it since childhood."

Her voice was shaking but she couldn't stop it. "His father, Carl Donetti, was a great swimming champion. My husband inherited his competitive spirit and talent from him. This morning Tony awoke at my side so excited about the race I believe his heart just couldn't handle everything required of it."

She paused for breath. "But on a happier side, maybe the baby we're expecting has inherited those famous Donetti genes. It's possible that twenty years down the road, the world will once again see the Donetti name on the sports pages."

Laura had been forced to make a split-second decision. Just as she knew it would, her revelation had created a minor explosion of excitement. But it was for Zach's protection, if anyone's.

She knew how gossip ran rife. As soon as someone found out she was pregnant, they wouldn't think twice about attributing her baby to another man, and Zach would be their number-one target. Even now, because he was with her, supporting her, they could be forgiven for thinking he held an important place in her life.

"It might even be a girl," she added to divert their

thoughts further. Because they were hanging on every word, she got an approving chuckle out of them. But it was the extra squeeze from Zach that told her she was on the right track with this.

"Since I'm going to be a mother—in my opinion the greatest career on earth—I plan to stay home and raise my child. Tony lost his parents in infancy, and he was reared by an aunt and uncle who adored him, who devoted their lives to him.

"I plan to do the same for our child, and I know this is what Tony would have wanted. But if you would be so kind as to give me twelve hours to inform the television studio of my decision to resign, I would be grateful."

Actually Laura wasn't worried. She'd be talking to her parents before long. In reality, they were her employers, so there *was* no problem.

An odd stillness had fallen over the crowd of reporters. She had the oddest impression they were really listening to her, something that had never happened before. Now would be the time to say what was vital.

"The man standing next to me, holding me up so I won't fall down in a heap, is no stranger to you. Zachary Wilde has been Tony's roommate all these months of training. There's no one my husband trusted more. Now I know why." Her voice broke.

She felt the tremor that shook Zach's body just then.

"He has let me know that the Ziff team is alive and well. They're going to finish the Tour de France as if

Tony were riding at the helm. In fact, who could refute that he won't be right there with them, egging them on?''

She paused for breath. ''When it's over, my family and Tony's will hold funeral services for him.''

She was starting to feel light-headed. ''Tony loved the thrill of competition with all its ups and downs. He would be the first person to tell everyone to get on with the race and remember the good times.''

There was a suspicious prickling behind her lids. ''I, for one, intend to do just that. Now if you'll please excuse me, my most difficult job is still ahead of me. I have to phone the relatives who loved him like a son and tell them Tony's gone.''

Absolute quiet reigned as everyone backed off, allowing her and Zach to proceed into the hotel.

Unbeknownst to her, the Ziff team, sponsors and owners had congregated in the foyer and must have heard her speech, because they began clapping. One by one they stepped out of line to embrace her and offer their condolences. Every eye was suspiciously bright. Especially Richard's and Bev's, who'd rejoined them without her being aware of it.

She heard smothered coughs and more clearing of throats. Emotions were running high.

By the time they finally reached the elevator, she clung to Zach for fear she'd collapse from too much feeling. No one tried to jam inside with them.

When the door closed, sealing them off from the others, Laura let out an audible sigh.

"My feelings exactly," Zach murmured into her hair. "You were wonderful out there."

"I thought that if—"

"I *know* what you thought," he interjected, his voice thick with emotion. "You were right to talk about the baby and me in reference to Tony. Your frankness will pay dividends when the reporters get busy on their story."

His eyes were deep wells of gray as he went on, "You spoke from your heart tonight. I felt the effect on the crowd. You mesmerised them. You mesmerised *me*." He shook his head slowly. "I stand in awe of you, Laura."

She grasped both his hands, studying them before she gazed up at him once more. "Then we're both in awe, because you were the one who convinced the doctors to save Tony's reputation. From the moment I arrived in St. Léger, you've been my guardian angel."

Keep saying it, Laura. Keep saying he's your guardian angel. Don't think of him as a man. You mustn't!

It was all she could do to rise on tiptoe and kiss only his cheek, instead of his mouth. Then she let go of his hands to exit the elevator.

He detained her long enough to say, "Here's your room key. Number forty-three. Richard handed it to me outside the hospital. Their room is across the hall in case you need anything."

Laura took the key from him, fighting the urge to ask him where *his* room was. It took all her willpower not to suggest he drop by her room when he'd finished talking to the team.

What would be her excuse for requesting even one minute of his valuable time?

I need you, Zach. Since I've met you, I don't want you out of my sight. When you're around, my world feels complete. Come inside and hold me.

Make love to me.

All she said was, "I won't be disturbing anyone. They need a good night's sleep, too. So do you."

His question was unexpected. "Do you think that's possible?"

Her head came up. She steeled herself to keep from breaking down. "No. Each of us is having to do the impossible. Right now it's your turn to go downstairs and infect the team with your brand of Wilde heroism."

His brows knit. *"Heroism?"* He acted as if he'd never heard of the word. *How like him!*

"A real hero just does what needs doing. That's *you*. Good night."

Zach did nothing to detain her, but when she closed the door on him, he couldn't make himself walk away.

Lord. How could she shut him out like that? Until a few minutes ago he could have sworn she felt exactly the same way he did.

He wanted, needed her so much that desire was coursing through his body, igniting dormant feelings, making them ooze from their hidden places to infiltrate his last line of defense.

But she obviously wasn't suffering from the same affliction.

Unlike Rosie's husband, Nick Armstrong, Tony Donetti would not be coming back from the dead to reclaim his wife. He'd done something much worse.

He'd left his ghost behind to do the fighting for him, an adversary more cunning, more dangerous and cruel than the living entity. In that kind of unequal struggle, no one came out the winner.

As Zach stood there agonizing, his hands tightened into fists. *Not this time, Wilde.*

A shudder racked his powerful body before he wheeled away from the door.

The minute Klaus saw him enter the foyer of the hotel, he moved toward him. Over the past few months, they'd become good friends. "That was one amazing speech Tony's wife made out there. You can castigate me if you want, but he did not deserve her."

Zach struggled for breath. "I agree."

"So—" he clasped Zach's shoulder "—we will ride to the finish line for her and the little one to come, *Ja?*"

"Yeah," Zach muttered. His path set, he said, "Klaus? Do you mind if I take you up on the offer to room with you and Vadim for the rest of the circuit? I think it's important that the team stick together until the end of the Tour."

The German gave an infectious grin. "I not only do not mind, I am delighted. As for Vadim, he has been moaning that the old team camaraderie has been missing lately."

You're right, Klaus. A woman has a way of wreaking havoc. But never again. You're out of my life, Laura Donetti.

"After we plan our moves for tomorrow," Zach said, "I'll grab my gear and join you. What's your room number?"

"Twenty-one. I'll tell the concierge to roll in another bed."

Two floors down. Good.

"I have another idea." Zach was suddenly full of them. "I saw a café a few doors away. Let's gather the team and head there."

"I know the exact one. The beer is average, but the local *freuleins* are nothing short of *wunderbar,* if you know what I mean."

"Why do you think I suggested it?"

"Ja?" The German eyed him speculatively. "The press refers to you as the dark horse from Newport Beach. I believe they are right. Have you been holding out on me?"

Zach's face broke out in a wolfish smile. *I'm fighting for my life, Klaus.* "They don't call me King of the Mountain for nothing. *Ja?*" he mimicked.

Klaus nodded. "That's right. We haven't celebrated your victory yet. An oversight we will rectify after we dedicate the first round of drinks to Tony." He turned to the others. "Hey? Guys?"

While Klaus shepherded everyone out the hotel entrance, Zach lagged slightly behind. He should have told Richard and Bev about the change in his accommodations so they wouldn't worry when he didn't show up at the room next door to them.

But Zach couldn't handle the kind of gut-level bare-bones interrogation his brother would subject him to. Morning would be soon enough for that.

As he stepped out into the fragrant summer night, its nocturnal beauty called to his aching heart and body like a siren's song, bringing a staggering wave of fresh pain.

Keep walking, Wilde. Just keep walking.

IT WAS AFTER MIDNIGHT when Bev heard the hotel-room door open and close. "Honey?" She hurried out of the bathroom, leaving her brush on the sink. "How's Zach?"

Richard grimaced. "I have no idea. I haven't seen him."

She closed the distance between them and threw her arms around his neck. "That means he's with Laura," she deduced with a growing excitement.

"No. He's not. The concierge said he left the hotel with the team hours ago, but he thought most of them were back by now."

Bev took a deep breath, aware of the hurt Zach's nonappearance had caused her husband. After such a traumatic day, she knew Richard would feel helpless until he could talk to his younger brother and find out what was really going on inside him.

Her love for her husband made her want to take away his pain. "I'm not surprised. The team has always looked to Zach for leadership. He's either with the coach or Leon, working out last-minute details. He'll probably knock on the door any minute to say good-night."

"Maybe."

"There's no 'maybe' about it. Come on. The kids are asleep." She slid her hands over his chest. "Get undressed and lie down," she whispered. "I'm going to give you one of my deluxe back rubs."

He covered her hands, stilling them. "Have I told you lately that I couldn't live without you?"

Her eyes misted over. "All the time. I love you, too. So very much."

"I know. It's what keeps me going. Is there something wrong with me that I want that happiness for my brother?" His voice was thick with tears.

She shook her head. "No, darling. I guess we're going to have to be patient a little longer while we wait for it to happen. In the meantime, we'll continue to give Zach all the support and love he needs."

"What if he disappears and we can't?"

"We'll find a way, no matter what."

But by morning that promise had already been sorely tested. Not only had Zach avoided coming to their room before going to bed, he made only a token appearance at breakfast, and that was to inform them that he'd hooked up with Vadim and Klaus for the duration of the Tour.

Laura hadn't yet come down to eat, but Bev noticed that Zach didn't even mention her. Given his total absorption with Tony's wife yesterday after the race, for him to suddenly display a complete lack of curiosity over her and her creature comforts today set off warning bells. When he gave each of them a brief hug and he went off with the rest of the team, Bev felt her heart contract painfully. If she was suffering this much, then she could just imagine her husband's tortured state of mind.

There was no question that Tony's death had caused something to snap in Zach, with tragic results. The thing she and her husband had worried about had come to pass: rather than be vulnerable again, Zach had decided to distance himself physically and emotionally from Laura. Clearly there was nothing Bev or Richard could do about it.

Because Laura would be riding in the van with their family, Zach didn't have to worry about her and could relinquish all caretaking responsibilities to them. But in the process, he was distancing himself from the family, too, and she could tell it was already hurting Richard.

Laura didn't make her way downstairs to the dining room for another ten or fifteen minutes. Bev had the disquieting suspicion that she'd waited upstairs on purpose, knowing Zach would have been up early.

After she arrived at the table, she, too, avoided making any references to *him*. Quietly she told Bev and Richard about her phone calls home, the combined shock and grief of both her parents and Tony's aunt and uncle. It had been decided that after a memorial service in Paris, the families would accompany Tony's body home to California, where funeral services would be held at their family's church. Then he would be buried next to his parents.

Other than letting Bev and Richard know she'd asked the hospital to ship Tony's body to a funeral home in Paris, she didn't touch on the personal again. If she was plagued by nausea, she didn't mention it and involved herself in the children's conversation. She was, Bev thought, behaving far too normally for a pregnant woman who had just lost her husband. But Richie was oblivious. He seemed to think the sun rose and set with her, and he fought constantly for her attention, winning out over the girls.

Though Laura had a natural way with young people, even Bev could see that she was overdoing the pretense that all was well. Whenever the children made a reference to Zach, she glossed over his name as if he meant nothing more to her than anyone else on the Ziff team.

Several times Richard's anguished glance darted to Bev, the message poignant and unmistakable. When he finally suggested they leave the table and get ready to follow the racers for the next stage, Bev rose from her chair with the awful premonition that getting through the next two weeks under these conditions would be a true test of the refiner's fire.

CHAPTER EIGHT

THOUSANDS OF PEOPLE jammed the Champs-Elysées near the L'Arc de Triomphe to watch the racers cross the final finish line of the Tour de France.

A roped-off area had been reserved for the Ziff-team support group and families. When Richard parked the van on a side street near their vantage point, Laura hurried on ahead. For one thing, there had been so much togetherness in the two weeks since Tony's death that she felt Bev and Richard deserved some time alone with their family.

But the most compelling reason for separating herself from them was her need to watch Zach as long as she could through the binoculars. Too soon she would be joined by her parents and Tony's aunt and uncle in the cordoned-off area. She wanted these few extra minutes to herself.

So far, all seven of the Ziff team had made a fantastic showing with no serious mishaps. She was so proud of them she could burst. Klaus and Vadim had won several stages on the flats. Day after day, kilometer after kilometer, through sunshine and cloudbursts, they had all ridden with unflagging stamina and courage. It was possible Klaus might finish up in the first six.

But anyone could see that it was Zach who set the grueling pace for the team. He was the rock who anchored the younger racers and kept them focused.

The past two weeks had also been an agonizing experience for Laura, because with each passing day, she knew the end was drawing near. After the memorial service, Zach would be gone from her life for good.

Not once had he sought her out during their free times, either before or after each day's race. Not once had he come to her room to inquire if she needed anything.

Though she'd taken many walks alone in the quaint towns of France where they'd spent their nights—hoping to bump into him—the desired result had never occurred. Clearly he wanted nothing more to do with her.

Because he'd drawn the line, she didn't dare cross it. Something told her that if she tried to approach him, he would reject her, and this would bring pain beyond enduring.

Tony's death had resulted in a different kind of grief, a sadness more than a sense of loss, but in two weeks she'd come to grips with it. The excruciating pain she was experiencing now had everything to do with Zach, because he'd cut himself off from her and his family. No one said anything, but she'd learned a great deal from the confidences Bev had shared with her during those first few days in St. Léger. His brother and sister-in-law were hurting, too.

Needing to see Zach, she inched her way through the crush of bodies in the ninety-plus heat. When she could see the racers, she lifted her binoculars and spotted Farramundi in the far distance.

That might have been Tony out in front if only… She felt a pang that this couldn't be her deceased husband's moment, but she kept her glasses raised in search of Zach.

Klaus was coming up fast, jockeying for a winning position among the German and Dutch team members behind Farramundi. Another group rode behind. She could barely make out Jacques. Then she saw Zach.

I love you, Zach. You'll never know how much.

She watched him as long as she could, then headed toward the Ziff-support area. The grief-stricken faces of Tony's aunt and uncle brought back bittersweet memories of the past. Then she spotted her parents. Everyone caught sight of her at the same time.

"Laura!" they all cried, and ran to embrace her. By this time Richard and his family had joined them, but the introductions had to be cut short because the racers were fast approaching the finish.

A roar went up from the crowd as Farramundi crossed over first. But Laura's gaze was riveted on the four Ziff team members whom the other racers had allowed to ride forward. They pedaled side by side, Klaus, Vadim, Jacques and Zach, each holding high a personal item from Tony's racing kit. As they passed Laura on their way to the finish line, they saluted her.

While Richard and Bev's children shouted exuberantly to Zach, the crowd went crazy and camera flashes went off by the thousands.

Throughout the pandemonium, however, it was the silvery eyes briefly piercing Laura's that stayed with her long after the champagne flowed and Farramundi donned the yellow jersey.

When she heard Klaus's name announced as the fourth-place winner—a feat that brought another roar from all the Ziff fans—she felt her mother's arm go around her shoulders. "Come on, darling. You look ill. This has been too much for you. Your father and I are taking you back to our hotel and putting you to bed."

Too many emotions and feelings had caught up with Laura for her to form an argument. She nodded docilely.

Bev grasped Laura's hand and squeezed it hard. "We *have* to talk later."

Laura knew exactly what she meant. By tacit agreement they hadn't discussed Zach during the race. But now that it was over, there were things that needed to be said.

She threw her arms around Bev, attempting to convey her love and gratitude for all she'd done for her.

Soon it was Richard's turn. "We love you," he murmured, enveloping her in a hug.

"I love you, too," she whispered, then lifted her

head and looked straight into his eyes. "*Every one* of
the Wildes."

There. Her secret was out. She was no longer able
to hold back the truth.

Richard's eyes darkened and he cleared his throat.
"Do us a favor, Laura. Go lie down and take care of
yourself. We'll see you at the church for the memorial
service in the morning. Afterward we'll talk, and that's
a promise."

"I can't wait." Her voice shook.

Holding on to Richard was like holding on to a
piece of Zach. So it was with great reluctance that she
finally let him go, and then her wet eyes frantically
searched the crowd. As was true of every day of the
race, Zach couldn't be found once the stage had ended.
In a city like Paris, he could have gone anywhere,
traveled down any street. To find him would be like
looking for a grain of sand.

"SO... YOU'RE GOING to pull out before the service
tomorrow?"

Klaus and Vadim had just come into the hotel room
where Zach was packing up his gear. He'd hoped to
be gone before they'd finished their celebrating, but
no such luck.

"That's right. I made a reservation to leave Paris
tonight."

"What's the hurry?" Vadim asked, his shrewd eyes
narrowed on Zach's hardened features.

"New horizons. I've seen enough of Europe to last me a lifetime."

Vadim rubbed his lower lip absently. "That's too bad. The rest of us were hoping you'd take off on a small climbing trip we've planned into the Pyrenees. You know, a little vacation before we all have to go home. The valleys are peaceful, the food excellent, and the women warm and willing."

The words of a single guy.

He gave Klaus and Vadim about three more years before they each fell hard for a woman and settled down to raise a family.

At least that was the way it was supposed to happen. Zach was living proof that life didn't always fall into place quite that neatly or easily.

As for Vadim's words, they had no power to tempt Zach's scarred soul.

Because of him, Tony had died on a mountain, blood doping or no. Since that day, the only reason food made it to his stomach was to preserve his pointless life. The only woman Zach could imagine wanting was Tony's pregnant widow, and she was forever off-limits.

After coveting Tony's wife, he had no moral right to Laura or her love. And one day, when she had to explain to her child why she or he didn't have a father, Laura's resentment of Zach and the key role he'd played in Tony's death would flare up and intensify. Zach already knew what it was like to try to win over the child of another man. Rosie's son, Cody, had never

accepted him, and that division had created monu-
mental problems. No way could Zach put himself
through something like that again. It was time to bail
out.

If his plan for the future was successful, tourists
would be coming to him for a sailing holiday in far-
off and unusual places. It sounded like a palatable life.

"I appreciate the invitation," he said to Vadim,
"but I'm afraid I'll have to turn it down."

Vadim nodded, and then Klaus moved closer, his
eyes fusing with Zach's. "Thanks to you, the team
pulled through and I was able to place. Next year, who
knows? Maybe someone on the Ziff squad will take
home the yellow."

Zach nodded. "I've already told Leon to give you
my bike as my congratulatory gift."

The German's face suffused with pleasure. "I am
honored."

"I'll be watching and rooting for you from wherever I am."

"You don't know where you'll be?" Vadim
showed his surprise.

"Not yet."

It wasn't a lie exactly. He did have a destination in
mind and would stay there if he liked it. But for reasons of his own, he had no intention of telling anyone
where he was going.

"Do me a favor tomorrow and light a candle in the
church for Tony?"

"Of course," they replied in unison.

"Wait, *mon ami*. I have your polka-dot jersey," Vadim said.

"Give it to my nephew, Richie, tomorrow after the service."

"*Bien.*"

"Any word for Laura?" Klaus asked.

Zach had wondered when her name would come up. He turned away and lifted his backpack, ready to go. "Tell her we're grateful for Tony's life. Otherwise none of us would ever have had the opportunity of knowing each other. It's been an illuminating experience, *ja?*" He smiled at Klaus.

The younger man smiled back before the three of them hugged. Then Zach slipped out the door and headed for the foyer.

Besides a letter he'd written for Richard and Bev, he wanted to return a book she'd lent him to read, along with the travel magazine she'd left in his room. After leaving everything with the front-desk clerk to be given to the Wildes in room 703, he stepped outside and hailed a taxi for the airport.

When he landed in New York, he would board another plane for Miami, then Quito, Ecuador, where he would meet with Russ Magneson, president of the Windjammer Connection Tours in the Galápagos. The renowned naturalist and sailor was a leading expert on the famous archipelago.

For the next two months Zach had signed on to help crew the Windjammer line of yachts traveling to the most noteworthy of the eighty or so islands. In that

amount of time he would either have saturated his curiosity about the area and moved on, or he would buy
a sailboat with a cuddy to run his own private tours
for a while.

Hopefully the experience would help bring on forgetfulness, that long-sought-after state of mind that
would allow him to survive the rest of his life.

"MONSIEUR WILDE?" the front-desk clerk called out.
"I have something for you. *Un moment.*"

Wondering if it could be a fax from the company
at home, Richard waited somewhat impatiently. Bev
had already gone upstairs with the children, who were
desperate to use the bathroom. As for Bev, she was so
broken up about Zach and Laura's situation, Richard
had an idea he would spend the rest of the night trying
to console her.

When he saw a paper bag in the clerk's hand, he
blinked in surprise and took it from him. Curious, he
wandered over to a pillar and rested against it while
he looked inside.

A magazine and a book?

He frowned and pulled out both items. In the process, a letter fell to the floor. He recognized Zach's
handwriting and suddenly had the feeling *he* would be
the one clinging fiercely to his wife in the next little
while.

Greetings, Big Brother—
There are no words to express my feelings ade-

quately. You've always been there. You were always my role model. You never let me down. Not once in my life.

Richard groaned. This was the goodbye letter. Richard had been expecting it, but not until after the service tomorrow. Apparently Zach had decided to leave the country today. He read on.

Everyone should be blessed to have a brother like you. Then again, no one should have to give years and years of themselves and their time for someone else. But that's what you've done for me.

As he kept on reading, Richard's heart grew heavier.

I'm not unaware that my needs have put a blight on your otherwise perfect marriage.

But no more, Richard. The Tour de France is over. I relinquish you of all further responsibility where I'm concerned. Bev needs her husband back. Talk about the patience of Job, but even Bev has her limits!

Bev would be devastated when she read this.

Don't grieve for me. I'm fine. I promise to keep in touch so the family doesn't worry. Just think of me as you would an adventurous brother back in the 1700s who took off for new lands.

Lately I've developed a hankering to see the world. With the race out of the way, there's nothing to stop me.

Take special care of yourself and your precious family. With another baby on the way, why don't you slow down a little and enjoy life? No one deserves all the good things more than you.

I love you, Richard. You'll always be my idol.

—Zach

Minutes later Richard entered into his family's hotel room. He could hear his wife in the adjoining room with the kids.

"Bev?"

She must have known something was wrong by the sound of his voice, because she hurried into their room and shut the door, bracing herself against it. Her gaze darted to the paper bag.

"What have you got there?"

"A book and magazine you lent Zach."

She blinked. "He's gone, hasn't he."

Richard nodded before tossing the bag on the bed. "The letter's inside whenever you want to read it."

"Honey, he may have left Paris, but it's not going to work. It's like shutting the barn door after the horse has gone."

"I realize that."

She moved toward him with a mysterious smile. "It

doesn't matter that he's flown to the other side of the earth. He'll think about her until it turns him inside out. His protective instincts will be working overtime because she's going to have a baby. He'll slowly go mad wondering what's happened to her.''

Richard gave a great sigh. ''But for all the obvious reasons, he won't act on his feelings.''

''No. You're definitely right about that. But we know someone who might, don't we? I suppose it all depends on how much she cares.''

''She's in love with him,'' Richard declared without hesitation.

''I know that, but what makes *you* so positive, my love?''

''She told me today.''

''She actually said so out loud?''

He nodded.

''Richard!'' Her eyes lit with joy. ''If she could admit that to you, then she doesn't have any of the hang-ups Zach thinks she has!''

His wife's words ignited a ray of hope, but it was extinguished by a bleak thought. ''Honey, we have no idea where he's gone.''

''That's true. But we'll find out.''

Richard shook his head. ''Even if we do locate him and she attempts to see him, he'll fight her. I hate to tell you this, but Zach makes a formidable adversary.''

''I've no doubt, but haven't you noticed she's a fighter, too?''

He stared at his wife, then nodded.

"Honey, after Tony died it would have been so much easier for her to fly straight home to California and not deal with any of the pain or unpleasantness. Instead, she faced the press, supported the entire team and kept our children better entertained than either set of grandparents could have done."

Richard's mouth broke into a half smile. "You're right. She's definitely Zach's match. Funny how you would never guess it to look at her."

Bev darted her husband a wry glance. "I'm not a man, but I would imagine Laura Donetti's beauty would keep him too busy to think about much else."

He chuckled and reached for her. "Now how am I supposed to answer that?"

"You're *not* supposed to agree with me." But she grinned as she said it and was rewarded with a kiss.

He hugged her. "When I walked in here a few minutes ago, I felt like it was the end of the world. But as usual, my wonderful wife has made the sun come out again."

"That's what wives are for. I have to tell you that your brother badly needs to be loved by a wife like Laura Donetti. For what it's worth, the look she gave him today contained enough love to fill the universe. Zach can put up all the fences he likes, but Laura will get around them. Mark my words."

"I'm marking them, honey. I'm marking them," he murmured into her hair.

AT QUARTER TO TEN the next morning, Laura stood outside the small church in Neuilly with her parents

and Tony's relatives. They were greeting those attending the service—mostly Tony's cycling friends, the
people who owned the various racing teams or
coached them and members of the press. In Laura's
opinion it was a great honor that Farramundi, the five-
time winner of the Tour de France, along with his
wife, were kind enough to pay their respects.

But the whole time she shook hands and thanked
everyone for the outpouring of affection and flowers,
her eyes glanced around desperately for Zach. She'd
raved about him to her family and Tony's, and
couldn't wait to introduce him to the people she loved
most.

Finally Richard and Bev arrived with their children.
Laura broke free of the informal line to hurry forward
and hug them. Now that the Tour was over, she
thought, of course, Zach would be with them.

Without her having to say a word, Bev's expressive
eyes conveyed the bad news. Laura's disappointment
that he hadn't come was so great she felt ill. But she
had no choice but to carry on as if his failure to show
didn't faze her.

At the end of the brief service, she learned she
wasn't going to see him at all. For Klaus and Vadim
told her that, before Zach had left Paris yesterday, he'd
asked them to light a candle in Tony's memory. By
the time they'd given Richie Zach's polka-dot jersey
and had left the church, the pain Laura felt was excruciating.

Damn your nobility, Zachary Wilde!

I was afraid it was going to be like this, her heart cried out in agony. *I was afraid you would vanish the second you'd done your part for Tony and the team.*

But I'm not going to let you get away with it. Wherever you've run, no matter how long it takes, I'm going to find you. I will!

I'm in love with you.

Do you hear me? I'm in love with you.

Please God, help me.

"Laura?"

At the sound of Bev's voice, she turned to find the pretty blonde at her elbow. They stared at each other while streams of unspoken thoughts flowed between them.

"I have an idea where he might have gone, but I realize this isn't the time or the place to discuss it," she said in hushed tones. "When we're all back in California and you've had time to put this behind you, call us. You know the number. We'll be waiting."

A wave of pure love for Bev swept over Laura. She reached out once more to embrace the woman who'd become her dearest friend. "You'll be hearing from me sooner than you think."

"That day can't come soon enough for us." Bev's voice shook with raw emotion. "Take care going home and God bless."

CHAPTER NINE

"ZACH? MIND IF I JOIN YOU?"

Zach was sitting in the hotel lounge. He recognized Gwenn Barker's voice before he even looked up from the itinerary he'd been studying in preparation for tomorrow's new eleven-day trip.

A member of the Windjammer staff, Gwenn was the naturalist who'd been aboard the *Flying Cloud* with him on their last two trips.

Besides being a master dive instructor, she knew her stuff and held tourists captive with her knowledge about the Santa Cruz highland rain forest, the lava tubes and a wealth of other information concerning the plant and animal life. He was indebted to her for what she'd taught him.

But he hoped it was her fascination with his expertise as an ocean-certified sailor and not his being a single male that had prompted her to seek him out during their free time.

"Be my guest," he murmured. His invitation was as redundant as her inquiry, since she'd already seated herself.

Instead of the normal shorts and shirt, she'd worn a sundress to dinner, revealing a considerable amount of bronzed skin. In place of a braid, her long blond hair cascaded over one shoulder from a side part. She was most certainly a head turner.

He'd learned enough on two trips with her to know that her eight-year-old daughter lived with her part of the year in the Florida Keys, the other part with her ex-husband in the mountains of Colorado. A joint-custody situation that had been working for some years now.

Zach couldn't imagine a worse scenario for a child, but then, he tended to compare every marriage to Richard's, so he kept his thoughts to himself. In any event, he had no interest in Gwenn beyond a professional one.

"Can I buy you a drink?" she asked.

That should have been *his* line, but all attempts at civility seemed to have died after the fifth stage in Val d'Isère when he'd heard the news of Tony's death.

"I just had dinner and enough to drink with it," he replied. "But I'll keep you company while you have one."

"Actually I don't drink. Since you and I will be working on different boats for the next two cruises, we'll only bump into each other on the various islands. Tonight I'd like to get to know the man behind the facade."

His brows quirked. "You don't like the man you see?"

"If I didn't, I wouldn't have invaded your space, which you guard oh, so jealously."

Her blunt speaking prompted him to do the same. "I had hoped we wouldn't have to have this conversation, Gwenn."

"Whew. You don't mince words, do you?"

"No. I can't afford to, and you're too terrific a person for me to hurt, intentionally or otherwise."

"I don't want to rehash our lives, Zach. I certainly don't want to talk about mine. I'm lonely tonight and sense you could use some company, too.

Can't we at least spend it together? No words. No expectations or morning afters."

Zach shuddered inwardly at the depth of her loneliness. "How long have you been divorced?"

"Three years, and believe it or not, you're the first man I've approached since my husband and I split up. Do you have any idea how much courage it took me to walk over to this table, fearing we might have this exact conversation?"

Her honesty reminded him of someone else's. Just the thought of Laura Donetti ripped him apart all over again. Six weeks ago he'd ridden past her on his bike, sought and found her beautiful brown eyes for the last time. They still haunted him.

He pushed himself away from the table and stood up, startling Gwenn.

"You're much too remarkable a woman to use for a night's comfort."

She got to her feet, also. "You're too remarkable a man to hide away from life much longer."

"Isn't that what *you're* doing?" he demanded quietly.

"No. My parents were naturalists from the Keys who raised me in these waters. The man I married thought he wanted this life, but he found out he didn't. I'm living the only life I know how to live. *You're not.*"

He frowned. "What makes you say that? I've been a water baby from day one."

"You're a lot more than that. I've read articles about you in sports magazines. Cycling and sailing are only a couple of your passions. You have strong family ties in California and a lucrative outdoor-sign business spanning three states.

"You've been on the verge of marriage twice, but neither relationship worked out. Tragedy followed you to France where your teammate, Tony Donetti, died of a heart attack during the race. I happen to know that Zachary Wilde, the man who was crowned King of the Mountain, has hung up his jersey and quit the racing world to crew in the Galápagos, but I still say you're sailing in waters way out of your element."

Zach blinked in amazement that she'd been curious enough to do her homework on him. He didn't see it as an invasion of privacy. Gwenn was a good woman and honestly interested in him. He couldn't blame her for that.

Her mouth curved in a compassionate smile. "I had hoped you and I might be able to forget our pain for a little while. Oddly enough, I do believe yours is even greater than mine. But if you should change your mind and crave a little companionship with a woman who's very interested in you, remember I'm always here and we'll be crossing each other's paths for the next three weeks. Think about it.''

Zach knew himself too well. "I've already thought about it, Gwenn, and the answer is no.''

"Don't be so hasty,'' she warned him. "For the past three years I've told every man who approached me that I wasn't interested. Then I met you.''

She turned and left the dining room, but her words remained. He felt as if someone had just walked over his grave. After Rosie, he'd been just as convinced that no woman could touch his life again.

Then, by some incredible twist of fate, Laura Donetti had happened to him.

She's still happening to you, Wilde. Every damn night when you're forced to be alone with your thoughts.

You can't forget the brush of her hip against yours as you walked out of the hospital together breathing the intoxicating scents of the night.

You can still feel the touch of her lips against your cheek at her hotel-room door.

Every night you go inside that room with her and shut out the world. But the dreams aren't enough anymore.

Damn Gwenn Barker for reminding you that you're human, that you have needs that are eating you alive....

"Laura? I thought you would never get here!"

Laura had barely gotten out of the car she'd driven down from Hollywood to Newport Beach before Bev was hugging her like long-lost family.

It was how Laura felt, too, and she returned Bev's hug fiercely. They clung to each other for long moments, both assailed by bittersweet memories.

And in the clinging they could feel how much thicker they were from their pregnancies. They eventually broke apart with giggles that ended in hysterical laughter.

When it finally subsided Laura wiped her eyes and exclaimed, "You look wonderful!"

"So do you," Bev said, her cheeks glistening with moisture. "When I told Richard you'd called and were coming down, he gave a whoop of joy and said he was taking off work. I expect him at any moment. The kids won't be home for a couple of hours. When they find out you're here, they'll go berserk!"

"I've missed you all so much."

"You don't know the meaning of the word," came Bev's emotional response. She linked her arm with Laura's and they started walking toward the large hacienda-type house with its wrought-iron balconies and masses of flowering shrubs.

"Your home is gorgeous."

"Thank you, we love it. Oh, Laura," Bev said. "I've been praying you would call! So many times I picked up the phone to talk to you, but then I thought I'd better not because you needed your space."

Laura groaned. "Every day I've wanted to phone you, too. But I've been in a lot of pain since the funeral. Even with all the details to attend to, I find myself remembering things. I've been concentrating on the good times with Tony. I—I did love him once, and though I did most of my grieving long before he died, I found there were still things I had to let go."

"Yes, I can imagine."

"Being with Tony's aunt and uncle has helped. George and Ann didn't believe he died of a heart attack. There'd been too many rumors about drugs, so I ended up telling them the truth. It hurt them terribly. That's when I suggested we could all benefit from professional counseling, so the three of us went."

"Good for you. So has it made a difference?" Bev asked as they entered the house, which was done in a breathtaking Spanish motif.

"Yes. I'd already decided in the hospital room at Val d'Isère that I wasn't going to let Tony's death make me take on any more guilt. But that's easier said than done. We talked a lot about guilt in our therapy sessions. It became clear that all of us should have been getting counseling for years where Tony's concerned. We've been walking victims."

"And now?" Bev met her gaze. Laura had the impression she was holding her breath.

Now I need Zach. My life will never be complete without him. He understands me. He understands about Tony. I love him.

"Well, now that I'm four months along and have

been given a clean bill of health from my obstetrician, I'm ready to get on with my life.''

"A-are you going back to university?'' Bev stammered.

Laura's heart was pounding. "Yes. But there's something I have to do first.'' She swallowed hard. "You *know* what it is.''

"Thank Heaven!'' Bev threw her arms around her again.

After a moment Laura stepped away. "Have you heard from him, Bev?''

"Only through Mom and Dad Wilde. Apparently Zach has written them several times, but a courier always brings the letter to their door with no return address or clue as to where he might be.''

At that crushing news, Laura felt the blood drain from her face. Bev took one look and made her sit down on the couch, then sat beside her.

"Laura, I told you in Paris that I had an idea where he is. I still think he's there. Richard happens to agree with me.''

"Where?''

"The Galápagos Islands. South America.''

Laura gasped. "Really?''

"It's just a hunch, but before Zach checked out of our Paris hotel, he asked the front desk to return this to me, along with a book I'd lent him.'' Bev reached for a travel magazine lying on the coffee table and put it into Laura's trembling hands.

"If you'll look carefully at the article on the Galápagos, you'll see there's a tiny checkmark made in pencil next to the island of Santa Fe.''

Laura hunted for the page, saw the mark, then looked up. ''But what does it mean?''

''*I* didn't put that checkmark there, Laura. Nor did anyone else, because I'd just bought it off the stand in St. Léger for something to read. When I finished it, I left it in Zach's room, in case he was interested.''

''Y-you think because of that…?''

''That, and the fact that sailing, not cycling, is Zach's passion. According to the article, the Galápagos Islands offer some of the greatest sailing in the world. You didn't know him long enough to learn that he and Richard are both certified to operate any ocean-going boats up to 125 feet in length. They're both certified scuba divers, and while they were in high school and college, they worked part-time for the company, and the rest of the time as beach lifeguards.''

She paused, then smiled as she went on, ''In fact, I met Richard and Zach when my girlfriend and I got caught in the undertow at the beach and they saved us from drowning.''

''You're kidding!''

''Nope. Richard gave me CPR. When I could finally talk, I asked him if he was my guardian angel.''

At those words, chills shot through Laura's body, making the hair stand up on the back of her neck.

''*Laura Donetti!* Is it really you?''

At the sound of Richard's voice, both women turned

around. In the next instant he'd pulled Laura up and into his arms.

At last he released her and said, "I'm not going to ask you why you took so long to get here. All I can say is, you've come and Bev and I are very happy." He cast his wife a loving glance. "Now the only important question is, how soon are you going to go find my brother and bring him back home?"

This was a time for honesty. She lowered herself again to the couch. "I won't stop until I find him, Richard, but I can't promise to bring him home. Not...not if he doesn't want to come."

Richard's jaw hardened, exactly like Zach's. Another heart-wrenching memory. "You're the only one who can work the miracle."

She bit her lip. "We're going to need one. Zach has lost two great loves. He's not about to become vulnerable again with a third. On top of that, he believes himself responsible for Tony's death. His guilt runs very deep. I've learned a lot about guilt in counseling. It's one of the most difficult emotions to eradicate from the soul."

Richard's hand tightened on her shoulder. "But you're going to try."

Laura sucked in a breath. "I have no choice. I'm desperately in love with your brother."

"Thank God."

He paced the floor for a minute, then came to a stop and said, "I presume Bev has told you where we think he is."

"Yes. I already have a plan."

"You do?" Bev said.

"Yes. Knowing Zach, he's probably warned the locals not to tell anyone he's there. If I asked questions about him ahead of time, someone would probably tip him off and I might never be able to find him."

"You're probably right about that," Richard muttered.

"So, I think I'll sign up for one of those trips and go from there."

"My thoughts exactly," Bev said as she handed Laura a travel brochure from the coffee table. "There are a lot to choose from, but on page five there's an eleven-day trip that lists Santa Fe on the itinerary."

Laura spotted it. "I'll start with that one. But the next sailing is just ten days from now. I doubt I could get a reservation in time."

"We've already made it for you," Bev admitted somewhat sheepishly.

But Richard's smile revealed no qualms as he added, "Just in case."

"Don't I need immunizations to travel there?"

Bev shook her head. "We checked and found out they don't require any shots unless you're taking a side trip into the Amazon, which you won't be."

"What name did you use?"

Richard's eyes twinkled. "We debated on that one before coming up with Mr. and Mrs. John Wallace. That way you would be ensured a double cabin to yourself...just in case."

Just in case, Laura thought, Zach was crewing the trip. Her heart turned over.

"As soon as Bev phoned me a little while ago," Richard said, "I dropped by the travel agency and told them to put the charge on my credit card. Here are all your travel documents." He handed her a packet. "Your flight for Quito has already been booked under your own name, because, of course, you'll have to show your passport."

Laura stood in awe of their determination to find Zach. It was just as great, if not greater, than hers. "You two are incredible."

"We feel the same way about you," Richard said, smiling.

"Well—" Laura still felt a little dazed by events "—since you've prepared my path before me, it looks like the only thing left to do is some shopping."

"How about right now?" Bev suggested. "We'll go to lunch and then I want to take you to this darling boutique along the waterfront. They have a maternity section with the most adorable mother-and-infant matching sailor outfits you've ever seen."

Fear warred with excitement, making it difficult for Laura to breathe. "If I do catch up with him, he'll see this pregnant lady and dive overboard."

Richard's expression sobered. "You don't know what you're talking about. I saw the way he looked at you in Paris. It could have set off a three-alarm fire."

A warm flush stole over her cheeks. "He's just got to be there, Richard."

"This may be a long shot, but my wife's instincts are never wrong. In my gut, I *know* he's there."

On a surfeit of emotion, she reached out to hug them again. "Then I'll find him."

TEN DAYS LATER on a golden Monday morning, Laura and the eight other people in their party—four of whom were members of the same family from Michigan—stepped off the plane at Baltra Island. Immediately they boarded a bus that drove them to a dock on an azure-blue bay.

The two older couples, the Devrys and the Olsons, were close friends and had kept pretty much to themselves during the preceding part of the trip—a stay in Quito and a city tour. But to Laura's chagrin, the Fisher clan, comprising the parents, Don and Sylvia, and their two sons, Brad and Pete—both in their early twenties—had been unable to get over her resemblance to Margo of TV-soap-opera fame.

Laura had laughed at their comment and answered that Don reminded her of Bob Stack, the host of the TV show "Unsolved Mysteries".

That observation had distracted them enough to finally leave the subject of her looking like Margo alone. Unfortunately the two sons, both on break from the University of Michigan, seemed delighted that the young widow was traveling with them.

Their unsolicited attention was something Laura hadn't planned on. So except for meals, she'd chosen not to join them on the city tour and opted to stay in her hotel room in Quito until it was time to fly to the Galápagos.

Both Brad and Pete attached themselves to her now as they all made their way down to the pier. A dark-bearded, middle-aged man stepped forward and extended a friendly hand to each of them. He commented that the birds they saw diving toward the water like shooting arrows from dizzying heights were called blue-footed boobies. It brought a smile to her lips.

Unlike her, their greeter didn't wear sunglasses, and his skin was burnished the color of teak. She noted the admiration on his face as his deep-set blue eyes scanned her face and figure.

Her newly purchased white maternity pants with a sleeveless loose-fitting blue-and-white sailor top, which hid her condition, felt comfortable in the mid-seventies temperature. But because of the Humboldt Current, she'd heard that the nights got cool, even cold, so she'd packed a sweater and windbreaker.

Those with a discerning eye might suspect she was pregnant, but according to Bev, it would be at least a couple of more months before Laura blossomed for the world to see.

She debated telling the Fisher sons that she was pregnant. The news would definitely kill their interest. But she also felt it would be better if no one on board knew she was expecting a baby. Aside from the fact it wasn't anyone else's business, she didn't want any sort of preferential treatment.

"Welcome aboard the *Puff Cloud*. I'm the skipper and my name's Nathaniel Simonds. I answer to Nate."

He seemed to be addressing only her, and so she murmured, "Nate it is. I'm Jean Wallace."

"Do you mind if I call you Jean? We're pretty informal around here."

"Not at all."

Laura had been christened Laura Jean Delaney after the first names of both grandmothers, so the middle name wasn't entirely foreign to her.

"Good. Correct me if I'm wrong, but I thought there was a *Mr.* Wallace coming aboard, as well."

On the flight from Miami to Quito, Laura had made the decision that until she found Zach, she would tell as much of the truth as possible without divulging her last name. Zach could be crewing aboard the beautiful sixty-six-foot yacht that Nate was skippering and that would be taking her to the various islands, but so far she hadn't seen any sign of the crew.

If it was at all possible, she wanted the element of surprise to be on her side when she first saw him again. *If* she saw him again, her heart cried.

There were many different tour companies that ran trips in the Galápagos, but because of the travel magazine's article on the man who headed the Windjammer Tours and his impressive sailing credentials, Bev and Richard had acted on the hunch that Zach might be working for this particular tour group.

"Recently my husband passed away, and I decided I needed a vacation. Since I didn't want to share a cabin with anyone, I booked the trip under both our names and paid the double fare. I hope that's all right.''

"If it's all right with you, of course it's all right with us. There's no better place to relax and enjoy nature. Hopefully this trip will bring you peace of mind and help you to get on with the rest of your life.''

"That's exactly why I've come. Thank you.'' She smiled in relief because he hadn't recognized her from TV. Furthermore, he accepted her explanation without question and didn't pry.

"I first heard about the Galápagos Islands when I was a schoolgirl. I think it was in science class and the teacher was discussing Darwin's theories on evolution. The slides on those enormous turtles and sea lions had me completely fascinated.''

He nodded. "I had a similar experience in my youth. I can promise you we're going to see those sights and a lot more before this trip is over. We're also extremely lucky to have Gwenn Barker along as our naturalist.

"She's lived a lot of her life out here—initially with her parents, but they're retired now. You couldn't have a better guide to introduce you to this wildlife sanctuary. No one's more qualified.''

"I'm looking forward to meeting her.''

"She'll be aboard shortly, along with our crew of three. In the meantime, your cabin is the first door on your right when you board the *Puff Cloud*.'' Just the mention of the crew sent a shiver of nervous excitement through her.

"We're all on hand to keep you safe and comfortable," he continued, oblivious to the chaos of her emotions. "Call on us at any time if we can be of assistance."

"Thank you," she said.

"In half an hour, we'll ask everyone to assemble in the dining area to meet Gwenn. Right now, go to your cabin and settle in. The crew will follow with your bags. You'll see we've left you some literature to read, and you've been supplied a selection of soft drinks and beer, so help yourself."

Needing no encouragement, she boarded the yacht and found her way below. Pete, the elder of the Fisher sons, hovered expectantly in the corridor watching her, obviously having already checked out his cabin.

Laura pretended not to notice as she entered her room and shut the door. She had no intention of making an appearance until everyone had been called together. The only thing on her mind was Zach. While she unpacked, she tried to imagine what would happen if he was assigned to the *Puff Cloud*.

She hid her face in her hands. It had been almost two months since she'd seen him. Too many long empty agonizing days and nights.

Have you thought about me at all, Zach?

If, or when, you discover I'm a member of the tour, will you ignore me in front of the others and wait until no one else is around before you confront me? Will you be angry?

There was a worse thought. Maybe he wouldn't seek her out at all.

That possibility struck fear in her heart.

Knowing Zach, he might simply acknowledge her with a nod, as he would any past acquaintance, and then go on about his business, never giving her an opening.

If that happened, Laura was determined to go after him and force him to listen while she poured out her heart. What he decided to do with that knowledge was anyone's guess, but it wasn't in her nature to play games.

A shudder passed through her. What if he couldn't return her love?

Traumatized by her thoughts, she still hadn't put her things away when Nate announced over the intercom that everyone was to proceed to the dining area at the other end of the yacht.

With alternating feelings of excitement and trepidation, Laura left the cabin still wearing sunglasses for camouflage, her gaze darting everywhere for signs of Zach.

The second she entered the common room, she caught sight of the three other crewmen and her heart plummeted.

Zach wasn't among them.

After the captain had made the introductions, she realized she would have to put her second plan into action—make friends with the crew and, without arousing suspicion, find out if Zach was an employee of Windjammer Tours. As Richard had said, this was a long shot, but now that she was here, she wasn't about to give up until she was convinced Zach hadn't come to the Galápagos at all.

Disappointed beyond belief, Laura only noticed Gwenn Barker after she felt the other woman's long probing gaze. Did she recognize Laura from her role on TV?

Somehow Laura doubted it. The naturalist spent most of her life here, away from the so-called amenities of civilization.

Not until Nate called upon the athletic-looking blonde to give a preliminary sketch of their itinerary did those penetrating yellow-green cat's eyes finally shift from Laura to the rest of the group.

She imagined that most men found their naturalist, who was probably in her midthirties, rather attractive. It was more than possible that Zach knew her.

Does he find her appealing?

Tortured by the thought, Laura could hardly concentrate on the woman's talk. She returned to her cabin as soon as the session broke up and it was announced they were setting sail.

Pete followed Laura down the corridor and asked her to join him for a drink in the cabin he shared with his brother. Deciding she'd better set the perimeters right now, she kindly but firmly refused him, hoping he'd get the point.

Once she'd shut the door, she opened her bags and put her things away in the drawers and closet. As she was placing her toiletries in the bathroom, she heard a knock on the door.

Afraid it was Pete, she decided not to answer it.

"Mrs. Wallace?" a female voice called.

It sounded like Gwenn Barker. For some unknown reason, the hairs prickled on the back of Laura's neck as she opened the door.

"Hi," Gwenn said. "Mind if we talk for a minute?"

After a slight hesitation Laura shook her head and told her to come in.

"I'll get straight to the point," Gwen said as soon as the door closed. "Part of my job as your guide is to know the passengers on board and adapt the tour to their individual needs."

Laura decided that Gwenn's womanly intuition had devined Laura's pregnancy, and so she needed to ascertain her state of health before the tour got under way.

Laura spoke up. "I know what you're going to say. It's true I'm pregnant, but my doctor told me I was in perfect health and he encouraged me to enjoy this trip. I went over the itinerary with him, and he said the exercise would do me good. I hope that reassures you."

Gwenn eyed her with a puzzled frown. "That's not why I'm here. We've had pregnant women on board before. I myself found out I was going to have a baby during a trip about nine years ago. As long as your doctor has given you the okay, that's fine with us.''

"I'm relieved. I-is there another problem, then?''

"Only to me.''

"I don't understand.''

"I have to work with the authorities when we're responsible for tourists entering Ecuador or Peru for one of our tours. They send me a list of passengers' names, in case there's an emergency of some kind.''

Laura knew what was coming and braced herself.

"Windjammer Tours has you down on our list as Mrs. Jean Wallace. But according to the name on your passport, you're Mrs. Laura Donetti. I recognized the name immediately. My mother is a huge fan of your soap opera.''

"I see.''

"It isn't a problem, Mrs. Donetti. If I was a celebrity, I'd travel under an assumed name and do everything in my power to keep attention away from me, too. I won't say a word of this to anyone, not even the captain. For this trip, you'll be Mrs. Jean Wallace.

"Off the record, may I offer my condolences over your recent loss. I read about your husband's accident in a magazine. I'm very sorry.''

Laura expelled the breath she was holding. "Thank you. It *was* awful. I won't pretend about that, but the worst is over, and I'm looking forward to this cruise.''

"I lost my husband through a divorce. The pain is not dissimilar, but I can tell you that your child will bring you incredible joy. I think you're very wise to give up your career to be a full-time mother. If I didn't have to earn a living, I'd stay home, too.''

"Thinking of my baby has been my one abiding comfort," Laura confessed, warming to the other woman. "Thank you for allowing me my privacy."

"You're welcome. Anytime you want some female conversation, don't hesitate to seek me out."

"I won't. Thanks again."

After Gwenn left the room, Laura gave in to her pain and flung herself across the bed, convulsed with sobs. Since Gwen had read about everything that had happened during the Tour de France in a magazine, then she would have seen Zach in the pictures. The fact that Gwenn didn't say a word about him or display any sign of recognition meant he didn't work for Windjammer Tours.

Richard and Bev had been so certain!

But maybe he'd hired on with another company in the Galápagos.

Laura suddenly sat up and wiped her eyes, determined to get to know their naturalist a great deal better. By the time this trip was over, she would prevail on Gwenn to help her find Zach.

If he's here to be found.

CHAPTER TEN

"HI, SAILOR. A penny for your thoughts."

At the sound of Gwenn's voice, Zach turned his head in her direction, hoping she'd happened upon him by accident, not by design. Because of the bright morning sun he had to squint to see her.

Two sea turtles were mating on the shore, a sight tourists paid thousands of dollars for the privilege of viewing. Once upon a time, the scene would have intrigued him. But coming to work in the Galápagos had only underlined an acute sense of loneliness brought on by his self-imposed exile.

If anything, his state of mind was worse than when he'd left Paris. After the trip ended tomorrow he had ten days' free time coming to him and he'd decided to fly to Quito.

Aside from the Galápagos, he hadn't spent any time in Ecuador. Maybe when he reached the mountains, he could find that joie de vivre he'd unexpectedly felt during the first few days of the Tour de France.

Be honest, Wilde. The magic started when you opened your hotel-room door and discovered Laura Donetti standing there.

"Hello, Gwenn. I didn't realize the *Puff Cloud* stopped on Bartolome Island this trip."

She hunkered down next to him. "That's the difference between the two of us. I knew the *Racing Cloud*'s itinerary by heart and figured the yacht you're crewing for had pulled into the other disembarkation point by now. My female intuition told me that when you went on break, I'd find you on this forgotten stretch of beach, instead of keeping watch over the people swimming among the penguins."

His mood black, Zach got to his feet. He and Gwenn were colleagues of a sort, but he'd walked through the mangroves to this part of the island to be alone. It would be better to put some distance between them before he hurt her anymore because of his inability to respond.

She shielded her eyes from the sun to look up at him. "Before you take off, could I ask you a question?"

"You already know the answer, Gwenn."

"I think maybe I do, but I'm going to ask it, anyway. How well acquainted were you with Tony Donetti's wife?"

The mention of Laura—particularly when she was never out of his thoughts—set Zach's heart thudding. He paused midstride and jerked around, stunned by the question.

Her shrewd regard missed little. "Well, now, I guess I have my answer."

He watched her get up, wiping the grains of sand

from her shorts. Though Gwenn couldn't help reading what was printed in the tabloids, he felt irrational anger at the media who'd turned the tragedy of Tony's death and its aftermath into the biggest moneymaker of the Tour de France. He was particularly angry at her for believing the lies and succumbing to the sensationalism.

"You disappoint me, Gwenn," he said in a withering tone. "I thought scientists like you always strive to get at the truth."

"That's right." She stood her ground. "The scientific method of discovery may be basic, but it gets the job done. Fact number one—Tony Donetti died during the race.

"Fact number two—you were a teammate of his.

"Fact number three—you were his roommate throughout the training period prior to the race.

"Fact number four—the press took pictures of you with your arm around Mrs. Donetti the night her husband died.

"Fact number five—you disappeared right after the finish of the race in Paris.

"Fact number six—no one has seen you since, not even your family.

"Fact number seven—out of the blue you showed up in the Galápagos, asking to crew for Windjammer Tours.

"Fact number eight—you're single and attractive, and I know in my gut you're not into an alternative life-style.

"Fact number nine—you've spurned me, the only eligible woman working for the same company as yourself.

"Now there's fact number ten..."

White-lipped, he muttered, "And that's?"

She shook her head. "I'll let you figure it out for yourself."

"What in hell are you talking about?"

"Who," she corrected him. "Ever heard of Mrs. John Wallace?"

Zach couldn't imagine what Gwenn was getting at. "I don't know anyone by that name."

Gwenn stared hard at him. "Oddly enough, I believe you. See you around, sailor."

"Oh, no, you don't!" In a lightning move, Zach grasped her arm to prevent her from leaving. "You had a definite reason for mentioning that woman's name to me. I want to know what it is."

"Just testing one of my theories. I've come up with a partial answer."

"Then let me in on it."

"Sorry." She looked pointedly at the hand still holding her wrist.

Only now did he realize how out of control he was. He'd never used force on a woman in his life. As if her arm were a burning coal, he let go of it. "Forgive me, Gwenn," he said. "I didn't mean to come on so strong."

"I know that. Obviously I've hit a nerve that runs deep. I have my own apologizing to do for driving you so hard. Trust me, I'll be leaving you alone from here on out. You're obviously on some kind of pilgrimage to forgetfulness and don't want to be found, let alone hassled. So, the next time we see each other, I'll just wave and keep on walking.''

He sucked in a breath. ''I've behaved badly.''

''None of us is at our best when we're in the kind of pain you're in,'' she said before walking off.

He didn't call her back. She'd opened up a wound that had been festering since the moment he'd laid eyes on Tony Donetti's wife and had wanted her for himself.

Zach took off on a run down the deserted pristine beach, but the exercise didn't wipe out the name Mrs. John Wallace. Why had Gwenn mentioned it?

Another couple of miles and the answer came to him.

Laura has remarried.

That's what Gwenn, with her keen intellect and perception, had been trying to tell him. Maybe she thought it would help him get over his heartache.

But the knowledge that Laura belonged to someone else, that another man had the right to kiss that exquisite mouth, to touch that gorgeous body, came like a tremendous blow to the midsection, incapacitating him. He collapsed on the sand with a groan.

He'd felt the brush of her lips on his cheek in gratitude; he'd crushed her grief-stricken body in his arms because she'd sought comfort. But never once had he been able to let loose his passion.

Now some other man had that privilege. Most likely

someone who knew her well in California and had wanted her, despite the fact that she didn't love him back. Zach buried his face in his arm.

Whoever he is, I know you couldn't possibly be in love him with him, Laura. Did you do it to give your baby a father?

Richard probably knew who the man was. All Zach had to do was get to the nearest phone and he could find out. But it would change nothing. If Zach hoped to forget her, the fewer details he was told about her remarriage, the better.

All he knew was that the faceless man who now claimed Laura for his wife had taken advantage of her pregnant condition, unable to wait a decent length of time before getting her into his bed.

And Laura let him. Dear God.

Three blasts of the yacht's horn returned Zach to an awareness of his surroundings. The *Racing Cloud* was getting ready to sail to North Seymour Island for its passengers' last afternoon and night aboard ship.

Jumping to his feet, he took off toward the boat. Realizing he was already late for report—his first infraction since arriving in the Galápagos—he poured on the speed. Zach had always prided himself on being the total professional. Unfortunately Gwenn's news had knocked the foundation out from under him, leaving him in utter chaos.

He went aboard and found a moment to apologize to Captain Martelli, who praised him for his performance thus far and told him not to worry about it.

Later in the day Zach volunteered for the night watch. His thoughts of Laura were so tortured he needed to keep busy, knowing he'd never be able to get to sleep.

When morning came and they'd pulled ashore at Baltra Island, he'd finish up last-minute chores, grab his gear and head for the plane that would fly him to Quito. He needed a change, anything to distract his thoughts. Otherwise… *Otherwise what, Wilde?*

THROUGHOUT THE TRIP, Laura had slowly been getting to know Gwenn Barker. Tonight, her last night aboard the *Puff Cloud,* she felt confident enough to approach the woman in her cabin. It would be a good time to tip her for being an outstanding guide, and it would allow her the privacy she needed to talk frankly.

She waited until dinner was almost over, then slipped away from the dining table before Pete could drum up some reason to detain her. She'd amassed dozens of pictures of the Ziff team for Tony's scrapbook and had brought a couple of photographs of Zach with her.

One newspaper article showed him in his cycling uniform and cap. The other picture had come from a magazine where he stood bareheaded and casually dressed with a group of people. Both were excellent pictures, easily identifiable.

But even if they weren't that clear, Zach was extraordinarily handsome. If Gwenn knew him, she would recognize him immediately. If she hadn't seen him, she might at least have heard of him. Laura didn't want to even consider the possibility that the other woman wouldn't be able to help her.

When she was ready, she glanced outside her cabin door to see if the coast was clear. Good. No one in the corridor. The sunsets in the Galápagos were spectacular, which meant their travel party was probably on deck enjoying the view one last time.

Normally Gwenn didn't mingle with the passengers after hours. Laura hoped that was true of their guide tonight as she hurried down the hall to her cabin.

To Laura's relief, on the second knock Gwenn told her to come in. Laura entered and shut the door, her heart starting to pick up speed. The fear that she might be headed toward a dead end made her mouth go dry.

She knew she was talking too fast when she thanked Gwenn for the fabulous trip and left some American money on the table for her. The woman cocked her head quizzically.

"Something's wrong. What is it? Has Pete been pulling more moves? He has a terrible crush on you, you know. It's a good thing he's going home tomorrow."

"Pete's been somewhat of a nuisance, but that isn't what's wrong. Gwenn—" she bit her lip "—I'm going to be honest with you about something because I don't know where else to turn.

"I came on this trip to find someone I have reason to believe might be working here in the Galápagos. Or rather, his brother, Richard thought he might be here, crewing on one of the yachts."

Gwenn eyed Laura in her usual direct way. "What's his name?"

"Zachary Wilde." Laura handed her the news clippings. "Since you heard about what happened to my husband during the Tour de France, it's possible you saw Zach's picture, as well, and would recognize him if he was in these waters."

"I saw him in the magazine article."

"I imagined you would have."

Gwenn gave her back the clippings. "He's so attractive he'd be impossible to miss."

This was a time for total honesty. "He's much more than that." Laura's voice shook. "He's the most wonderful man I've ever met. Gwenn, have you seen him? I *have* to find him. I'm...I'm deeply in love with him."

"Is he the father of your baby?"

Laura felt as if someone had just stabbed her. "No, but I knew the gossip surrounding Tony's death would construe things that way. If the truth be known, though, I wish Zach *was* the father," she whispered brokenheartedly.

"He knew I was pregnant before I did, and he took expert care of me in France while I was green with morning sickness. Tony died without knowing.

"You see, the pregnancy was an accident. Tony didn't want children, and I was afraid to tell him until the Tour was over." Laura covered her face with her hands. "I didn't want anything to upset him. I knew he wanted a divorce as much as I did, but he'd been so consumed with winning the Tour de France we never got the chance to talk about it. Then he died from some drug he'd been taking. Zach left Paris before the memorial service and no one's seen him since.''

Gwenn cocked her head again. ''I thought your husband died from a heart attack.''

''That's what Zach told the press to avoid any scandal that might hurt me or my baby. That's the kind of man he is. If Zach has a fatal flaw, he's *too* noble.'' She sighed. ''He's like the proverbial knight in shining armor and won't let anyone see his pain. Please, Gwenn, don't tell anyone else what I just told you. That secret is the only thing holding my sanity intact.''

The woman nodded. ''You have my word.''

''Thank you.''

''Look, Laura, I wish I could help you.''

She felt Gwenn's sincerity, but lost the battle with tears and wiped them away furiously. ''This means Richard's intuition was wrong. He and his wife had convinced me I'd find Zach here. They were depending on me. I—I dread calling them with the awful news. Richard and Zach, you see, are closer than twins. His disappearance has put a blight on their marriage. I'm not the only one suffering.''

She took a shuddering breath. ''Well… I've just got to start a new search someplace else, because I'm not going to quit until I find him. He has this mistaken idea that he was responsible for Ton—'' She stopped abruptly.

"I'm sorry, Gwenn." She sniffed and pulled herself together. "This isn't your problem. Please forgive me. You're not only the best guide around, you kept my secret from the others. When I get an opportunity, I'm going to write your company and tell them how lucky they are to have you in their employ."

She started to leave when Gwenn said, "Wait."

Laura wheeled around.

"What is it? Did you remember something?"

"Maybe I'm doing the wrong thing, but I can't lie to you. Zach *does* work for Windjammer."

"*Gwenn*—does he know I'm here?"

"No. Just give me a little time and I'll find him."

"You would do that for me?" she blurted joyously.

"Sure. Do you have to go home tomorrow?"

"No!"

"I'm assuming that money is no problem."

"No."

"I tell you what. The *Puff Cloud* is taking on another group of passengers tomorrow and it's fully booked. But if you want, you can room with me. Sometimes my daughter joins me, but not this trip, so it wouldn't be a problem. I'll arrange it with Nate tonight. He won't care as long as the company gets paid for your passage."

"Really?"

"Of course. I'll make inquiries at head office to find out where Zach is exactly. Then I'll leave a message that you're on board the *Puff Cloud* looking for him. How's that?"

"That's…that's wonderful!"

Without conscious thought, Laura threw her arms around Gwenn. "One day I'll find a way to really thank you."

AS IT TURNED OUT, Zach was the last to board the plane taking off for Quito. He found the only available seat next to a talkative guy who introduced himself as Pete and looked about twenty-two or -three.

Zach wasn't in the mood to deal with anyone, let alone Pete and his brother, Brad, who sat directly behind them. After shutting his eyes, he sat back, pretending to sleep. He needed it desperately, but feared that sought-after state would elude him for a long time to come.

Unfortunately he couldn't tune out the conversation going on next to him, which not surprisingly centered on some breathtaking creature they'd met aboard their yacht, rather than the sights they'd seen in the Galápagos. Zach could hardly remember being that age, when anything, everything was possible.…

"She thinks she's gotten rid of me," Pete was saying in low tones to his brother, "but she's in for a big surprise."

"Are you going to fly out to California?"

"Yup. On my next break."

"Where are you going to get the money?"

"I'll work more shifts at that pizza place after classes."

"If she didn't want to be with you on the boat, then I don't think she's going to be that happy to see you."

"Mom and Dad were around. That's why she avoided me."

"I don't think so. She's older than us. Besides, Mom says she's pregnant and wants to be left alone."

"Tough. I'm going to go see her, anyway."

"How are you going to find her? You don't have her address."

"I'll find her. Even if there is no John Wallace listed in the directory, I can get Walt to help me. His dad works for the passport office."

John Wallace?

Zach sat up with a start, experiencing a suffocating feeling in his chest.

He turned to Pete. "I couldn't help but overhear you guys talking. What yacht did you say you were on?"

"The *Puff Cloud*."

His jaw hardened. *Gwenn knew…*

When he'd forced himself to calm down, he said, "My yacht was full of retired couples."

Pete grinned. "We lucked out," he admitted, eager to talk. "Man, she's one hot babe."

"She's a widow, too," his brother, Brad, added.

Zach's eyes closed tightly. Laura hadn't remarried, after all. The relief he felt was exquisite.

"How come she's not on this flight?" he asked when he'd recovered.

Pete shrugged. "She said something about wanting to see more of the islands, so she stayed on board for another tour. If I'd had the money, I would've stayed on with her.''

A fresh surge of adrenaline almost drove Zach from his seat. "What did she look like?"

"Have you got all day?"

"At least until Quito."

"Have you ever seen that soap 'The Way Things Are'?"

"I've caught a few segments," he lied without compunction.

"She looks exactly like Margo, the attorney," Brad said.

"Nope." Pete shook his head. "She's much better-looking. Black curly hair, dark brown eyes. You oughtta see her in a bathing suit. Whoa—is she built! Her legs go on forever. I get the hots every time I think about her."

At that point, Zach excused himself on the pretext of needing to use the rest room. If he'd had to endure one more word, he would have bashed Pete's teeth down his throat.

Once he'd locked the door, he leaned back against it, trying to make sense of what he'd learned.

It didn't surprise him that Laura would travel under an assumed name.

She'd lived through so much hounding from the media, she probably dreaded stepping outside her house to get the newspaper. *If that, in fact, is her usual habit,* he thought. He had no clue how she lived her life.

What really preyed on his mind was the reason she'd come to the Galápagos.

No one, not even Richard, could have known where he'd gone when he'd left Paris, least of all Laura. But both him and Laura being here in Ecuador at the same time was too great a coincidence.

His brows knitted into a fierce frown. Nothing added up. Laura had to be at least three or four months pregnant by now. Even if she was in excellent health, it shocked him that she would travel on her own to this remote region of the globe. In case of an emergency, the closest expert medical care was hundreds of miles away by air. For her to sign on for another cruise defied logic.

Unless she was looking for him.

But if that was true and she'd enlisted Gwenn's help, then why hadn't Gwenn told him yesterday?

He raked his hands through his hair.

Because it's more than possible Laura isn't looking for you, Wilde. And if that's the case, then Gwenn had no choice but to believe Laura is here for a vacation. Nothing else.

Maybe after recognizing Laura from the tabloids, Gwenn had been prompted to come on a little fishing expedition of her own yesterday.

The more he thought about it, the more he realized that, when he'd refused to answer her question about Laura, Gwenn had mentioned the name Mrs. John Wallace just to see what kind of a reaction she'd get from him.

When Zach said he'd never heard of the woman, Gwenn had closed up. In retrospect, he couldn't blame her, not after he'd all but told her to leave him alone.

Which was exactly what she'd done. She'd delivered her cryptic message, then left him to his own devices.

A few minutes ago Pete had unwittingly decoded that message. Now it was up to him whether or not he acted on the information.

Lord. Laura was here in the Galápagos. She'd been here for the past ten days.

What if she doesn't want to see you, Wilde?

What if she's trying as hard as you are to bury painful memories?

Even if you do see her again, it can only end in disaster. That's the pattern. Haven't you learned anything?

By the time he left the washroom, he'd made up his mind that when they landed in Quito, he'd take that trip into the mountains where, at 21,000 feet, the air thinned dangerously. They said a man could pass out from lack of oxygen long before he reached that height. Well, he'd find out. In fact, he looked forward to it.

But after he'd disembarked and had made it as far as the passenger-information desk at the terminal, he suddenly found himself walking toward the airline desk to book the next flight back to Baltra.

While he waited to board the plane for the return trip, he phoned company headquarters located in the heart of Quito and asked to speak to Paquita. She was the manager in charge of staffing.

He needed to know the *Puff Cloud*'s itinerary. When he'd ascertained the yacht's next disembarkation point, he'd ask Paquita to locate another boat going to the same location from Santa Cruz and hitch a ride.

Though everything inside him screamed the warning not to put himself in any more emotional jeopardy, Zach found he couldn't fight the overwhelming desire to see her again. The desire had translated itself into a compulsion totally beyond his control.

CHAPTER ELEVEN

LAURA HAD BEEN LYING on her bed taking a nap when she heard Gwenn's voice over the intercom.

"Attention, everybody. We're alongside the peninsula of Santa Fe Island. At lunch I promised you a swim with some sea lions, and we've got sea lions heading our way as I speak. Report on deck with your snorkel gear."

Much as Laura enjoyed snorkeling, she decided to take Gwenn's advice and only participate if she could wade out into the impossibly blue water from the shore. Here they had to jump from the boat and couldn't touch bottom. If Laura should develop a cramp or a complication...

Since the baby's health came first, Laura opted to be sensible and remain on deck to watch the others, maybe do some filming. It went without saying that Gwenn would be relieved, since she and the crew were responsible for everyone's safety.

Laura's real reason for joining in as much as possible was to avoid being alone with her own thoughts and emotions, which ranged from elation that he was here to fear that he wouldn't want to see her.

"Mrs. Wallace?"

Laura didn't recognize the male voice, but that didn't surprise her. Except for the captain, they had a different crew this trip and it was only their second day out. Most likely Gwenn had sent someone to tell her to come up on deck.

"Just a minute, please."

Sliding off the bed, she pulled on a clean pair of white maternity shorts and matching cotton overblouse before padding to the door in her bare feet.

But the sight that greeted her eyes when she opened it sent her into shock.

Zach!

A gasp escaped her throat. She put a hand over her heart because it hurt so much.

Gwenn, it seemed, had wasted no time finding him. Her hungry eyes feasted on him without reservation, cataloging every detail. His tall powerful physique clothed in a T-shirt and shorts. His tanned skin that the strong equatorial sun had burnished to a rich mahogany. His hair, no longer the short-cropped racer's style, its sun-bleached tips making him more attractive than ever.

"Zach." She finally managed to say his name.

"Hello, Laura."

His narrowed gaze played over her tanned features, then dropped lower to register the changes to her figure the pregnancy had caused. There was something in his look that was so erotic he might as well have been touching her. She couldn't swallow, couldn't think.

"A-are you very angry?" she asked.

His well-defined brows met in a puzzled frown. "Angry?"

"Because I—I've been looking for you," she explained in a shaking voice.

His chest heaved as if he was having difficulty dealing with conflicting emotions of his own. She closed her eyes. At least he wasn't indifferent to her.

When he didn't respond, she opened them again. "Please...come in."

Dear God. The way her voice throbbed, she sounded as if she was begging him.

She could sense the struggle going on inside him before he finally stepped over the threshold, dwarfing the tiny cabin as she shut the door. Terrified he would change his mind and leave, she rested her back against it, her palms flat on the metal.

His taut body stood planted in the center of the room, which meant they weren't more than three feet apart. She could feel the heat radiating from him, smell the scent of the soap he used in the shower.

"How did Gwenn find you so fast?"

"She didn't, but that's another story," he said darkly. Close to him like this, she could see lines around his mouth that hadn't been there two months ago, giving him an almost hunted look. "More to the point, how did you know I was here?"

"Th-that's another story, too." Now was not the time to mention his brother. An invisible shield had been lowered around his heart.

His every emotion had gone into deep freeze—except his guilt, which was alive and doing well. And that guilt, compounded by the problem of his fear of ever being vulnerable to loss again, had driven him away. She knew that now.

Since she and Tony's family had been through therapy, Laura had a strong conviction that the only way she was going to penetrate that shield was *through* his guilt. Fighting fire with fire.

"Okay, then why have you been looking for me?" he asked next.

Zach wasn't a man to mince words. He'd always been open and direct, one of the many qualities she adored about him. But this was one time she'd have given anything if he hadn't wanted to get straight to the point. Not when she was aching for him to take her in his arms—they'd been apart for so long! There was so much to say.

"I need help," she whispered achingly.

While he absorbed that, a tension-filled silence hovered between them.

At last he asked, "Are you in trouble of some kind?"

"Yes."

His jaw hardened. "Why me?"

She'd been expecting that question. Whatever she said now would determine whether or not Zach disappeared from her life within the next sixty seconds.

"I have a confession to make to you. When I flew

to Belgium to support Tony in the Tour de France, I—
I had another agenda.''

She saw Zach's hard-muscled body stiffen in reaction. The past was every bit as painful for him as it
was for her.

"The demons driving Tony ruined our marriage
from the day we took our vows. Over time I came to
realize that deep in Tony's psyche, he wanted a divorce. But for various reasons, not the least of which
was his fear of his aunt and uncle's disapproval after
all they'd done for him, he couldn't bring himself to
ask me for one.

"On a subconscious level I realized it was up to me
if we were ever to be free of each other. But like most
young wives, I had hopes that I could change him,
that I could make our marriage work.

"When he turned pro the first year, I saw the writing on the wall, but I still clung to the idealistic dream
that everything would be all right if I just had patience.
His aunt and uncle encouraged me in this of course.
However, it was the wrong thing to do, and for the
next five years everything went downhill.

"Four and a half months ago, Tony came home for
a two-day visit because his uncle demanded it. We
hadn't been intimate in almost a year. We had sex
once, but you couldn't call it making love. It was like
we were programmed to do our duty or something. It
was awful. That's when I realized I couldn't go on
like that and I was determined to ask him for a divorce, no matter how his aunt and uncle felt about it.

"But with the Tour de France coming up so soon, I thought it would be better to broach the subject when it was over. That's when the idea came to me that if his father's scrapbook could help Tony to focus, he might win the yellow jersey. If that happened, he would be on such a high, it would numb him to any guilt and he'd agree to the divorce."

She sighed. "Then I found out I was pregnant. I didn't know what to do. I didn't want the baby to be the reason he stayed with me, but I realized he had to know the truth. So again, I decided to put off telling him the news until after the race."

Zach shifted his weight. "And because of me and my desire to give him a hard time for treating you like he did, his life was cut short," he said bitterly, wounding her heart all over again.

I loved you for that, Zach. I loved you, and still love you, so much, you can't possibly imagine.

"Obviously we both have regrets where Tony is concerned," she rushed to agree. Arguing with him would get her nowhere. "It's true that neither of us can do anything about the past. It's over and done. But there's still something to be salvaged from all the pain, something that could bring us both a lot of peace. That's why I'm here."

"I don't follow," came the hollow rejoinder.

"I have a defenseless baby growing inside me, a little life who only asks for a mother and father to give it love." She took a deep breath. *It's now or never,*

Laura. "How would you like to help me raise this child?"

The second the words left her lips, his head lifted in shock.

"In my mind," she went on, as determined as she'd ever been in her life, "you've always been the father. You were the one who discovered I was pregnant. *I* didn't even know!" She made a noise somewhere between a laugh and a sob.

"When you wiped my mouth with a cloth and helped me to the bed, brought me food and looked after me, it felt like *you* were my husband. And if you remember, *you* were the one who worried about my driving the circuit alone and made those arrangements with your brother. It was *you* who phoned me the night of Klaus's accident to make sure I was all right, to see if I needed anything. Not Tony.

"Now that I'm alone, I'm afraid to raise this baby by myself, Zach. Naturally I'm not talking about the physical aspects. I have the money and a wonderful support system with my family. What I'm talking about is my baby's emotional development.

"You lived with Tony long enough to see what being deprived of a father did to him. It denied him an identity. Tragically his uncle treated him like an uncle, rather than the father he desperately needed. I don't want that to happen to my baby. My baby deserves a father. But not just any father."

She saw Zach's lips thin, but was pretty sure he was still listening.

"Because you know things about my marriage to Tony and the circumstances surrounding his death no one else knows except me, that makes you the only man who'd have a vested interest in my baby's welfare. Don't you see? Tony is a bond between us."

By now, fear of his rejection had released another surge of adrenaline, forcing the blood to pound in her ears. Taking a calculated risk, she said, "If you and I worked hard at it, we could shower this child with love and attention, the kind Tony wouldn't let anyone give him after he lost his parents."

"Marriage isn't in my plans, Laura."

She'd been waiting for that wintry salvo and was several steps ahead of him.

"That doesn't surprise me, not after losing two fiancées." Again Laura saw his body stiffen, but she went on talking as if she hadn't noticed. "Unlike you, I was never engaged, much to my regret. If Tony had been forced to wait three or four months before the ceremony, I probably would've seen enough evidence of his insatiable drive and inner struggles to realize a good marriage with him would be difficult, if not impossible, to achieve.

"Perhaps Tony knew this, subconsciously at least, which was why he rushed me off my feet. I was too inexperienced to understand what was going on. At the time we met, many of my friends were married or engaged. I'm afraid I was in love with love and got swept along with the tide."

She drew a ragged breath. "Once I was married to

him and realized my mistake, I didn't know how to end the pain. I was so riddled with guilt it took me six years to gather the courage to confront him. When he came home for that two-day visit in May, I should have asked for a divorce right then.

"But once again I chickened out. When you guessed I was pregnant even before I did, you encouraged me to tell him right away. But I couldn't bring myself to do it. I was afraid to hurt him—he was very fragile inside and I was terrified of the consequences."

She drew in another ragged breath. "After living through so much pain with Tony, I'm a little nervous of it right now." That wasn't true, but she didn't want to frighten him off by making him think he *had* to marry her.

"But please don't get me wrong," she said, her hands spread in front of her. "I've seen some wonderful marriages. Especially your brother's."

"Richard and Bev share something unique," he admitted in a gravelly tone.

"Yes, they do," she agreed, "and I know why. They're both unselfish and put the other person's happiness first, *every time.* No matter how trying the circumstances, they forget self and reach out to comfort the other. It's a revelation to me. I don't think many couples attain that kind of joy."

"You're right about that."

"Communication was certainly not a strong point in my marriage to Tony. He wasn't home enough."

"Surely that's not your fault."

"No. I no longer take the blame for a lot of things that did or didn't happen, but I am sorry he died without knowing he was going to be a father."

"I'm sorry, too, Laura. But he was on the verge of winning the most important race of his career. Knowing Tony as I did, plus having witnessed the precarious state of your marriage, I think the news would have thrown him. In retrospect, I believe you did the right thing by keeping quiet."

Thank you for saying that, Zach. "Maybe. But that wasn't your gut reaction when you saw me throwing up in the hotel bathroom on the morning of the time trials. You urged me to tell Tony."

He straightened to his full height. "I didn't know all the facts then."

Even now you're defending me, Zach. If you only knew how much I love you.

"Nevertheless you always have the right instincts. In that regard, you and Richard are very much alike."

"You know what they say, Laura. Hindsight's twenty-twenty."

"That's exactly what you have *all* the time! It's the reason you're an exceptional human being. That's why I want you to be in my baby's life on a permanent basis. I need a good man I can trust."

Her cheeks had grown warm. "I grew up with a wonderful dad. The thought of depriving my own child of that experience hurts me. If you're honest, you'll agree with me, since I happen to know that you and your brothers share a special bond with your father.''

''I don't deny it.''

''That's why I would like permission to hang around you as much as you would allow. There would be no expectations, just the quiet knowledge that you're there.'' *She held her breath.*

''My work is here, Laura. You work and live in Hollywood.''

''No, I don't.''

''What are you saying?''

''As I told the press that night in Val d'Isère, I've given up my acting job. A few weeks ago I gave up the apartment. Everything I own is in storage. There's no place I call home anymore. The only spot I want to be is near you because you make me feel...*safe.*''

He blinked.

''It's true!'' she said from her heart. ''When we first met and I couldn't find Tony, you did everything in your power to help me, even to arranging for me to drive around the circuit with your brother. Don't you see? When you realized I was pregnant, you took care of me, watched over me.

''The night you called me from the hospital because Klaus had been hurt, I realized then how much I needed you and had come to depend on you. Because you're not a woman who's expecting a baby, you couldn't possibly understand how much that caring meant to me.''

Swallowing hard, she said, ''I realize you're a

sailor, but you have to come ashore once in a while. I understand there are houses for rent in Puerto Ayora on Santa Cruz Island. If I lived there, you could drop in for meals at the end of a cruise, stay all night. Whatever suited you.

"Just knowing I could see you from time to time would bring a measure of comfort and relief I haven't experienced since before you left Paris." She looked away, fighting tears. "When Klaus and Jacques came to the church and told me you'd gone, I felt like...my rock had deserted me. It was the worst feeling I've ever had."

She saw the color drain from his face and went on, "Of course I couldn't blame you for leaving. You'd shouldered everyone's pain to help the Ziff team succeed, but no one shouldered yours." Her voice caught. "I couldn't come after you right then because I was still getting over the trauma of Tony's death, and I had responsibilities. There were loose ends to tie up, and Tony's aunt and uncle needed me. But now that I'm free and have put the worst of my grief behind me, I want to be with you in any capacity you'll allow."

A groan escaped his throat. "That would be insanity, Laura. We're hundreds of miles from the nearest hospital," he muttered almost as an afterthought, making her heart leap, because though his rejection was clear, somewhere in his complicated psyche, he was still entertaining the idea.

"I'm not expecting this baby for more than four months, and the doctor has told me my pregnancy is going along perfectly. If an emergency arose, I could fly to Quito.''

He rubbed the back of his neck. ''I only have three more cruises with the company, then I'm leaving the Galápagos and sailing my own boat to other waters around the world.''

Every time he opened his mouth, she was put on an emotional seesaw. One minute hope flared. The next he said something to extinguish it.

''Would you consider taking me with you? If nothing else, I'm an excellent cook and I've always wanted to learn how to sail. The baby would get her sea legs early.''

''Her?''

She'd been waiting for the propitious moment to drop that little piece of news.

''Yes. I had an ultrasound and the doctor is pretty sure it's a girl. She could learn everything about the oceans and sailing from you. I can't imagine a better education for a California girl, can you?''

''For a dozen reasons, Laura, it's out of the question.''

Taking a calculated risk, she said, ''If the idea had any appeal, none of those reasons would apply. Please forgive me. You've heard about a mother who would face a burning building to save her ch—''

''Have you ever seen the ocean during a storm?'' he broke in harshly.

''No.''

''Right now it looks like your friend, blue and

placid. But then a wind comes up. In an instant everything changes. The ocean becomes the enemy and you start fighting for your life. Under those circumstances, how could I protect you and the baby?''

As their gazes fused, a certain calm descended. ''Because you're a Wilde. I have no doubt you would find a way.'' She knew the conviction in her voice reached him because he looked away, but not before she saw the flash of torment in his eyes.

Undaunted, she made one final plea. ''Obviously the answer is no, but maybe you wouldn't mind if I came along on your next cruise with the company before I make definite plans. When you're not on duty, I could use a sounding board.''

''The *Wind Cloud* is fully booked,'' he said a trifle too quickly.

Nervousness was not an emotion she would have attributed to him. It brought her another modicum of hope.

''Are the crew's quarters fully booked, too?'' When he didn't answer right away, she rushed on, ''The captain gave me permission to share Gwenn's room with her. Maybe I could bunk with you on your yacht if you had an extra bed. I've already paid for another ten-day cruise.''

There was a marked rise and fall of his chest. ''I wouldn't be good company. After the watch I crave sleep.''

Blackness descended. ''All right, I understand. However, I'm not sorry I came to the Galápagos. At least I know I *tried* to do the right thing for Tony's child.''

His face became an inscrutable mask. ''Where are you going when you leave here?''

''I have several options. Maybe I'll figure everything out while I'm on this cruise with Gwenn. She has a lot of wisdom, having lived through a divorce, which I understand is even more difficult than getting over the death of a spouse.''

''Gwenn's roots are here, Laura. You need your family.''

''I would have thought you did, too.''

''I'm not pregnant,'' he said.

''That's right. You're a man who can move about freely with no unwanted baggage. No ties, no obligations. How lucky men are.''

''Don't talk that way.'' He sounded angry. ''Cynicism doesn't become you.''

''Ah…forgive me, but I had a great teacher in Tony. His legacy to me and my baby.''

''Laura…'' She could see his throat working.

''Don't worry, Zach. I'm not your responsibility. I never was. There are lots of men out there who want a relationship without the ceremony. Since I refuse to let my daughter grow up without a father figure, I'm sure it won't take long to find someone. Maybe I'll get lucky and he'll like children. Maybe he'll even stick around long enough to help me raise my daughter. Maybe not.

''I would have preferred that man to be you, but

you've made your feelings quite clear. I'd be lying if I didn't tell you I'm disappointed. Nevertheless, I knew I could count on you to be honest with me.''

She forced herself to stay calm. "Thank you for that, and thank you for coming aboard to talk to me when you didn't have to. Obviously you sailed here on another yacht. You probably need to get going.''

She turned around with the intention of opening the door for him. To her joy, he made no move to leave.

"Are you feeling all right, Laura?"

Thank God your heart hasn't hardened completely.

"Since the morning sickness went away, I've never felt better. But I have to admit the movement of the yacht makes me sleepy. I generally take a nap this time of day. The rocking motion is sort of like a giant cradle. No doubt the baby likes it, too.''

She smiled as she turned back to him.

By contrast, his jaw hardened. After a long silence he said, "You look good.''

"Thank you. So do you. I can see you're in your element.''

His expression revealed surprise. "How did you know?''

"Bev told me about your passion for sailing.''

After a sustained pause, he asked, "When are you due?" He changed the subject so fast she didn't have time to blink.

"February twentieth.''

"What happened to Margo?" he asked.

"One of the evil mob bosses hired a doctor to do

plastic surgery on her while she was in her coma. A few weeks ago she woke up with a new face and a new life.''

Zach didn't smile. ''The old one was better.''

She eyed him saucily. ''Have you been holding out on me? I thought you never watched TV.''

''You're right. However I *do* have eyes in my head, and what I'm looking at right now could never be improved upon.''

Laura trembled in every cell of her body. ''You *do* know how to make an old pregnant lady feel attractive.''

''Every old pregnant lady should look so attractive.''

''Then it's a good thing you won't be seeing me again. Give me a few more weeks, and I'll look like a beached whale.'' She hoped her joke covered her fragmented emotions.

A bleakness entered his eyes. ''You must have some idea of where you think you'll live.''

She nodded. *I can keep this up as long as you can, my darling.* ''I've always loved the beach. The only reason Tony and I settled in Hollywood was because he wanted to be with his racing buddies who'd formed a cycling club there.''

She shook her head. ''If I'd had my way, we wouldn't have lived anywhere *near* Hollywood, and I would have found a job doing something else. But Tony insisted I stay on the set and keeping working because it brought in more money than either of us could have earned any other way. He needed funds and expected me to help him,'' she added quietly.

Zach's jaw tautened. "I wondered about that.''

"When he left the States to race in other countries, it suited him to tell everyone I was too busy at home being a TV star to join him. The truth is, he wanted more and more money to support his expensive life-style—the clothes, the parties, cars...women. He bought that Ferrari in Italy with the money I'd given him to attend law school. Little did I know he'd never intended to be a lawyer.

"Since his death, I received a bill for a wardrobe he'd had designed for himself in Italy. Obviously he was attempting to create a sort of sports superstar im-age for himself.''

Zach was still listening, so she decided to tell him everything. "You know what Tony was like. He had delusions of grandeur that turned him into a stranger. He never really wanted me—only what I could do for him. When we first met, he told me I was beautiful. Every woman wants to hear that from the man she loves. But as time went on, I realized that my physical beauty was *all* he cared about. If I'd been less attrac-tive, he would never have pursued me because I wouldn't have fit the image he had in mind for the woman he wanted hanging on his arm—say, for a pub-licity shoot. I didn't realize this until it was too late.'' She sighed. "Tony never intended to get to know the person I really am. He led a frighteningly shallow ex-istence.

"But that's all in the past now, and I like to think he's found peace at last. As for me, I want nothing more to do with acting or filmmaking. I've got a degree in English, and maybe one day I'll go back for a master's. In the meantime, I'd like to stay in contact with Bev. We're both expecting around the same time, you know."

His features looked chiseled. "You've been with them recently?"

"Yes. I asked for their help in finding you. I hope you don't mind." *Please don't mind.* "Bev thought you might have come to the Galápagos because of that travel magazine she lent you. It seems she was right. It also seems as if all I've ever done is prevail on them for favors. I love both of them. A lot."

Zach stared at her for an uncomfortably long moment.

I've said too much.

"My condo is for sale."

What? She reeled in shock and stayed firmly planted against the door.

"You can buy it if you want. It's right on the water and has three bedrooms, one of which could easily be transformed into a nursery. What furnishings are there you can keep or sell."

Her heart plummeted.

"It's been vacant for months," he went on, oblivious to her pain. "Richard and Bev have been keeping an eye on it the past six years while I've been in and out of the country. But I told Richard at the beginning of the Tour de France that I was going to let it go because I wasn't returning to California.

"You're welcome to it, Laura. In fact, I'd like to sell it so that it wouldn't be a burden to my brother any longer. You'd only be two blocks away from them."

Steady, Laura. Don't fall apart in front of him. If he's being deliberately cruel to get rid of you, he's doing an excellent job....

"Does your brother have power of attorney?" She managed to keep her voice level, unemotional, despite her pain.

He nodded, but she noticed the shadow that entered his eyes. It expressed her question had surprised him. *Good.* "Well—" she forced her lips into a smile "—that's an incredible offer, but I probably won't take you up on it, since I may not be residing in California at all."

"Why's that?"

"Because I'm seriously considering moving to Hawaii." *At least, I am now!*

He looked as if she'd just slapped his face. "That doesn't make any sense."

"Actually it does. Before I met Tony, I'd started dating a man named Michael Shipp. He worked as a realtor for his dad, who has an agency in Hawaii and California. Naturally because of Tony, our relationship came to a premature end.

"To my surprise he showed up at Tony's funeral service in Hollywood to pay his respects. When he learned I was going to move and wanted a place on the water, he invited me to fly over so he could show me some beach properties I might be able to afford.'' *And it would be far away from you, my darling. Maybe that's exactly what I need.*

"Is he married?" Zach demanded.

"No."

"Does he know you're expecting a baby?"

"Everyone knows and seems eager to be of assistance."

"You'd be much wiser to stay near family."

After a pause she said, "No matter what happens, I think I've prevailed on the Wildes altruism long enough, don't you? I told you in Belgium that I looked upon you as my guardian angel. When I arrived in St. Léger, I needed one desperately and there you were—ready to keep my world from falling apart. But you left Paris before I could thank you for everything. I'm glad I've had this chance now. I think you know I couldn't have gotten through that period without you."

"Klaus would have taken over," he murmured. "He thought the world of you."

"I liked him, too, but there's only one Zach Wilde."

"That's nice to hear." He glanced at his watch. "Unfortunately I can't stay any longer to talk. Is there anything I can do for you before I go? Do you want me to ask one of the crew to get you a drink or a sandwich?"

Laura had thought she could handle it, but now she had to fight not to react to the horrifying realization that he was about to disappear again.

"Nothing, thank you. They feed you like kings on here. I had this huge lunch and I'm going back to L.A. plump as a hen. No one'll recognize me. Maybe that's not such a bad thing, after all. I'm so sick of publicity it's wonderful to be anonymous again." She chuckled softly though her heart was breaking. "God bless you, Zach. No one deserves the best in life more than you."

Needing something to do with her hands, she turned and opened the door for him. Out of a sense of preservation, she stepped back to make sure their bodies didn't touch as he moved past her.

When he was in the corridor, he faced her one last time, his gray eyes dark slits. "The captain says you'll be stopping at South Plaza Island tomorrow. I know the cactus is in flower and the sight is spectacular, but it's a difficult walk even for someone who isn't pregnant. Stay on the yacht."

She nodded. "Since you're the one warning me, I'll do as you say." The desire to touch him was so strong she thought she might die from the wanting. But he obviously wasn't suffering the same way.

Face it. He's beyond feeling, and somehow you're going to have to get over him.

"Goodbye, Laura." That note of finality in his voice devastated her.

"Goodbye."

After shutting the door, she sank onto her bed in

frozen silence, her anguish too deep for tears. She would give him an hour, then she would prevail on Gwenn to help her find a way to get back to Puerto Ayora on another yacht.

Zach had gone away believing she would finish out her ten-day tour on the *Puff Cloud*. But she couldn't bear to stay another minute in the Galápagos knowing he was so close, yet so unreachable.

If he could give up his home in Newport Beach, then he truly intended to cut all ties with his old life.

Your guardian angel has done all he can do for you, Laura. Now he's flown elsewhere and you'll never see him again.

CHAPTER TWELVE

THE BARTENDER at the Del Mar Hotel in Puerto Ayora looked surprised when Zach sat down and ordered a double whiskey.

"You haven't drunk anything for a whole week, and *now* you want a double this early in the morning?" he asked with a friendly smile as he handed Zach his drink. "What gives?"

Ignoring the question, Zach swallowed the entire content of the glass in one go.

The bartender kept up the chatter, oblivious to Zach's mood. "You must be the kind of guy who doesn't usually drink, but when you do, you go all out. Am I right?"

"Yeah," Zach muttered, setting the glass down with more force than was necessary. "Do me again."

This one he sipped, his mind elsewhere. Every day he'd gotten up thinking he'd fly to Lima for a little diversion. But since his meeting with Laura, he had trouble deciding whether to get out of bed in the morning, let alone decide how to fill the long pointless hours. The free time given him had been exactly what he *hadn't* needed right now.

What I need is for you to be gone from the Galá-

*pagos, Laura. Then everything will get back to nor-
mal.*

"How soon will the *Puff Cloud* be in?" he asked
the bartender, thinking the man was a bit too nosy
about the people who worked for Windjammer Connection Tours.

The bartender shot him a surprised glance. "She
was in an hour ago. Why? You crewing her later today?"

"No. I'm assigned to the *Wind Cloud*. She won't
be sailing until tomorrow." He slid off the bar stool
and slapped a couple of bills on the counter for the
drinks. "Do me a favor? When Gwenn Barker shows
up, ask her to come to my room."

The bartender grinned. "So *she's* the reason you're
drinking doubles."

Zach didn't bother to enlighten him and headed
back to his room. The only thing that mattered was
that Laura had left Ecuador; he could find out from
Gwenn. Until he knew she'd flown out, he didn't dare
show his face in town. He might run into her, which
was the last thing he wanted. One more meeting with
her and he wouldn't be able to walk away again.

Toward noon he heard a knock on the door. As soon
as he opened it, Gwenn said, "Hi, sailor. You wanted
to see me about something?"

"I do. Come in."

"I don't think so. I can smell the alcohol on your
breath. Obviously the only reason you want to talk to
me is Laura Donetti."

"Gwenn, I was hoping we could talk for a few minutes."

"There isn't anything to say, because Laura isn't here."

"You saw her get on the plane?"

"No. I mean she sailed back here on the *Riptide* the same day you saw her. I haven't seen her since and all I know is that she said she was leaving on the next flight out of here. Sorry," she said before turning and walking off.

Laura hasn't been in the Galápagos for the past ten days?

He felt exactly the way he had when he'd been sailing on the Pacific years ago with his brother and a sudden squall had sent the boom crashing the wrong way. He'd been knocked overboard, unconscious. If Richard hadn't grabbed him and held on, he'd have been lost in the depths of the sea.

Okay, Wilde, you got exactly what you wanted. You sent Laura Donetti away, and now she's well and truly out of your life. Some other man who saw her first is eagerly awaiting the opportunity to get to know her better. She and her unborn baby will be well taken care of. It's nothing to do with you.

No words of love ever passed her lips or yours.

Be thankful it's a clean break. You're free from the possibility of ever having to lose her because she was never yours to begin with. It's time to celebrate.

"SO NOW THAT WE'VE TALKED you out of moving to Hawaii, why can't we get you to even consider *renting*

Zach's condo?''

Laura stirred restlessly in the passenger seat of
Bev's car. They were parked in front of the bougain-
villea-covered house overlooking the ocean where
Richie was taking his piano lesson.

Bev's argument against Laura's moving to Hawaii
was valid. If Laura had been emotionally involved
with Michael six years ago, then Tony's advent in her
life wouldn't have resulted in marriage. So it wouldn't
be fair to go to Hawaii now and raise Michael's hopes
when clearly none existed.

*Not when I'm painfully in love with, Zach. But I
couldn't live in his house. It would tear me apart.*

''The offer is tempting, Bev, but much as I'd love
to act on it, I can't. Put yourself in my place. Could
you live in Richard's house if he was no longer in
your life?''

Bev sighed in defeat. ''Probably not. But it's a crying shame, because Zach's condo is exactly what
you've been looking for. Nothing you've found is as
close to us or as ideally suited to your needs.''

''That's true, but if one day Zach does change his
mind and wants to come back to Newport, he should
be able to return to his own home. My presence would
keep him away.''

''I think you're wrong,'' Bev said. ''If he truly
wanted to get rid of you, offering you his condo would
be the last thing he'd do, wouldn't it? So maybe he
had another agenda for suggesting what he did. He

may be thousands of miles away, but it's apparent to me that he wants you exactly where he can find you at any given moment.''

Her argument made Laura's heart race, but every time she remembered the tone in Zach's voice when he'd told her goodbye, she was jolted back to reality.

''I—I wish I dared, but I'm too afraid of doing the wrong thing. I think I'm going to rent that apartment we saw yesterday.''

Bev grimaced. ''It's not what you want. It's too small and nowhere near the beach. I've already told you that you can move into our spare bedroom until you find something permanent.''

''No, Bev. I wouldn't dream of disrupting your family like that. Besides, the apartment is near the college, and I can put a crib in the bedroom with me.''

''You're so stubborn! Well…what kind of lease agreement is it?''

''One year.'' At Bev's groan she said, ''I know. I'm not happy about it, either. If I find something I really like before the twelve months are up, I'll worry about breaking it then.''

''Oh, well, since I can't change your mind about Zach's condo, I should be thankful you're moving to Newport at all. The other night I told Richard that if you went to Hawaii, I'd be devastated.''

''Oh, Bev, I feel the same way. That's why I'm moving here.''

It was true. An unbearable sense of loneliness swept over her every time she even so much as considered the idea of living apart from Bev and Richard and their children.

Just then she saw Richie burst out of the house. He spotted the station wagon and ran over to it. "Laura! Mom!" he exclaimed through the open passenger-side window. "I didn't know you guys were coming here!"

"Your mother suggested we come so I could invite you to go to the ball game with my dad and sister tonight. You can sleep over at my parents', and I'll bring you back tomorrow. Would you like that?"

"*Would* I!" He looked ready to burst with excitement. "Mom, is it okay?"

"Of course. That's why we're here. Stick your bike in the back and let's go home. I've already put your toothbrush and a change of clothes in your backpack so you and Laura can get away as soon as possible."

"All right!"

Fifteen minutes later Laura had said goodbye to Bev and she and Richie were on their way.

"This is a rad car."

"It's a Passat. You like it?"

"Yeah. Uncle Zach used to have one."

"Really?"

"Yeah. He says German cars are the best, but Dad only buys American." He cocked his head. "Rachel has a poster of Tony driving a Ferrari. Did you ever ride in it?"

"No," she said quietly. "He bought it in Europe. I never did see it."

"Where's it now?"

"I had it sold."

"How come you didn't keep it?"

Oh, Richie. If you only knew. "Because I like German cars best, just like your uncle."

"I miss Uncle Zach."

"So do I."

"Do you think he'll ever come home?"

"I hope so, Richie."

"You love him, huh?"

"Yes."

"I think he's upset because you're going to have a baby."

She blinked. "Why do you say that?"

"Because Rosie's son hated him."

The words made Laura cringe for the pain Zach had been forced to suffer.

"A baby doesn't know how to hate. If my little girl is lucky enough to be around your uncle, she'd adore him."

Richie pondered that for a moment. "If you married Uncle Zach, then you could have more babies and they'd be my cousins, right?"

"Yep," she said softly. "We'd all be related."

"That would be the *best!*"

Her heart filled to overflowing. "No matter what happens, Richie Wilde, we'll always be friends, won't we?"

"Uh-huh."

"You know what? I thought I had enough gas to

get us there, but I'd better not take a chance on running out on the freeway, so we're going to stop at the first place we find.''

On the outskirts of Newport she pulled up in front of the pumps at a convenience store. Hers was the only car there.

''Can I get a candy bar?'' Richie asked.

''Sure. Tell the clerk to put it on my bill.''

''I can use my allowance, but thanks, anyway.''

What a wonderful kid. Laura watched him fondly as he disappeared inside. She got out of the car and went around to put her credit card in the slot. The next thing she knew, she was on the ground and it felt as if someone was shaking her. Glass shattered behind her.

Earthquake.

The tremor went on for endless seconds, and Laura heard a scream and the sound of crashes coming from the store. She cried out Richie's name, and when at last the ground stopped moving, she staggered to her feet and dashed to the store entryway. To her horror she saw that the window on the door and the plateglass window on the front wall had shattered. Inside, grocery items littered the floor. The middle-aged female clerk stood in the midst of the debris, panting and dazed.

''Richie!'' Laura shouted again, unable to see him anywhere.

''I'm in the washroom!''

Thank God. ''Are you all right?'' she cried.

"Yeah, but I can't open the door!"

She made her way gingerly through the mess toward the men's room in the back. Most of the shelving had fallen, and one large metal cabinet had shifted and now lay directly in front of the washroom door. It was open as far as the cabinet allowed, and she could see Richie through the crack.

"Are you really okay, honey?"

"Yeah. That quake was awesome. Are *you* okay?"

"Oh, just a bump on my elbow, but I'm fine, especially now that I know you didn't get hurt. Wait just a minute while I try to move this thing."

"I'll get the other end," the clerk volunteered. Together the two of them managed to push the heavy cabinet a good ten inches from the door. Richie squeezed out and within moments was hugging Laura fiercely. Over his dark-blond head Laura asked the clerk if she was all right.

"I'll make it, but I just checked the phone and it's dead."

"That's not surprising," Laura murmured. "If you're really okay, I'm going to try and get Richie home. His parents will be frantic."

"So will my husband. His work isn't far from here. I'm sure he'll come before long."

Laura nodded. "Good. But to be safe, let's exchange names and phone numbers. Whoever can get through first for help, we'll do it."

When that was accomplished, she put her arm

around Richie's shoulders. "Come on, honey. Let's get going."

No telling how many of the streets were impassable. She would just have to weave her away around and pray they'd be able to reach Bev and Richard's house before the aftershocks began.

AT NINE THAT NIGHT Zach went off duty. Tomorrow the *Wind Cloud* would put in at Puerto Ayora and he'd have two days off before the next cruise. Forty-eight endless hours he couldn't bear to face because they gave him too much time to think, and thinking only sent him on a downward spiral.

The last nine days of work aboard the yacht had done nothing to lessen his despondency. Inside him was a great yawning emptiness, robbing him of the smallest pleasure. Even the thought of sailing the boat he planned to buy in another couple of weeks meant less than nothing to him.

Up until the moment he'd confronted Laura aboard the *Puff Cloud,* he'd had the idea that he could carry out his plan to go into the sailing business for himself, if not in the Galápagos, then some other place. But the unsettling news that Laura had slipped away unbeknownst to him seemed to have drained him of that desire or any other. He felt as if all life had been sucked out of him.

Alarmed by his morbid state of mind, he started for his cabin.

"Zach?"

Pausing midstep, he turned to see Sean McClintock, the captain of the *Wind Cloud,* headed in his direction.

"I'm glad I caught you before you went to bed."

"Is there a problem?"

"We just received word over the radio that a major earthquake hit Southern California about three hours ago. There was a massive tidal wave, too, and casualties are mounting. You have family there so I thought you'd want to know."

Zach was jerked for once out of the immobilizing bleakness of his soul. "Do you have any idea which area was hardest hit?"

"I heard something about the epicenter being near Costa Mesa in Orange County."

"Costa Mesa is only a few miles north of Newport." His words were calm, but his insides were in turmoil as pictures of the people he loved flashed through his mind. And Laura. Where was Laura? *Had* she gone to Hawaii or was she still in California? Bev and Richard adored her. If they had anything to say about it, she'd be ensconced in his condo right now. Dear God. If anything happened to her or the baby...

Sean gripped his shoulder. "Come on. You're welcome to listen to any reports over the yacht radio and try to make contact with someone who can give you details."

Unfortunately, after settling in the pilothouse, Zach only heard the same news repeated at intervals throughout the rest of the night: phone service had been interrupted in the hardest-hit areas; anyone wanting information about relatives could phone a special number set up by the Red Cross...

It was the news he *didn't* hear that caused one horrifying scenario after another to run through his mind. By dawn his anxiety had reached its peak. The captain took one look at him and said, "As soon as we dock, you have my permission to take the first plane out of Baltra."

"Thanks, Sean. I hate letting you or the company down, but—"

"Don't worry about it," Sean broke in. "Someone else will always be happy to crew in your place, but you can never replace family."

His words pierced Zach like a knife.

"You're one of the finest sailors I've ever had the pleasure of working with," the captain added. "Nate Simonds agrees with me. We'd hate to lose you. But it's obvious you've been going through some sort of personal hell while you've been out here. Coupled with the news of this disaster, I don't see that you have a choice except to go home. Otherwise you'll never have peace of mind."

Zach knew this, though he'd failed to acknowledge it before hearing about the earthquake. Now he couldn't get back to California fast enough.

"You're right, Sean. I won't." He raked shaking hands through his hair. "As soon as I reach Quito, I'll contact the head office and explain my situation."

"You can do that now and make a reservation for your flight to the States at the same time."

TWELVE HOURS LATER Zach was heading north from the San Diego airport in a rental car. He'd purposely avoided flying to the airport in L.A. because he wanted to avoid what he was sure would be chaos. This drive was much longer, but in the end he'd get to Newport faster.

Every radio station carried the same news. Costa Mesa had been hardest hit, with severe damage to oceanfront property and marinas stretching as far north as Sunset Beach and as far south as Corona Del Mar. Fatalities were in the hundreds. Damage to boats and waterfronts were estimated to be in the millions.

He cringed when he heard that major sections of the coastal highway from Huntington to Newport Beach were closed due to damage. Following that report was an announcement that the governor had just declared a state of emergency and was deploying National Guard units.

Zach took it all in with a sickening sense of dread. All the people he'd ever cared about—his parents, his brothers and their families—lived in Newport. And maybe Laura, too. He could only pray she *had* gone to Hawaii.

When he'd first arrived in San Diego and was waiting for his rental car, he'd tried reaching everyone, including Laura's parents in Hollywood, but hadn't been able to get through. All he could do was call a local number for emergency services and give them the names. He'd been told it might be twelve hours before they had any information they could pass on to him. In that amount of time he would already have reached his destination and would know the situation firsthand.

Using alternative routes, he drove into Newport a little after two in the morning and headed straight for his parents' house. They weren't there, and one of their cars was missing, but everything looked good. He didn't notice any damage. Their caller ID showed they hadn't been getting their messages for the past three days. They were probably out of town. That should have relieved him, but it didn't.

He drove to his younger brother's condo several blocks away. No one was home there, either, and one of their cars was missing. Their answering machine had a few messages, but Zach couldn't ascertain times or dates. Again everything seemed all right structurally.

Where is everyone? On a trip?

He didn't want to think the other possibility, that they might all be over at Richard's, whose house was on a private canal leading to the marina. The damage would have been the greatest there.

On impulse he left the rental car in Mike's driveway and took off for the marina on Mike's bike. As he had learned better than anyone, a bicycle could go anywhere—and get past police barricades if necessary.

No one was going to prevent him from reaching Richard and Bev's. Not only did they mean the world to him, they were his only link to Laura.

"LAURA?"

She whirled around, milk glass in hand, thinking she was the only person awake in the Wilde household. "Hi, honey. Couldn't you sleep, either?"

Richie shook his head. "I keep waiting for another aftershock."

Laura shuddered. "So do I."

"I'm glad you're up. My sisters are in bed with Mom and Dad and they're all asleep."

She smiled at him and ruffled his hair. "Want some milk?"

"No, thanks."

"Do you want to come back to bed with me?"

"Can I?"

"Are you kidding? Bring your baseball cards and we'll see who wins. I've improved since our last game in France."

Richie left the Spanish-styled kitchen at a run. Laura rinsed her glass, then reached for the makeshift ice pack.

Her elbow was throbbing and swollen. She didn't dare take any painkillers until she'd checked with her obstetrician. But thank heaven it was her elbow, not the baby, that had taken the brunt of the impact. So other than a bruise below her right knee, she couldn't really complain. Nevertheless, if her elbow didn't start to improve in the next few days, she'd have to see a doctor about it.

After turning off the light, she tiptoed through the house and hurried up the wide staircase to the upper level. Richie was waiting for her in the guest bedroom, his box of baseball cards at the ready.

No sooner were they sitting cross-legged facing each other on top of the covers when they heard an ominous creak. Richie's face paled. "Another tremor's starting."

"Maybe," Laura said calmly. "Let's play, anyway. My turn to ask a question first. What year did Mickey Mant—"

"There it goes again," Richie said.

She gave a resigned sigh. "I don't think it's a tremor. More like someone walking around. Probably your dad."

"Do you think?"

"I do. Okay, here's the question again. What year did—"

"*Uncle Zach!*"

CHAPTER THIRTEEN

RICHIE'S JOYFUL CRY would have woken the dead. He flew off the bed to greet the uncle he idolized, knocking the cards to the floor. Laura's eyes darted to the doorway where stood an achingly familiar man in hip-hugging jeans and a T-shirt.

Zach. She mouthed his name silently as their gazes met and locked over Richie's head. Within seconds the house was filled with shrieks of excitement and joy as the entire family converged on the guest bedroom. Laura's eyes filled with tears as she watched Richard grab his brother and crush him in a hug. Bev was next, and then she explained that his parents were in San Francisco, and Mike and his wife and baby were visiting her parents in Sacramento, so there was no need to worry about anyone's safety.

Laura climbed off the bed, making sure the belt of her lime green terry bathrobe was fastened over her nightgown. She'd blossomed a lot in the past few weeks, and judging by the way Zach looked at her, the changes in her shape were readily apparent.

"Thank God everyone is all right," he said as Robin squeezed him for all she was worth. "We heard

the news about the earthquake over the yacht's radio.
I left the Galápagos on the first flight out of Baltra.''

Robin stayed in his arms and patted his burnished
face. "Our swimming pool has a *huge* crack in it, and
water ran over the edge and ruined the flowers
Mommy just planted.''

"Yeah, and your condo kinda got ruined, Uncle
Zach,'' Rachel blurted, despite Richard's attempt to
shush her.

Zach's eyes hadn't left Laura's. "As long as no one
was in it, it doesn't matter.''

She cleared her throat. "Richie and I were on our
way to a baseball game in my car when the quake
hit.''

"Yeah… It was scary, Uncle Zach. I got barricaded
in the gas-station washroom and Laura had to push
this huge thing outta the way. She's a really cool
driver, too, and has a Passat, just like you.''

"Hmm. I saw it in the driveway and wondered
whose it was,'' his uncle said.

"She got us back home like a shot. I bet she could
handle anything, even a Formula One racing car!''

"Richie," Laura said warningly, her face flushed,
"that was supposed to be our secret.''

The family burst into laughter. In the face of such
unrepentant hilarity, Laura shook her head and joined
in.

"By now you ought to know there are no secrets in
this house,'' Zach said. "After the Tour de France I
thought I'd picked a spot where no one could find me,

only to discover that all along my clever sister-in-law knew exactly where I'd gone.''

A further burst of laughter from Bev, who still looked too young to be the mother of three and expecting her fourth. But Laura couldn't help feeling a little nervous because, after all, she'd been the one to follow him when he hadn't wanted to be followed. Still, if he was angry, it didn't show. At least he wasn't allowing it to show in front of his family.

''Come on, guys,'' Richard said finally. ''Everyone back to bed. Your uncle has just flown thousands of miles and needs his rest. Girls, you go in with your mother. Richie, I'm sleeping with you.''

''That's okay, Dad. Laura said I could stay with her. We're gonna have a contest.''

''That can wait until tomorrow.''

''But—''

''No buts, son.'' Richard's stern voice surprised even Laura.

''All right,'' Richie muttered crossly. He began gathering the spilled cards.

Laura leaned over to help him. ''I'll play with you in the morning,'' she whispered.

''Promise?''

''Promise.''

''You're the greatest!'' He gave her a hug, then flung his arms around Zach one more time before disappearing.

As abruptly as the room had filled, it emptied, leaving a trembling Laura alone with the man who'd be-

come her whole world. But she wasn't about to delude
herself that he'd come back to California because of
her, not when his goodbye on the *Puff Cloud* had been
so final.

"I'm sorry you had to find me here," she said. "Because of the aftershocks, Richard insisted I stay the
ni—"

"Is this yours?" he broke in without apology,
scooping her makeshift ice bag from the floor.

"Oh—" her hands made an impotent gesture
"—it's nothing."

His gaze flicked to hers, his expression sober. "If
that was the case, you wouldn't have found a need for
this." He held up the bag. "Show me where you've
been hurt."

She took a step back. "It's nothing. Really."

"Let me see." He came closer. His nearness constricted her breathing. "You and Richie were caught
by the quake. He's obviously fine, but you're not.
What happened?"

Something in his stance, his demeanor, told her he
wasn't about to let it go.

"When the ground shook, I fell and landed on my
elbow."

His brows knit. "I've done that more than once on
my bike. Let me see how bad it is."

Terrified to be this close for fear she wouldn't be
able to resist reaching out and touching him, she
backed up all the way to the bed. To her consternation,
there was no place else to go.

"Take off your robe, Laura, or I'll remove it for you."

"Please, no…"

Her resistance only made him more determined. Without conscious thought Zach found himself untying her belt. Beneath the cotton nightgown he felt the hardness of her enlarged belly with a sense of wonder.

A faint citrus scent emanated from her. This close, her warmth caught at his senses, kindling the ache that had never gone away since the first moment he'd seen her standing in the doorway of his hotel room in Belgium. As he slipped the robe off her shoulders, he leaned closer, letting the black glistening curls of her hair, soft as butterfly wings, brush against his unshaven jaw.

Compelled by an urge he no longer had the power to control, he skimmed his hands down her arms, unable to credit that Laura Donetti, the phantom lover of his dreams, stood before him in the flesh, vital and trembling.

He was so entranced he forgot the reason her robe had come off in the first place. That is, until his fingers inadvertently found the tender area around her right elbow. Though the pressure was ever so slight, it elicited a wince.

"Forgive me for hurting you," came the husky apology as he carefully examined her injury. All the time he was touching her, he could sense the blood coursing through her veins. It seemed to match the wild rush of his own.

"You're not," she said, lifting her face to his. That lovely face whose features he'd imagined exploring with his lips over and over again in the solitude of his empty bed.

"You have too much mobility for it to be broken," he murmured, "but it'll be sore for a while."

"That's what I thought." She sounded breathless.

The effort to speak appeared as difficult for her as for him.

Only now did he recognize the difference between fantasy and reality. Dreams had a way of obscuring details—like the faint freckles on her nose, the laughter lines around her heavily lashed eyes.

This was no dream. When he gazed into those liquid brown irises, he saw that same look of nervousness and vulnerability he'd seen in Belgium. He saw something else. Fear of *him,* maybe? *Why?*

"Don't you know I would never intentionally hurt you?"

"I know." Her breath seemed to be coming in pants. The beguiling curve of her mouth was only a whisper away.

Her mouth. It was all he could think about.

"I want to kiss you, Laura. I *have* to kiss you."

"Zach…"

If crying his name was an attempt to stop him, it had come too late. He could no more deny the desire driving him than he could deny the air he breathed.

When his mouth closed hungrily over hers, Laura almost fainted from too much feeling. She'd been praying for this day, longing for this moment. Zach could have no inkling of the depth of her love or her desire.

She'd promised herself that if he ever reached out, she would respond slowly, carefully, so as not to frighten him off.

What a joke! How delusional could she have been? The way she was kissing him back, you'd have thought she was a lovesick teenager caught up in the out-of-control passion of first love.

Laura was just like that. Out of control. She knew she was, but she couldn't stop what was happening, couldn't stop her response to him. Zach's kiss went on and on. She wanted it to go on forever.

Her subconscious fear that he would regret this momentary lapse made her lose all inhibitions. She pressed her body closer and wound her fingers into his hair. She pulled her lips from his and moved them with restless intensity over the rugged features of his face.

"Dear God, Laura..." he groaned, then urged her with him onto the bed. Her voluptuous body felt hot to the touch. His insatiable need for her drove him to kiss the perfumed satin of her skin everywhere the cotton nightgown didn't cover.

She brought him so much pleasure it was almost pain. Her gorgeous long legs intertwined with his, locking them together. Her mouth was another miracle, like an endless fount where he could drink long and deeply.

He loved the healthy ebony sheen of her short curls.

Every inch of her hair and body smelled like flowers. The first time he'd ever laid eyes on her, he'd thought her the ultimate of femininity. The thought had only intensified.

"Do you have any idea how beautiful you are?" he said into the scented hollow of her neck.

"I was thinking the same thing about you," she confessed as her hands roamed over his T-shirt-clad chest and broad shoulders. "Bev told me you have Viking blood in your ancestry. If these were days of old and you'd come to kidnap me and take me away in your longboat, I would have gone willingly."

He crushed her mouth beneath his again, electrified by her nearness, by her breathtaking response. Laura was different from any woman he'd ever known. She had this amazing ability to give her body *and* her soul, holding nothing back. It was a revelation to him.

"Willing or not," he whispered against her lips, "I would have thrown you over my shoulder and claimed you for myself."

The fierceness of his tone thrilled Laura. She inched closer. "I wouldn't have wanted anyone to come after us and rescue me."

"You think I would have let them?" His voice was gruff.

"Maybe…after you'd grown bored of the distraction." Heat stormed her cheeks. "As you've learned for yourself, I'm afraid I'm not your typical demure maiden, shy and unsure."

He rose up on one elbow. "You really think I could be held by such a woman?"

"I don't know," she answered honestly.

Somehow their lovemaking had become something else. She began to feel uneasy about the serious turn their conversation was taking.

Talking only complicated everything. She didn't want to talk, but when she tried to bring her mouth to his again, he stopped her by pinning her shoulder to the mattress with his free hand.

"Come on. Explain what you mean." The steel in his voice alarmed her.

She sucked in a breath. "You and I said our good-byes back in the Galápagos. If there'd been no earthquake, you wouldn't be here now, compelled to deal with *my* presence."

"Compelled?"

Her brows knit delicately. "Did Richard leave you any choice when he ordered everyone else to bed?"

"Since childhood my brother and I have communicated without words. Richard did exactly the right thing—he knew I wanted to be alone with you."

She could feel his searching gaze, but averted her eyes for fear he'd read too much in them. "In case you were wishing you hadn't offered it, I never considered buying your condo, Zach."

His ruthless silence prompted her to keep on talking, which she did—faster and faster.

"Richard and Bev begged me to at least rent it, but

I told them that if you ever came back to Newport, you would want to return to your own home.''

She felt his hand tighten almost painfully on her shoulder. He could have no idea of his strength, yet she welcomed it because the unconscious gesture proved he wasn't indifferent to her.

"I'm glad you put my needs first," he said. "Otherwise, considering what the quake did to my condo, you could be nursing more than an injured elbow."

In the next instant he bent his head to kiss her shoulder where his hand had been. "So when are you leaving for Hawaii?" he murmured against her sensitized skin.

She couldn't think, not when his mouth was inching closer to hers. "I decided it wasn't a good idea, after all." The words came out so faintly and tremulously she wasn't certain he'd even heard them.

He had. "You're right," he said in a silky whisper, burying his face in her hair. "So what's your plan?"

With a thudding heart she said, "There's an apartment complex here in Newp—"

"Which one?" he cut in, brushing her cheek with his lips.

"The Riviera."

"It's too far from the beach, but it will do as well as anyplace else until the condo's repaired."

"No, Zach. I've already told you I'm not moving into your home."

After gently biting her earlobe he said, "I thought you wanted me around to help you raise your daughter. Has that idea lost all its appeal since you left Ecuador?''

Confused, Laura tried to sit up, but his hard body kept her pinned. ''You know it hasn't, but you made it clear to me you weren't returning to Calif—''

''Earthquakes have a way of putting a man's priorities in order. I owe Tony—not only for baiting him without mercy, but for the greater sin of coveting his wife. Since you're willing, I'm prepared to make restitution, provided we get married immediately. Anything less wouldn't do.''

Laura couldn't prevent the gasp that escaped her throat.

Before she'd gone to the Galápagos, her plan to win Zach's love had been based first on appealing to him to be a father to her baby. At the time she'd thought it a good idea. It seemed her plan had finally succeeded, but the results were tearing her apart—because she'd forgotten one thing. *Zach's not in love with you. Remember your conversation with Bev?*

The lovely Rosie Armstrong was the woman who would always hold Zach's heart.

''Think about it,'' he said, ''and let me know in the morning.''

And then he gave her a hard kiss and levered himself from the bed.

Her gaze followed his retreating back until the door closed behind him.

What am I going to do?

She buried her face in her hands, shattered.

The next hour passed like an eternity. She felt feverish. In this anxiety-laden state, it wouldn't be long before she was really sick.

Zach had told her to give him her answer in the morning.

But you already know the answer, Laura. You have no shame where he's concerned. Admit it. Go to him now and tell him the truth.

Bare your soul.

If he still wants to marry you knowing you love him, then so be it. At least we'll both know exactly where we stand. We'll have honesty. That's more than a lot of couples have.

Her mind made up, she got off the bed and reached for her robe. Then she tiptoed out of the room.

He was probably asleep on the pullout couch downstairs. It would be cruel to wake him up after his long flight, but this couldn't wait. If she didn't tell him now, she might not be able to find the courage in the morning.

The large family room off the kitchen was her favorite place in the Wilde household. Besides books and games, there was an old player piano everyone enjoyed. Laura particularly loved the comfy furniture.

The aquarium in one corner gave off enough light for her to distinguish shapes in the darkness. Her gaze sought the couch, expecting to see Zach's stretched from end to end.

"You're looking in the wrong place."

She wheeled around in surprise. Zach, still dressed,

stood in the doorway. "Why aren't you in bed?" she asked.

"Why aren't *you?*"

Zach had a way of knocking her off balance. "I haven't just flown in from Ecuador. You must be exhausted!"

"If I am, my body doesn't know it yet. I've been outside inspecting the damage to the swimming pool. Richard's lucky his house is still in one piece. Luckier still that everyone is safe."

"I couldn't agree more," she said quietly.

"Is your elbow keeping you awake?"

"No."

There was something about the middle of the night that created intimacy and made it difficult to lie about anything.

Nervous and frightened of the outcome, she rubbed moist palms against the side of her robe. "I need to talk to you, but I was afraid I would have to wake you first."

"I'm listening."

Isn't this what you wanted, Laura?

"All right. I've only told you one untruth since we've known each other. No, that's not exactly true. I've told *two* untruths," she blurted, then moaned because it had come out all wrong. "That's not exactly true, either." She fidgeted with the ends of her belt. "Since Tony died I've been keeping something from you—" her voice shook "—and I've been hating myself for it ever since. I should have just been honest when you came to the cabin on the *Puff Cloud,* but..."

"For the love of heaven, Laura," he said impatiently, "just *say* it. You think I don't know that deep down you could never marry me because you've never stopped loving your husband no matter what he did to you?"

"No, Zach!" she cried in horror, because he was so wrong. So very wrong. "That isn't what I'm trying to tel—"

"Don't deny it," he warned, sending a thrill of alarm through her body. "I witnessed your devotion to him, saw it in a dozen different ways, remember? But the proof was in your eyes the night I accompanied you to your hotel room after Tony died."

Her heart turned over just remembering that moment she'd almost committed the unpardonable and invited him inside.

"*What* proof?"

"Do you really need me to spell it out for you?"

"I do. What is it you think was going on inside me?"

Something in her tone must have alerted Zach, because she sensed his hesitation, a rare thing for him.

"You were in so much pain you didn't want or need anybody."

"You're right," she said. "You saw pain. Excruciating pain. Perhaps now you have some idea of what it cost me not to ask you to spend the night with me."

Even in the dim light of the room, she perceived

his shock. There was an electric silence. The time to tell all had come.

"I'm far from perfect, Zach. Maybe you'll understand why I underwent therapy after the Tour de France was over."

"Therapy?"

"Yes. I knew that if I didn't talk to a professional about my guilt over wanting you, I'd be endangering my health and ultimately the baby's. I'm not proud of what I'm about to tell you, but it has to be said because it's the truth.

"I fell in love with you, Zach." Her voice caught. "It happened after you answered the hotel-room door and introduced yourself as Tony's roommate. When you asked me to come in and wait for him, a little voice warned me this was wrong, told me I should run away and not look back. But I chose to ignore it. That's how fast and how…naturally it happened."

She heard a low groan. It could have meant anything, but she'd started this and had to finish it. "I'm at a loss to explain how or why. All I can tell you is that…my life changed that day.

"In the beginning I lied to myself. I told myself I was only attracted to you because you were so kind to me. I rationalized that my pitiful marriage had made me vulnerable to any decent man's attentions. But when you phoned me from the hospital to tell me about Klaus, I had to admit that my feelings for you went far beyond anything remotely resembling gratitude.

"As terrible as this sounds, I didn't want to hang up. I wanted our conversation to go on and on. I wanted to beg you to come back to the hotel and be with me."

She paused to draw a deep shuddering breath. "The more circumstances separated us, the more my feelings for you grew. By the time I'd finished shedding my tears for Tony, I had to face the truth. I loved *you*. My heart, my soul knew it. And so did my body."

Laura heard Zach groan again. In admitting the truth she risked everything, even his revulsion. But it had to be said.

"When you walked me to my hotel room that night, I struggled not to break down and invite you in. I feared what you would think of me if I did." She paused once more. "Do you understand what I'm saying?" she cried, barely holding on to her emotions. "Only a few hours before, Tony had collapsed and died! And there I was, wanting you in all the ways a woman could ever want a man."

Tears rolled down her hot cheeks. "I was convinced there had to be something wrong with me, something evil. How could I want you when the body of the man I'd promised before God to love and honor hadn't even been buried?"

She choked down a sob. "This gets worse. Only one thing prevented me from begging you to stay the night. To my shame, it wasn't God. It was *Rosie Armstrong*."

At the sound of his ex-fiancée's name, she saw Zach

recoil. Proof, as far as she was concerned, that he'd given everything to Rosie. There could be no more.

"Bev told me all about her, that she was the great love of your life, so it's pointless for you to deny it."

"I wasn't about to."

You knew this could backfire on you, but you didn't know how agonizing it was going to be.

Head bowed, she murmured, "Even Richie let me know how much her son's jealousy of you brought you grief."

Finish it. Just finish it. "It's obvious to me and everyone else you've never gotten over her. I *know* what that kind of love is like, because it's the same kind of love I feel for you. The forever kind. It defies time and…and logic. It drove me to lie to you in the Galápagos about not wanting to be married. I thought I'd be clever and pretend marriage didn't matter to me as long as you'd let me stay in your life, in whatever capacity you chose. But from the beginning, I fantasized about what it would be like to really belong to you, to have your baby."

She lifted her chin. "But therapy taught me many things. Like the fact I'd been in mourning my whole marriage and had done most of my grieving long before Tony died. Thus the reason I was ready to get into a new relationship.

"Therapy also helped me understand that it's unhealthy to live with guilt and secrets. In the end, you find you've only destroyed yourself.

"That's why I decided I'd better tell you all this

tonight. I'm not about to hang around you, let alone try to lock you into a loveless marriage. I realize that if both parties don't feel the same, it doesn't work and wouldn't be good for a child.''

She had to get out of here, and she started for the kitchen. ''Please,'' she called over her shoulder, ''let me be. Forgive me for flying to the Galápagos uninvited. It was wrong of me. You went there to nurse your wounds. All I managed to do was stir up the past and embarrass you. I promise it won't happen again, Zach.''

She hurried through the house and up the stairs, anxious to be gone from here before morning. It was time to close the chapter on the Wildes before she made any more mistakes.

A FEW MINUTES LATER Zach opened Richie's bedroom door, seeking Richard. He didn't care if his brother was asleep. He had to talk to him or he'd go out of his mind.

''Come all the way in,'' Richard said, ''I've been waiting for you.''

Relief swept through Zach. ''Where's Richie?''

''I think the quake scared him more than he wants to admit. He had so much trouble settling down, I went to the kitchen to make him some hot chocolate. That's when I heard voices coming from the family room and figured you might need to talk later. I told him to get in bed with Bev and the girls.''

''What would I do without you? How come I'm one

of the lucky ones in life who was given a brother and best friend rolled into one?''

Richard turned on the light by Richie's bed. Dressed only in a T-shirt and boxers, he threw off the covers and sat on the edge of the bed, eyeing Zach for a long sober moment.

''Welcome home. It's good to see you again, too. I've missed you more than you know.''

''Want to bet?'' Zach fired back. ''I don't think I realized just how deep my feelings went until the captain of the *Wind Cloud* told me there'd been an earthquake in Southern California. When he said the epicenter was in Costa Mesa…'' Zach couldn't finish.

''It was something, all right. I was in the office when everything went flying off the desks and cabinets. For once I was glad you were thousands of miles away. Luckily no one at the office or home was hurt.''

''Except for Laura.''

Richard leaped to his feet. ''She never said anything.''

''You know her. She's so self-sacrificing she didn't want to alarm Richie.''

''She's not going to miscarry, is she?''

''No, no. It's not that bad. But when the quake hit, it knocked her to the ground. She banged her elbow pretty hard and I saw an ugly bruise below her knee.''

Richard quirked and eyebrow. ''The knee, huh? That must have been *before* you left her bedroom to go downstairs.'' He chuckled.

''Zach, when are you going to break down and admit she's the reason you flew home on the next plane?'' He paused, ''You know you're in love with her.''

''I've known that since day one.''

''Is there the slightest doubt in your mind that she's hopelessly in love with you, too?''

''Not anymore. Tonight she told me exactly how she felt.'' Her confession had transformed him. ''*Lord*, Richard. She loves me the way Bev loves you. I didn't think that kind of love was possible for me.''

Richard's eyes moistened. ''Destiny must have known what was down the road when you were asked to train for the Tour de France. Let me tell you something. Bev and I *watched* the two of you fall in love. It happened fast. Now answer me one question. What are you doing here in Richie's room, instead of hers?''

''She thinks—no, she's *convinced* I'm still in love with Rosie.''

''That's Bev's fault,'' Richard confided. ''The day of the time trials she told Laura about your past without realizing the damage it would do. She's hated herself for it ever since.''

Zach shook his head. ''I love Bev and could never blame her for anything. It's *my* behavior that's the problem. When Laura came to see me in the Galápagos, she offered herself to me in any capacity I was willing to consider. I was so afraid she didn't love me the way I loved her, I turned her down flat.''

''Tell me something I don't know,'' Richard said, shaking his head. ''She came home shattered.''

"Then you have some idea of the state I was in when I found out she'd left the Galápagos without my knowledge. The hell of it is, tonight I made another fatal mistake by telling her I'd marry her to atone for my guilt over the part I played in Tony's death."

"You *what?*"

"Yeah," Zach admitted. "I told her to give me her answer in the morning. As you found out when you went downstairs, she chose not to wait until the sun came up to tell me no thank you." He began to pace. "You should have heard her tonight. If I'd tried to tell her how I really felt about her, if I'd made one move toward her in the state she was in, she would have run out of the house and I might not have been able to find her again."

"You mean like *you* did in Paris? Without leaving a forwarding address?"

Zach's hands balled into fists. "Okay, I deserved that."

"Hey—" Richard gave him another hug "—don't be so hard on yourself. You did what you felt you had to do. Tony's death shocked all of us. But that's in the past. You *are* home to stay, aren't you?"

They stared at each other.

"I don't ever want to be anyplace else."

"Then you need to tell Laura."

"I need to tell her a lot of things."

"I agree. So go in to her right now and start talking." Richard took him fiercely by the shoulders. "I mean a knock-down-drag-out heart-to-heart. Don't

stop until she's listened to you—and *believes* you!
Whether it takes two hours or twenty, I'll make sure
the kids stay away.''

Zach's thoughts raced ahead. ''Does the guest-room
door have a lock?''

''No.'' Richard grinned. ''When the house was
built, I made a last-minute decision not to bother.''

''That was a wise decision.'' He grinned back.
''Otherwise there might have been more to repair than
your swimming pool.''

But Zach's grin faded as he left the bedroom and
approached Laura's. Fearing she wouldn't answer him
if he knocked, Zach made the split-second decision to
go in unannounced and uninvited.

Quietly he turned the knob and entered.

The sight that greeted his eyes would live with him
forever.

A gasp escaped Laura as she frantically attempted
to cover herself with the end of Richie's bedspread.
The movement knocked her clothes to the floor. She
must have just come out of the shower and was about
to get dressed, Zach thought.

*No doubt she has a secret plan to leave Newport
without saying goodbye.*

''Going somewhere?'' he asked. Acting on instincts
older than time, he closed the distance between them
and picked her up in his arms. ''I don't think, so.'' he
whispered against her lips.

''No, Zach!'' She turned her head and fought with
surprising strength, but she was still no match for him.

With only a bedspread separating him from her gorgeous body, he recognized his advantage for what it was and chose to use it.

In wonderment he watched a rose tint suffuse her cheeks and proceed down the breathtaking length of her.

As he'd once told Richie— "All's fair in love, war and the Tour de France." With the race out of the way, they were now down to the love and war part. He remembered that the family-room door *did* have a lock and he planned to show no mercy.

"Please put me down," she begged.

"I will when I'm good and ready, but first we're going to have a long undisturbed talk." So saying, he started for the door.

"What are you doing? And we've already talked."

"What happened to my raven-haired captive who said she'd come with me anywhere willingly? And no, we have *not* talked."

"But you don't want me!" she wailed plaintively before burying her face in his shoulder.

"You don't have the faintest idea *what* I want because I let you say everything that was on your mind first. Once we're where no one can bother us, it's going to be my turn to talk and yours to listen. Without interruption."

He opened the door and headed for the staircase.

"Let me at least take my clothes!"

"I'll let you come back for them later."

Enjoying the role of marauder, Zach stole through

the house with his treasure, pleased that she'd gone all silent on him.

Once the family-room door was closed and he heard the satisfying click of the lock, he could concentrate fully on Laura. The thought of making love to her on the sofa bed Bev had made up for him almost sent his heart into fibrillation.

But if he gave in to the desire racking his body, there'd be no talking. Richard's easy chair would accommodate both of them. Locked in his arms, she would have to stay put, and he'd still have the power to think and speak.

Or so he'd thought.

Too late he discovered that the small amount of light from the aquarium had given the smooth skin of her arms and shoulders a pearly luster. The reality of her physical presence, her natural beauty, every curve of her face and body, played havoc with his senses. The enticing dishevelment of her curls, still damp from the shower, the lovely mouth with its full lower lip made him forget what he was about.

Suppressing his yearning while he still could, he got up with her from the chair and carefully lowered her onto the sofa bed.

Her astonishment at being dispatched well out of his reach would have made him laugh if the situation wasn't so crucial to his existence. Though he'd lived through two relationships that had caused him great heartache, he'd been able to get on with his life. Not this time, though.

As long ago as Belgium, he'd realized that if he was privileged to live the rest of his life with her—as her husband—he would be one of those mortals lucky enough to scale the full height of human experience. In the Galápagos he'd discovered that without her, he would suffer a kind of death and be irrevocably lost.

She made no move to escape. Like an obedient child she lay there with Richie's bedspread cocooning her, her dark eyes anxiously peering out from the fringe.

The mixture of innocence and womanly beauty melted his insides.

"Before any more time passes," he said, "I want you to know everything there is to know about me. That way there'll be no secrets between us after we're married."

CHAPTER FOURTEEN

AFTER WE'RE MARRIED? Do you really mean it, Zach?

With extreme effort, she managed to sit up and still keep the bedspread in place.

His eyes followed every movement. "Because you were a married woman when we met, I didn't have the right to share everything with you like I'm going to do now."

"You'll never know how much I wanted you to," she said.

"You think I didn't?" He sucked in a breath. "I'm afraid you're in for a long siege, Laura. Many of the things I'm about to tell you, no one else knows. Not even Richard."

Because she'd never known two brothers more devoted, this statement made an impact. She stared at him, wide-eyed.

"As you've already divined," he began, "I have several glaring flaws. But one stands out from the rest. I've always put Richard on a pedestal. Everything I ever did, aimed for, achieved, had to be measured by his standards. He didn't ask for his little brother's hero-worship. Unfortunately for him it just happened, an accident of birth in the family constellation. I followed him around like a puppy and he had to bear the burden.''

"That happens in lots of families," Laura said, rushing to his defense.

"In our case I took it too far. I'm afraid I became a nuisance, as well as a responsibility. Being Richard, he took me on because that's the kind of man he is.'' Zach paused. "After saving Bev from drowning, he fell in love with her.''

"Yes. She told me about that.''

His eyes flashed. "Did she tell you how jealous I was because she'd taken him away from me?''

Laura's heart went out to him. "No.''

"Maybe I did a better job of hiding my dark side than I thought. Anyway, there were moments in my teenage years when I disliked her intensely.'' His brows knit. "If you can imagine anyone disliking Bev, then you'll have an idea of just how dark I can be. Anyway, at their wedding, I felt like I'd lost my best friend. I couldn't tag along anymore. The only people they associated with were other engaged or married couples. Life just wasn't the same, particularly when a few months after the ceremony I heard they were expecting a baby.''

"Zach, many younger brothers and sisters feel bereft when an older sibling leaves the nest. It's a huge adjustment for everyone. I went through it myself.''

He shook his head. "My case was unique. I could have benefited from therapy. But that word wasn't in our family's vocabulary and I went from bad to worse.

I figured that if I found myself a girlfriend and got married, Richard would allow me into that inner circle and we'd be buddies again. So began my quest to find the perfect woman.''

"And she turned out to be a carbon copy of Bev," Laura guessed. But she'd spoken without thinking.

Zach stared at her before nodding. "She could have been Bev's twin. Superficially they resembled each other. Cathy had Bev's sunny disposition. Richard approved of her, so that was all that mattered. To my delight, they let me bring her over to their apartment for dinner. The four of us went sailing together. After Richie was born, we saw even more of one another. When it looked like my plan was working, I bought her a ring and we set a date for our wedding.

"The only shadow on that particular horizon were the migraines Cathy suffered. Sometimes she'd be too sick to go anywhere. Though I never said the words out loud, I'm ashamed to admit that I used to resent her for ruining an evening we'd planned with Richard and Bev."

He blew out a sigh. "Obviously I was too emotionally immature to be involved in a serious relationship of any kind, certainly not one that had been engineered by my own selfish agenda. Because Richard had always handled everything so well, I thought I could carry things off just like he did.

"Reality struck when Cathy had to be hospitalized after a bad migraine attack. She was frightened and reached out to me for support. I couldn't comfort her the way she needed. Don't get me wrong—I cared for her a great deal, but I didn't know what real love was. I didn't dare admit that to anyone. That was the hell of it. About now my guilt kicked in.

"It was a sobering experience for a number of reasons. I'd never been around a really ill person before, in this case my fiancée. For the first time in my life I had to forget my needs and desires to be there for her. I had to pretend things I didn't feel in front of her family and mine because I didn't want anyone to know my turmoil, particularly Richard."

"Zach—"

"You see what I'm talking about? I had real problems and promised myself that when she got better, I would try to make it up to her." Another sigh. "It never dawned on me that Cathy would die. My imagination didn't stretch that far. When the doctor told me she'd passed away in her sleep because of a brain tumor, I simply didn't believe him. Like all young people, I thought we were immortal.

"Her death was not only a tragedy, it forced me to continue living a kind of lie. Everyone assumed I was grieving for my lost love. Of course I felt horrible about it, but part of my pain had to do with my own wretchedness."

Laura understood only too well.

"My guilt deepened and I went into a depression. Of course no one knew what I was going through. The family rallied around me, but for once their love couldn't fix what was wrong. Poor Richard, forever my champion, made a suggestion he thought would help me get over losing Cathy.''

''What was that?''

''He felt a new hobby unassociated with the past would force me to channel my energy into something positive. The next thing I knew, we were out buying racing bikes. His idea. I would never have thought of it on my own.'' He shook his head.

''Oddly enough, her death brought us close together again. It was wonderful being with Richard in the old buddy way, but my guilt—compounded by more guilt because I knew he ought to be home with Bev—prevented me from enjoying the situation.

''I concentrated, instead, on pushing myself to the edge. Cycling happened to be the only sport at which I was better than my brother. It felt good to beat him at something. I needed to redeem myself, be a person worthy of his respect. When I saw he was proud of me, I worked out harder and began entering local competitions.

''That was about the time Bev announced she was pregnant again. She suffered terrible morning sickness, and Richard couldn't come with me as often. But it no longer mattered as much. Between my work in the family business and the cycling, a certain amount of healing started to take place. So even though Richard never knew the truth, his idea had turned out to be a good one.

''Those years following Cathy's death were a time of growth for me. I won a lot of national and international races. I traveled a great deal and met a scout representing a European-based sponsor of a cycling team.''

Zach told Laura how they'd been looking to include some Americans on a new pro team they were putting together to train in Park City, Utah, for the Tour de France. Though he'd had no burning desire to win a competition like that, the idea of seeing new places had sounded interesting.

''Of course old habits die hard,'' he said, ''and I had to discuss it with Richard before I did anything as drastic as uprooting myself to live in Utah. He thought I ought to consider it because my hobby kept me from dwelling on the past, and I was good, really good, at cycling. Dad encouraged me, as well, and offered to sponsor me so I could devote full time to the grueling training involved. I began to see that if I did this, it would make the family happy. Since I felt I owed them, I thought, why not try it?''

Laura pondered this last revelation. Guilt was responsible for more pain than just about anything she could think of.

''I realized an offer like that didn't come your way very often. Being at loose ends, I accepted it and moved to Park City. The Rockies provided me with a whole new set of problems, but I thrived on adversity. It took time to acclimatize. At such a high altitude, I learned endurance and found the steep grades challenging.

''I also discovered loneliness and began seeing

women. Over a period of time I met all types, from sports buffs to party girls.''

That's something I didn't know, Laura thought. *I don't think Bev and Richard know it, either.*

''To some extent I enjoyed the experience, but I never felt anything lasting. As soon as I sensed they wanted a commitment, I moved on with the excuse that I'd be leaving the States before long to live in Europe.

''One day on a mountain road, I was racing around a corner and almost bumped into this woman who was out riding bikes with her son and his friends. She apologized for being in the way. When the near-accident was clearly my fault, I found her generosity refreshing.''

He smiled at the memory. ''Rosie had a sunny disposition. The absence of any artifice or superficiality made her really appealing. Unlike the other women I'd met, she had stability in both her career as a teacher and role as a mother. She didn't come on strong.''

In fact, Zach said to Laura, it had been her reticence that had drawn him to her. He'd known instinctively that she would make no demands on him. He'd needed that because he wasn't ready for a deep emotional commitment.

''She was a widow and quite content with her life. She didn't need me to complete it, didn't want something from me. I could tell she was a good parent, too. Her son, Cody, was friendly at first. But as soon as he realized I enjoyed being with his mother, he didn't like me at all. Since I was out of town a lot, it didn't bother me. Our dates were sporadic.

"But little by little, love grew. In time I discovered that I liked coming home from a racing event to one woman. The bachelor life began to pall, as did the cycling circuit. I gave up the idea of training for the Tour de France and, instead, started up a branch of our family business in Salt Lake.

"At that point Rosie's son declared war. Between him and her in-laws interference, I had the fight of my life on my hands. Despite the love Rosie and I shared, the second year of our relationship resembled a battle-field with Cody outmaneuvering me at every turn.

"Unfortunately Cody's behavior had created sort of a smokescreen that masked a much more serious prob-lem for Rosie."

"What was that?" Laura asked in a haunted voice.

"Rosie was still in love with the husband who'd died in the war." He started to pace. Laura watched him, her heart breaking for him. "I knew all along she wasn't completely over him, but I told myself it didn't matter. What we had was here and now. It was similar to what I'd told myself about loving Cathy when I knew the kind of love I had for her wasn't enough."

Laura shivered involuntarily, afraid of what was to come.

"I knew in my gut it was pointless to keep seeing Rosie. But so much time had been invested, I made one last-ditch effort and invited her and Cody on a cruise. If nothing came of it, I was going to leave Salt Lake.

"To my surprise, she proposed to me aboard ship and told me she wouldn't let Cody stand in the way of our happiness. She swore she loved me and I believed her. Of course I knew her feelings for me were different from what she'd felt for her husband. I told myself that in time, though, our love would take on a life of its own. I had gotten to the point where I wanted to settle down. I didn't want to look anywhere else."

He stopped pacing and put his hands on his hips. "We probably would have achieved a solid marriage if her husband hadn't returned. But the second she phoned me and told me the news that he was alive, I knew it was over. So did she."

"How were you able to do it?" Laura asked. "How were you able to let go?"

"It was hard. I won't lie about that. We'd been friends a long time."

"And lovers," she whispered.

"No, Laura, that's where you're wrong. We never slept together."

She couldn't comprehend what he was telling her. "You mean that over a two-year period you nev—"

"No," he cut in. "I didn't want to make love to her until I knew it would be *me* in her bed, not Nick. You see, I thought it didn't matter that she still clung to her first love. But when it came right down to it, I was greedy. I wanted it all. When I couldn't have it,

I decided to play a waiting game. I could afford to. I wasn't going anywhere.''

He sat down on the edge of the bed and ran a hand through his hair. Laura found *herself* wanting to do that, but she stayed still and listened. ''Because of that decision, we were both fortunate enough to walk away in the end without *that* complication to deal with. She was able to resume her marriage to Nick and not look back. They have an incredible relationship, like Richard and Bev's. Needless to say it made Cody deliriously happy.''

''Stop being so noble, Zach!'' she exclaimed. ''What about *your* happiness?''

''*My* happiness?'' He turned to her and his eyes narrowed. ''She's sitting right in front of me, exactly where I want her.'' His voice sounded husky.

Laura heard the words with a sense of unreality. ''Be serious.''

''I've never been more serious in my life. Haven't you listened to anything I've been saying?''

The next thing she knew, he stood up and reached for her, pulling her, still clutching the bedspread, into his arms.

''I've only known one great love, my darling. *You.*''

She couldn't deny the power of his declaration. All the emotion, all the love that was in him, had found the path straight to her heart. A small cry of joy escaped her. ''I love you, too, Zach.''

He molded her body to his, worshipping her with his hands and mouth. She couldn't get close enough.

"I never believed a person could fall in love at first sight, Laura, but it happened to me when I opened my hotel-room door and saw you standing there."

"That day was like a wonderful dream," she said. "I never wanted to wake up."

Zach sighed. "By the time I'd made up the excuse that I was out of razor blades so I could walk you to your hotel, I was in love. I knew you were Tony's wife, but it didn't seem to matter. You weren't anything like I'd imagined. I didn't want to leave your side, or you to leave mine."

"I know, darling, I know. Why do you think I invited you in *my* hotel room and fed you those granola bars? I was desperate to think up any idiotic excuse to detain you."

Burying his face in her neck, he whispered, "I loved those bars. With every delicious bite, I cursed the Fates that had made you Tony's wife, instead of mine. Talk about desperation…"

Laura clung to him, almost mindless with passion.

"The attraction I felt for you," he said, "drove me to inveigle Richard into taking you around the circuit with him. Not that he needed any coaxing once he'd met you. It was the only plan I could think of to legitimately see you every morning and every night."

"Then why did you stop joining the family?" she cried in remembered pain.

He held her away from him and shook her gently. "You *know* why. I'd already passed beyond the bounds of decency when I called you from the hospital.

"No, you—"

"Laura," he interrupted, "all my life I've tried to live by a certain code of ethics. Making love to another man's wife has always been verboten. I don't frighten easily, but that night when I knew you were alone, I came close to breaking that vow and I experienced real fear."

She closed her eyes tightly and buried her face in his chest. "You were right not to come. How could I have refused you? Not even Tony's death made a difference. After that scene with the press, I just wanted to curl up with you alone somewhere and shut out the world. I'll never know how I found the strength to turn away from you."

A tremor shook his powerful body. "I don't want to think about that. The only matter of any importance is marrying you. If it was up to me, I'd drive us to Nevada right now. But if you want a big wedding..."

She chuckled. "I'm afraid the wedding arrangements might already be out of our hands."

He looked down at her, confused. "What are you talking about?"

"Bev and Richard have been hoping for months that we'd get together. They'd be crushed if we just drove off without letting them plan a celebration."

"I love and need you so badly I don't know if I can wait. But since it's Richard and Bev—"

Laura silenced his mouth with her own. He returned

her kiss with an ardor that blocked out the rest of the world. When he finally let her catch her breath, she murmured, "Let's go upstairs and tell them the happy news. It's already morning. The sun's up. And you *know* they've been awake all night just waiting to find out if all their plots have hatched the way they hoped."

Zach smiled at her. "You love them as much as I do. That's just one of the many things I adore about you."

"They're the most wonderful people I've ever known."

"I agree."

So saying, he picked her up in his arms and headed for the door.

"First we'll have to go by the guest room so I can get dressed," she said.

"Really."

She blinked.

"Zach—"

"Hush, woman!"

Effortlessly he carried her up the stairs. Something told her she was in trouble.

"Zach, you can't let anyone see me like this!"

He cast her a positively wolfish leer. "Any spoils must be presented to the master of this house first. He and he alone will decide your fate."

"Uncle Zach!"

Richie appeared out of nowhere. "What're you do-ing with Laura and how come she's wrapped in my bedspread?'' He spoke loudly enough for all to hear. Within seconds the girls had run out of the master bedroom.

"Is she sick?" Rachel wanted to know.

"How come she's not saying anything?" Robin demanded.

Fire raged in Laura's cheeks. All she could do was hide her face in Zach's neck.

"She's in shock, Robin."

"Does that mean the baby's coming?"

Laura could feel Zach shake with suppressed laughter. "It better not be. We've got to get married first."

"Hooray!" the girls shouted.

"It's about time, Uncle Zach," Richie declared.

"Is *that* right, Richie."

"Yeah. Laura's the best. She's already part of the family."

"Did you hear that, my love?" Zach said in her ear as they swept through the doorway of Bev and Richard's room. "No greater praise."

"Come all the way in, little brother. Let's see what you've got bundled up in there."

"I've returned with precious plunder after a great voyage in my longboat."

"What's a longboat?" Robin wanted to know, but nobody answered.

"Come closer so I can inspect the goods," came the command.

"Richard Thorald Wilde!" Bev cried indignantly on Laura's behalf.

"You started this, *wife*," Richard teased.

Laura had the sinking feeling there was no stopping Zach or his brother. He carried her over to Richard's side of the king-size bed.

Richard reached out to smooth the fringe of Richie's bedspread away from her face. He winked. "What's this? A woman with strange black hair and dark eyes that can put the pox on a man so he doesn't know where he is or what he's doing. Don't you know this kind of creature makes a man useless and causes trouble in our world of blond-haired blue-eyed giants?"

"Richard, that's enough!" Bev tried again.

"She's with child, too, but I still want her." Zach swooped down and gave her a kiss in front of everyone.

"Hmm, yes, I can see that you do." Richard put a finger to his cheek thoughtfully. "If you claim her, you can't go on any more voyages."

"I don't want to go on any more voyages. I want my own castle, my own lands...my own woman."

"From here on out you'll have to do your share of the work and not cause any more havoc for me and mine."

"I swear by the oath of Thorald I shall."

"By the oath of Thorald, huh? In that case, she's yours! What do you call this creature?"

"Laura."

"That's a strange name."

"But I like it."

"The child's name will have to be Astrid in honor

of our great-great-grandmother, Queen Astrid, isn't that right, *wife?*"

"*Astrid?*" The shock in Zach's voice made Laura chuckle.

"It's Astrid, or there will be no ceremony."

Zach looked down at her in puzzlement. "Laura?"

"Do you mind?" Her eyes begged him. "She's going to be your daughter. I want her to be a true Wilde."

Zach's stunned gaze flicked back to Richard. "Astrid it is."

A huge grin transformed Richard's face. "I told you those brown eyes were going to be your downfall. Wife." He turned to Bev. "Name the date for the ceremony."

"Wednesday."

"But that's five days from now!" Zach protested. "I'm not waiting that—"

"Wednesday it is," Richard proclaimed with kingly authority. "Until then, this creature will have to stay with the womenfolk and be prepared."

Rachel squirmed her way through to sit on her father's lap.

"Daddy, you're funny."

"Yeah, Daddy—"

Robin was cut off by the ringing of the phone. It was a sound no one had heard since the quake.

"The phone's back on, thank goodness. Now we can call everybody and invite them!" Bev reached for the receiver and said hello. But the shining happiness in her face faded as she listened to whomever was on the other end.

Fearing it was bad news, everyone in the room fell quiet. Laura clung to Zach.

"He's fine. In fact, he's right here," Bev said quietly, her apprehensive blue eyes darting to her brother-in-law.

Covering the mouthpiece, she said, "It's for you, Zach. Salt Lake calling. You can take it downstairs. I'll wait and then hang up."

Laura felt as if someone had just slugged her in the stomach. *It's Rosie.*

She stiffened in Zach's arms. "Put me down in the hall, then go take your call," she urged him in a shaky voice.

Ignoring her request, Zach held her even closer in his arms and walked around to the phone on Bev's side of the bed.

"Hold the receiver up for me, will you, darling?"

In shock, Laura did as he asked, but her fingers were trembling.

"Rosie?" he began. "Is that you?"

"Yes. When I heard that the Newport area had been hit by the quake, I had to call to find out if you and your family were all right."

Warmed by her concern, Zach felt like he was talking to an old friend, nothing more. He could have no greater proof of his total and complete love for Laura. She was his whole world. Nothing else mattered.

He cleared his throat. "We were lucky," he murmured, looking at Laura, who stared up at him half-fearfully. "No one got hurt except my fiancée, and even she escaped with only minor injuries."

"Oh, Zach!" Rosie said happily. "You're engaged?"

"Yes. We're being married on Wednesday." He paused to kiss Laura on the mouth. He'd never get enough. "You were given your heart's desire when Nick returned from the war. Now that I've found mine I understand why you could never let him go. If I lost Laura…" He couldn't even think about it.

"Never," Laura mouthed before relaxing against him in total contentment.

"Your news has made me happier than you'll ever know," Rosie said.

"Laura's love has made me feel reborn."

"I can tell. God bless you, Zach."

"God bless you, too, Rosie. Give my best to Nick and Cody."

When he hung up the phone, the last door to his troubled past had closed. Zach lowered his head to kiss the woman who'd become his future, his *life*.

"Okay, everybody," Richard announced as he climbed out of bed. "It's time for breakfast. Last person downstairs has to do the dishes and clean up the kitchen!"

"That'll be Uncle Zach," Richie grumbled near the doorway. "If he ever *does* come down."

"I wouldn't count on it," his mother said, glancing at the oblivious couple locked in an embrace.

"But Laura promised to play baseball cards with me."

"I'm afraid you're going to have a long wait, son," Richard said. "Since I don't have to go to work today, how about me standing in for her?"

"You?" There was a brief silence. "Okay," he agreed, not sounding quite as grumpy, "but nobody's as smart as Laura."

"We don't have to go to school on Wednesday, do we, mommy."

"Of course not, Rachel honey. I'm going to need you girls' help to get everything ready. We want Zach and Laura's wedding day to be perfect!"

"Yeah!" they all chimed in at once.

CHAPTER FIFTEEN

"GOODBYE! HAVE A wonderful time!"

While family and friends stood on the front porch and waved to Zach and Laura as they drove off with *Just Married* spray painted on the trunk of the car, Richard reached for his wife. For some odd reason, he needed her more than usual tonight.

Loving her pregnant shape, he slid his hands around her from behind and instinctively searched for movement in her abdomen. He would never take the process of conception and birth for granted. Each time he felt the evidence of the baby they'd made inside her, he relived the wonder of it all—especially tonight because the brother he adored was finally going to experience real joy as a husband and father, too. In fact, he would probably end up having several children in quick succession to make up for lost time.

Suddenly Bev whirled around to face him. "I'm so happy I feel like I'm going to burst! Have you ever seen two people more in love? Honey, I can't believe I'm saying this, but I'm glad Zach had to go through what he did first. Otherwise he would never have met the perfect woman for him."

As Richard took in his wife's radiant beauty, his

heart overflowed with love. Swallowing with difficulty, he murmured, "If it hadn't been for you, if you didn't love him as much as you do..." He gave up and simply crushed her in his arms.

"Hey," she whispered, nestling even closer. "I have a surprise for you."

When her words had fully computed, he pulled far enough away to look down at her questioningly.

"I decided to save it until now to help you get over your separation anxiety."

One brow quirked. "Separation anxiety?"

"Yes. You think I don't know you're feeling a little abandoned now that your brother has cut the cord for good, so to speak?"

Bev knows everything. How I love her.

"When Laura and I went in for our ultrasounds, I found out we're going to have a new version of Zach running around the house pretty soon."

"We're having another boy?" Richard almost shouted. His parents and Laura's, who were standing nearby talking, started to laugh.

Bev sent him a teasing smile.

"I thought that might cheer you up. In your old old age you'll have this cute little towheaded guy who'll follow you everywhere, who'll gaze up at you with adoration in his eyes and think you're the greatest man alive. Which, of course, you are."

As soon as Laura was dressed, she left the examining room and more or less shuffled into her doctor's office.

"Full term" had taken on new meaning in the past couple of weeks, for both her *and* Zach.

Hard to believe February had finally arrived. With Valentine's Day just around the corner, this could be her last visit before the baby came.

Zach stood up as she entered the room. He gave her a hug and the doctor told them to be seated. Though her husband tried not to show it, he'd been on edge all week.

Yesterday he'd hung around their newly remodeled condo all morning with the excuse that he didn't need to go into work until later. Today he'd taken the whole day off just to accompany her to the doctor's office.

Of course, Laura wasn't complaining. She deemed any time she could spend with him precious. But she didn't like that brooding expression on his handsome face. It was too great a reminder of the Zach she'd confronted in the Galápagos.

Without preamble, Cindy Stewart, Laura's obstetrician, explained that everything looked good.

"The baby has dropped and you're two centimeters dilated. Don't plan another sailing trip down to Baja right now." She winked as she said it, but Laura noticed that Cindy's teasing had been wasted on Zach. He'd gone pale beneath his tan.

Now he got to his feet, rubbing his neck absently. "What you're saying is, our baby could come any time now."

"That's right. If you have some questions, I'd be glad to answer them."

Laura's heart went out to her husband, whose anxious gaze flicked from Cindy to her. "Do you have any, darling?"

"No."

She had several actually, but in Zach's nervous state, she thought it wiser not to voice them.

"If that's the case, I'll leave you two and go see my next patient." Cindy rose from her chair. "Call me when the pains start. You have the number of my beeper."

Laura nodded. "Thank you so much for everything."

"It's my pleasure, believe me." On her way out of the room the doctor patted Zach's arm. "Your wife is going to be fine."

Her reassurance didn't make a dent. The second she was out the door Zach cupped Laura's elbow. "Let's go home."

"All right."

On their way out to the parking lot her stomach grumbled, reminding her that it had been a long time since lunch. "Do you care if we stop for some souvlaki on the way?"

Grim-faced, he muttered, "We'll phone for take-out."

Laura frowned. As far as she knew, there were no Greek restaurants in the area that delivered. Her husband simply wasn't thinking clearly. He'd been cooped up all day and needed an outlet.

"I've got a better idea. Let's take a walk down on

the pier and find us a cozy little place that serves stuffed shrimp.''

It was a favorite dish of theirs, but judging by her husband's next question, it seemed he couldn't be tempted.

''Do you think that's wise this close to your time?''

She leaned into his side and kissed his cheek before they got in the car. ''Darling, we both have to eat. As for walking, a little exercise is good for me.''

His jaw hardened. She recognized the signs.

''On second thought, home does sound inviting. Come to think of it, one of your Spanish omelettes sounds even better.''

''You'd like that?''

Obviously she'd said the right thing to temporarily appease him.

''I'd love it.''

Within minutes they'd arrived at the condo. The double decks overlooking the water had been destroyed by the quake and recently rebuilt. It was the kind of beachfront property Laura had always dreamed of.

Possessing a green thumb like her dad's, she had plants and tubs of potted flowers growing inside and out. Together she and Zach had chosen a Hapsburg-yellow color scheme, which they teamed with light oak and rattan furniture. The decor had transformed his former domicile into a comfortable sunny haven of beauty. Especially the nursery.

Of all the bedrooms in the house, the baby's room

had claimed her husband's undivided attention. Never had any expectant father taken his role so seriously. From the walnut-colored French-provincial-style crib to the colorful mobile of the seven dwarfs, everything was perfect.

For the past four months they'd been ecstatically happy. Why, she worried, had Zach's behavior undergone such a drastic change?

The second they entered the house he put his hands on her shoulders from behind and said, "Why don't you go on up and take a nice relaxing bath. By the time you're out, I'll have dinner ready and bring it to you in bed."

Laura didn't turn around.

You're frightened, my darling. What's wrong?

She kissed the hand nearest her warm cheek. She was always warm these days. "You must have been reading my mind. I'll be waiting for you."

All three bedrooms faced the water and so each had a spectacular view. Laura entered the master bedroom, her mind trying to fathom what was going on inside her husband.

By the time she'd had her bath and slipped into a fresh nightie, she'd made up her mind to get to the bottom of it.

No sooner had she climbed into their king-size bed than he appeared with a tray. She sat up against the headboard, already salivating over the omelette's delicious aroma.

"Mmm," she said as he placed the tray on her lap.

"Thank you, darling. Everything looks wonderful. Where's *your* dinner?"

His eyes were veiled. "I'll eat later."

Knowing better than to coax him, she started to eat and chatted about inconsequential matters. He sat in one of the chairs near the bed and watched her.

Ever vigilant, as soon as she'd eaten the last green pepper and drained her glass of lemonade, he took the tray and put it on the magazine table next to his chair.

As far as she was concerned, it was time for a serious talk.

After praising him for the superb cuisine, she patted his side of the bed. "Come and join me," she invited, her voice husky. "I miss you next to me."

It was true. Up until a week ago they'd been making love morning, noon and night, whenever they could. Every time was like the first time, filling her with rapture.

Then suddenly he'd stopped touching her. For the past few nights when he'd thought she was sleeping, he'd left their bed to stand out on the deck, sometimes until the morning fog rolled in.

Zach's hands tightened on the arms of the chair, but he made no move to get up. "I don't think that's a good idea."

She frowned. "I think it's a very good idea. All I want you to do is hold me."

"It's almost impossible for me to just hold you," he said gruffly.

"Then I'll hold *you*."

She heard his sharp intake of breath. "Don't, Laura."

"Don't what? Ask my husband to come to bed with me? It's a perfectly natural request—unless you've stopped loving me."

His savage imprecation made her jump. Like lightning he shot out of the chair, his hands balled into fists at his sides. "Don't ever say that!"

"Darling!" she cried, aghast. "What's wrong? For the past week you've been acting like a stranger. *Talk* to me! Please. Tell me why you're so upset."

His continued silence devastated her. He was in pain. On an impulse she asked, "Are you afraid something's going to happen to me?"

The second the question left her lips she saw the hardening of his features and knew she'd hit home.

"You heard the doctor. I'm going to be fine."

"Can she guarantee it?" he fired back.

Laura had been listening with all her senses. Suddenly her thoughts flashed back to his first fiancée, and then to Tony.

He thinks there's a chance I'm going to die.

She tossed the covers aside. Forgetting her protruding stomach, she pushed herself off the bed and threw her arms around his neck.

"Millions of women are having babies every day. You're going to be right there with me, holding my hand. How could anything go wrong? You'll be the first one to see our daughter born. I can picture you parading around with her right now."

His gray eyes had darkened with emotion. "If anything happened to you…"

She trembled. "Don't you think I feel the same way about you every time you leave this house to go to work? Every time you're out of my sight? All it proves is how much we love each other. But we can't let the past dominate our lives, not when we have everything to live for."

"I know," he whispered, but his eyes were glazed with moisture. For a moment she saw into his soul and read his anguished cry for help. Something else was still worrying him.

"Are you afraid for the baby? You don't have to be. The ultrasound indicates our baby is perfect."

He didn't say anything. The bleakness in his eyes alarmed her. Then she remembered a comment Richie had made to her in the car.

"Zach, you're going to be the first person our baby sees when she's born. You'll be her father, now and always. Someday when she's old enough, we'll tell her about Tony, but if you think for one second that will make any difference to her, you couldn't be more wrong."

"But every time you look at her, you'll—"

"No, darling. Haven't you been listening to me? Since the moment you guessed I was pregnant, I have always thought of you as her father. In fact, I can't remember a single second when I didn't. Her birth is going to make us even closer, because she'll be the best part of Tony. She's a gift we'll treasure forever."

They were the right words to say. Zach reached for her and they clung. Then, grasping him by the hand, she drew him onto the bed and into her arms. Thus began a communication of bodies and spirits that lasted well into the night. At some point they finally fell asleep with her back against his chest, his arm around her and the baby.

AROUND FIVE in the morning Laura was awakened by a dragging sensation that swept around from her lower back to the front. There was only one thing that feeling could be.

For a long time she lay there in awed silence, pondering the event that was about to happen.

By six she was convinced the pains coming at regular intervals weren't going to go away. When her first really hard contraction began, she let out a cry of surprise at its intensity.

With a smothered imprecation, Zach said, "I felt that, too!"

Masculine hands that could be at once provocative and tender moved over her taut belly.

"How incredible!" he said. "Where did you put Dr. Stewart's number? I have to call her. We've got to get to the hospital."

"It's written on the appointment card in my purse, but there's no big hurry. She says the first baby usually takes a while."

"Our baby is really coming!"

"Yes." Her face broke out in a grin because he

sounded so excited. The demons of last night seemed to have vanished. "We're about to become parents. Do you think you're ready?"

"As long as you never stop loving me, I'm ready for anything, Mrs. Wilde."

"FOR CRYING OUT LOUD, Uncle Zach, when's it going to be my turn to hold Astrid?"

Richie's frustrated voice carried from the nursery into the bedroom where Laura and Bev were having a heart-to-heart.

Leaving Richard and Zach with the awesome responsibility of deciding how long each child should be given time with the adorable new dark-haired arrival, Bev heaved a weary sigh and stretched out on the bed so she was facing Laura.

"Here I am, still great with child, and you're lying there looking gorgeous when you only gave birth five days ago. It's not fair!"

"A lot *you* know. As soon as I'm given permission, I'm going to have to whip out my mother's old exercise board, otherwise Zach will turn me in for a new model."

"That'll be the day. Honestly, Laura, you have my brother-in-law so womped, I don't recognize him anymore."

Laura's eyes shone. "You think?"

"Was there ever any question?" She raised herself on one elbow and said seriously, "There's a marked difference in him from a few days ago, too." She paused, then confided, "I know this might sound strange, but his behavior, I thought, was most peculiar lately. Then suddenly it's like this hidden part of him emerged. There's a new confidence I've never seen before."

Laura nodded sagely. "It's called *relief,* and it's because I didn't die in childbirth." The other reason didn't matter anymore. Besides, it was something private between her and her husband.

Bev's smile faded. The two of them stared hard at each other with an understanding born out of their love for Zach.

"I should have figured that one out long before now."

"Tell me about it," Laura groaned. "I was beginning to think he'd fallen out of love with me. Then it came like a revelation what was really going on. I'm afraid I've married a very complicated man."

Bev smiled. "Join the club. All the Wilde men are the same. Complex, but s-o-o-o wonderful. We just have to learn to stay one step ahead of them. Did you know Richard almost fell apart when Zach drove off with you after the reception?"

"You're kidding."

"Nope. For once in his life Richard had to face the fact that you now came first in his younger brother's life. After being the kingpin all these years, it was hard to relinquish it."

She patted her stomach. "That's why it's a good thing my baby is about to make an appearance. Little

Zach ought to expand my husband's role of guardian of the realm.''

Laura was shocked. ''Bev, I had no idea. Honestly, Zach and I have been so happy I guess we've kind of ignored everyone else.''

''Don't you *dare* apologize!''

''Apologize for what?'' Zach said from the doorway. He was holding their hungry infant. Laura could see he was a natural-born father and so crazy about the baby his every fear had fled.

She smiled up at him. ''For going into labor before *she* did.''

An answering smile transformed his features. ''They don't call me King of the Mountain for nothing! Are you ready to feed my little girl?''

''I recognize that look,'' Bev whispered. ''He wants to be alone with you. I'll gather up our brood and call you tomorrow. It might even be from the hospital.''

''I hope so.'' Laura squeezed Bev's hand. ''I've got my fingers crossed. Thank you for the darling outfit and booties.''

''Anytime.''

With some difficulty Bev got off the bed and gave the baby's head a kiss on her way out of the room. The minute the door closed Laura held out her arms.

''I want both of you here with me.''

Zach eyed his wife for a moment. It seemed his life had always been a race toward something elusive, something that had no name. But as he stood there with their daughter in his arms, Laura's face aglow with love, he knew that long race was over. He knew what it was he'd been running toward all this time.

His share of heaven on earth.

READER SERVICE

The best romantic fiction direct to your door

Our guarantee to you...

*The Reader Service involves you in no obligation
to purchase, and is truly a service to you!*

*There are many extra benefits including a free
monthly Newsletter with author interviews,
book previews and much more.*

*Your books are sent direct to your door
on 14 days no obligation home approval.*

*We offer free postage and packing for subscribers
in the UK—we guarantee you won't find any
hidden extras.*

*Plus, we have a dedicated Customer Care team
on hand to answer all your queries on
(UK) 0181 288 2888
(Ireland) 01 278 2062.*

There is also a 24 hour message facility on this number.

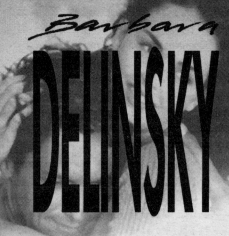

CATHERINE LANIGAN
in love's
SHADOW

ON A COLD DECEMBER EVENING, A SHOT
RANG OUT IN A WEALTHY CHICAGO SUBURB
AND THE LIVES OF THREE WOMEN WERE
CHANGED FOREVER. BUD PULASKI, SUC-
CESSFUL BUSINESSMAN, COMMITTED SUI-
CIDE, LEAVING BEHIND A SHATTERED WIFE,
AN ESTRANGED SISTER, A BITTER MISTRESS
AND MANY UNANSWERED QUESTIONS.

THEY ARE THREE WOMEN—SEARCHING FOR
ANSWERS THAT WILL AFFECT THE REST OF
THEIR LIVES. SEARCHING FOR A RAY OF
HOPE IN LOVE'S SHADOW.

**Available in August
from The Reader Service™**